IN TH

SHADOW OF EVIL

The Countess De Couvegne Letters

TONY COLLINS

BLACK ROSE
writing™

ISBN: 978-1-61296-303-7

PUBLISHED BY BLACK ROSE WRITING

www.blackrosewriting.com

Printed in the United States of America

In The Dark Shadow Of Evil is printed in Andalus

To Heather
Best Wishes

Tony Cottey

To my friends Marjorie and Lydia for their valued advice
and my wonderful wife Jill.

IN THE DARK SHADOW OF EVIL

THE COUNTESS DE COUVEGNE LETTERS

CHAPTER 1

THE COUNTESS DE COUVEGNE LETTERS

Brittany France 2010

The buildings along the street were shrouded in darkness; only their outlines were reflected on the cobblestone road, which was cast in a silvery luminescence following a recent downpour.

Every step of the way sent him into even murkier extremes. The amber street lamps shone dimly as an enveloping mist blocked out much of their light, casting an eerie glow that played on the wet flagged pavement.

A dog barked from behind a closed gate causing an animal to squeal, and in response a dustbin lid clattered to the ground noisily, as the fleeting shadow of a cat made a speedy retreat.

Baxter momentarily froze for he was not at ease in these surroundings and neither was he familiar with them. He was a town man used to the hustle and bustle of the brightly lit London streets. He loved the noise of fast urban life and the way people in the city were constantly galvanized into a hectic rush.

In stark contrast here was solitude, silence and a world of elongated shadows; a milieu that was far outside his zone of comfort.

The wind was building, causing the street lamps to gently rock; he thought perhaps their movement was responsible for his feelings of apprehension; feelings which were heightened by uncertainty brought about by a road deserted by any sign of human presence.

Baxter could have quite easily jumped into his car and driven to his destination; he would have taken the ring road. However, the short cut up the narrow, winding lane was less than a mile distant and despite the forecast of an imminent gale, he had decided to take the fresh night air. It would blow away the cobwebs and work off the large meal and bottle of Medoc he had just consumed in the hotel restaurant.

With little pollution and few smells of human origin, his nose had become sensitive over the past few days, something which could never happen in the busy, odiferous streets of London.

He was walking, stooped slightly forward up the steep cobbled lane with the wind behind, but the going was slow on account of the incline and the unevenness of the paved surface. For some time, he had been aware of a familiar aroma that appeared to be following him, a pungent and distinctive smell, which he recognised as French tobacco.

He stopped in his tracks, listened for a few seconds and then, spinning on his heels, turned just in time to see an orange glow illuminating the iron grill on a window embrasure just a few yards away. The smell of cigarette smoke wafted stronger, more potent as a draught of wind passed him by.

Bourge-Vilaine was a small, medieval town perched uncomfortably on a hilltop, with its fortified castle built on a rocky outcrop overlooking the open countryside. The buildings were almost exclusively half-timber frame structures with colour-washed rendered walls in a variety of muted colours. Roofs were wide-ranging in height and angle, often clumsily pitched against their neighbours and varying considerably in size, indicating the differing degrees of wealth of their owners. Whatever their status or size, the roofs in this part of the town were either a wonderful moss-covered riven stone or more often slate; plain or decoratively hung.

This architectural mish-mash was an expression of the town's past wealth, a legacy from the fifteenth century hemp-linen industry, which had flourished here for over two centuries.

The streets and dark alleyways were a palimpsest of cobbled arteries; every one of them steep and challenging as they meandered up to the only signs of nocturnal activity; the bars and small bistros that were clustered around the old marketplace on top of the hill.

He knew he had to keep moving upwards towards the centre of town and although these backwaters appeared to be deserted of all human life, he was in no doubt that he was not alone. Someone was secretively following him and because he didn't know who or why, that made him nervous.

For a second time he paused, listening for footsteps but there were none. He held his breath for a minute and thought he heard a slight throat murmur. He turned quickly and once again an orange glow alerted him to a human presence as it lit up the stonework on the corner of a building to his rear. His pulse was hammering, painfully exerting pressure on his lungs and his forehead was beginning to perspire. He spotted a profile reflected on the wet cobbles by the street lights overhead, but within a split second it had melted away into the darkness of shadows.

He waited in silence, weighing up his options. He was faced with a trilemma; a choice of three unfavourable possibilities. He could run and attempt to lose his follower, but with a hill this steep and on cobbles, which at the best of times were capable of mis-footing even the slowest pedestrian, he realised that might not be so easy. Also, he had already noted how the paving sets were wet and slippery under foot. Alternatively, he could carry on regardless in the pretence of not knowing or caring that he was being followed. However, he realised he had now compromised his situation by pausing like this. He'd let his would-be mugger know 'he knew' the man or woman was following in his footsteps. The third option was to make a challenge, this was probably the least favourable, but without thinking, he launched into a dialogue.

'Hello who's there?' he called out brazenly, but got no reply. He walked into the middle of the road. 'I know you're following me, I've just called the police,' he lied. He caught yet another glimpse of an orange glow as his follower drew heavily on a cigarette and then melted once again into the shadows.

Deciding he didn't have the necessary courage to challenge his follower any further, he continued up the hill, now at an aggressive pace fuelled by a sense of urgency.

He was trying to flush his would-be follower out by forcing him to break cover. If the sinister character was going to keep up then he would have to leave the shadows of doorways and corners and break out into the open, and that Baxter doubted he would wish to do.

One last concerted effort and Baxter finally reached the top of the winding street and with muscles tightening in the backs of his legs he paused, sitting on a low wall while catching his breath.

He looked back the way he had come, it was dark down towards the lower end but even so there was no sign of his follower. A tinkling of a bell preceded the spectacle of a little old lady struggling up the steep incline with a goat reluctantly dragging behind on a short length of rope.

Here at the top of the hill there was no protection from the wind, exposed, he was forced to turn his body slightly sideways.

Spread out before him on a flat plateau was the town centre. Here was a large open space outlined with buildings in marked contrast to this otherwise densely occupied settlement. The Medieval castle tower dominated everything else. Occupying much of the western side, the neatly cut sandstone walls were once a testimony to wealth and power. Famous for housing the Parliament of Brittany during the great plague, they now stood in darkness, redundant once the daily queue of tourists had departed.

On the other side of the square a few people were scurrying across the exposed cobbled market place angling their bodies in reaction to the strong wind, much like Lowry matchstick men and women.

Baxter got up and made his unhurried way towards the far side of the square. He stopped in front of a bistro. The restaurant in itself wasn't unusual, but sandwiched between two ancient timber-framed buildings it presented a collision of scale of the proportions one wouldn't expect to see in an historic environment like this.

The combination of floodlights and a modern plastic façade

ablaze with bright clashing colours insulted his senses, but were supposedly intended to express modernity and quality, and perhaps for many it did. A waiter came out and casually leant against the door slowly drawing on his cigarette, he looked across at Baxter and they exchanged the usual polite nod of the head.

He continued his way through the town centre towards the old market square where a solitary fishmonger was packing away his empty polystyrene boxes. A door opened some distance away and the muted sound of laughter followed as a group of men headed off in earnest to their night time rendezvous.

Unfortunately the bar Baxter was looking for was not here where the townscape was brightly lit and becoming reassuringly busy, but in the dark side street he had just reached.

His way was a narrow downward road, characteristically cobbled but unlike most of the streets in this mediaeval town it was unlit by street lamps, deserted and certainly very desolate. Baxter found the prospect of venturing further quite intimidating despite the lack of any sign of activity, confrontational or not.

Baxter stopped to check he had arrived at the right place. The blue and white sign on the corner read Rue des Meurtrier; a chilling reminder from the past when this area was part of the abattoir quarter. Half way down the street he could see a meagre pool of light glistening on the cobbled road. He headed down towards it.

When he reached the spot, a flickering fluorescent light on a fascia buzzed loudly as it made its very last effort to produce illumination. Baxter looked back up the street half expecting to see some evidence of his tail, or at least catch the distinctive smell of French tobacco, but it seemed his shadow had not followed him this far.

The sign above the door was crudely fashioned in wood, the paint had been slowly peeling for many years, but he could just make out the name- Bar Rat De Cave.

Not quite certain what to expect in this backwater end of town he took a deep breath before entering via the dark uninviting lobby.

As he pushed open the glass panelled doors he was met with a rush of stale tobacco smoke which was sucked past him on its way to meet the fresh air in the lobby.

Inside the single roomed bar the décor was well past its normal life expectancy. A sweet pungency of Turkish tobacco, sweat and overheating lamps confirmed this was obviously no place for tourists or indeed anyone with any sense of taste. The once garish wall panels painted in orange and yellow gloss were now universally toned brown from years of co-habiting with nicotine. Tobacco smoke hung from the ceiling like clouds, yet the whirring of the long-bladed fan did little to disperse the pollution. Along the opposite wall a bar counter had been recently built using fake timbers, the plastic panels and beams over emphasizing the pine grain to such an extent that it no longer looked like wood.

He spotted the proprietor, dressed in an off white apron carelessly draped over a blue checked shirt that needed ironing. The man briefly looked up as Baxter entered but then seemed to dismiss him as inconsequential as he continued to lean on the bar reading his newspaper.

Baxter surveyed the room; business was slack and the atmosphere was decidedly chill. The clientele who were propped up against the bar were as one might expect to find in the rundown part of any rural French town. Archetypally huddled in a small group at one end of the bar, they were to a man typically dressed in overalls or dark blue trousers and drab mis-matched jackets, and without exception all decked a cap or beret which was characteristically balanced at an absurd slant. A wizened cigarette hung from every one of their mouths, a cloud of smoke slowly rose and then lay suspended above them. Of course smoking in public places was against the law here in France, it had been since February two thousand and seven, but obviously few if any Gendarmes bothered to pay this dive a visit and certainly very few tourists would wish to linger here.

As he slowly made his way further into the room, the clientele perched on their stools sluggishly turned, sizing him up. Every one of them had eyes it was unwise to catch and faces which signalled a dislike for strangers, a distrust of anyone who did not immediately fit the local stereotype, their stereotype. Baxter knew they would have few scruples and would probably slit his throat for the price of Pernod or perhaps even for the fun of it.

He quickly satisfied himself that the man he was here to meet had not yet arrived. Even though he didn't have a clue what he looked like, there was certainly no one here who even vaguely fitted the bill, so he ambled nonchalantly across the room until he reached a table, the one which was furthest away from the disagreeable patrons at the bar.

Baxter looked across towards the counter where the barman continued to read his newspaper. He couldn't possibly go up to the bar to order a drink as that would be his death knoll with the regulars, for it would classify him as a tourist. Baxter was determined not to give in to the sullen proprietor, even though it would have been so much simpler to go up to the counter and order a drink. By ignoring him the barman was clearly pushing him to submit and order his drink at the bar, but he was quite happy sitting here waiting for his contact. If the man didn't come over to take his order, then that was fine by him.

At thirty five years old, the ups and downs of life had drawn few lines on Baxter's face, a face which was moderately good-looking and one which suggested a degree of intelligence, despite the light brown wiry hair which these days nudged his shoulders. He was wearing what he invariably wore, the blue Thomas Pink Dunlop check shirt, open at the neck of course. Vintage-washed beige corduroy trousers and light brown Tarpit leather jacket which was comfortably worn-in and reassuringly supple.

Waiting anxiously he found himself tracing his own path of

success.

Both his parents had been killed in a tragic car accident when he was barely eight years old. Baxter was gathered up by his two great aunts Matilda and Rosamond, neither had married and so both treated him as their own special little boy. The aunts were moderately well off, living in a house in Knightsbridge, a rambling London mansion which was far too large for them, but a legacy that had been handed down over several generations.

Right from the beginning the aunts recognized Baxter was most educable and were determined he would have the very best education. They were also firmly convinced that the attainment of languages held the key to a wide and varied career path and so even before he'd reached the age of nine he had his own personal French and Latin tutors. At that age his abilities were variable. His English was very good as was his understanding of history and geography and he excelled in Latin, but the likes of algebra and logarithms were a complete disaster. The aunts would have been delighted if he had passed the entrance examinations for Harrow or Eton, but Baxter failed to come up to the minimum requirements, but then he would have been a very different person today if he had gone through that scholastic route.

Belford in Berkshire was a public school set in magnificent grounds designed by Capability Brown. The school had an excellent reputation for its languages and boasted many distinguished old pupils. The Palladian building was a treasure house of antiques, a veritable glossary of English and European art which inspired Baxter more than he realised, for how soon in life the die is cast? For Baxter it was cast in stone at that very moment in time. The daily exposure to artifacts from every corner of the world would shape his future career path and provide an appreciation of art which from this embryonic beginning would blossom into a cauldron of knowledge.

Baxter liked it here and quickly established himself as a model pupil and successfully achieved the necessary A-levels to gain entry into university. At Oxford he gained a degree reading the history of art and then an MA at the Faculty of Oriental Studies, again at

Oxford. He spent a further three years studying for a language degree in Chinese Mandarin. He then moved down to London and went on to study Chinese ceramics at the Percival David foundation before taking up a two year stint in the Far Eastern galleries at the British Museum.

Despite all those years in academia, Baxter was desperate to be free and do his own thing. He was convinced there was good money to be made from dealing in antiques and so armed with his considerable knowledge of Oriental and European art he entered the sometimes shady world of the antique dealer.

Baxter had no desire to operate from shop premises, averse to the thought of spending long hours sitting, waiting for the next customer to browse his stock. No, he wanted to be out on the road hunting down that overlooked gem. He *loved* to be in the midst of the foray when word went out that a certain class of antique was suddenly en vogue and at the top of rich buyers' shopping lists. He needed to raise his game and fight for the attention of wealthy Russian oligarchs, American collectors from California and investment companies in interest-strapped Britain.

So for the past few years he had been a freelance antique dealer, although some would classify him as a runner, a term he hated immensely as it conjured up the shadiest side of antique dealing. He considered himself a consultant who sourced specific antiques for numerous dealers and trade outlets. If an antique dealer in say, the Kings Road in London had a client who wanted a particular piece of Georgian silver, then the dealer would leak this information to his network of runners. Of course each would be led to believe they had a unique lead, but in reality often hundreds would be out hunting the same shopping list. Last week it was an eighteenth century silver punch bowl which had to be by Hester Bateman, one of the few female silversmiths of that period, and whose work could be difficult to find, especially such large pieces. Despite calling on all his contacts, unfortunately on that occasion Baxter had not been successful. Indeed, it was a rat race, whoever produced what was on the wants list first, got the deal, but the rewards could be high at times, in fact they could be potentially enormous, and had been for some lucky dealers.

Two days ago Baxter had received information from a friend of a friend who had a French contact in the trade who had been approached by a man regarding some letters that had apparently been found here locally and were now to be sold in the little Bourge-Vilaine auction rooms. His contact had told him that there would be people who would pay handsomely for them, so he guessed these were no ordinary pieces of correspondence.

Even though he had no idea as to why these letters might be of interest to him, his contact had in the past opened opportunities which were hard to come by. This man had a knack for sniffing out things which other people would miss. The French informant had by all accounts not been the one who had discovered the papers, but he claimed to know something about them that others did not, a secret which made them highly important, in fact positively explosive, in the right person's hand.

And this is why Baxter had made the long journey here by ferry and car from England, a trip he suspected might end in disappointment. However, Baxter's philosophy in life was simple. '*Only those who are brave enough to take the plunge stand a chance of reaping the rewards.*' So although this particular challenge was outside his normal scope, he was going to see it through.

Baxter continued to wait at his table, still totally ignored by the bartender, his only ally was the whirring ceiling fan above. He could sense all in the room were talking about him, those squatting at the bar half turning to see what he was doing, or perhaps not doing, and then a sudden burst of laughter followed, presumably at his expense. The barman stood up and topped up the glasses, then glanced over towards Baxter, uttered a few indistinct words and another roar of laughter followed.

A man came in and one by one shook the hands of all those gathered at the bar. *This must be my contact* Baxter said to himself, but the man simply bought a packet of cigarettes and then made for the door. Before he reached the exit a tall auburn- haired woman entered. The departing man sported a look of surprise, perhaps anxiety even, as he moved sideways to let her by. She nodded casually at the proprietor then sat at a table in the corner and proceeded to light a long cigarette. To Baxter's annoyance the barman promptly went into motion, his coffee machine screamed into action and he wasted no time delivering a small cup of coffee, which he placed on the table in front of her.

No matter how hard he tried he couldn't take his eyes off this woman who had been bold enough to come here apparently unaccompanied, here to this seedy dive where she stood out like a sore thumb. He wondered if like him she was waiting for someone else to arrive, perhaps her partner or even a secret lover. His attention was now solely on the mystery woman, she was at least a distraction from the monotony of waiting without so much as a drink for company. He continued to attempt to make out the features of her face but she was sitting in a dark corner and never once looked his way, she was deliberately denying him the opportunity to study her.

He guessed she would have a stunning face, he couldn't imagine anything less than that. He had noticed her figure when she came in and it was evident her body was as perfect as a body could be, the envy of most women, but then he guessed she probably knew that and was able to use it to her advantage.

The door suddenly swung open, the handle banging loudly against the frame.

'Bonsoir Fabian' the timbre of the voice was packed with familiarity and confidence as it greeted the barman.

'Bonsoir Marcel,' the bartender muttered taking his hand in a firm grip. As the man turned towards his table Baxter blew a sigh of relief. This at last must be his contact.

'Marcel Didier?' Baxter enquired

'Shhh, don't mention my name again, it is most important you do not,' he said in broken English. He paused to look over his shoulder taking particular note of the woman in the corner.

'We speak in minute or two,' he added, nervously twitching his large brows in a mad overstated fashion.

The barman folded his newspaper, wiped his hands on his off-white apron and came over to serve them.

'Ca va?' he asked Marcel who replied he was well. The bartender stared at Baxter, a long questioning glower, and then turned to face Marcel with a look which demanded an explanation for Baxter's presence here in his bar. When he didn't receive any form of enlightenment from Marcel he switched his gaze back to Baxter, his face now emitted a look of malevolence as he waited to take their order.

'Vin rouge,' Marcel said to the barman, and then half turned and raised his eyebrows to Baxter.

'Le même chose pour moi,' Baxter nodded to the barman who returned a disgruntled snort. He thought it would be easiest to have the same, but hoped it wasn't the cheapest bottle in the rack, but afterwards considered it probably would be by the look of his companion.

Marcel was none too pretty. His face was tanned a walnut brown, but not in an attractive way, it bore evidence of a rough outdoor life, old beyond his years, and framed by long black lank hair, tinged by grey around the edges which fell to a point way past his shoulders and the heavy stubble on his chin was at least a week old. He was a large man, taller than most and with hands the size of shovels, hands which were tempered by years of hard physical work and his left wrist sported a tattoo with the initials M.D separated by a seraphim. His arms had extended muscles and looked massive enough to crush an oak tree, but when he spoke, his voice was genteel, slow and calculating, and surprisingly, for someone of such apparent background, his English was good.

Baxter leaned forward, 'So tell me about these letters, Marcel.'

The man looked around the room once again nervously checking those sitting at the bar and his eyes lingered for several seconds on the woman in the corner before he turned to face Baxter.

'As I tell to you in my note I 'ave information regarding some letters you will much want.' He stopped as the barman approached, slammed down a bottle and two glasses and then without saying a word sauntered away. Marcel picked up the bottle of red and filled two glasses, pushing one over to Baxter. He fumbled for a cigarette, lit it and took several drags which he deeply inhaled and then coughed violently. Baxter moved back to avoid his spit.

'I'm all ears Marcel, tell me more,' he urged. Baxter noted the man's sombre expression as he took a long swig of his wine and then immediately refilled his glass. His face creased as he leaned closer, too close, for Baxter could smell the acerbic garlic laced breath of his informant as he coughed after another sharp drag of his wizened cigarette, followed by a hiss as he blew smoke from the corner of his mouth.

'But first my friend, if you please, we talk about money, it is most important to discuss this before we commence.'

'No' replied Baxter firmly, 'I want to know more about what I'm buying before I decide if it's worth anything to me.'

The man sat back in his seat and began scratching the stubble on his chin, an involuntary action brought on by his need to take the measure of his punter. It also gave him valuable minutes in which to try and gauge how interested Baxter was for the information? Had he woven enough intrigue to lure his buyer, could he add more bait without giving too much away?

Baxter was likewise weighing up his informant and had come to the conclusion the man desperately needed money, probably enough to buy the week's wine and perhaps a little cannabis and of course, tobacco.

'I'll tell to you then my friend,' began Marcel 'but you must understand others would pay at least one thousand euros for this information, but I come to you first because Philippe Fresne tell me you are fair man and I believe 'im.'

'Fresne! How on earth did you have contact with him?

'Ah, my friend, Marcel also 'ave contacts in places most high.' His face flashed a momentary smile.

Baxter knew Philippe Fresne. He owned a high class antique shop at the fashionable end of Bond Street in London and had returned a favour by giving him this particular tip off. But he couldn't possibly imagine how someone like Marcel Didier, living as he undoubtedly did in rural France, would have reason to converse with a top London antique dealer like Fresne.

'So tell to me if you please, do you want the information I 'ave?' The man leant forward eagerly awaiting Baxter's reply.

'I am indeed fair and if the information is worth a thousand euros then you'll get it, but I feel I have to warn you that I very much doubt if it's worth anything like that much.'

'Shhhh' Marcel placed a finger to his lips, and then once again looked nervously over towards the bar. He turned and faced Baxter.

'ave you 'eard of the celebrated Countess de Couvegne?' he asked.

Baxter's ears reacted, the name Couvegne did ring a bell. He racked his brains and then it came to him, yes that was it, on his way here he had seen the outlines of the chateau de Couvegne, a popular tourist stop if the line of coaches outside was anything to go by.

'Yes a little,' he said 'but tell me more.'

'Well mon amis, the Countess de Couvegne was born Marie de Echantel. 'Er father was Baron de Echantel and 'er mother the French aristocrat Marie de Valois. She went on to marry Henri de Couvegne and after 'e 'wers killed in a duel so tragic, she inherited much wealth.'

'So what has that got to do with some old letters Marcel?'

'I was to that point just coming. Marie was a letter writer most prolific, 'eet is said great quantities were written to her daughter. But by the year eighteen fifty eight Countess de Couvegne's letters were being copied, and sold as the article most genuine, so she 'ad the majority destroyed. I tell to you the genuine signed examples are rare indeed. However, a year ago a bundle of some one hundred and twenty letters turned up here in Bourge-Vilaine; all were signed, every single one of them.'

'That sounds interesting, but I'm still not quite certain why you think they could possibly be of any interest to me.'

'*Alors*, my friend, they contain facts most grave about the goings on in the Royal French court of Louis Philippe. In those letters are details which many in high places would not want to be broadcast, they would 'ave to pay, indeed, a very high price for them.'

'But surely in that case those people in high places will be bidding for them won't they?'

'Ah, no my friend, you see I think no one else knows what 'es in that bundle of letters which are lost in that very large chest of bills and paperwork of little interest.'

'Okay, so why are you not bidding on them yourself?' Baxter was suddenly very suspicious of his informant's intentions, or the lack of them.

'My friend, the problem is the chest they are in is seventeenth century and will command a price of perhaps one thousand five hundred euros, maybe more. I am but a poor man and cannot find that sort of money.' He again looked furtively over his shoulder to check all was well, then leaned across the table and poured himself another glass of wine. It was then Baxter noticed the empty table in the corner, the solitary woman had quietly left. He shouldn't have been surprised, but for some unexplained reason he was. Apart from her un noticed departure, everything else remained the same. The men at the bar were now rather noisier and the proprietor continued reading his paper but something disturbed Baxter, he just couldn't put his finger on what it was but something wasn't quite right.

'Marcel, did you see a woman sitting alone in that corner over there when you came in?'

'I tell to you she is someone you do not see.' he looked nervously towards the group at the bar. 'Don't mention her again or I will 'ave to leave. Now, tell to me what do you say to my most interesting proposition. It is good, yes?'

The man was pressing him to make a speedy decision, but Baxter was still uncertain and struggling to make that judgment. He was torn between the possibility of making a quick buck and suspicion of Marcel's claim to the possession of this potentially valuable information. True the letters did sound as though they might have potential, but did he have the right contacts in England? He wasn't at all convinced; in fact he doubted his ability to do them justice.

He mulled it over, then decided that if he was going to get a seventeenth century chest, then perhaps he could offer Marcel something, but certainly not a thousand euros. He knew by now that Marcel was desperate and had few trump cards to play with.

'Five hundred euros' Baxter offered Marcel who met his gaze with what he knew was a palpable and open dislike.

'Five hundred! You rob me mon amis, that information I give to you is worth more than five hundred euros you know it is.' The look in his eyes could only be described as pitiful. His words were now of someone who had long outlived their purpose. He shook his head and took another swig from his glass.

'I tell to you it is a cadeau at one thousand euros, I think you don't like to part with money so dear to you.' His jaw was set with determination, but even now Baxter could see the man's resolve was slowly melting away.

Baxter shook his head and got up to leave, Marcel grabbed his arm.

'Please to stay, don't go yet,' he implored, switching his hold to Baxter's wrist and exerting enough strength to ease him back into his chair.

Baxter deliberately hardened his expression and then slowly and purposefully counted out five hundred in brown crisp fifty euro notes; Marcel grabbed the money and hastily folded it before slipping it into his breast pocket.

'So tell me what I need to know, and it had better be worth what I have just paid you.' Marcel grabbed his shoulder pulling him close then whispered in his ear. 'Lot seventy six, just to trust me, now go and be very careful, it is most dangerous out there.'

'Thank you.' was all Baxter could utter; there didn't seem to be any point in saying anything else.

'There are ruthless people in this business,' Marcel murmured, largely to himself because Baxter was already leaving the table and heading for the door. He stopped before departing, turned to look back one last time at the sorry excuse for a drinking establishment. The proprietor continued reading his newspaper, but two of the regulars at the bar turned on their stools and gave him a look which sent alarm bells ringing.

Baxter was relieved to be out of the besmirched smoke-filled Rat de Cave and once again in the fresh night air. A slight chill in the brisk wind made him shiver as he walked away from the bar and began climbing the steep hill back towards the town centre. A loud sound from behind was the door to the Rat de Cave slamming loudly and he naturally thought it was Marcel. He turned and saw it wasn't his informant at all but two of the characters who had been sitting at the counter. They spotted him, shouted something he didn't catch and then started running towards him. Startled, Baxter turned on his heels and began sprinting. He straightaway discovered the going was difficult on account of the wet and uneven cobbles and almost immediately lost his footfall and stumbled. Suddenly a hand grabbed him from behind forcing him head first onto the pavement. He turned and was rewarded with a punch which caught him squarely on the chin.

With self-preservation in mind he kicked out wildly, catching his assailant in the shin causing him to give out a high-pitched yell.

The other man, who was of considerably larger size and of the sort of proportions which were going to hinder his agility, dived recklessly for Baxter who managed to roll aside before the large body mass crumpled onto the pavement. Baxter sprung to his feet ducking a swing from the first man and landed a punch which found a gap in his defences and slammed into his face causing a jet of blood to spurt from his nose. The fat man came at him again, dragging him upright before sending a breath restricting punch into his stomach. The next thing he knew hands were rifling through his jacket pockets, roughly and without any regard for his discomfort. He head-butted the man thumbing through his inside pockets and was rewarded with a punch which would have caught him squarely on the face had he not moved at the last moment, glancing the bow to the side of his head. Baxter struggled to get up, but his arm was pulled behind his back in a half nelson and a knee pushed hard into the crease of his spine. The other man took a long-bladed knife out of his pocket and Baxter caught the menacing sight of the blade as it drew close to his neck. Suddenly a gunshot sounded, it echoed loudly between the buildings, a single volley but its resonance continued for several seconds. His first reaction was to cower, thinking he had been shot, but then to his relief he realised there was no sensation of pain. His attackers yelped in surprise and suddenly let go of him, the smaller man kicked him in the stomach before grabbing the big man and running off down the street.

Scrambling to his feet Baxter looked around to see who his saviour had been. He caught a brief sight of a moving shadow disappearing down an alleyway to his left, but it melted away in the blink of an eye. Although the main street appeared empty he could still hear the pounding of his attackers running away down the hill.

He was left alone wondering if it had been a real gunshot. It now seemed highly unlikely, but just then he caught the pungent whiff of nitro-glycerine, the distinctive smell of sawdust soaked powder propellant which is released after a bullet has been fired.

Baxter lost little time making his way back to the town square and the moment he spotted a taxi sporting a green light, he didn't have to think twice before flagging it down. He jumped in and directed the driver to take him the short journey back to his hotel. As the cab bumped over the cobbles, he checked to make certain his wallet was still in his zipped trouser pocket and to his relief it was, but his mobile phone was gone and the loose change in his coat pockets had also been taken. He wondered why those men from the bar had attacked him. Surely it wasn't simply a mugging, but more to the point who had scared them off with the single gunshot? Was it the same person who had been following him earlier? Wait a minute; he thought to himself, I bet that was Marcel following me. But then when he thought about it he quickly concluded that the man must have been nimble and light footed. He couldn't imagine Didier hiding his hunk of a body behind corners, although a woman could, and that gave him some room for thought.

The small hotel where he had earlier booked a room was comfortable enough, but lacked any signs of refinement or welcoming hospitality, but this was to be no more than a place to lay his head and sleep. He opened the bottle of malt whisky he had bought on the ferry and poured himself a generous measure.

Exhausted from the evening's adventure, he sat back on the small settee sipping the spirit. He immediately felt the soporific effects of the liquor as it passed easily down his throat, far too easily for someone who was trying to kick the habit. This relaxed his tensions and gave him the opportunity to mull over the day's extraordinary events, but no logical conclusions would be cemented into a coherent pattern this night.

Marcel spent another hour drinking, and as was his way he drank on his own. He certainly didn't like the company at the bar although there were only two left propping up the counter. Those left in the Rat de Cave, including Marcel, had heard the gunshot outside, they could hardly miss such a loud crack at that time of night, but it was nothing to do with them. By the time his third bottle of rough red had come to an end, Marcel staggered out of the bar and fell backwards onto the cobbled street before passing out in a drunken stupor.

CHAPTER 2

LOT 365

THE PROPERTY OF A GENTLEMAN.

The LCD numbers on his bedside clock displayed ten thirty, Baxter blinked and looked again in disbelief for he hadn't intended to sleep this late, a larger than usual intake of whisky the night before had been responsible for that. Although he had no particular desire to leave the comfort of his bed, there was work to do today and he needed to get galvanised and that meant getting his day kick-started.

He walked across the room and threw back the wooden shutters. The street outside was narrow and the buildings tall, yet the sun had already climbed high enough to peep over the roofs opposite, emitting a thin shaft of light which cut through the darkness of the road below. This was a brief window of light, in stark contrast to the shadows which engaged most of the narrow streets here in Bourge-Vilaine. Just as he was turning away he noticed a solitary woman standing opposite, leaning against the lamp post, her feet casually crossed, he thought in the manner of a prostitute, but she was certainly never a lady of questionable virtue. He took in her attractive profile. Her dress was smart and very understated her shoes plain and black. She held a newspaper level with her head so once again he couldn't make out the woman's face, but he felt certain she was the same lady he had seen the night before sitting in the corner of the bar Rat de cave. But what was she doing here? Was she spying on him? And if so had she been his follower the previous evening? Perhaps it was just a coincidence but Baxter had never trusted coincidence, it had a knack of preying on the mind. He had known others in his profession, admittedly dealers on the outer fringes of respectability, who had come to a sticky end because they believed in coincidence.

By the time he left the small hotel the street was completely deserted, the mystery woman whoever she was had disappeared and he even found himself doubting his earlier assertions that it was the same person. After all, he reasoned, he had barely seen her features in that dimly lit bar. He told himself he was being paranoid, he usually was, that was his way; to his annoyance people were always telling him that so he guessed there must be some truth in it.

He popped into the boulangerie on the corner, bought a couple of croissants and a bottle of Perrier water and as he made his way to the saleroom he greedily tucked into his make-do breakfast.

The Salle des Vent in Bourge-Vilaine was a typical provincial auction room straight out of nineteenth century France, unchanged by time and appearing to be unchallenged by modern standards.

The building looked much like any other along the street, but it was so much larger than the street frontage suggested. A long converted warehouse behind the front façade was the auction room proper. The small entrance vestibule had a long shop window covered with posters citing terms and conditions and a simple poster advertising today's sale. People crowded around the front counter filling in forms as they waited for their bidding number which was simply written on a square piece of card.

The catalogue consisted of ten photocopied pages listing four hundred and twenty five lots. It was an unsophisticated publication in black and white and with no illustrations but surprisingly at the bottom of the absentee bidding form he spotted an internet address, salledesventeBourge-Vilaine@orange.fr. So his assumption as to the primeval appearance of this auction room was quite mistaken, they were up to speed with modern internet technology and that meant he might just have some competition here.

He skimmed his eyes down the list until he came to lot seventy six. '*A good seventeenth-eighteenth century chest*'. Marcel was right, there was very little in that description to excite anyone, a fact which raised his hopes significantly. Lot seventy six did not particularly stand out amongst the numerous coffers, armoires and time worn nineteenth century chairs and settees. When he lifted the lid and riffled through the papers inside, he could see nothing of any obvious interest. The large bundles wrapped in brown paper denied the inquisitor any hint of their content, if they had been opened and read, then someone had gone to great trouble to hide the fact.

The auction commenced at eleven o'clock, not sharp, but characteristically five minutes late, but that in French parlance was etiquette. The first lots went slowly, agonisingly so, without any hint of a need to get on and reach the better pieces. He couldn't understand who would want to bid on half a dozen mis-matched plain glass drinking tumblers or an assortment of empty whisky bottles or even more bizarrely, a collection of one hundred beer caps, but some of these strange lots attracted aggressive bidding. Gradually, slightly better quality lots and sometimes items of an antique nature were being auctioned.

His eyes wandered around the room as he tried to calculate who the serious bidders were. Most of those here looked like casual opportunists waiting to snap up a low-priced bargain that could be sold on for a tiny profit. He could usually spot the serious buyers; it was to his advantage if he could identify them and keep them under scrutiny for later on when the important bidding started.

Then he spotted something from the corner of his eye. He squinted and held his gaze for several seconds. He couldn't quite make it out from that distance but something over there looked interesting, in fact it appeared to be potentially wonderful, but then he knew from experience it could be something or nothing. The mystery object was partly hidden behind an armoire in the far right hand corner of the saleroom. He needed to find out exactly what it was, and quickly in case it came up for sale in the next few minutes.

He surveyed the room and was relieved to see that all eyes were on the auctioneer, or rather his assistant who held up a frayed Persian carpet. The porter had the room in fits of laughter as he poked his head through a gaping hole in the middle. Baxter rose then sidled over to the far end of the saleroom and casually leant his arm on the side of an armoire. He went through the motions of weighing up the tall cupboard, but he was really scrutinizing the blue and white vase partly concealed behind it. His heart started to pound, he was looking at that magical combination of blue and white, not any old blue, but a cobalt blue of great intensity and depth and a white of slightly green tinted marble. At that moment he knew he was looking at something special, something very special indeed.

'Baxter!' A familiar voice from behind made him jump.

'Shirley, Shirley, he declared with surprise.

'Watch it,' she said eyeing him cheekily, 'you're not too old to go over my knee.'

This was a long standing charade. In the trade she was affectionately called Shirley Shirley, simply because Shirley had an antiques shop in the Shirley suburbs of Southampton.

He kissed her cheeks one after the other in the normal French manner.

'So what brings you down here Shirley?

'Oh a bit of this and a bit of that, I went to Le Mans yesterday.'

'Any good?' he asked, not particularly interested, but he enquired as a matter of polite courtesy.

'Not bad, some antique textiles, you know the sort of thing.'

He certainly did and that was why he was baffled that she should be here in the little Bourge-Vilaine auction rooms. Surely Marcel hadn't told Shirley about the letters as well, but then why wouldn't he cash in as much as he could. What he did know was that Shirley did rather well buying old documents. Her trick was to roll them up two or three at a time, then tie a pink or red ribbon around them, and sell them in a glass dome jar to Americans who eagerly snap them up for coffee table talking pieces.

Shirley wandered back to the middle of the room and took a seat close to the right hand side and Baxter followed.

Several times he almost nodded off, the auction was that exciting! Had it not been for Shirley's constant chat, he probably would have.

He didn't even hear the auctioneer pronounce lot seventy six, the good seventeenth century chest he had been preoccupied chatting to Shirley.

'I'm selling lot seventy six then,' the auctioneer shouted in an excitable tone. Baxter suddenly came to his senses.

'Are there any more bids?' he barked surveying those gathered in front of him.

Since discovering the Chinese vase, Baxter had largely lost interest in the letters; however, the chest was still worth bidding on. The problem now was what had the bids risen to? He looked at Shirley, he hadn't noticed her put her hand up, but he could hardly ask her what the current bid was. Had she deliberately distracted him so he would miss out? He decided it couldn't possibly have gone that high and most likely only reached five hundred or so. He waved his numbered card.

A gasp rose in the room, and it was then he sensed there might just be a small problem.

'I'm impressed Baxter, I dropped out at five hundred.' Shirley announced. He hadn't even seen her bid, but then he knew she always saw off her rivals by using the discreet wink technique.

'I have a new bidder.' The auctioneer beamed at him. 'At four thousand five hundred euros then, are we all done?'

Baxter gulped what had he done? He couldn't possibly find that sort of money. Who on earth had bid it up that high?

'I'm selling lot seventy six then for four thousand five hundred euros.' He raised and then held his gavel in anticipation and surveyed the room for the very last time.

'Five thousand' the high-pitched voice came from his assistant who was manning the telephone at his side. Baxter had never been so glad to be outbid and when the auctioneer looked at him for a further response, he firmly shook his head.

Baxter surveyed the gathered crowd, waiting for the auctioneer to drop his gavel.

'Are we all finished then? It's on the telephone at five thousand euros.' The gavel landed loudly.

Because the winner was a telephone bidder Baxter was denied any opportunity to see who had bought the chest of enigmatic letters and for so large a sum of money.

'So… who is your admirer back there?' Shirley asked, half tilting her head sideways. He looked at her puzzled. She had a twinkle in her eye as she dropped her head and raised her eyebrows waiting for his reply.

He looked behind, the three or four rows of chairs were occupied by a mixed collection of spectators, mostly middle aged or above, some engrossed in their catalogues others eagerly watching the auctioneer. But there she was at the far end of the saleroom sitting with her catalogue in front of her face, the mystery woman who still refused to reveal her identity.

'I haven't a clue who you're talking about,' he said dismissively.

Shirley half turned 'Just over, ah she's just got up and left, that's strange.'

'I'm sure she couldn't have been an admirer,' he replied.

'Well.' Shirley placed her hands on her hips, 'she couldn't keep her eyes off you, watched your every move for the last hour.'

'How do you know.' he asked puzzled at her ability to see what was going on behind her.

'You really don't know much about auctions do you,' she said raising her eyes and then slowly shaking her head. 'See that mirror over there,' she said pointing to a dressing table amongst the line of furniture on her right.

'Yes I do.' He confessed. It now dawned on him. 'You use that conveniently angled mirror to watch your competitors from behind, very clever Shirley.'

She just smirked; she loved to get one over him.

'What did she look like Shirley?'

'Well she was quite nice looking if you like that sort of thing,' she said dismissively, tossing her hair to one side.

'Shirley!'

'Alright, she was gorgeous, red hair, long at the sides, well dressed oh and nice eyes, I did notice her eyes, they were very pretty, I hate her,' she said in jest.

Shirley bid on and won a mixed lot of vintage chateau curtains, some ormolu bronze fittings, and a large trunk of old textiles which could only be described as scruffy chic.

'You're buying well Shirley?'

'Not bad, but I've got to get out of here fast.'

'Why what's wrong?' he said gently.

She shook her head to and fro rather gingerly; 'I get headaches, quite bad ones sometimes, so must dash, pop into Simply Chic sometime, you never know you might find something you really can't live without.'

He somehow doubted that, but promised to try and pay a visit one of these days, if not he would see her around, he often did.

Baxter estimated the auction rate was about ninety lots per hour, so taking into account the traditional French lunch break from twelve until two- he predicted it should be shortly after five when the Chinese vase would come under the hammer, but there were a few other Oriental lots before that so he decided to return early.

Back in his hotel room, Baxter relaxed on the bed pondering the morning's auction. He would have quite liked to have won the chest, it was decorative and had a good resale value and probably even the letters would have returned a profit had the lot been five or six hundred, but five thousand euros! Someone certainly wanted those letters very badly, and as far as he was concerned, that someone could only have been the French Government. But then he considered, apart from him, there must have been at least one other serious bidder to push it up that high.

His mind returned to the rather more exciting Chinese vase. Standing three feet high, it had the classic dragon winding its way around the belly, but it was the colour of the blue which excited him the most. It was that brilliant cobalt with inky black tones which told him this piece of Chinese porcelain was from the early Ming dynasty. The problem on Baxter's mind now was who had seen the vase, did anyone else realize its value, and how much was it likely to sell for? After paying Didier five hundred euros he still had two thousand eight hundred to play with and could raise another three hundred from the nearby cash machine. He decided he was prepared to bid up to twelve thousand euros, but would have to ask his friend Keith to wire the money through on his behalf should that be necessary. He just about had that level of funds, but no means to access such a large amount from here in France.

The auction proceeded slowly and rather uneventfully at first, and then just before three o'clock the auctioneer announced the withdrawal of one hundred and ten lots, due, he said, to a last minute legal dispute over ownership. The room erupted in uproar, people shouted angrily, robbed of the opportunity to buy some of the best pieces on offer that afternoon and in particular some very fine eighteenth century Sevres porcelain. As a result, just after four o'clock, an hour earlier than expected, the auctioneer had reached lot three hundred and sixty five. It was listed as '*The property of a Gentleman.*'

A large blue and white Oriental vase in good order.

The auctioneer started the bidding at a modest one hundred euros and at first it looked as though there wasn't even going to be a maiden bid. He was just about to raise his hand when a young man made the first move. Baxter saw his bid and raised it. The auctioneer glanced at the first bidder but he shook his head. Baxter though he was going to get his vase for a measly one hundred and fifty but another bidder entered the arena, and pushed the price up to six hundred and fifty. The whole thing was over in less than two minutes. The hammer went down to Baxter at seven hundred euros.

He couldn't believe his luck as he watched two other lots of Chinese porcelain go under the hammer, not bothering to bid, but curious to see how much they went down for, and to his amusement, one insignificant piece outdid his vase.

The relative hush of the auction room was suddenly interrupted by a loud commotion in the front lobby. Heads turned to see what the fuss was all about and despite the auctioneer raising his voice to try and compensate; it had become difficult for the crowd to concentrate on the proceedings, and so the auctioneer called for a break while he went to sort out the cause of the disturbance.

Baxter took this opportunity to leave as there was nothing else to interest him in the sale, or at least he doubted there would be.

As he left the auction room he was aware of a commotion up ahead and as he reached the entrance lobby it had turned into what could only be described as a battle scene. A number of people were jostling around the enquiries desk shouting loudly, waving arms in the air, the screaming was raising the temperature to fever point. As Baxter looked on in amazement, a handful of men were arguing fiercely with the clerk, while several others behind tugged at their shoulders trying to push their way forward. He suddenly realised the protagonists were angry over the way the auction had been conducted, some furious over the withdrawal of one hundred choice lots, and others that a Chinese vase had already been sold a good hour before it should have been. It transpired that some of these unhappy punters had travelled some distance to bid on that particular piece, they were angry to have been robbed of the opportunity to bid for it. To a man they were demanding that it be re submitted for sale, saying there should have been an adjournment in the proceedings to make up for the mis-timing of later lots.

The clerk was most apologetic but despite his attempts to pacify the crowd it was clear he was unable to manage the rapidly deteriorating situation. Auctioneer's clerks have to cope with all sorts of problems, smooth out the grumbles of many an awkward customer, but this was a situation which this clerk had never before experienced. Suddenly, to his relief, he saw the auctioneer making his way through the crowd. He rushed to meet him.

'We have a riot out here Monsieur Renaud,' the clerk said in a voice that shook with fear and confusion. 'They're angry because you moved the auction list forward.'

'Alright leave it to me, I'll deal with it,' the auctioneer said. He suddenly homed in on Baxter standing in the doorway. 'Wait there,' he shouted sternly wagging his finger at him. 'Sorry Sir,' he said composing himself 'will you please wait out there for a few moments, I won't keep you long.'

He turned back to his clerk. 'Before we let that gentleman over there clear his lot,' he said pointing to Baxter, 'we have to deal with this unfortunate situation here.'

He held his hands up and clapped loudly; the noise abated. 'If all of you would care to come this way,' he said as he ushered the protesters into his side office. With the area all but cleared, Baxter noticed three immaculately suited men left behind standing by the door. But what caught his attention was the fact that two of them were Oriental, a comparatively rare sight in rural France. The third man however, was European, probably French and quite compact.

All three were deep in conversation and whilst Baxter couldn't understand a word they were saying, he could read their body language and that told him in no uncertain terms that they were cross, very cross indeed. If their displeasure was over the Chinese vase, and as two of them were Asians he thought it probably was, then he wondered why they hadn't joined the others to continue the dispute in the auctioneer's office.

Baxter saw his chance and quickly moved towards the counter. 'I want to pay for my lot it's three hundred and sixty five.' He showed the man the lot entry neatly circled red, then removed his wallet and started counting the crisp notes.

'I'm sorry sir, replied the clerk, but I have to check with the, ah here he is.' The auctioneer emerged from his office followed by the disgruntled clientele, many of whom were still demanding the lot be re-offered for sale. The auctioneer turned back to face them once again and for the umpteenth time explained why that was not possible. He told them it was out of his hands, the lot was sold and that was final.

'Mr Baxter would like to pay for lot three hundred and sixty five,' the clerk said. The auctioneer turned on his heels and glared at his assistant, amazed at how insensitive the man had been considering the escalating situation here in the foyer.

The crowd closed in behind Baxter, intimidating and jostling. Little was actually said, but their mood was such that it made words quite unnecessary.

The auctioneer sensed impending danger to one of his customers, and with little likelihood of the crowd dispersing any time soon, he grabbed Baxter's arm and escorted him into his office quickly locking the door behind them. He snatched up his telephone and instructed his porter to take lot three hundred and six five to the loading bay and wait with it there until he arrived. Baxter eagerly handed over the correct amount for his lot and the auctioneer folded the notes and put them in his desk drawer without even counting them. He opened his outside office door, looked up and down the road and then escorted Baxter across the street to his parked car. Two porters carried the vase round from the rear of the building and placed it carefully on the back seat of his vehicle, the auctioneer shook his hand and bade him farewell, adding a note of caution.

The rear entrance road was no more than a side street providing warehouse access to the auction gallery as well as a couple of smaller artisan workshops. It also offered convenient parking for twenty or so cars but was normally full well before the auctions began and so Baxter had been fortunate to have secured a place here. Leaving the deserted lane he turned into the main street and spotted the two ominous looking Chinese gents standing at the auction room entrance, they spotted him and turned. Baxter resolved to avoid making any eye contact with them, but no matter how hard he tried, he couldn't resist looking across the road as he drove past. It suddenly dawned on him that his vase had probably been on somebodies want list, and if there had been a Chinese syndicate after it, then that type of person could be very unreasonable. He knew from experience that Asian art was something the Chinese considered to be their cultural right. Whatever the case, he had evidently upset quite a few people; the sooner he distanced himself from the auction room and Bourge-Vilaine the safer he was likely to be.

CHAPTER 3

PURSUIT

Baxter was now faced with the vexed problem of how to get his vase safely back to England. He wasn't naïve enough to think those he had just upset would quietly melt away. No, he had stirred the cauldron and now it was about to boil over. He knew most of those involved would be hatching plots to intercept him, rob him of his bounty, and there would be many opportunities during the long journey back to England.

He was now driving around Bourge-Vilaine circumnavigating its lower ring road, giving himself time and opportunity to weigh up his options and come up with a solution and one which would solve the dilemma he was faced with. He knew he had to act quickly. Remaining in the town was not an option, or at least not with a large Chinese vase in the back of his car, but yet it would be dark in a couple of hours and the thought of making the long journey home at night was not one he relished. It then dawned on him that there wouldn't be another ferry out of Cherbourg until tomorrow morning anyway, so another solution had to be found.

Baxter knew next to nothing about cars and unlike the average male, he didn't care to take note of types, shapes or especially colours, they didn't interest him one little bit, except of course for his prized Celica. But in his rear view mirror he realised the same vehicle had been behind him for quite some time. A black Citroen appeared to be shadowing him closely, it was distinctive with its gleaming chrome trim, large elongated lights and it was a right hand drive on French plates, but other than that it was just another car but one which had uniquely caught his attention.

He had now reached the straight length of road which paralleled the old town walls, he put his foot down on the gas but the Citroen kept a constant pace behind. He spotted a supermarket advertisement on a large roadside hoarding warning the would-be shopper that the superstore was one hundred metres on the right. The store, close to the road frontage had a large central pedestrian entrance, but the car park was situated at the rear, its only access was through an old narrow arched coaching entrance, an historical mediaeval gateway which had been preserved and incorporated into the new building layout.

Spotting a gap in the queue waiting to access the gateway, he manoeuvred himself between two vehicles, upset one driver in the process and was awarded with an irritable and very rude gesture from a man in a battered Renault van. He shot through the opening and arrived in the rear car park while the Citroen was forced to wait its turn. Baxter swung into an empty bay, parking tightly between a large white van and car. He unclipped his seat belt and lowered his body below the steering wheel, angled his wing mirror and watched the Citroen drive slowly past the parking lots, pause and then turn right and disappear out of sight.

This gave Baxter the opportunity to leave by the rear exit. He swung his car to the left and put his foot down. Within a few minutes he was forced to break quite abruptly when he caught up with a short queue waiting to re-join the ring road.

He tapped on his dashboard, urging the couple of cars ahead to make some effort to breakout and join the fast paced flow of traffic. *We are going to be here all day at this rate,* he said to himself. *Come on, there's plenty of room to get out now* he muttered out aloud. He opened his window and waved at the driver in front, a gesture to get moving. He checked his rear mirror and of course the Citroen was once again behind, but fortunately there were two other cars between them so if he could get out reasonably swiftly, he felt confident he would lose them again.

While he was waiting he dipped into his dashboard compartment, found his other mobile phone, plugged it into the cigarette lighter slot and rang London Shipping agents Royle and Bevis. He had used their services a number of times over the years and especially during his time at the British museum. Baxter was in luck, his contact informed him they were due to ship a consignment to England from the museum in nearby Rennes. It was for a temporary loan exhibition on Brittany folk art to be staged at the Horniman Museum in London's Forest Hill. If he could take his Chinese vase to the museum in Rennes, the man at Royle and Bevis said, for a small handling fee they would ship it back for him the day after tomorrow and keep it until he collected it back in London.

A plan was beginning to come together, but first he had to find a way of shaking off his pursuers and that wasn't going to be easy.

At last the car ahead moved out into the traffic. Without stopping Baxter followed. Veering right he narrowly missed colliding into a speeding car as he shuffled behind another fast moving vehicle.

Once again on the ring road he took a sharp left and climbed up the steep cobbled hill which took him to the centre of town. He ducked down several side streets, and once again joined the ring road. He checked his rear mirror and to his horror, the Citroen was once again a couple of cars behind. He needed to take some drastic action and soon if he was to shake them off so he could head for Rennes, and before the museum closed for the night.

This was the third time he had circumnavigated the town by the ring road, up ahead the traffic lights were on green. He slowed hoping they might turn just before he reached them and miraculously they did. *Perfect* he said to himself *I've got you this time* he thought as he sailed past the amber light. In his rear mirror he watched the car behind stop and breathed a sigh of relief as he put his foot down once again. But what he didn't see was the Citroen sailing through the red light. Cars meeting it in the middle of the road screeched to halt and horns sounded from all directions, but the Citroen just carried on regardless.

It wasn't long before Baxter spotted his tail pacing him once more. He was lapping the large sprawling industrial estate, the same one he had passed three times previously. He spotted the sign for a tyre and exhaust service centre and thought maybe, just maybe.

The inspection booth ahead was empty as he screeched to a halt inside its portals. The Citroen had stopped at the service centre entrance waiting to see what Baxter's next move was going to be.

A mechanic came out of a side room and walked up to Baxter's nearside window.

'You have to go to the office first sir,' he told Baxter.

He nodded and drove slowly out of the far end of the booth. He was still weighing up his options, as were his pursuers who continued to wait by the entrance. Baxter sedately made for the rear exit road which fed into other parts of the industrial estate. The Citroen driver thinking Baxter was making a run for it out the back way, reversed and at speed shot back onto the ring road and disappeared with the intention of intercepting Baxter when he re-emerged a little further on. But Baxter didn't actually leave the service centre exit, instead he thrust his car in reverse and backed into the service booth. The French mechanic with arms folded watched his antics with a look of incredulity, the mien on his face was priceless, but then Baxter guessed the man was probably used to crazy Englishmen, most French service providers were.

Baxter explained he had a problem for which he was willing to pay generously if the man could help him out. He told him he needed his car kept out of sight for an hour and perhaps the mechanic would check the oil and tyre pressures, give it a wash and then deliver the vehicle back to his hotel.

'I have to check with front office first,' the mechanic said adding 'this is a very unusual request and besides there might be another car booked in.'

Baxter took two fifty euro notes out of his wallet and waved them in front of the man's face.

'Actually sir it *is* getting late, I doubt there will be any other cars booked in now.' He went to take the money, but Baxter lowered his hand. 'So you don't have to check with the front office first then,' he said waving the notes once again. The mechanic agreed that wouldn't be necessary and stuffed the notes in his top bib pocket. Pleased with the generous one hundred euro tip, he quickly pressed the button which sent the hydraulic doors down hiding Baxter's car from public view. Baxter rang a local taxi company and the cab arrived surprisingly quickly, it had obviously been nearby when the driver received the call. Baxter put the vase in the back of the cab and asked the driver to take him to Rennes Museum, a thirty minute drive on what was a moderately fast and busy road.

He stretched his legs as the cab pulled away, quickly picking up speed as it raced down the ring road. Baxter spotted the Citroen coming in the opposite direction. On instinct he ducked his head out of sight and smiled, wondering what they would do next.

The taxi was now cruising through the open countryside. He leaned back, all he could see now were the tops of trees rushing past his window and for the first time in countless days he was relaxed enough to close his eyes and catch a brief but welcome nap.

The journey to Rennes was uneventful, which made a pleasant change from his recent exploits and once the vase was in the safe hands of the shippers, he jumped back in his taxi and made the short journey back to Bourge-Vilaine.

Arriving back at his hotel it was just getting dark as he stepped out of the cab. His sleek silver Toyota Celica was once again neatly parked outside the hotel. Thanks to the garage mechanic, it now gleamed like a new pin.

Although it was now almost six years old, this car was his baby, he loved the fact that the name Celica came from the Latin heavenly or celestial as it had been a heavenly gift to him after he had found a very rare silver Monteith. Baxter had stumbled on the silver punch bowl in a respectable Surrey antique shop. It was labelled *A silver punchbowl by Paul Peppard 1846 price eight hundred pounds.* Baxter knew right away this was wrong; the piece was a classic *sleeper,* a term used in the trade to denote an item which has been incorrectly identified and priced too low. It was certainly not nineteenth century as the label claimed, but a very rare example of a late seventeenth century Monteith. The piece in question was in essence a large silver bowl with notched rim for suspending wine glasses in the basin which held iced water. But what made this piece early and rare, was its detachable rim and fine Chinoiserie decoration. The final points which had been completely missed by the dealer, was the position of the hallmarks on the side of the vessel rather than underneath, also the P.P. was not Paul Peppard but the most famous Huguenot silversmith of all time Pierre Platel.

Baxter had little difficulty finding a buyer willing to pay forty five thousand pounds for it, and as it was cash, the taxman never knew anything about it. The Celica GT he had dreamed of was then his.

It was now eight o'clock as he skipped up the hotel steps. At the counter he palmed the top of the bell twice and waited. It was several minutes before the proprietor emerged from a dimly lit back room from where the muffled sounds betrayed the fact that he had been passing away the long tedious hours watching television.

Baxter told him he wanted to pay his hotel bill as he expected to leave quite early the following day. He always liked getting that bit over and done with as it meant he had the freedom to leave whenever he wanted to. The man did not enquire as to whether the room had been satisfactory, or if Baxter had enjoyed his stay in Bourge-Vilaine, but was quick to ask if he had heard about the terrible killing outside the bar Rat de Cave the previous night? The proprietor seemed to take great pleasure relating how the man's throat had been cut, adding that he had been shot several times and his lifeless body thrown down a flight of stone steps landing outside the church of Sainte Pierre. Baxter didn't for one minute believe the man was recounting fact, but making most of it up as he went along and typically exaggerating the details. But why was he telling him all this? It was almost as though the man knew Baxter had been in the bar Rat de Cave the previous night!

Baxter confirmed he hadn't heard anything about the incident and asked who the poor victim had been.

'It was a most hideous creature,' he said screwing up his face with a look of disgust. 'They say he was a giant, a full three metres high and more.' He held his hand above his head to illustrate the height. 'Those who saw him said he was half man half beast, probably a werewolf, it was a terrible, terrible sight.' He rolled his head from side to side.

'Really,' was all Baxter could say? He would have been quite amused by this ridiculous, over-embroidered description had it not been for his experiences outside the bar the previous night and particularly that gunshot.

'So what was his name?' he asked suddenly suspecting who the victim might have been.

'They say he was a man without a name, he had some strange Chinese message pinned to his back and the tattooed initials MD on his arm.'

A chill went down Baxter's back as he realised who the so-called giant was, it would have been his informant Marcel Didier, but why? Had Marcel refused to divulge Baxter's name to some thug who was desperate to buy those letters? If that was the case then what was in those Marie de Couvegne letters that made someone kill to ensure they got them and just who had paid so much for them? No it didn't make any sense; Didier wouldn't risk his own life for anyone and especially not for him, of that he was certain.

He was in no doubt that a conspiracy was behind the whole business. His mugging, Marcel's killing, none of it made any sense.

In many ways he was relieved he hadn't bought the letters and instead secured the Chinese vase. He suddenly felt a little foolish, amazed at the way he had gone to all that trouble to take the vase to Rennes. Nobody was interested in him, it was all to do with the letters, except for that black Citroen of course! Whatever was going on here, the sooner he left Bourge-Vilaine, the happier he would be.

Back in his hotel room he relaxed with a generous glass of whisky, mulling over the events of the past twenty four hours. He was generally satisfied with the way the day had panned out but still unable to put all the pieces of the jigsaw into their rightful places.

It was another bright and clear day as Baxter jumped into his car and made an early start on his way home. The first rays of sunshine impaired his vision causing him to squint, but he was in no hurry as he headed back towards Cherbourg and his ferry home to good old England.

Quickly leaving Bourge-Vilaine in the distance he was now on the road to Avranches happily whistling to himself and feeling relaxed and refreshed after the stress of the previous day, a day which had presented so many ups and downs and thankfully a day which was now behind him.

He suddenly spotted in his rear view mirror something he really didn't want to see, but perhaps it wasn't the same black Citroen that had followed him around Bourge-Vilaine the previous day. He looked again and although he couldn't be one hundred percent certain it *was* the same car, but he could see it was a right hand drive on French plates as it paced him, and that made him suddenly nervous.

Baxter wasn't in any rush today; he had at least seven hours before his ferry departed from Cherbourg on route for Portsmouth, a journey which should take no more than five hours, so he was intending to enjoy a leisurely drive through the glorious French countryside. French drivers rarely dawdle, they like to drive bumper to bumper and overtake, even on bends, no especially on bends with little visibility, but this driver was maintaining a constant distance and that was worrying Baxter. The other thing he realised for the first time was that the other vehicle was a right-hand drive with French plates, not that unusual but even so he was still surprised.

Every time Baxter pressed on the accelerator, the car behind maintained the same distance between them even to the extent of denying any other vehicle the option to close the gap.

After a while he wondered if he should call their bluff by pulling into one of the roadside laybys to see what they did. If the other car stopped he would know it was following him. On the other hand he reasoned, if they wrongly believed he was carrying a valuable Chinese vase then stopping in so remote an area could be a dangerous option and perhaps just what they were hoping he might do.

He decided to up the pace and keep moving, after all he would be in Avranches in twenty minutes or so, and in a city that large he felt confident he could give them the slip, whoever they were. But who were these men, were they really trying to steal his vase? As he maintained a constant speed, he tried to put the pieces together, but none of it made any sense; was this all a dream, was he going to wake up in a few moments?

As he rounded the next corner he got his first view of the impressive cable-stayed road bridge sweeping across a wide natural gorge linking the countryside of Brittany to the sprawling outskirts of Avranches. In normal circumstances he would take time to admire the stunning way the bridge complimented the beautiful rolling countryside, but today he was more concerned about those who were following him.

Suddenly he heard a roar of acceleration as the Citroen came up fast on his left hand side, pulling in front, forcing Baxter to slow down, but he had no intention of being manipulated by them. He felt a rush of excitement as he braced himself and then braked suddenly, opening a gap between the two cars and then threw his gears into first and accelerated fast catching them off guard as he swerved to his left and overtook the other car.

Within minutes they were catching him up rapidly but he maintained his speed as he approached the beginning of the bridge which spanned the large Cameau ravine. The sharp incline forced him to change down a gear. At that moment he was catapulted forward by a jolt, followed in quick succession by further battering to the rear of his car throwing him violently forward his seat belt countering painfully against his chest.

He fought desperately to remain in control as his vehicle veered to the nearside, his tyres bouncing uncomfortably on the concrete kerb causing his steering wheel to judder violently in his hands.

In his wing mirror he could see the black Citroen swerving sideways once again making an attempt to overtake him on the left hand side, its tyres squealing as the driver negotiated this dangerous manoeuvre. He now knew this most certainly was no dream, and he wasn't going to escape its consequences by simply waking up. Baxter put his foot down hard on the accelerator and his powerful Celica GT released all its one hundred and eighty eight horsepower. The front end reared up and his body was forced into the back of his seat as he raced towards the top of the bridge.

At this point the gorge bottom was two hundred metres below, and despite the trees which softened its profile, it was nonetheless a terrifying sight for anyone like Baxter who was scared of heights.

He had suffered from acrophobia since an early age when he fell off his father's step ladder. That mishap had only been a tumble of a couple of metres, but to a five year old it was like falling from the heavens, an experience that had never completely left him.

Through his rear mirror he could see the black Citroen gaining pace and soon both vehicles raced down the sloping bridge. Several more cars and another van were recklessly overtaken leaving the road ahead completely empty.

The black Citroen came alongside, its smokey black windows screened the driver from view making him even more sinister. A split second later the Citroen ploughed into Baxter's rear offside door forcing the back of his car to bounce along the roadside barrier. He slewed the steering wheel left and the car vaulted back on to the carriageway with an uncomfortable bump.

He accelerated harder which caused his body to lurch backwards once again, almost snapping his neck in the process. The dial hit one hundred and forty, fifty and now reached one hundred and sixty kilometres an hour. He heard a strange ping but couldn't think what the sound was until a second louder clang reverberated above his head and he realised the sounds were bullets ricocheting off the open sun roof bar. The other car was once again paralleling him on his left hand side, the front window was open and an Oriental man was struggling to control his steering wheel whilst at the same time waving a gun in Baxter's direction. Another two gunshots sounded in quick succession, one missing altogether but the other impacting into his bonnet sending sparks flying across his windscreen.

He realised this was no longer a game of cat and mouse. Up until now he had found this pursuit quite invigorating in a funny sort of way, but things were no longer balanced in his favour, the guy was now clearly out to finish him off and he had the means to do it.

Baxter braced himself, pushing his back firmly against his driving seat. At this heart wrenching speed he knew his next action was going to be little short of terrifying and possibly even suicidal. Baxter gripped the steering wheel as tightly as he could and then jumped on the brakes. His car protested aggressively, shuddering violently like a machine gun in reaction to the unreasonable expectations of its owner. The anti-lock braking system responded immediately forcing all four wheels to maintain the same rotational speed which encouraged his car to keep tractive contact with the road. The seat belt tightened gripping his chest like a vice as he left his seat and lurched towards the windscreen only narrowly avoiding impact. His car had decelerated to a touch under one hundred kilometres an hour and the other car slowed in response but despite pumping his brakes, his Celica was still rapidly closing the gap on the steep downward slope. Seconds later he was involuntarily overtaking the other car on the inside. Further gunshots sounded and in blind panic Baxter spun his steering wheel sharply to the left. His Celica made contact with the front of the Citroen sending its rear end into a spin. The driver pumped his brakes frantically, desperately fighting to maintain his cars centre of gravity, but it was an old vehicle which lacked any form of assisted braking.

The Citroen suddenly fishtailed swerving from side to side as the rear end of the car spun around and bounced against the left hand barrier. Baxter watched in amazement as the Citroen shot upwards spiralling to the left before it was hit by an oncoming lorry on the opposite carriageway. The impact at that speed was immense sending the Citroen catapulting into the air and spinning cleanly over the safety barrier. With its engine whirring loudly it dived down to the gorge below bouncing noisily against the rock sides before exploding with a muffled bang several seconds later.

Baxter didn't stop even though he knew he should have waited at the scene, but carried on eager to distance himself from what had just taken place. His car was obviously in a sorry state, he could hear dislodged parts clattering loudly as they dragged on the road surface and the steering was now difficult to control. Baxter continued to gently brake bringing his speed down to a more comfortable sixty kilometres an hour. Just as he began levelling out close to the end of the bridge, he took one last look backwards in his rear mirror. The lorry had stopped a few metres from where his vehicle had collided with the Citroen and the driver was walking back to the spot where two other cars were pulling up at the scene.

As soon as the bridge was out of sight, Baxter pulled into the first layby. He could have cried as he walked around the battered wreck which until a few minutes ago had been his beloved car. He had taken so much trouble over the years to keep it in near pristine condition, and now he didn't even know if it was going to get him back to England. Still, at least he was alive, unlike the Citroen driver and his passenger.

He pulled the dented bumper away from the back wheel and threw it into the bushes and then lifted the double exhaust pipe, lashing it to his boot so as to raise it from dragging on the road.

He was soon on the road again but no longer enjoying his drive through the French countryside. His car continued to groan every time he accelerated and on every bend he had to fight to control his steering wheel. It wasn't only his car which was distressed, his head was in turmoil as he struggled to control his nerves which were in tatters, whipped to fever point every time he thought about the events that had just taken place.

He was within sight of Avranches when he first heard the distant sound of a siren, possibly a fire fighting vehicle, but he suspected it was more likely a police car. He wondered if it was chasing after him, perhaps it had picked up his trail following the tragic accident on the bridge.

His concerns were mounting as he began to ponder the vexed question which was would the French police believe his story, would it appear too fantastic? Also how much should he tell them and what part should he keep quiet about?

He could now see the vehicle with the siren, a blue Renault with flashing light was rapidly closing the distance between them.

The police car pulled him to a halt.

'Is this your car Sir?'

'Yes it is,' he replied

'It appears to be in a rather sorry state.' The officer raised his eyebrows as he walked around Baxter's battered vehicle.

Baxter realised he was now in trouble but decided not to say any more than he needed to and so pretended he hadn't understood what they'd said. He often found it useful to use the excuse of *being English* in order to side step awkward French situations.

The policeman demanded his papers, and then ordered him into the back seat of the police car while the other officer took the wheel of Baxter's vehicle.

CHAPTER 4

ON SUSPICION OF MURDER

On arriving in the centre of Avranches, the police car pulled up outside a red-brick two storey building, obviously constructed shortly after the D-Day destruction of much of this part of the town.

Baxter was led to a desk where a sergeant checked him in, the officer nodded to the policemen who marched him into interview room two. This was a functional but bland room and even on that summer afternoon the interior glossy painted walls gave out a decided chill.

Baxter had not been told why he had been stopped and brought here to police headquarters, only that he was invited, as the sergeant put it 'to have a chat with the inspector of police'.

Sitting on a long hard bench he looked across at the policeman who stood motionless by the door, but got no reaction whatsoever.

Baxter decided at the outset to say no more than was necessary. One thing puzzled him and that was how quickly they had apprehended him, barely fifteen minutes after the accident on the bridge. He was nervously aware they were probably going to throw the book at him for not waiting at the scene, and might even charge him with manslaughter? His car certainly had enough evidence to keep the local prosecutor happy.

The door opened, the policeman stiffened and smartly saluted a tall uniformed officer who entered, nodded and then sat down at the table. His subordinate handed him a file which he opened, slowly turning the pages, all the while twisting his large moustache between his fingers. The French Gendarmerie Inspector in dark blue jacket and pale ice green shirt, was wearing a tall flat képi hat with the usual exploding grenade motif. He was obviously from the 'old school' and judging by his proudly worn coloured ribbons or batons, he was highly decorated for service abroad. He looked hostile from the outset.

The Inspector straitened his white tie. 'So Monsieur Baxter,' he began in a cavernous voice, 'tell me, who did you meet in the bar Rat de Cave in Bourge-Vilaine on Wednesday evening?'

Baxter blew a sigh of relief, the question was an easy one compared to the difficult one he had feared. He wasn't expecting to be questioned about the Rat de Cave- he thought he'd been dragged in to be grilled about the car that went over the bridge.

He was a little disappointed the policeman hadn't spoken in French as that would have given him a slight edge. He lowered his eyebrows attempting to give the impression he didn't know what they were talking about and then took a deep breath before launching into the lie. 'The bar Rat de Cave! I have never heard of it, definitely not,' he said dismissively.

'If you please Monsieur Baxter, we know you were in the Rat de Cave on Wednesday evening.'

Baxter scratched his head 'Ah I did go for a drink in a little bar, that might have been on Wednesday evening, yes, I believe it was but I have no idea what it was called though.'

'So who were you with?'

'I wasn't really with anyone as you put it, but I did pass a few words with a local, I believe his name was Marcel something,' he offered, still attempting to act vague.

'Marcel Didier was it?' the inspector snapped.

'Yes that was it, Marcel Didier.'

'Well that wasn't his name,' the Inspector pronounced triumphantly, his lips distorted into a peculiar smile, 'the man you met was Andre Poisson.'

'Really, well you seem to be better informed than I am.'

'I'm not so certain about that Monsieur Baxter because I think you know rather more than you tell us, is that not correct.'

Baxter wasn't entirely surprised his informant was not who he had claimed to be, after all there was no doubt in his mind the man had been a shady and probably disreputable character.

'Ah,' he raised his finger 'the barman called him Marcel and so *he* clearly knew him by that name.'

The Inspector leaned back in his chair, twisted his moustache and gave a little nod, though whether as an expression of acceptance, or otherwise, Baxter couldn't tell.

'That may be so Monsieur Baxter but tell me what the meeting was about? I want to know what Poisson was offering you?'

'Well to be honest Inspector I didn't really know the fellow, he contacted me via a friend who said the man had some information he wanted to sell me.'

'Some information!' The Inspector swung in his chair and leant over the table facing Baxter. 'And what information was that?'

'Just details of an old antique chest which was coming up in the next day's auction room in Bourge-Vilaine and that's all.'

'You've travelled a long way to buy this so-called chest.' he wagged his finger. 'And did you buy it, because if you did I would like to know where it is?'

'No Inspector I didn't, someone was prepared to pay substantially more than I could afford.'

'Tell me why it is that you treat me as a fool?'

'I don't inspector, I'm telling you the truth.'

'I don't believe your story Monsieur Baxter,' he said at great speed. 'I think you tell me lies and I will get to the truth of this matter.'

Baxter could see he had his back against the wall. The Inspector's face was reddening as he banged his fist on the table. He suspected the man was used to people being afraid of him and the fact that Baxter wasn't, or at least not yet, was most likely affecting his ability to control his composure

Baxter swallowed hard. 'okay' he offered,' it wasn't just the chest, the man told me there were letters inside which he thought were valuable, but I can tell you now that I didn't see any of them.'

'These letters tell me, what was so special about them?'

'Well that's the strange thing.' he screwed up his face to create an impression of empathy towards the Inspector; he went on 'I gave him a few euros for the tip off, but he didn't tell me anything except that they were written by a certain Countess de Couvegne, but I haven't a clue why they were so important. But I'll tell you one thing Inspector,' he said with enforced authority, 'someone thought they were rather special to pay five thousand euros for them.'

'Five thousand euros!' The Inspector blew a long sustained whistle through his pursed lips. He got up and opened the door.

'Henri,' he shouted across to the desk sergeant, 'get the Bourge-Vilaine auction rooms on the phone, I want details of,' he paused and turned back to Baxter 'What lot number was it?'

'Lot seventy six'

'That's lot seventy six,' he bellowed across the corridor.

He returned to his desk and scribbled some notes, then searched for something in the file. 'Ah here it is,' he looked up, 'and I see you paid him five hundred for that tip off, quite a lot of money for so little information, wouldn't you say.'

'But...' Baxter was suddenly taken aback by the Inspector's knowledge of facts he thought only he knew, 'what makes you think I gave him five hundred?'

'It says so here in this report but we will come to that later.' The Inspector rubbed his chin then went on. 'So tell me did you see anyone else in the bar Rat de Cave that night?'

'Err, well yes, there were some shifty characters sitting at the bar, I didn't like the look of them, I thought they were rather rough characters, and it turned out two of them were.'

'Rough characters, I see,' the Inspector said with a look of amusement, 'please continue.'

'I also didn't like the look of the barman, he was a very unfriendly man, and I don't think he liked the English.'

'So we have a rough looking clientele and an unfriendly barman who did not like Englishmen, and anyone else you didn't like the look of?' he asked mockingly.

'A man came in for some cigarettes, he didn't stay, oh and a woman, she sat by the window and had a cup of coffee.'

'Can you describe her?' he said raising his eyebrows, 'and was she a rough type also, as you like to say?'

'Well, no, not at all, actually she was rather elegant.' Baxter chuckled.

'This is not a laughing matter monsieur; we may be charging you with murder, I don't think you will be laughing then, do you?'

'Look Inspector I didn't see her properly but I think she had reddish hair, she was tall with long slim legs and I suppose in her early thirties, but that's about it.'

'You see Monsieur Baxter, the authorities have been watching your Marcel Didier or should I say Andre Poisson, for some weeks now but someone killed him before they could find out what he was up to.'

'There is one other thing I should add Inspector.'

'Carry on, I'm all ears,' he said

'Well when I left the bar, two of the men who had been inside, jumped me and stole my mobile and some money.'

'And you think they were customers from the Rat de Cave do you?'

'I know they were Inspector, but that's not all, you see someone fired a shot and it frightened them off, otherwise they might have killed me.'

'And who precisely fired the shot, you do realise this is now a most serious development?' he said eying his subordinate.

'I don't know Inspector but is this going to take long because I have a ferry to catch in a couple of hours?'

'I don't think you will be going very far today. In fact unless I can find out rather more about you and what you're doing here, you may well be staying in France for a very long time.' He cleared his throat. 'Tell me did you kill the man you called Marcel Didier?'

'No of course not, that's ridiculous Inspector. I hardly know what to say. I admit I did meet him in the Rat de Cave, but I can assure you I know nothing about the circumstances leading to his death. '

It was now dawning on him that he was in a tricky situation and worse, he didn't have an alibi for that night which meant he was a murder suspect? He only hoped the Inspector didn't know about the bridge incident as well because that would really put him in the frame as a ruthless killer.

His lame response didn't go down well. The inspector stood up, banged his fist on the table. 'Ridiculous you say,' he began shouting in a high pitched voice. 'I think you did kill that man, brutally and savagely with a knife and all because he knew something it was dangerous to know, something which was a threat to you or your dealings down in Bourge-Vilaine.'

Baxter shook his head and remained silent.

'Have you seen this before?' he asked holding up a crude drawing of four flying bats encircling Chinese letters.

'No I most certainly haven't, why should I?'

'Because Monsieur Baxter, whoever killed Poisson pinned this to his jacket, and I'll wager that person was you.'

Baxter forced a laugh 'I'm sorry Inspector but you're on the wrong trail here. I would suggest looking closer to the Orient.'

'Oh am I Monsieur Baxter, you see I think you are a contract killer sent by someone, I don't know who, but you come here to silence this poor man, but the mistake you make was to leave the money you gave him in his pocket, that measly sum of five hundred euros in crisp new notes. You see Monsieur Baxter, a man like that might spend some of it on wine, but I doubt it was of a fine quality. A man like Poisson doesn't have that sort of money and certainly not in crisp new notes, so we know he wasn't killed for his money by a mugger, so that only leaves you Monsieur Baxter; I put it to you that you are the killer.'

Baxter turned on a forced laugh; the inspector spun on his heels and grabbed Baxter's neck from behind. 'You laugh at me again, you will not be laughing when I have finished with you, you are a cold and calculated killer and I'm going to make certain you spend a very long time in prison.'

A rap on the door and a very attractive female sergeant looked in the gap.

'Come,' retorted the Inspector

The door inched open and the nervous officer entered; the

Inspector released his grip on Baxter's neck. The officer whispered something in the Inspector's ear before handing him a singled sided note. She glanced sideways at Baxter as she left the room.

'The Bourge-Vilaine auction rooms have told my sergeant here that you bid four thousand five hundred euros for the letters, that is most certainly a great deal of money Monsieur.'

'That was a mistake actually; I didn't realize the bids had gone that high, you see I wasn't concentrating, but I can tell you now that I was relieved when somebody outbid me.'

'You're lying to me, I think that is another very convenient story you are telling me, but,' he leaned across the table his face practically touching Baxter's 'I don't believe you and I will find the proof; I will most certainly discover it.'

Another officer came in waving a piece of typed paper and whispered a few words in the Inspector's ear. Baxter heard the name Atterbury mentioned and his ears pricked in recognition, the name was familiar but he couldn't put a face to it. A few moments of reflective silence followed as the policeman gazed at the piece of paper and then without a word the Inspector stood bolt upright and marched briskly out of the room leaving the other officer behind.

Baxter was left pondering his fate and trying to piece together what appeared to be disparate and unbridgeable parts. Firstly, who had killed Didier, and why? And what exactly did those Chinese symbols mean? Also, why had the authorities, whoever they were, been watching Didier? He was hardly a big name within the criminal world, in fact that wasn't even his real name, so why did he use an alias. He also had a nagging feeling that the car chase incident was in some way related, but apart from the Chinese connection with the note on Didier's back, that was as far as that line of reasoning took him.

It had been barely five minutes when the door opened again and the Inspector returned, this time smiling apologetically.

'Goodbye Monsieur Baxter and be quick or you'll miss your ferry home.'

'Is that it,' Baxter reeled in shock.

'Yes Monsieur Baxter you can go home now.'

'So tell me Inspector, just who did kill Marcel Didier, I'm intrigued to know?'

'Marcel Didier! Never heard of the man,' the Inspector quipped.

'Alright then, Andre Poisson, if that was his real name.'

'You are mistaken Monsieur Baxter, there has been no murder, no murder at all, you must forget all this now and go home.'

'But…' he protested.

The Inspector put his hand on Baxter's shoulder. 'If you please, I think you should go quickly,' his voice dropped to a whisper 'oh and by the way drive most carefully, your car does not look very safe. If I didn't know better I would have said it has been in a very nasty accident, perhaps on a bridge or something like that.' He shrugged his shoulders and ushered Baxter out of the room.

Baxter didn't need telling twice, it was obvious the Inspector knew far more than he was letting on, but why hadn't he questioned him about the incident on the bridge? Surely the death of two people in an accident which could easily be linked to Baxter's car was important to somebody, but apparently not.

As he passed the Sergeant's desk he was just in time to see a red-haired woman disappear into a side room. This time Baxter knew it was his mysterious lady from the bar, but who was she and why was she always on his tail?

As he left the police station he was still trying to work out who the mystery woman was, if she had in some way been responsible for his release, then at least he had that to thank her for.

He felt robbed that so little of what had happened over the last few days had made any sense. Baxter liked a good mystery, but this one, one he was clearly part of, made no sense at all. He was sorry to be leaving it all behind, unanswered, unresolved and shrouded in uncertainty here in France.

CHAPTER 5

LA CERAMIQUE CHINOIS

Baxter loved London, the streets were fast and noisy and the smells were reassuringly familiar, such was the contrast to the last few days over in France. His adventure there had left him with a mixture of emotions; events which had turned his life upside down were still swirling around in his head. The overriding sensation was one of relief, a realisation he was free following his release from the police station in Avranches. He certainly had nothing to do with Didier's death but at the same time he was still concerned regarding his involvement with the fatal car incident on the bridge, an event which the French police had apparently ignored, but why?

He also had a sense of bewilderment over the bizarre letters which had sold for such an extraordinary sum of money, but was he finding tenuous mystery where no mystery existed? The more he thought about the recent events, the darker the story became. But as he pulled himself together all sensations of self-doubt and irrationality were far outweighed by excitement and elation over his discovery and successful purchase of the Chinese vase.

Baxter arrived back at his Chelsea mews cottage late that night, tired and irritable but relieved to be once more back in the safety of his home. His address in this most fashionable quarter might suggest he was a man of means, but that was far from the case. He had inherited the cottage from his aunt Matilda. When her older sister Rosamond died Matilda sold the big mansion in Knightsbridge and bought the Chelsea mews cottage, a much smaller place in which to spend her final years. For ten years she lived there on her own, virtually as a recluse. When she first acquired the property it had been hastily converted from the stable block belonging to a large house, to a mews cottage. She never spent a penny on the property and whiled away her last days in what could only be described as poverty.

When Aunt Matilda died she left everything to Baxter. At first he considered selling the run-down cottage believing he couldn't afford to carry out the essential repairs which had been brought about by so many years of neglect. He had all but handed over its destiny to a local estate agent when he made an unexpected discovery.

Being the only heir to his aunt's estate the cottage had been left to him lock stock and barrel, exactly as it was the day she passed away. The contents were very much outmoded by modern standards, but scattered around the property were some reasonable antiques, mainly furniture and a few pictures, but at first sight little of any great value. However, after some initial research he discovered one of the maps on her wall was potentially valuable. It was a copy of the legendary 'Americae sive Novi Orbis by Abraham Ortelius' considered by many to be one of the most important early maps of the Americas and always in great demand on that Continent.

He had taken it along to Windsor and Park auctioneers who gave him the good news. They confirmed the rare map was indeed genuine. It was not only in mint condition but was from the first edition of Ortelius 'Theatrum orbis terrarum' and dated 1570.

Six months later it came up for sale in the Bond Street auction rooms selling for the princely sum of eleven thousand six hundred pounds. Baxter used the proceeds to have the property renovated and had lived there ever since.

The main problem now on Baxter's mind as he tossed and turned in a desperate effort to sleep, was what to do with the Chinese vase. It was a purchase he didn't intend to keep and so he had to consider very carefully how best to sell it on.

He was certain it had a reasonable value, in decorative terms certainly in the low thousands, but potentially he knew it could be a lost masterpiece from the fifteenth century and if that was the case, then it would be worth a considerable amount of money.

If the furore at the auction room was anything to go by, there were others who thought the same. It was those others he had upset that concerned him the most as he was convinced they would be out to steal it from under his nose if they had the slightest opportunity.

He had managed to stay ahead of the game so far, but only just bearing in mind his conflict with the Chinese in Brittany. One way or another he knew he was going to have to be smart if he was going to hang on to his treasure.

Before he could do anything, he needed to collect it from the Horniman Museum in Forest Gate. The shippers Royal and Bevis had told him it would be ready for collection after ten o'clock tomorrow morning, from that moment on he would be at risk so he had to think this one out very carefully.

Once the vase was back in his possession he would need to have it assessed by an expert, he knew just the man to consult, but the prospect of carrying it around London was not an appealing one. He decided photographs would be the solution and provided they were of good enough quality they would convey much of the information his expert would need.

There was nothing for it, he just couldn't sleep, there was just too much going on in his head, so he jumped out of bed and began searching his mews cottage for a suitable hiding place for the vase. After hunting in every corner and alcove, dismissing all the obvious hiding places he came to the conclusion there was only one possible hidey hole for a three foot high vase, and that was in his hot water cylinder. It was perfect; he could cut off the copper top, drop the vase inside and replace the top with the heating element inside the vessel and then solder the top securely back. Once the lagging was neatly replaced no one was going to find it in there, he felt certain of that. He would naturally turn the thermostat down a little, but he knew the impervious porcelain would withstand very hot water provided there were no cracks or potting faults, he would check carefully beforehand.

Sleep was still eluding him and so he slumped into his armchair, opened his laptop computer and started researching the internet. Past auction results have always been a good place to begin when looking for comparable examples, but he quickly realised he was not seeing anything even remotely similar to the vase he had bought. Deciding he wasn't getting anywhere on the various internet auction result sites, he locked into the British Library on line portal and went straight to OPAC to browse the online catalogue. This fantastic resource lists some twelve million records. He selected ten books and then clicked 'my reading room requests' and designated them for the following day. This was his usual way of pre-ordering his books and thereby avoiding long waits alongside the one thousand or more people who visit the library every day.

Despite a restless night, Baxter was up early and by nine had already prepared the copper water cylinder. He was excited at the prospect of collecting his vase and having the opportunity to examine it properly. During his time in Bourge-Vilaine he hadn't once had the chance to study it in any great detail and so was naturally desperate to satisfy himself that it really was as good as he had imagined. So often he'd experienced the phenomenon of buying a treasure too good to be true, only to find out later on close scrutiny, that it was indeed too good to be true and not at all what the piece had appeared to be when first snapped up in the heat of the moment.

The other point of contention was why the Bourge-Vilaine auctioneer had placed such a low estimate on the vase. Were his expectations really that low? It certainly made him wonder if he really had over rated it.

Baxter looked out of his window checking the street below, on his guard against people watching him, waiting for him to make a move, poised ready to intercept him if given the opportunity. The road in both directions appeared to be deserted. He needed to get across London but his car was in such a distressed condition he doubted it was legal to drive in the U.K and besides, he had to maintain vigilance in case he was still under observation, so he decided to call a taxi for his first appointment of the day.

'The Horniman Museum' he instructed the driver Steve, whom he knew very well. As the cab pulled away from the curb and joined the moving traffic in the Broadway he looked listlessly out the window watching people thronging the pavements. He wondered where on earth they were all heading, so many people marching briskly in both directions; each would have their own agenda, as did Baxter on this bright summer's morning. Despite the usual traffic congestion the journey to the Horniman took less than twenty minutes, and to his relief his vase was waiting in the collection bay. He shouldn't have been, but he was impressed by the way it had been carefully packed before transit. Past experience should have told him that would be the case as the shippers Royal and Bevis were used by museums worldwide and were second to none as far as their reputation was concerned.

It was now mid-day as he arrived back at his cottage with the Chinese vase still in its packing crate. His hands trembled as he prized apart the wooden slats, unravelled the bubble wrap and finally lifted the vase out of the polystyrene box. He lifted it onto his coffee table and examined it closely for the very first time.

The intensity of the cobalt blue was superb, it had a rich soft tone with heaped and piled effect highlighting the design and when he turned it over the unglazed foot rim was wedge-shaped in section. All these pointers were characteristic of very early Ming dynasty pieces. It really was as good as he had imagined, better than he'd dared hope. He stuck to his decision to hide it away, after everything that had happened since the auction, he was in no doubt it was too risky to carry around London in the back of a car. But before secreting it he took a dozen and more photographs, taking particular care to obtain good images of the inscription. With the vase safely tucked away inside the prepared water cylinder, he replaced the top, soldered it in place, turned the thermostat down and re-filled it with water.

Excitement was mounting in the well of his stomach as it started to dawn on him as to exactly what he might have bought. He was confident the piece dated from as early as the Ming dynasty, but was it late sixteenth or early seventeenth century or a piece of extremely rare Yuan dynasty porcelain? If it was the latter then it would be very valuable indeed. He also wanted to know what the strange inscription down the side meant as that would quite likely have a bearing on its identification.

The next problem was his battered car sitting in his garage; he decided not to risk driving it even the short distance to his local repair centre, so rang them requesting an urgent assessment for insurance purposes.

The mechanic shook his head in dismay as he surveyed the damage to Baxter's car. He had known the Toyota Celica for six long years, lavished all the care and attention a car of that marque and quality deserved. To see it in this state was painful.

'What do you think then?' Baxter asked trying to gauge the man's expression, which was desolate at best, 'that bad is it?'

'Pretty much so, yes,' he replied, slowly tugging at the rear wing causing it to fall clattering to the ground.

'I hardly need tell you it requires a new wing,' he said pointing to the gaping hole in the side, 'the passenger door has had it, a new bumper and twin exhaust system and if I didn't know better, I would have said these are bullet holes here along the roof gutter.' He looked expectantly waiting for an alternative explanation but he didn't get one from Baxter who merely shrugged.

'Not to mention rear lights and a re-spray which will be expensive for a car of this age?'

He pressed the green button on the car lift.

'Come under here,' the mechanic said waving his inspection lamp, 'look at that, the chassis is twisted out of alignment. What on earth have you been doing? You're normally such a careful driver.'

'I am, but the other guy wasn't, he can't be repaired but this can, can't it?'

'I'm afraid you're wrong about that. Shock treatment of this nature can never be put right; the car's a write-off.'

'But surely there must be something you can do.' Baxter was desperate to save his car from the scrap yard but despite all his protestations, the mechanic wouldn't budge, the car was definitely a write-off and he would inform the insurance company to that effect. He offered Baxter a Vauxhall to use until the insurance was paid out in full.

The mechanic felt certain he spotted a tear in Baxter's eye as he said his goodbyes to his beloved car.

The British Library has been described by some as an unfashionable building. Moved from its original location at The British Museum, the St. Pancras replacement is a red brick and slate grey multi-layered edifice. Opened in 1988, it's the world's largest library with one hundred and fifty million items which include fourteen million books, so naturally it's a building of impressive size and complexity.

Baxter handed in his premier reader's pass at the main foyer and proceeded to the third floor where the Asian and African studies were located. Because he had pre-ordered his books, they were brought to him almost immediately.

He first thumbed through a modern copy of The Great Yongle collectanea together with its translation in English. This monumental piece of work was commissioned by the Ming Emperor in the fourteenth century. The project had involved copying and preserving all known literature up to 1408 and contained some twenty three thousand sections or Juan as they were known. Unfortunately a great fire destroyed all but seven hundred sections, of which this was the last. Although it had much information on Chinese porcelain, it was not specific enough to help identify Baxter's vase.

He moved on to study the catalogues of A.W.Franks, the great benefactor to the British Museum, and found references to blue and white temple vases, but all of later Ming date. Von Brandt's letters from eighteen ninety four mentioned the porcelain looted from the Summer Palace in Peking, but contained very few specific details and nothing that would identify individual pieces. The works of Hobson in the twenties pointed him to a pair of vases acquired by the great collector Percival David and for the first time he could see a direct link with his vase, but more importantly the mention of another one, which was apparently illustrated in 'La Ceramique Chinoise' by Ernest Grandidier. Fortunately Baxter had the foresight to order this large folio and quickly thumbed through the pages until he reached plate one hundred and three. It was not there. He could clearly see a slightly jagged edge where it had been torn from the book. Someone had evidently stolen it.

'It's err Baxter isn't it?' A voice quietly enquired from behind. Baxter shot around to see a tall distinguished man in his late fifties holding out his hand. Baxter took it and the handshake was firm.

'Assistant Commissioner.' he responded in surprise, surprised the man had recognised him as they only rubbed shoulders very occasionally and only at the Oriental Society meetings.

'Atterbury, just call me Atterbury,' he said in a matter of fact way, 'I don't like titles out in the public gaze, too many eyes and ears.' He looked around taking note of who was in earshot.

Of course, Baxter said to himself *that's Atterbury and that's whose name was mentioned at the Avranches police station!*

'So I see you're swatting up on La Ceramique Chinoise, you must be researching something important,' he said peering over Baxter's shoulder.

'Not really, just general study.' What about you?'

'Just passing through, but a word of caution, I have it on good account that there is an important piece of Chinese porcelain about to surface, the buzz is going around so if you do come across anything of that nature then be very careful who you trust,' he said giving him a knowing look. He went to leave, then turned suddenly. 'By the way Baxter, should you need any advice or help then don't hesitate to give me a call at the Yard, here's my number,' he said handing Baxter his card.

Baxter took the card noting his department was the Specialist Crime & Operations Directorate. He felt a certain warmth in the knowledge that he had an ally in Scotland Yard, and one who had presumably had something to do with his sudden release from the police station in Avranches.

Unsuccessful from his researches, Baxter made his way along the third floor walkway, and then he spotted her, the familiar mystery woman. It was definitely her, no doubt about it, three floors down walking slowly yet purposefully past the foyer. She briefly looked up and then turned quickly, hiding her face, deliberately looking away from him.

He ran to the lift and stumbled in his panic. Two men helped him to his feet, he apologised and embarrassed at his clumsiness he blamed his fall on the highly polished stone floor. However, their faces suggested they thought he had perhaps over indulged in lunchtime drinks. Reaching the lift he travelled to the ground floor then rushed across the large entrance vestibule, past the front foyer and out through the revolving doors and into the courtyard. The mystery woman was nowhere in sight, as was her normal forte' she had simply vanished, an act which she always seemed to perform quite effortlessly.

He sat on one of the benches regaining his breath. The chequer-board brick and stone outside sitting area with terracotta planters was a pleasant place to rest and reflect. He wasn't alone, a number of people sat around the quadrangle eating sandwiches, typically with a book in one hand and a small plastic box balanced on a lap. One man was still working, busily tapping the keys on his laptop. Several people were in conversation on their mobile phones; their faces suggested they were talking to loved ones or perhaps unashamedly flirting.

Baxter reflected on his failure to find any direct references to his vase, but he was now convinced it really was of some importance. And what about the detached coloured plate mentioned by Hobson. He had informed the library assistant of its removal just in case they thought *he* had taken it.

The thought that kept returning was what Atterbury had really meant when he referred to 'an important piece of Chinese porcelain'. Was he possibly meaning *his* find? And why was the assistant commissioner of Scotland Yard suddenly being so pally and offering his assistance?

He finally came back to the conclusion he had made the previous day. There was only one person who could tell him about his vase, he was clearly wasting his time trying to research it himself, so he resolved to pay the Professor a visit first thing the following morning.

Baxter was once again having a poor night's sleep, something which always seemed to follow when events of the day resulted in a mind in turmoil. He tossed and turned trying to shake away the thoughts which continually invaded his mind. What on earth was going on, what secrets lay behind his Chinese vase and how was Atterbury of the Specialist Crime & Operations Directorate involved, if at all? But the overriding question had to be who the mystery woman was? He had asked himself the same question time and again. She was the key to the whole affair, but he couldn't understand how she fitted into the jigsaw.

He closed his eyes but he couldn't sleep because the images of the woman kept filling his mind.

A dozen times or more he had awakened after sweating profusely, acutely aware of the dream which wouldn't go away. The mystery woman was constantly there, but never her face, it was always turned away from his gaze. He so desperately wanted to see it but he just couldn't.

He needed to know if she had the most beautiful and sexy face he had ever set eyes upon or was it horribly disfigured and one which challenged all but the strongest to look at. To make matters even more complicated Baxter was aware he rarely, if ever, saw any face during his dreams. People who visited his nocturnal adventures always seemed to be blurred, distorted; their faces were there but not discernible in any way. Strangely he always knew who the person was, even though he couldn't see their face.

He had read all the normal theories which claimed how the human mind was not capable of inventing faces during dreams and those which were seen were real faces of real people, people who had been observed during one's lifetime, but not necessarily people they knew or remembered.

He had seen hundreds of thousands of faces throughout his life, so there was an endless supply of characters which his brain could choose from. But he had never seen the face of the mystery woman and that was why in his dreams his brain was unable to find it.

Finally, deciding sleep was going to pass him by, he got up and jotted a few notes on his computer; a set of questions which would jolt his memory on specific points. He printed off the notes and pushed them into his jacket pocket.

CHAPTER 6

8 BEDFORD SQUARE

As was his way, Baxter parked the loan car where it was cheaper and easy to do so even though it was some half a mile away from his place of appointment. Today, for a change, he wasn't in a rush so he ambled along the endless rows of austere grey stone buildings whose re-invented facades were a sad reminder of distant days of affluent commerce.

Baxter loved this part of central London; its diversity of architecture and the relationship with its recreational spaces, those leafy islands which unexpectedly appear in the middle of the built up environment. He had long savoured the thought that maybe someone had forgotten they were there, secreted between the countless rows of buildings, but that was far from the truth, they were highly regarded by residents and locals alike.

Bedford square in Bloomsbury was typical of these green spots.

The houses on three sides were Georgian and perhaps some of the best preserved in London. Typically five stories high, they had once been well to do family homes with additional holiday apartments for relatives, Great Aunt's, nephews, cousins and the like. At the very top of the house where the ceilings were pitched below the roof, servants quarters and in the basement below pavement level, the kitchens, butler's office and housekeeping department.

The age of extravagance was long gone; the First World War marked the beginning of the end when so many young men, servants and heirs alike, failed to return from the trenches. Today every one of these houses had been divided into more affordable apartments.

Baxter looked up at the black and white chequer-board arch above number eight before climbing the four stone steps between the fluted columns. He rang the bell to flat two. The muted sound was distant but quite distinct, and so he waited.

The man he was here to visit was Professor Adrian Hadley, formerly keeper of the Far Eastern section at the British Museum, a very respectable and venerable post.

Baxter had worked for the Professor in the late nineteen nineties when co-coordinating a Chinese exhibition under the auspices of the Chinese Secretary General of the Chinese People's Association for Friendship with Foreign Countries. This had been the first time a major exhibition illustrating the cultural history of China had been held in the west.

Baxter with his newly acquired Oxford MA from the Faculty of Oriental Studies had landed the job of editing the British edition of the vast catalogue of exhibits, a task which had been laborious but at the same time highly educational for him.

He heard confident footsteps on hard vitrified tiles, slow and unhurried, the clinking of keys and the fumbled attempt to find the keyhole.

The door swung open.

'Ah, come in, come in dear boy.' Hadley swung his arm out in the direction of the darkened hallway, his other hand grasped Baxter's, shaking it firmly. 'It's err...' he fumbled

'Baxter.'

'Of course, Baxter yes, so nice to see you dear boy.'

'Do go in,' he said pointing to a pool of light which played on the carpet at the far end of the hall illuminating an open door, 'oh and I'm ashamed to say you'll have to take me as you find me, not too used to visitors these days.'

'Don't worry about that Professor,' Baxter said.

'Just give me a minute, Oh and do find yourself a seat.'

He scurried away muttering incoherently leaving Baxter standing alone in the middle of the room.

This was not a typical Georgian drawing room, or at least, architecturally it was but visually it certainly wasn't. The room was archetypal of every University lecturer's personal quarters. Clearly not a place to sit and relax in elegant Adam style luxury but an extension of the professor's lifelong work, a huge repository of information. Hundreds of volumes lingered in mahogany break-front book cases and equally vast numbers were casually strewn over every table and chair. Stacks of learned journals stood like sentinels on the floor and others, open, were covered in yellow Sticky Notes.

He had only ever been here a couple of times before and that was many years ago, but from memory it appeared to be untouched by any evidence of modernity.

Despite the chaotic nature of the room, it was such an exciting space with so many fascinating items of interest. He wandered over to the far end where a small but interesting oak case was attached to the wall. Inside behind protective glass, a small book was accompanied by a brass plaque entitled *Letters of Indulgence by Joanne Guttenberg 1448*.

'I see you've spotted my Guttenberg,' exclaimed Hadley as he came back into the room.

'Yes 1448, that's rather impressive professor.'

'Rather impressive!' he bellowed. 'That my dear boy is one of the earliest examples of a printed book from anywhere in the world, except China of course and is number two of only three examples known to exist.' He blew on the glass and wiped it with his cardigan cuff. 'Now do take a seat; there are lots of chairs somewhere.' his eyes scoured the room desperately seeking a vacant seat or chair.

He suddenly rushed over to a partially hidden chaise longue and with a swipe from the back of his hand sent quantities of paperwork and magazines onto the floor. 'Here we are,' he declared patting the leather seat. 'Do sit dear boy.'

The professor pulled out a smoker's bow from under his desk and sat opposite with his hands behind his head. He had obviously quickly combed through his silver tousled hair in response to Baxter's unexpected arrival, but had clearly not dressed that morning with a visitor in mind. The long sloppy jumper had a large hole in one arm revealing an off white shirt underneath and also traces of darning from earlier repairs. Trails of food down his jumper suggested he didn't often sit at a table to eat, and his corduroy trousers, dark green when they were new, were now faded and shiny around the knees and his slippers were a clear sign of domesticity.

'Well it's so good to see you after all this time, how many years is it, three, four?'

'Actually it's over ten years Professor.'

'Ten years, is it really that long?' Hadley said in a slow drawn out voice. 'Where does the time go? I'm rapidly running out of years you know.'

'I last saw you at the Royal Academy you were giving a talk on Chinese blanc-de-chine wares.'

'Ah yes I remember it well.' He beamed then leant forward, removing his glasses, squinting in Baxter's direction as though checking or trying to remember exactly who he was.

Hadley had never been too good with names and the same applied to faces. So… many people had crossed his path over the years, but his fuddled brain had little capacity to store irrevelant details, it was dedicated almost entirely to research.

He unfolded a tightly pressed handkerchief from his top pocket, vigorously wiped his glasses and then put them back on.

'So tell me what brings you here to Bedford Square then dear boy, surely it's a tad out of your way?' he said looking over the top of the thick-rimmed glasses which were now perched precariously on the end of his pointed nose.

'I have brought you some photographs of an interesting Chinese blue and white porcelain vase,' he said nervously taking the photographs out of the folder. 'It's of meiping form with what looks like a Yuan dynasty inscription.' He handed the Professor the pictures.

'I realise it's not likely to be mark and period or anything like that,' he hastily added, 'it's the inscription that I'm having problems with as it isn't in ordinary Chinese script.'

The Professor went to the window to examine the photographs in a better light.

Since retiring, Professor Hadley had spent his time researching the development of Ming and earlier porcelain and had gained notoriety for his incongruous articles in the Transactions of the Oriental Society. His well-respected work had discredited a number of important examples in major collections in various parts of the world. In a number of instances he claimed to have evidence which proved some so-called fourteenth century Yuan dynasty works of art were in fact later Ming copies and subsequently worth only a fraction of their supposed historical and monetary value. In one particular case an American consortium had purchased a small but highly important collection in Amsterdam. Hadley had controversially declared the collection to be all later Ming dynasty copies. As a result some people stood to lose a fortune.

Baxter could see the old man's eyes flickering wildly behind his thick-rimmed spectacles.

'Incredible dear boy, absolutely incredible.' he cocked an eyebrow in surprise,' 'but you're surely not going to tell me you actually have the vase in these photographs?'

'Well yes I do but I'm sure it's only a Ming period copy?'

'A Ming copy!' he roared, shaking his head in disbelief, 'you really don't know what you've stumbled upon do you?'

'Well no, I'm not at all certain and that's why I've come to see you professor,' he replied quickly, suddenly embarrassed at the prospect that he might just have pulled off the big one this time.

Hadley rushed over to the far side of the room and pulled out a handful of books from the mahogany bookcase. He returned to his seat frantically scouring through the tomes, dismissing them one after the other, carelessly tossing them onto the floor.

Baxter homed in on a hand painted drawing pinned to the wall.

知己知彼，百戰不殆。

He translated the Chinese proverb out loud and with ease. *If you know both yourself and your enemy, you can win numerous battles without jeopardy.*

'There's a lot of truth in that,' Baxter exclaimed but Hadley hadn't heard a word he had said, too busy as he was in his search for an answer.

'No…. it can't possibly be Ming,' Hadley asserted, throwing down the last of the books he had skimmed through. He looked back towards his bookcase, his eyes lit up. 'Ah of course I know where I have seen that vase,' he said, rising to his feet and stumbling awkwardly across the book-littered room.

'Here we are.' He lifted out a large folio and carried it back to his chair. With a sweep of his arm he sent papers, books and magazines flying to the floor, exposing a desk top.

He laid the large volume down and flipped over the pages of highly colourful illustrations.

'That's a very impressive book Professor.'

'La Ceramique Chinois and its signed by no less than Grandidier himself. Look he signed it on the frontispiece,' he said heaving the pages back to the front cover.

'I looked at the same folio in the British Library,' Baxter said 'but I couldn't find anything similar to my piece, although there *was* a missing plate.' He added.

'Now I know it's here somewhere.' Hadley mumbled as he continued to rifle through the valuable pages. 'Ah yes,' he shouted, causing Baxter to jump in alarm. 'Here we are, just as I thought, the missing Henri de Montaigne vase.'

'The Henri de Montaigne vase?' Baxter repeated

'I take it you've heard of the Henri de Montaigne story?' Hadley enquired expectantly, peering over the top of his glasses.

'Sorry professor, it sounds as though I should have, but I don't believe I have.' He suddenly felt embarrassed, like a schoolboy who had forgotten his seven times table. Then his eyes fell upon the wonderful coloured engraving the Professor had laid open. Baxter was taken aback for here was his vase, the very same one he had hidden away in his cottage. Every detail had been carefully drawn, coloured and then printed, and it was no real surprise that the plate number was one hundred and three, the missing plate in the British Library copy.

'Yes that's it Professor,' he said jubilantly, 'that's the very same vase I have at home.'

'No, that's not *your* vase dear boy.' The professor asserted.

'But you said it was I…' he began but was cut short.

74

'I was going to say the Chinese vessel in your photograph is the *missing* Henri de Montaigne vase, not the one in this book.'

'But I don't understand.' Baxter suddenly felt deflated.

'Tell me dear boy, where did you find this vase, the one you claim to have at home? Did you buy it, and if you did where on earth from?'

'I found it in a little auction room in a small french town called Bourge-Vilaine.'

'Bourge-Vilaine,' Hadley shrieked, 'after all these years the missing Henri de Montaigne vase was in Bourge-Vilaine all the time, incredible just incredible.'

'I don't quite understand the significance of Bourge-Vilaine Professor.'

'General Henri de Montaigne who led the Opium wars in the eighteen sixties and gave his name to the vase illustrated in this book, had a flirtatious and long standing relationship with the Countess de Couvegne of Bourge-Vilaine.'

'From the nearby chateau' Baxter cut in.

'That's right my boy, but the interesting point is that the Count was a prolific collector of works of art, mainly Chinese porcelain, which he housed in a little museum in the Chateau de Couvegne.'

'I see the link with Bourge-Vilaine now.'

Hadley continued 'It's strange that the missing vase should come to the surface now, I would love to know where it has been all these years?'

'At the Chateau?' Baxter suggested glibly.

'Well no it hasn't, because you see it wasn't there when the current Countess contacted me a few years ago asking if I had any knowledge of its whereabouts. She invited me to look in various parts of the chateau and I can tell you now it wasn't there at that time.

Baxter couldn't throw any light on the matter but did point out that the auction described it as *the property of a Gentleman.*

Hadley dismissed Baxter's last remark saying 'That means nothing at all. Auctioneers say things like that all the time, they think it makes a lot sound as though it has a respectable provenance, in my experience that's rarely the case. By the way dear boy, I would be most careful not to reveal to anyone else the fact that you have illegally taken that vase out of France, could be a bit tricky if the authorities over there found out, you know what I mean,' he said raising his bushy eyebrows.

'But I bought it quite legitimately in an auction room.'

'That may well be the case dear boy, but for a work of art of that cultural importance and value you should have applied for a passport before taking it out of the country and I can tell you now they wouldn't have given you one, not in a million years.'

Hadley went over to the sideboard and reached for a hidden key then unlocked a silver mounted Tantalus. He lifted out two cut glass tumblers and a decanter and poured a generous and precisely equal measure of malt whisky into each of the glasses.

'Now dear boy I'll tell you all,' he said as he handed Baxter a tumbler of Scotch. 'Let me explain. You see your vase is the other one to the piece illustrated in this book. Now we know from the Henri de Montaigne records that there were originally a pair of them, but only the one illustrated here had been thought to survive, the other presumed lost or destroyed sometime during the early twentieth century.' He paused to sip his drink. 'The one we do know about, this one here,' he said pointing to the coloured book illustration, 'was sold in nineteen hundred and eight by a Mr. R. Pope of London who acquired it from the old Countess at chateau de Couvegne, but we don't know who purchased it at that time and like your vase, it hasn't been seen since. However, it's rumoured that it might now be in the Max Veerman collection in London, but how he acquired it is a mystery.'

Baxter had listened to the graphic story told by Professor Hadley and it had been most revealing, but one point still puzzled him.

'Just one thing Professor, how can you be so certain this coloured illustration isn't my Henri de Montaigne vase?'

'Ah now that's the interesting part. Firstly this one is recorded as the one sold by Pope in nineteen hundred and eight but more to the point, I take it you've noticed the Arabic script running down your vase?'

'Yes I have, but I can't read a word of it.'

'No, of course you can't, very few scholars can because it's written in ancient Sanskrit. It was intended to confuse all except the very highest Chinese scholars who worked in the Royal Palace, but I can translate Sanskrit. Now the vase in this illustration translated reads; *The rock of Batuta lives.* And that's it, there is no more.'

'That's a very strange and enigmatic statement to make on a piece of porcelain.' Professor.

'Well I have never come across anything like it before but it is said that in the Royal summer palace many secrets of great fortune were hidden in full view using the Chinese art of anhua which means,'

Baxter cut in. 'Hidden words or designs.'

'Quite right my boy, so I think these Sanskrit words must be part of a message, a sacred record of where something has been hidden'

'Okay, so what are you trying to tell me Professor?'

'I believe the rock referred to is a diamond but not any old gem but the diamond of Batuta; a legendary cut stone of immense size which was presented by the Arabian dignitary, Ibn Batuta to the Muslim eunuchs at the Chinese court sometime in the mid fourteenth century. Now when the Mongol dynasty was overthrown by the Ming, all Koranic influences were expelled and valuable gems were stolen, that is those which hadn't been hidden away, but where is this legendary diamond? It has to be in existence somewhere, unless it has been cut-up of course. So although the sentence is incomplete, it would make sense if there were a second matching vase, and I believe yours is the other half to the pair.

Baxter held up one of his photographs. 'So Professor what does my inscription say then?'

'Not so fast, Koranic inscriptions are not easy to translate, as I just pointed out, they were intended to baffle all but Lamaistic Buddhists. I think the first part may be *Mani Pad,* but it will take me a few days to decipher it with any certainty, so leave me the photographs and do give me a ring, say middle of next week. Oh and dear boy, do keep that vase safe, it's worth rather a lot of money and perhaps a great deal more if it unlocks the secret to the diamond of Batuta.'

'I realize that Professor I think I might have already upset a few people since I acquired it, and for a mere pittance.'

'Not Chinese! do tell me they were Europeans and not Orientals.' Hadley asked, clearly shaken by what Baxter has just told him.

'Most of those at the auction room were European but there were some Asians, probably Chinese buyers, along with a tall man. I think he might have been French, but I'm not certain. I must admit there were a few angry punters there and all because they had missed the opportunity to bid on the vase. Another thing I should perhaps mention is that my French informant was murdered.'

'Oh dear.' said Hadley 'that news does not bode well.'

'That's not all Professor, when the police found him he had a note pinned to his back with a strange symbolic message written in Chinese script.'

'Draw it for me dear boy, it could be important.'

Baxter did his best, the bats were simple enough, but the Chinese text was very blurred in his recollections.

Hadley looked over Baxter's shoulder. 'That's something to do with a secret Chinese organisation, I have seen reference to it before somewhere, but it eludes me right now.' He snatched off his glasses and unfolded a tightly pressed handkerchief to vigorously wipe them.

'That's bad news my boy, very very bad news indeed. We must all take care. In the meantime I'll look into the Chinese bat symbols just in case they are connected in some way.' He thought for a minute then raised his bushy eyebrows. 'If anything untoward should happen to me just remember the Guttenberg over there, it might just be didactic the next time you see it'

'Didactic?' Baxter enquired

'Come dear boy I thought you had a good understanding of cryptology and symbolism. Didactic simply means containing a hidden message or clue, a bit like Chinese anhua but I'll say no more. Now away with you and do ring me next week.'

He led Baxter down the passage. Opening the front door, he turned. 'Goodbye my boy. Oh and do be careful, we have entered very dangerous waters, very dangerous waters indeed.'

CHAPTER 7

THE CARTEL

The headquarters of the London and Hong Kong cartel, known by the respectable name of Beaux-arts d'Asie, was built on one of the many sites of bomb damaged London. Two decades after the Luftwaffe dropped their last incendiary this war torn area was redeveloped with shop and office premises. Today Jermyn Street consists of complete re-builds and a few old Georgian buildings hidden behind more recent facades. Here is a Mecca for antiquarian bookshops, bric-a-brac and collectible arcades along with up-market antiquity galleries. The maze of backstreet shops offers everything from Greek and Roman pots to reproduction resin netsuke. Here in the shadow of the British Museum an industry flourishes supplying the vast numbers of hungry tourists with a taste of the past, a souvenir to mark their visit which had begun in the marbled galleries across the road. True, many a respectable Roman oil lamp or Greek coin could be purchased at a reasonable price, but the unwary could just as easily return home with a very clever reproduction. Perhaps the majority of people were quite content in their own innocence because if they believed the clay pot they had just bought had been last touched by a Roman soldier two thousand years ago, it no doubt served its purpose, whether it be genuine or reproduction.

However, many respectable and genuine antiquities of the scale and importance of the ones in the collections at the British Museum could be bought here by those tourists with large enough wallets. Gallery Twenty One was such a shop and here everything was most definitely genuine and of the highest quality.

Despite displaying one of the best collections of Oriental art, the most important pieces were not for sale but hidden away two floors below in a steel vault; they rarely saw the light of day and certainly not on view to anyone outside the cartel executive.

Gallery Twenty One was an offshoot of its main showroom in Hong Kong and part of the secret European headquarters of the

Beaux-arts d'Asie cartel. Formed in the early nineteen sixties the cartel was an organisation which consisted of twenty one wealthy collectors and investors, nine from the United States, Five from China, six from Hong Kong and one from England. They were all wealthy long term investors in early Chinese pottery and porcelain and every one of them had made fortunes from investing in this lucrative commodity.

During the last four decades the cross-border trade in illicitly obtained or stolen Asian art works had slowly developed. However, over the last few years the international black market for Chinese cultural objects had burgeoned alongside economic globalization. The authorities claimed the black market for Chinese art today followed closely behind narcotics in terms of monetary gain.

This illegal trade had been largely fuelled by recent changes in China as a result of modern development, which led to the unearthing of more and more priceless pieces. The humble labourer had little trouble finding an eager buyer for the illicit sale of antiquities. There was for some however, a downside to this increase in available cultural art and that was the de-valuing of long term investment pieces the collectors had so carefully put away. One of the biggest problems of recent date was the wonderful large Tang dynasty sancai glazed horses and camels which had been discovered in small numbers during nineteenth century railway construction work in China. They were made to be buried as grave goods and had lain undisturbed for thirteen hundred years. They were one of the many casualties of the railway pioneers. Some of these spectacular pieces were quickly acquired by museums, mostly from outside China, but a few were soon in the possession of private collectors.

Throughout the twentieth century these pieces were almost akin to currency as every serious collector wanted one and a number of fortunes were made as a result.

The more recent level of exposure of cultural relics by modern construction work in China had resulted in objects like the Tang dynasty horses and camels now changing hands for a fraction of the prices hitherto reached. The same was true for Imperial pottery and now Yuan dynasty blue and white porcelain, previously rarely seen in the west was suddenly finding its way into the auction rooms. Some big names were losing a lot of money and so the cartel was formed with the objective to buy every specimen which might devalue their own pieces, and then sit on them. In recent years the prices had been restored, largely as a result of the Chinese Governments crack-down on this illicit trade. Now the cartel's holdings were being slowly released on to the open market, but in a controlled and measured way.

The principal aims of the cartel were therefore to create a single-channel marketing system which involved directing all available major works of Asian art into one monopolistic system held in several clearing houses throughout the world, and in such a way so that nobody knew the source of art when sold. In this way the cartel could maintain prices by regulating the supply and putting competitive parties at a trading disadvantage. All this was of course illegal under the European Union competition laws of articles eighty one and also one hundred and one of the Lisbon treaty.

Max Veerman, a Dutchman from California had been president of the cartel organisation in Britain for the past twenty two years. His brief from his Chinese superiors was to 'Keep the dragon in the box,' a reference to their desire to stop Chinese art disappearing into western collections. Unknown to his superiors in Hong Kong Veerman was guilty of doing just that and had lined his own pockets to quite a considerable extent.

The cartel building here in Jermyn Street was large and spacious and occupied all five floors. The hub of the organisation operated from the extensive offices on the second floor which accommodated the research team who spent most of their time on the internet or scanning newspapers from twenty countries, hunting down auctions in both town and country. Only Asian art is on their shopping list and it's down to their expertise to decide what is worth buying within the remit of their search.

Generally the cartel would buy items on two levels. The most important are pieces made for the Chinese market, but they would also purchase export wares if their quality is first class. Objects successfully acquired at auction were distributed according to their genre. All important Jades, manuscripts and items of cultural interest were sent to Hong Kong. Enamels, bronzes, porcelain and paintings would be divided between California and here in London. Items which were considered to be suitable for long term investment and those considered necessary for storing to prevent over supply to the market, were kept in the secure vaults here in Jermyn Street.

The showroom on the ground level was the showcase for items for sale to the public. This outlet was partly to help finance the operation, but also to provide what would appear to be the respectable face of the cartel.

The cartel was supported by a secret Chinese organisation based in London and Paris known as the Shāqi, a ruthless society who maintained a strict hierarchy and controlled the cartel activities by ruthless means. The Lugartenientes or lieutenants were the commanders who directly controlled the hit men and assassins who were all recruited from the ranks of the Chinese Shāqi organisation. The Falcons were the Shāqi eyes and ears on the streets. They were in the lowest grade of the society, but crucial to its success as they reported on the activities of the members and rival organisations. The researchers, buyers and administrative staff were all Europeans, employed directly by the cartel and mostly locally sourced. They were generally segregated from the cartel and its clandestine affairs. However, from time to time their activities would be monitored and if they were considered to be working *outside* the organisation they would come under the watchful eye of the Chinese Falcon agents.

The activities of the Cartel were nefarious, often illegal and almost always included violence. However, the cartel never did their own dirty work; the Chinese secret agents travelled the world to carry out the orders, assassinations and the shopping lists for the cartel. The latter included the illegal exportation of artworks via the Shāqi network.

A week ago Chinese agents escorted a cartel buyer to the Bourge-Vilaine auction rooms and had been there the day Baxter scooped the early vase and like the other disgruntled buyers, had been caught out by the withdrawal of one hundred lots. Max Veerman, the cartel president was furious, because he had in his possession the first Henri de Montaigne vase, it had been in his collection for over forty years and he knew it was one of a pair. He had spent much of his life trying to track down the other vase. He knew it had existed shortly after nineteen hundred and so had no reason to doubt its survival somewhere in the world. For more than twenty years Max Veerman's staff had obtained copies of every auction world wide which had Chinese porcelain included in the sale. Every likely candidate was assessed and many viewed, including the vase Baxter had bought at Bourge-Vilaine. Veerman had hotly considered this piece to be a possible contender. He was prepared to pay thousands to acquire it, even though he couldn't be certain that it really was the missing Henri de Montaigne piece. To this end he had sent his agents down to the Bourge-Vilaine auction rooms and told them in no uncertain terms to acquire the lot.

Two weeks before the auction Veerman had received a tip off that Baxter, the Chinese ceramics dealer, was also going down to Bourge-Vilaine and so he had him under close surveillance. In the end, after spending most of his life trying to track it down, Veerman had missed his precious Chinese vase by a whisker, and what made him even more furious was the ludicrous price Baxter had paid for it.

The headquarters in Jermyn Street were the respectable face of the cartel. A modern concrete built construction. The showy side had a fine façade which mirrored the Georgian houses which had graced this street until their destruction during the Second World War. Balusters and columns enhanced the upper casements while at pavement level enormous plate glass windows provided the showcase for this remarkable collection.

Above the public galleries was a network of offices, store rooms and several workshops. On the top floor Veerman had his luxurious penthouse apartment.

In marked contrast, situated some three metres below street level, the vaults were bereft of any embellishment whatsoever. Constructed before the rest of the building they consisted of a one and a half metre thick concrete shell, reinforced with high tensile steel with top-rated coefficient thermal expansion. The vault lining was thirty seven millimetres gauge super duplex stainless steel, reinforced with Zeron one hundred.

Fifteen years later a new underground car park had been constructed behind in Bedford square, built to serve the growing numbers of office workers and tourists. Some, like Max Veerman, had their own personal garage included within the new underground complex.

Veerman continually insisted that the building and in particular the vaults benefited from the latest and best detection devices that money could buy. He had recently installed within the vault, a microwave detection system with high RFI and EMI immunity. A transmitter constantly generated a close-knit series of invisible but highly sensitive beams across layered zones which meant that as soon as the transmitter detected a difference within any zone, the system would analyse the anomaly and if the pre-determined criterion for intrusion was met, then the alarms would be triggered. If this were not enough, the entire building had been fitted with thermal vision with multi-level sensitivity along with metal detector and bullet resistive warning alert technology. All important locks were fitted with iris and retina-pattern authentication and state of the art DNA recognition pads which were connected to the central computer and could check an individual's DNA in a matter of seconds.

The building with the exception of the galleries was fitted with a voice waveform recognition system. Every office, passageway and even the lifts had sensors which could detect voice patterns which were not authorized and would automatically send an intruder alert to the central security point.

Security was upmost in Veerman's philosophy and over the years he had spent large sums of the cartel money on it. His specialized security unit occupied the best part of one floor and comprised his security officers, of which he employed eight, and his technical support team. Between them they were responsible for monitoring all detection systems, communications and internet security.

Max Veerman had no doubt whatsoever that his organisation was one hundred percent secure, no one could possibly hope to break his security, of that he was certain.

Chapter 8

Baxter's Lament

Within minutes of arriving home following his visit to Professor Hadley, Baxter knew something was wrong, very wrong indeed. He could see no initial signs of any disturbance and nothing to suggest anyone had been in his cottage, but he instinctively sensed someone *had* been there. It was not the smell of alien aftershave or foreign body perspiration because there was none. No, it was an indefinable mix of apprehension and caution which triggered something in his inner senses. Baxter had always been a very tidy person, some would say fastidious although that wasn't strictly speaking true as it was only order which was an obsession, fussing over little details that most people would turn a blind eye to. Many of his friends, both male and female had long tagged him with the label of 'an obsessive compulsive' but that also wasn't a true definition of his make-up. He suffered from the similar but less severe 'symmetry disorder condition.

This meant he was compelled to ensure all objects around him were perfectly aligned and in particular, pairs of items had to match exactly, like candlesticks on his dining room table, or the pair of Derby porcelain figures on his mantelpiece. Even in places like his kitchen, items had to be stacked by category and graded by height. Although he would rarely let it show, he would become agitated if someone disrupted his things, the everyday possessions he had arranged with care for their symmetry. Baxter had been known to perspire profusely when unable to put things right and at the first possible opportunity, rush to regain order. He insisted that everything in each of his rooms always remained in exactly the same position. If anything had to be moved for cleaning, enormous care needed to be taken to replace it exactly where it was before. Baxter was fully aware of his obsessions which even he knew went way beyond normal tidiness.

He first noticed a brass swan neck handle on his bureau was standing upright, unlike all the others which hung down in the normal fashion. He could never tolerate that lack of symmetry and would have to put it right before he could get on with any other task, but he had not left it that way, of that he was certain. Then he noticed to his horror, on the shelf above, an error in the order of arrangement of his books. The nineteen eighty five edition of his antiques guide was next to nineteen eighty three and even worse, nineteen eighty eight was next to nineteen ninety one! Someone had clearly removed books and replaced them in the wrong order, but who had been here and more to the point, what had they been looking for amongst his books?

He rushed into the bathroom and here again he spotted a problem. The airing cupboard door was slightly open and when he looked inside the pile of neatly folded towels were not in perfect alignment, one was further forward than the rest, and the bottom one was partly turned over, but to his relief the copper cylinder was still sealed.

He spun around at the sound of water to find the hot tap on his washbasin was not fully closed; he couldn't stand a dripping tap and would never have left it like that. Someone had clearly opened the hot tap on his washbasin to make certain there was hot water in the cylinder. He realised how important it had been to let the tank refill after hiding his vase in it.

He went outside and looked carefully at his front door and garage gates but there was no evidence of a break-in. All windows were securely closed, not one of them displayed a single scratch or sign of having been tampered with.

Despite this he knew someone had been there and they had made a very thorough search, looking for something specific.

He was certain this had not been a random burglary attempt because whoever had been here did not want to leave any trace of their nefarious activity. The worst part was that someone had violated his privacy and in some ways it upset him more knowing they had done so with such calculating secrecy but if it was his Chinese vase they were after, they had fortunately been unsuccessful.

He retired to his laptop but within seconds of logging in discovered his mouse wasn't working. He hated computers and the way they seemed to have a mind of their own. One minute everything would be fine and then for no apparent reason something very silly would upset the entire system and without the kind of mind which could analyse and delve, he would be at the mercy of his local computer repair shop. He had never really taken to information technology micro-codes, tristate buffers and CPU's were like a foreign language to Baxter. In fact, one of his closest friends once called him a 404 man, jargon for someone who is clueless in regards to digital literacy. It was only two years ago since he had bowed down to the pressures to own a computer and that was due to the twenty first century trading advantage which it would give him.

He checked the mouse's lead, pushing, it went in the rest of the way. But something was very wrong; the lead was not in the USB port next to the printer line, but in the third port, leaving an empty terminal in the middle. Baxter couldn't have done that, it was once again the sort of thing which triggered his symmetry disorder condition. This alerted him to the fact that his mysterious intruders had also been tampering with his laptop. He quickly came to the realization that they had removed his mouse and in its place inserted a memory stick and copied what? His files he suspected although he couldn't imagine what they hoped to discover.

He spent several minutes delving into his laptop's root directory, trying to find out if he could detect what files had been copied, hoping this would explain why his cottage had been searched. Some entries were encrypted including one with today's date against it.

This was obviously the entry he was looking for but with his limited ability he was never going to learn anything more than the fact that his private particulars had been copied. He scanned down the list of documents and was relieved when he reached the bottom of the list without finding any reference concerning his Chinese vase, but there was one document which sent an instantaneous flutter of concern. With the heading 'Questions relating to a meeting with Adrian Hadley' he quickly opened the file to remind himself of the contents.

1. Almost identical vase illustrated in Grandidier La Ceramique Chinois. Known as The Henri de Montaigne vase. How old is my vase/period etc.?

2. Ask Hadley to translate the Koranic verse.

3. Ask about Chinese secret organisations–note pinned to Didier's back with Batwing symbols and Chinese characters, what do they mean? Did this organisation kill Didier? And if so why and who are they?

He poured himself a large Scotch and then sat back reflecting on the likely implications that the contents in the file might have in the hands of someone else, but he couldn't really see how they would help anyone trying to find his vase. But, he was aware he had now implicated the Professor and just hoped he hadn't put the man in any danger. He would ring him in the morning and warn him to take care. He picked up his laptop again and tapped the keyboard and the search engine page flashed into full screen. He began looking for any entries relating to General Henri de Montaigne on the internet site. Within a short while he was rewarded with a hundred results and soon discovered the Count had died in Paris in nineteen hundred after contracting an acute infection while in the port of Canton, China and was buried in the Montmartre cemetery.

Another entry was an inventory of Henri de Montaigne documents and papers held in the Musée d'Orsay in Paris. There were no specific details of their contents, but the dates were significant as they spanned the years from the eighteen forties until his death in nineteen hundred. It was therefore more than likely that at least some of them would relate to the Counts exploits in China during the Opium wars and the priceless porcelain which was taken from the Imperial Palaces and which he, like others, shipped back to Europe in large numbers.

Rather than rush over to Paris to continue his research, he decided to await Hadley's conclusions as they would likely answer if not all, then most of his questions. A trip to Paris was an attractive proposition, the French city was one of Baxter's favourite places, but with so much resting on the identification and safety of his vase, he decided to leave that option on the back burner for the time being.

Baxter spent the next few days looking at some of the major Asian collections in London. The Victoria and Albert Museum had a few pieces with Sanskrit writing but nothing which paralleled his vase. The two large elephant handled vases in the Percival David collection were of a similar shape and the same intensity of cobalt blue. They also had an inscription but not in Sanskrit, dating them to thirteen fifty one, a very early date for blue and white porcelain. These famous specimens formed an important group which represented some of the first examples of blue and white made in Asia. These distinguished Percival David vases had at one time caused heated debate for although auction catalogues of the nineteen thirties eagerly accepted similar pieces as pre-Ming fourteenth century, there followed many years of doubt and disagreement. Scholarly connoisseurs from as early as nineteen twenty nine had claimed an early date for these celebrated examples, but few others could accept that pieces of such refinement and brilliance could have possibly been made before the sixteenth century. The turning point came with the pioneering work by Baxter's former colleague Professor Adrian Hadley during his years as keeper of the Far Eastern section at the British Museum. What excited Baxter most was the possibility that his vase could just possibly be contemporary with these illustrious examples, but he would only have confirmation of this if the professor said that was the case.

Hadley was recognised by many as the foremost authority on

early Chinese porcelain, and as a result of his studies, some in the cartel had made fortunes from the professor's published work. However, recent research by him was now casting doubt on some of their earlier and more important pieces and unless they could rectify the current nervousness in the trade, they stood to lose significant sums of money.

A week had passed since Baxter's visit to Professor Hadley. As instructed he rang his former colleague the previous night and had been amazed at the old man's excitement, although it was quite evident that his exuberance was very much fuelled by an excess of alcohol. 'Wonderful news' he kept saying, but he wouldn't divulge any further information over the telephone. 'The telegraph wires have ears, you can hear the buzz' he used to say and most likely he was right.

It was a bright and early Monday morning when Baxter once again climbed the steps to 8 Bedford square; he couldn't wait to receive the professor's verdict. He rang the bell to flat number two, the resonance sounded in the far distance as he hovered from foot to foot, barely able to contain his excitement. Several agonizing minutes passed but he still hadn't heard any reassuring footsteps so he rang it again and waited, but still no response.

He was about to give up and depart when he heard footfalls in the hallway but they were not reassuringly heavy but light and quick paced as they neared the entrance. The front door opened and a middle-aged woman emerged wearing, what was thirty years ago, a posh Aquascutum cashmere camel coloured wrap style coat with belt and loosely tied headscarf. She stopped in her tracks and noticeably jarred as she came face to face with him.

'I'm looking for' he began but she ignored him and scurried quickly past. Baxter swiftly placed his foot in the door stopping it from slamming shut and as soon as she was out of sight, slipped inside the hallway.

Half way down the passage the door to number two was slightly ajar. As he drew closer he spotted paint flakes on the black and white tiled floor and splintered wood scarring the left hand door panel. He pushed the door fully open and stepped over an ugly mutilated section of architrave which lay on the floor close to where it had been torn from the door jamb.

He could see the professor with his back to him, sitting in his high-backed leather armchair, his left foot against the edge of the table, both hands clasping his knee, but his head was curiously drooped.

'Are you alright, Professor?' Baxter asked as he fought his way across the ephemera littered room. There was no reply. He made haste battling his way through the muddle, he swung the professor's chair around and the man's left leg dropped to the floor, his arms fell to his waist and his head slumped forward. Baxter fought to right the stricken man, avoiding touching his blood-soaked body, dark red and long congealed. Baxter studied the old man's face, his eyes were open but as Baxter lifted his arm to feel for a pulse, he knew he had been dead for some time. Baxter continued to stare, transfixed by the sight of someone who was dead, yet he looked for the most part as though he was still alive. He strangely felt no sorrow, that was to come later, but he had regret, no, if he were to be honest, he was angry with the professor for denying him the opportunity to solve the riddle of his vase.

He realised Hadley had been shot in the back of the neck, probably whilst asleep. He often dozed off in this position after drinking too much whisky. But what really alarmed Baxter most was the note pinned to the back of the man's jacket. Even though it was reddened from blood seeping from Hadley's coat, Baxter recognised the drawing of four bats encircling a Chinese text. It was the same symbol he had been shown by the Inspector at Avranches police station and the one he himself had attempted to draw for the Professor.

The room had always looked as though it had been ransacked, but this was different. There had previously been a kind of order to the disorder in Hadley's life, but this disorder was total.

The bookshelves had been swept clean of every book, and even more manuscripts, papers and magazines universally littered the floor along with ornaments and trophies, deliberately smashed. Cupboard doors hung open, their tightly packed interiors rifled, their contents added to the mess? Someone had certainly gone to great efforts to search his apartment but had they found what they were looking for? He couldn't see his photographs of the vase although he guessed they could be lying hidden under the jumble on the floor. He had a sinking feeling that all was now lost, his one and only chance to discover what his vase was all about had been snatched from under his nose, He was in no doubt that it was his photographs or perhaps even the vase itself that the intruders had been searching for.

He spotted Hadley's Guttenberg and remembered the old man's words 'If anything untoward happens to me just remember the Guttenberg, it might reveal all'

His heart began beating as he clambered over the debris, he had no regard for what he was stepping on even though he knew some of the books and manuscripts were highly valuable. He lifted the framed Guttenberg off the wall and sure enough a piece of folded paper had been taped to the back.

'So you did leave me a didactic message after all then, Professor,' he said removing it from the back of the frame. And then a chill went down his back as he heard sirens in the distance. Slipping the note into his back pocket he quickly hung the frame back on the wall and was about to leave when the sound of sirens screamed outside and blue flashing circles reflected through the front window panes. Car doors slammed, followed seconds later by the rush of hurried footsteps as the first of countless police officers burst into the room.

Baxter was immediately escorted outside and made to wait in one of the police cars in company of a young female police constable.

'I just found him like that,' he said in an attempt to break the silence between them, but she merely nodded.

The whole street now seemed to come alive as white vans with forensic support teams arrived. Men suddenly slipping on white protective suits, shoe covers and latex gloves before entering the building. He clearly saw multiple blue strobe flashes illuminating Hadley's window and guessed the police photographer was inside recording the scene. It was about twenty minutes later when another police officer, a detective this time, jumped in the car and they headed off on the short journey to the local station.

The police headquarters in Paddington Green was in marked contrast to the one in Avranches. It was both modern and somehow reassuringly efficient but more to the point they spoke in perfect not pigeon English.

He had been taken to block C which was a separate wing from the rest of the main building. The sign on the entrance had the bold letters B.O.C.U, then underneath the caption Borough Operational Command Unit. After passing innumerable doors and offices they arrived at the Sergeants desk where the police constable gave Baxter's details, before showing him into a side room.

The chair he had been told to sit on was not at all comfortable. It was a fairly standard iron s-frame type with moulded plywood seat, but had an inclination which forced the body slightly forward. He felt certain this was intentional to stop those being interrogated from relaxing. The room was barely furnished with little else other than an empty desk and a tape recording machine on a table. He wasn't alone, a young police constable stood legs apart just inside the door. He tried to make conversation, but the officer refused to respond, choosing to remain straight-faced.

A middle-aged plain clothed officer entered and settled himself behind the desk. The policeman flicked open a file and slowly thumbed through the notes, shuffled in his chair making himself comfortable and then looked up at Baxter

'Would you care for one?' he asked as he slowly un-wrapped a toffee and held the bag towards Baxter.

'No thank you, they play havoc with my teeth,' he replied, stunned by the policeman's casual introduction.

The man popped one in his mouth; Baxter watched the officer's cheeks as he moved the sweet from side to side.

'I am Detective Chief Inspector Monroe,' he said drily.

Baxter nodded.

'So Mr. Baxter, thank you for agreeing to help us with our enquiries. Now what can you tell us about the circumstances that led you to be on the premises of Professor Adrian Hadley this morning?'

Baxter was taken aback by the Inspectors expression of polite interest, he quite expected him to plough straight into damning accusations, particularly as he had been discovered red-handed at the scene.

The Inspector raised his eyebrows. Rattling the toffee between his teeth he was taking note of Baxter's actions, but also searching for thoughts on the man's face, he had long learnt the art of recognising facial mendacity, but in this case he was struggling to see any signs of it.

Baxter on the other hand desperately wanted to keep quiet about his real reason for being in the professor's apartment, after all he didn't really know if he could trust the local police. Hadley had told him how organisations like the cartel were known to have very extensive connections which in the opinion of the professor, included corrupt police officers.

'Funny, I had an inkling you were going to ask me that,' Baxter finally said.

'Don't try and be witty with me Mr. Baxter, you're in a very serious situation here, now tell me what were you doing there?'

'I was calling to see Adrian Hadley; I telephoned him last night and he suggested I call around for a chat.'

'A chat you say' the inspector leant forward raising a quizzical brow, 'and what time did he ring you?'

'Eight thirty or so, I don't know exactly.'

'Now that's interesting because the professor was killed at about twenty one hundred hours. That is only a rough estimate and based purely on the fact that his clock was broken and stopped at that time.' He looked up at the ceiling, deep in thought. 'So... you're telling me you were at home at around twenty one hundred hours?'

'Yes, I certainly was.'

'And someone can confirm that can they?'

'No, I was on my own.'

'I see, so you were on your own.' His face flashed a momentary infectious grin which rapidly faded into a look of redolence as the solid line of his eyebrows returned to their normal disposition.

'Yes, and the telephone records will confirm I made the call from my home address at that time.

'I'm afraid that's not much of an alibi Mr. Baxter. How long would it take you to go from your cottage to the Professor's flat, twenty minutes, half an hour?'

'I don't really know Inspector, but'…..

Monroe cut him short. 'I can tell you now, at that time of night it's possible to travel from your cottage to the professor's flat in less than ten minutes.'

Baxter didn't reply.

Monroe said 'From what you remember from your previous visit to the Professor's apartment, would you say anything was missing.'

'Missing,' Baxter repeated, unsure what the Inspector meant.

'Stolen,' he said slightly impatiently.

He thought back carefully. 'His collection of Russian silver in the glass-fronted Edwardian cabinet was definitely still there,' he said 'and I did notice his silver and cut-glass spirit Tantalus was as well, but as for anything else, I wouldn't know.'

'Did you see anyone else in or near the Professor's house this morning?'

Of course, he suddenly remembered the lady who opened the door and inadvertently let him in. 'There was a lady coming out of the front door when I arrived, in fact that's how I got in.'

'And can you describe this woman?'

'I only got a brief glimpse of her, but she was middle-aged, quite tall with black…. no I didn't see her hair because she wore a headscarf. But one thing I did notice.' He paused to recollect the exact details.

'And that was?' Monroe quizzed.

'She was wearing a nineteen eighties Aquascutum cashmere

camel-coloured wrap style coat with belt. I noticed it because these days retro pieces such as that are normally only worn by youngsters who think it's trendy to re-invent the past.'

'You seem to be remarkably well informed regarding women's clothing Mr. Baxter.'

'Not really, but I do try to keep in touch with trends in the retro market. There's a lot of money to be made out it.'

Monroe rose from his chair and opened the interview room door and called out 'Johnson, a minute please.'

'Sir,' the desk sergeant stood with a stack of papers in his arms.

'Get on to PC Carter; he'll still be in Bedford Square. I want to know if he has taken a statement yet from a lady in a camel-hair coat. Oh and Johnson, she's wearing a headscarf. I want anything he's got and right away.'

'Yes Sir.' the sergeant replied, and left, closing the door behind him.

Monroe returned to his desk, looked at his notes and then looked up and gave Baxter a hard stare which gradually transformed into an expression of curiosity. 'You say you were at number eight Bedford Square on the invitation of Professor Hadley, so tell me why would an eminent Professor wish to chat with you, did you know him?'

'Well yes, rather well in fact, we worked together for some time at the British Museum.'

'The British Museum' The Inspector arched a quizzical brow.' I think we'd better start at the beginning don't you?' He leaned closer. 'Now tell me about your relationship with the professor.'

Baxter was desperate not to divulge too much, or at least not yet. He wasn't at all certain how to deal with this fast developing situation or for that matter how best to protect his potential windfall, if that was what it was. He was also anxious to know what was in Hadley's note as that could well have an influence on how he should handle this situation and dictate what his next move should be.

He wove a tale wrapped in strands of reality but one which failed to mention his vase or trip to France and although Inspector Monroe seemed to accept his story, it prompted further questioning.

'So you're a bit of an expert in Chinese art are you Mr. Baxter?'

'Not really an expert, at least not compared with the late professor, but I studied Asian art for a few years.'

'Ah good, in that case I imagine you can tell me what this means?' he held up a clear plastic bag which contained the piece of blood-stained paper that had been pinned to the Professor's jacket.

The Shāqi Batwing Insignia

Baxter of course recognised it straight away, after all he had seen it himself on the Professor's back, but he preferred to pretend he hadn't.

'I don't know if I can translate it as such,' he said taking it from the Inspector and looking at it close up, trying to delve into its emblematic meaning. 'It's very representational.' He offered scratching his head.

'I know it's representational as you put it, but what does it actually mean or say Mr. Baxter?'

'The bats are probably symbolic of longevity, serenity and that sort of thing. Now the Chinese characters are arranged as a star configuration known as qī shā cháo dòu gé, but they're not immediately familiar to me, I would imagine they relate to some kind of organisation. I'm certain I can get them properly translated for you Inspector.'

Exasperated Monroe stood up and paced to the window.

'We can have it translated ourselves Mr. Baxter,' his voice rose, 'but what I want to know is, was it you who drew it and did you pin it on the dead man? Because I think maybe you did.'

'I can assure you Inspector I had absolutely nothing to do with Adrian Hadley's death or that note pinned to his back.'

The Inspector's attention was focused on the drawing of the batwing symbols. 'You see Mr. Baxter, we have several things which relate to one another and then we have this.' He held up the drawing. 'This appears to be outside the pattern of evidence, but it's not, of that I'm certain, but I will get to the bottom of it, I can assure you.

A knock on the door and Sergeant Johnson entered the room with an A4 sheet of paper in his hand. 'We've just had this faxed through from PC Carter,' he said placing the note in front of the Inspector. Monroe spent a few minutes reading the contents then sat back in his chair looking up at the ceiling.

'Just out of interest Inspector, who telephoned to report the Professor's death? I was just about to when your men arrived.'

'Were you really,' Monroe said with a slightly cynical look.

Baxter was irritated by the Inspector's measured voice. 'Well come on Inspector, if I killed the Professor last night, do you really think I would have come back again this morning?'

'There's nought as strange as folk, or so they say, but at the same time I have to admit you may have been set up.'

'At last you are taking me seriously,' he said, 'but tell me Inspector why the second thoughts about my involvement?'

'Well you see, it may be nothing, but it is strange that we

received the anonymous telephone call minutes after you claimed to have arrived at Hadley's house. That in itself means very little unless we can establish at what time you arrived at number eight.'

'I suppose I can't really,' Baxter confessed.

'Well actually I can tell you, it was ten thirty five precisely. And before you ask, one of my officers has just spoken to the Professor's neighbour a Mrs Morrison, the lady you met on the doorstep. Apparently, she leaves home every morning for the corner shop at exactly ten thirty five, after Grierson's makeover has finished.'

'Grierson's makeover? '

'A television programme apparently; anyway she has corroborated your story, but,' he added with a tone of caution, 'it doesn't necessary mean you're off the hook, but I admit, as I said just now, you may be the victim of a set up.'

'So that means someone was watching the house and waiting for me to go in before telephoning the police.'

Monroe didn't reply but jotted down a few points on the pad in front of him.

'I would like to make a telephone call, is that alright?' Baxter said.

The Inspector raised his brow and nodded. 'Yes I suppose that will be alright. Who to?'

'Assistant Commissioner Terrence Atterbury at The Yard,' he said pulling the visiting card out of his wallet.

The Inspector glanced at it briefly, 'I can't allow that,' Monroe said rising from his chair, 'completely out of the question.'

'But why? I know he is head of Specialist Crime & Operations Directorate, but he's also a friend of mine and I'm certain he will be able to help clear this matter up.'

Monroe didn't reply, instead he left the room leaving Baxter puzzled by the policeman's reluctance to allow him to speak with Atterbury.

The one thing that did baffle him was why he was being

questioned by a Detective Chief Inspector and more to the point, in block C, the Metropolitan police borough operational command unit for this part of London.

He had been sitting in the same chair for the best part of half an hour, his only companion the young police constable who seemed to be quite content to sit out this silent interlude to his normal working day.

The door opened and Sergeant Johnson walked in. He didn't take a seat, instead he walked up to Baxter and told him he was free to go home.

'Free to go, I don't understand, you lot were accusing me of murder an hour ago, have you caught the perpetrator?'

'I really can't say Sir, just that Chief Inspector Monroe sends his sincere apologies for the inconvenience. There has been a misunderstanding and he trusts you won't mention it to anyone else, and that includes other police officers.'

'Sorry,' Baxter said, 'but I don't buy that.'

'I think it best you forget all about Professor Hadley Sir,' he concluded giving Baxter a knowing eye.

'Déjà vu,' Baxter said to himself, we've been here before!

Instead of making his way back to where his car was parked, Baxter stopped in nearby Bedford Square Gardens. This was one of his favourite places in the centre of London where ash and plane trees lined three sides of a large grassy area. Here was one of those tranquil spots where office workers came each day to eat their sandwiches away from the city bustle. Baxter took a seat on a bench opposite Hadley's apartment block. His thoughts immediately shifted to the Professor as he looked up at the curtained windows and suddenly felt saddened by his good friend's terrible demise. The man's death had been a horrible one; the academic world was going to be shocked by the loss of one of its foremost experts on Asian art. Baxter's grief was intensified by pangs of guilt, he was certain the professor had been killed because of *his* involvement in something *he* didn't understand. And to make matters worse, if that was possible, he couldn't shake off the speculation that it was all down to the notes he had made on his laptop, the document saved as 'Adrian Hadley' the one which had been copied by who knows who?

He was still confused over his interrogation by the local police and their reluctance to let him talk to Atterbury and then the sudden stand down. This was not after all the first time this had happened, as the same thing occurred in the Avranches police station in France. He was finding it hard to believe there wasn't some form of complicity wrapped up in this mystery. Perhaps, he pondered, Atterbury had after all pulled some strings and that was why he had been released on both occasions, but why the secrecy?

He felt his inside pocket and removed the folded note.

As he fully expected, it was didactic and would be completely impossible to untangle by any normal person, but Hadley knew Baxter would be able to decipher it.

The note began with 漢語拼音 As soon as he saw that, he knew Hadley's note was written in the secret Chinese code called *Hànyǔ Pīnyīn*. He blew a sigh of relief; at least the professor hadn't encoded it in 'I Ching' the sixty four tetrahedron codes that Hadley so loved to play around with, that would have been impossible for *him* to decipher, but then the Professor would have known that.

He took his diary from his inside pocket, licked the lead of his pencil and started translating the Chinese characters into Latin. This was the only way it could be deciphered, it couldn't be translated directly into the English language; he knew that was impossible. This is what made it such a secure and secret code as very few people would realize that point and would waste their time in fruitless labour. For Baxter this was not so very difficult an exercise, every Mandarin syllable could be spelled with exactly one initial followed by one final character.

Once he had the text in Latin he quickly translated it into the English language.

'Dear boy' it began. 'If you're reading this and of course you are, then that means I am no longer of this world. Your Chinese piece is indeed the other Henri de Montaigne vase, the missing piece to a one hundred and forty year old riddle. As you already know the inscription on the first vase reads The rock of Batuta lives. I can now tell you the Sanskrit inscription on your one reads In Kuan Yao which as you know means Imperial ware, that's porcelain made in Ching Te Chen for the Imperial court. So together the two inscriptions say the rock of Batuta is in porcelain made for the Imperial Court. Now the interesting point is where is this piece of porcelain which was made for the Imperial Court? There is I think, just one other clue and that's General Henri de Montaigne and perhaps the Couvegne letters.

Now as for the strange symbolic message that was pinned to your informant's back. I have done some research and I found the four bat motif was often used on Chinese porcelain, but is nearly always composed of five bats representing the five blessings namely; longevity, riches, serenity, the cultivation of virtue and completion of life's work. It's rare to find a group of four like this, but if the letters were as follows – 七殺朝斗格 then the monosyllabic Chinese script translated is a Chinese star configuration known as qī shā cháo dòu gé. Quite simply it means ennoblement, but in Chinese iconography it is a code which encourages the individual to take to his own destiny but within the internal organisation. He must strive for might and power and often resort to murder in order to meet his goals. This ancient and very secret organisation known as the Shāqi was thought to have long disappeared as there had been no mention of them for several decades. After the handover in nineteen ninety seven when Hong Kong sovereignty was transferred back to China under the Sino-British Joint Declaration, the Shāqi organisation was outlawed by the Chinese Government. However, there have for many years since been rumours that they are still active and operating in the west. Now I have no direct evidence, but I believe the Shāqi organisation are linked to a London and Hong Kong cartel known as Beaux-arts d'Asie whose headquarters are

above Gallery Twenty One in Jermyn Street. But do be very careful as some of these people can be most unpleasant. Anyway I hope this is of help and good luck dear boy, I wish I could be with you when you find the Batuta stone, and find it, I'm certain you will.
    A.J.Hadley.'

As Baxter walked among the manicured beds of summer flowers, he pondered the professor's words. The man had clearly feared for his own life and that was why he had left the note with the vital last part of the riddle. But in ignorance of the true facts, Baxter feared someone must have found his photographs and therefore would soon know the second part of the riddle and that someone had to be the man Hadley had called Max Veerman.

But what did it all mean? He now knew General Henri de Montaigne did have both vases and it appeared to be the case that he had more than a passing association with the celebrated Countess de Couvegne, but surely the missing clue wasn't likely to be back in France. One thought did warm him though, and that was if, as he suspected the cartel had found the photographs, then perhaps they wouldn't be looking for his vase anymore and so that would surely make him now of less interest to them.

Baxter continued to meander along the winding path which encircled the square. He stopped to read a sign; its message conveyed an intrusion which destroyed all the senses which had told him this was an untouched sanctuary. Despite all outward appearances this park was not after all a place of natural beauty free from the demands of London planning. It wasn't an island which had been largely spared the requirements of twentieth century redevelopment. But amazingly, below the gardens and lawns, the sign told him there was an underground car park hidden below several metres of concrete and turf. Its presence distilled any illusion that this was a piece of untouched London.

The entrance to the car park was located at the far end where Second World War bomb damage had all but wiped out one side of the square and here the backs of less attractive buildings sat slightly uncomfortably in this historic setting.

He had been quietly sitting there for twenty minutes or so mulling over the events of the last few weeks when a very strange thing happened and one for which he could find no logical answer. A long black Daimler car stopped opposite the car park entrance and waited. A few minutes later two men walked briskly towards him. And this is where the incident became interesting because they were Chinese gentlemen. Probably because they were Asian and smartly dressed, he straight away questioned 'had they been the individuals he had seen at the Bourge-Vilaine auction rooms'?

He knew it was notoriously difficult for Europeans to distinguish individual Oriental faces, but all these coincidences were piling up. The only problem he had with this surmise was that if they were the disgruntled characters who had been unable to buy the Chinese vase at Bourge-Vilaine, then they were not the same men he had forced off the road bridge because they were certainly very dead.

The two Chinese men appeared not to recognize him as they scurried past at great speed. He watched as they got into the waiting Daimler, which then glided down the approach road into the subterranean car park. *Now that's strange*, he muttered to himself. *Why would they be picked up and taken into an underground car park?* He decided to delay departing as he wanted to see how this peculiar situation panned out.

After an hour it became clear the Daimler was not going to re-emerge and neither were the occupants. He reluctantly decided it was time to go home and try to forget all the strange thoughts which were swirling around in his head.

In nearby Jermyn Street, Max Veerman was patiently waiting for his agents return. He was hoping they were going to bring him the news he needed, in fact craved for, to such an extent that he couldn't focus on anything else. He had ordered the visit to Hadley's flat in

Bedford Square, but not in his capacity as head of the cartel, this was a personal matter and strictly outside the remit of his position.

His Shāqi secret agents, the same ones who had earlier searched Baxter's cottage and found and copied the documents on his computer, had been instructed to pay the Professor a visit. Thanks to Baxter's notes, Veerman now knew who had bought the other vase and the Professor's involvement in deciphering its legend. He also suspected the likelihood that the vase itself was in Hadley's apartment.

When the Chinese Shāqi agents forced open the door to his flat they discovered the professor fast asleep with a half empty decanter of whisky on his desk. Their boss had ordered the death of Hadley, partly because the Professor's recent research had exposed details which de-valued some of his and the cartel's collection. He also didn't intend to allow him to pass on any details which might help Baxter find the diamond.

With the evil deed done the Chinese Shāqi agents set about hunting for the vase, photographs, drawings and any notes relating to it, but despite turning the flat upside down, the only thing they discovered was his copy of La Ceramique Chinois and that was only because he had foolishly left the page with the coloured plate open. Before they departed they pinned the customary symbolic message on the dead body.

'What do you mean you found nothing?' barked Veerman at the two Chinese agents standing sheepishly before him.

'We find book open on this page,' one of the agents offered in broken English.

'But that's only an illustration of my vase, not the missing one.'

The agents both shrugged.

'What about photographs? Hadley had to have some details of the other vase; are you certain you searched his flat properly?'

'We search velly well Mister Veerman.'

The photographs Baxter had taken when he first met up with Hadley were not found in the flat by the Chinese agents or later on by the police, because once Hadley had translated the inscription, he knew full well how explosive those images would be if they got into the wrong hands and so he chemically wiped them clean.

'And you killed him afterwards?'

'We kill him velly well Mr. Veerman.' The other agent nodded in agreement.

'Yes velly well indeed.'

'And no silly Shāqi notes this time?'

'Ah no.' the agent lied. Veerman looked at the other man who momentarily paused and then shook his head in agreement.

CHAPTER 9

DANGEROUS ENCOUNTERS

It was the following day and Bedford Square Gardens seemed busier than normal. Sitting on his usual park bench with a small pile of auction catalogues alongside, he was struck by the larger than usual numbers of small children. It was a noisier place, today the normal tranquillity of the gardens was shattered by screams and excited voices. He looked over to the adjacent seat where two office workers sat eating their packed lunch. They shrugged their shoulders in silent agreement at the noisier than normal environment. It must be school holiday time, he concluded.

He scanned the auction catalogues looking for possible sleepers, items which may have escaped the auctioneer's attention.

These are often antiques which appear quite mundane, run of the mill, but illustrations in catalogues can often provide the sharp experienced eye with vital clues, which suggest they have far more value than their description implies.

Over the years Baxter had scooped a number of such sleepers and profited quite well from his level of expertise.

A gentle hum broke his concentration and once again a black Daimler slowly made its way towards the car park entrance, where it stopped as before.

Baxter watched, fascinated and then decided to casually wander over to that side of the gardens. He wouldn't get too close or show any signs of inquisitiveness, but pretend to take interest in the colourful beds of summer flowers and shrubs.

His faux attention to the flower beds was interrupted when he heard the sound of heavy feet on tarmac, and as he looked up, two Chinese men quickly marched towards the car and once inside, it again slowly glided down the ramp disappearing into the underground car park.

Baxter ran over to the entrance. He glanced nervously behind but no one appeared to be watching him, or if they were, they showed no obvious interest in his behaviour.

Despite the sign forbidding pedestrians, he sprinted down the slope into the poorly lit underground car park.

He jumped in surprise as a car sped down the access road to his left, its tyres squealing as it negotiated the narrow roadway between the parking bays, but it was certainly not the Daimler. Within minutes it had left by the exit tunnel leaving the underground bays in silence. All was not completely quiet though, for he could hear a distant whirring sound, a hollow mechanical motorized buzz, but in the half-light he could see no obvious movement. He slowly patrolled the parking bays searching for the Daimler. It was not a particularly large underground car park, there were bays for maybe a hundred cars, but after navigating all the parking lots twice it was clear the Daimler wasn't there, yet he knew it couldn't have left without him seeing it.

Eventually he gave up and went back out into the sunshine to continue his reading.

Baxter was in no doubt that something mysterious was going on in that underground car park, and although he had tried to convince himself that it was nothing to do with him, he knew that wasn't the case. For a start how could he possibly explain why two Chinese men should have any reason for getting into a Daimler which then disappears somewhere inside the underground car park? And where does the mysterious car go, when there is no obvious hiding place down there?

Baxter certainly didn't believe in magic, in fact he had always been a highly sceptical sort of person and had often been criticized for his stubborn cynicism to anything which didn't fit into a normal-shaped box. He knew there had to be a logical explanation behind these going on, even though he didn't have a handle on it just yet. What's more, he was now convinced there was a connection between the killings of Marcel Didier, the car chase and bridge incident and the death of his friend Professor Hadley. Not to mention the Chinese vase and the searching of his Chelsea mews cottage, but what exactly was the common denominator which linked them all together? He made the decision to shift all his efforts into cracking the mystery.

The first step, he decided, was to keep a watch on the underground car park; he was convinced it was here in the subterranean concrete parking bays where he would find, if not the answer, the beginning of the trail which would eventually lead him to the heart of the conspiracy.

The following morning Baxter set out early for Bedford Square.

Driving past the gardens he stopped at the entrance to the underground car park, shelled out twelve pounds for an all-day ticket and then selected a vacant bay close to where he had previously heard the whirring sound and waited.

Most of the parking activity took place before nine o'clock, with people working locally taking up the bays closest to the exit. After that the barrier only occasionally went up to let in a casual parker, often a mother with noisy children.

Baxter wasn't intending to idle his day away, he'd brought a spring file along with a copy of the notes he had compiled concerning General Henri de Montaigne, early Chinese blue and white porcelain and missing treasures from the Opium wars.

He had been there a little over three hours when two strange, although probably unrelated events took place. First he was suddenly aware of singing, although the tag 'singing' wasn't exactly appropriate for such an unmelodic din, which was slowly getting closer. Within a few minutes a figure unsteadily emerged into view. The man took two steps forward and then the same number sideways before bashing into a car. This went on as the drunk got closer. Baxter didn't want to be confronted by the idiot so ducked right down low so the fellow wouldn't see him and was relieved a few minutes later when he disappeared into the distant gloom of the car park. The second incident occurred shortly afterwards when two burly characters, in long black coats, walked towards his car. One tapped on his window, he wound it down. 'Yes can I help you?'

'It's time you left,' was all he said.

'Maybe I don't want to leave just yet,' he said rebuffed.

'I think you do want to leave,' said the other man as they both produced baseball bats, slapping them against the palms of their hands.

'Perhaps you're right,' Baxter said turning the key in the ignition.

He circled Bedford Square Gardens twice, trying to decide what to do next. It was clear someone didn't want him snooping around their secret goings on in the car park, and he realised he had likely been observed waiting there. He couldn't help but wonder if that drunk had been putting on an act and had actually seen him. That would explain how the thugs had known he was there, but more to the point, it suggested there was something which they didn't want him to see, something which was important enough to guard against snoopers. He realised he couldn't go back in there by car, so he parked up in a side street and walked back to the gardens.

It was now late afternoon. He had discreetly crept into the underground car park and squatted for the past four hours behind a white van. His patience was suddenly rewarded when he spotted the lights of a large car approach the entrance barrier. The driver didn't stop and pay but the barrier rose nonetheless. As the car came closer Baxter realised it was the Daimler, he ducked his head low watching it drive into a 'Strictly Reserved' bay, where it stopped. The engine carried on ticking over as a section of the steel car park wall began slowly rising, revealing a brilliantly lit area inside. The Daimler passed between the opening and the door immediately descended. Baxter then heard the whirring sound he had heard previously, but he just couldn't quite put his finger on exactly what was making the strange sound.

He considered for a moment. This underground car park backed onto Jermyn Street, which had been largely rebuilt after the Second World War, but more to the point some of the buildings there abutted the underground car park. He tried to orientate himself and soon came to the conclusion he was very close to the rear of Gallery Twenty One.

Surly this couldn't be another coincidence. Professor Hadley had been certain that the Chinese Shāqi organisation was linked to the London and Hong Kong cartel known as Beaux-arts d'Asie whose headquarters were apparently above Gallery Twenty One.

Baxter jumped to his feet and ran out of the car park and into the late afternoon sunshine. Back once more in his car, he put his foot down hard on the accelerator and sped around the corner towards Jermyn Street. He didn't have much time as he suspected Gallery Twenty One would close at six o'clock. He was pinning his hopes on an empty car parking space outside the front of the shop and was fortunate enough to find one just behind a vintage Austin Healy. Baxter wasn't particularly brave, but equally he was not one to shy away from confrontation, so despite recent developments he decided a visit to the shop might provide him with some answers; but what the questions were, he just didn't know at this stage.

Gallery Twenty One in fashionable Jermyn Street was known to Baxter. He had entered its mighty portals on a few occasions, sometimes to sell, though rarely to buy. This great emporium was more than just a prestigious shop selling Asian art, it was every bit as much a museum as the Victoria and Albert in Kensington or the British Museum just across the road. Its collections included some of the finest specimens in the country and provided an excellent reference library for student and scholar alike. Whilst the lavish showrooms looked respectable enough, most in the trade knew of the shady dealings which were secretly carried out here and many suspected cartel connections.

A liveried doorman stood motionless in front of the brass and glass entrance, a statement of exclusivity, sending a message to the passing window shopper that this was an expensive showroom, not the sort of place where the casual browser would feel, or for that matter *be* welcome.

Inside the vast showroom he found a marble palace. Its walls and floors were veneered in expensive Pietra Dorata marble, a dazzling white with golden yellow streaks. A thousand concealed spotlights gave the spacious gallery a superb brilliance, pin pointing light to where it had the maximum effect. The showroom boasted a large reserved area in the centre where a splendid octagonal display cabinet under a pagoda roof housed the finest blue and white specimens of Ming porcelain. Here, leather benches faced out towards the brightly lit cabinets which paralleled the long side walls. The army of glass cases housed a vast and colourful array of Oriental antiques with groups of Famille Rose and Famille Verte. Perhaps the most discerning and academically the most interesting cabinet was the monochromes. Here the decoration was not painstakingly applied with a brush, but the result of firing conditions, carefully manipulated to produce glaze colour combinations. Glazes with names such as Robins egg blue, iron rust, and pieces mottled with peach bloom. There were celadon vases, bowls and dishes; the better examples with a fine crackle glaze. Although pottery and porcelain were the main areas of interest, there was for the metal ware collector, cloisonné with brightly enamelled cells. A bronze bell with long inscription and great ritual Han dynasty vessels, sometimes of massive proportions and always green, a testimony to their great age, which often went back to the Han dynasty and beyond.

Baxter compared sketches in his file with some of the examples in the cabinets and added various notes as he wandered around, pretending to be browsing, when in reality he was trying to make some sense of the place.

'Hello Mr. Baxter.' A bright airy voice greeted him from behind.

Startled, he swung round to see a tall elegant woman with

auburn hair and stunning green eyes and they were beaming at *him*.

'You!' he stuttered, barely able to believe his eyes. The lady standing before him was the same woman he had seen in the Rat de Cave bar in Bourge-Vilaine and then outside his hotel window the following day. She had also popped up in the police station in Avranches and again at the British Library; in short, she was Baxter's mystery woman.

'You look surprised Mr. Baxter.'

'I think to say I'm surprised to see you here, close up, would be an understatement.'

'Not an unpleasant one, I hope.' She smiled coyly.

'No, no, not at all.' He found himself floundering.

He guessed she was about thirty, perhaps plus a couple of years, but no more and very attractively dressed. To his relief she *was* beautiful, his dreams had obviously saved the best part until last.

'So you recognize me. I am flattered; that's a compliment coming from an Englishman,' she declared, with a voice which was marked with a distinct French accent, yet her English vocabulary was fluent.

'Yes I do.' he snapped back, annoyed at her sardonic manner 'how could I possibly *not* remember you? You were...'

'Shhhh' she put her finger to her mouth then lowered her voice.

'Not in here, let's go for a drink somewhere, if that's alright with you.'

'Yes of course,' he found himself saying, as though it was a perfectly reasonable suggestion, which of course it wasn't, coming from someone who was a complete stranger in all but appearance.

Outside the gallery he discovered the owner of the Austin Healey he'd parked behind, was the woman. He smiled to himself; of course, that is exactly the type of car she would drive. She followed close behind as he weaved through several side streets, until he pulled up outside a smart public house.

As he waited to order his drinks, Baxter knew he should be feeling suspicious and edgy, but he wasn't. In fact he felt relaxed and quite excited about his new company.

Although he had never been in this particular public house before, this was *his* kind of pub. The interior of the Crown and Sceptre was typical of the many London drinking establishments in this part of the city. Built in the early Edwardian period, it had seen many changes over the years, but to the average person it appeared untouched by time. The first giveaway Baxter noticed was the row of cast iron posts, quite decorative where they met the ceiling, but evidence for the removal of walls at some point in its history.

Baxter placed his foot on the gleaming brass rail which spanned the long mahogany bar, and perched his bottom on a leather-topped cast iron bar stool. The barman took his order and retreated to the optics behind. Here was a stunning backdrop of mirrors, all magnificently engraved, most in the Art Nouveau taste. As an antique dealer Baxter appreciated the beauty and the value of such mirrors. A long row of mahogany and brass pumps stood upright like sentinels; they spanned the entire length of the counter. The lighting was sombre, the orange tulip shades on the brass hanging lights did little to illuminate the surroundings, but then that was the ambience the designers had sought to create.

With two glasses fully charged and his file tucked under his arm he weaved his way between the tables and chairs to the far end where the woman sat waiting in one of the intimate cubicles. These compartments or booths were set aside as places for private conversation. They provided a comfortable and sequestered arrangement of leather benches and mahogany tables, behind small maroon velvet tasselled curtains.

'A Campari and soda for you,' he said placing the drink carefully in front of her. He caught a whiff of her perfume and detected a hint of Egypt, a definite subtle blend of frankincense and myrrh, intoxicating as it teased his nostrils.

'Mmm…., that smells like Baccarats Les Larmes Sacrees de Thebe'

'That is most astute of you Mr. Baxter.' She looked at him curiously, 'I have to say I'm impressed,' she added in a voice which was soft and refined.'

'Don't be,' he casually replied, 'just a lucky guess, no more.'

It was of course no lucky guess. He once had a girl friend who worked for Baccarat and that was her favourite perfume. However, Baxter had never bought it for her as he couldn't possibly afford it at nine hundred pounds a time, even though it was contained in a pyramid shaped flask made from Baccarat crystal. His ex-girlfriend had occasionally managed to acquire a free sample in a plain bottle.

He wondered how this woman sitting opposite could afford such luxury; perhaps she had a rich husband or benefactor, or did she also purloin sample bottles. He somehow doubted the latter?

'Is that orange juice you're drinking? She asked, narrowing her eyes as though disapproving of his abstinence.

'I never drink when I'm working.'

'Surely you're not working now, or are you a policeman Mr. Baxter?'

'By the way, how do you know my name?' he said, quickly changing the subject.

She leant forward and clasped her hands together 'I know a great deal about you Mr. Baxter, but I would very much like to know more.' Her eyes sparkled as she carefully picked her words, slowly and purposefully, 'much more, because you interest me.'

He met her glaze, leaned forward and rested his chin in his hands.

'Why on earth should I interest you when I don't even know who you are? The only thing I know about you is that you have been following me for the past two weeks.'

She smiled over the wineglass, a very nice warm, but guarded smile. 'I'm surprised you took note, I'm flattered Mr. Baxter.' She fluttered her eye lashes a little and then smiled again.

Baxter returned her smile, realizing at that moment that his breathing had become irregular and his heart was missing a beat or two. His stomach suddenly felt oddly hollow, was it excitement, or nerves? He wasn't certain. *Her lips are so kissable,* he said to himself, *in fact she is probably, no, she is* he concluded, *the most attractive woman I have ever sat and talked to and I desperately want to know her better, much better.*

She was discreetly dressed in designer jeans, expensive ones at that, and an attractive white ruffled blouse under a blue velvet blouson jacket. She seemed to be lost in her thoughts. Her smile faltered for a brief moment. 'So I wonder why you should particularly remember *me* Mr. Baxter,' she asked in a playful tone.

He chewed on the question as he took a sip of his drink.

'I always notice pretty women,' he replied swallowing nervously, but wishing afterwards he hadn't said that, as it was a stupid and very obvious remark to make and he felt certain she would see right through it.

As a typical French woman, she would never interpret Baxter's remarks as a come-on, as a pretty girl would be told frequently in the street by men and boys alike 'You are a very pretty mademoiselle', and that most certainly did not mean the man wanted to sleep with her, but was paying a compliment in true French fashion.

Baxter tried to lessen the impact of his last remark by casually looking away, taking note of the cubicle, but he couldn't take his eyes off her. No matter how hard he tried, he was compelled to make eye contact; her eyes were always waiting to engage with his.

She had without doubt been at the front of the queue when looks were handed out, she was without any reservation, what could only be described as eye catching. Her long auburn hair was tied back in ringlets, swept back, neatly outlining an angular face with pronounced high cheekbones, which drew attention to her eyes, and what eyes! They were slightly slanted like a cats, but it was the colour which made them outstanding. Her eyes were as green as emeralds and highlighted by her long lustrous lashes, black and devastatingly sexy. Baxter, like most men, considered green eyes to be the sexiest of all. Perhaps it was because they are by far the rarest eye colour that they are commonly defined as exotic, a hiding place for secret unleashed emotions. Her facial features were complimented by an endearing collection of pale golden freckles which snuggled between the tops of her blushed cheeks and the corners of her eyes. She had an unwavering stare which was deadly attractive, yet suggested she was in control and this was reinforced by the well-known fact that women with green eyes were reputed to be short-fused and temperamental.

She had a slim yet well-defined figure and had clearly taken care of herself. Like any red-blooded male, Baxter couldn't help noticing her breasts, straining inside the white frilly blouse, they were large and beautifully proportioned.

She had clearly observed Baxter visually undressing her. Her lips encircled the glass very slowly, seductively, her eyes never leaving his as she took a gauged sip from her drink.

She leaned back in her seat. 'I'm so sorry, I should have introduced myself earlier,' she said softly and then held out her hand, 'my name is Magali.'

'Magali! What a wonderful name,' he exclaimed as he felt her fingers tighten in his hand. He then sensed a certain nervousness in her fingers as she released her grip.

'So Magali?' he said prompting a follow up surname.

'Couvegne,' she swiftly replied

'Wow' was all he could say, but her expression suggested she expected rather more than a mere wow.

'So am I right in thinking you're a de Couvegne from the chateau at Bourge-Vilaine?'

'Why yes Mr. Baxter, you know it, do you?'

'I saw the chateau on a recent visit, and read a description in the Tourist Information Office, but then you already know that don't you,' he said accusingly.

'You see Mr. Baxter, or do you have another name I can call you?'

'Just Baxter will do.'

She frowned. 'You see Baxter, my grandmother Countess Marie

de Couvegne was keen to buy the letters you bid on, in fact you made her pay rather more than she had expected, but that's another matter. I suspected Marcel Didier was in Bourge-Vilaine to sell you information regarding the letters, and when you two met, my suspicions were confirmed.'

He shot her a glance. 'And so you killed him?'

'No, certainly not,' she replied evasively, 'I don't know who killed him, but his death made no difference to us. You see all we wanted to know was who would be bidding and how much they were likely to be prepared to pay for them.'

'And was anyone else interested in them?'

'Actually there was. An English woman put in a few early bids, but she dropped out at five hundred, but the auctioneer had a commission bidder and although we've no way of knowing who that was, Grandmother thinks he or she was most likely bidding on behalf of the French Government. When you put your last minute bid in, the commission bid had stopped at four thousand Euros.'

'So what on earth was in those letters that made your Grandmother pay so dearly to secure them?'

'It wasn't so much their content, more that she didn't want French officials to see what indiscretions her ancestors had written about certain people in high places. Still, I don't want to go into those sorts of personal details any further.'

There was general laughter in the bar, but that had gone largely unnoticed by the two of them, engaged as they were in each other's company.

Suddenly the curtain rings jangled and a head popped through into the cubicle. 'Hi Baxter, I thought I heard your voice'

It was Shirley, the dealer from Shirley. 'So your admirer from Bourge-Vilaine was real after all. You're a dark one, aren't you?' Before he could explain she said 'I won't intrude, au revoir' and was gone.

'So tell me, *were* you watching me at the Bourge-Vilaine auction rooms?'

'Maybe,' Magali replied remaining firmly noncommittal.

'And at the Rat de Cave bar?'

'Possibly,' she replied sheepishly

'And I believe it was you waiting outside my hotel window an hour before the auction, and don't deny it, I saw you?'

'I don't intend to deny anything Mr. Baxter. You see I had to find out if you were going to bid at the auction, I'd planned to have a word with you in an attempt to try and bribe you not to bid on the letters, but then I thought better of it.'

'Actually you might have been successful, because I was buying them for a customer; but personally I only really wanted the coffer.'

She raised her eyebrows, prompting a response.

Baxter shrugged, choosing to ignore her silent comment.

'You were buying them for a customer, that's interesting; can you tell me who that customer was? No of course you can't,' she said dismissively, 'oh well it doesn't matter. So that's about it I suppose'

'Well it's not really, is it Magali?'

She starred at him blankly and then forced a rueful smile. 'I don't understand what you're getting at.' her face had a tortured, hurt expression.

'What about the police station in Avranches? Don't tell me you were not there, because I saw you?'

'Ah yes, you don't miss much do you Baxter. Well, this is a bit tricky.' She raised her head and cleared her throat. ' I trust you'll keep what I'm going to tell you to yourself.'

He hesitated, and then shrugged 'Yes of course, no problem if that's what you want.'

She glanced around, looking uncomfortable. She said in a soft low voice, 'Marcel Didier was killed on the orders of someone in a very high position, don't ask me who because I don't know, and nor do I know why, but the police in Bourge-Vilaine thought you had done it and contacted their counterparts in Avranches. Naturally you were a prime candidate until they contacted my grandmother for details about her purchase of the letters. She sent me straight to Avranches to explain and whilst I was doing that, a telephone call came through from an English police official.'

'The name wasn't by any chance Atterbury was it?'

'Yes that was it, I'm certain it was. Anyway, the Inspector immediately told me to go home and I believe he released you at the same time.'

'So it wasn't you who secured my release then.'

'Good heavens no Baxter, goodness me I don't have that sort of influence.' Her face once again sported a look of innocence. 'But' she added hesitantly 'someone in a high place had something to do with your release, perhaps you have a guardian angel.'

'I think that's most unlikely, but what about the British Library? I know I saw you there,' he said raising his brows prompting her reply.

'Please don't interrogate me like this, I didn't mean you any harm, in fact quite the opposite.'

'So your reasons were?' he pressed her for a reply

'Well if you must know I was concerned for your safety. I don't think you know what you've got yourself into, do you?'

'So tell me Magali de Couvegne, just what have I got myself into?'

She swallowed, clearing her throat. 'I wish I could tell you Baxter, but I can't,' she said with a heavy sigh.

'And you were looking after me were you?' he said with a wry smile.

'Yes I was and I have no excuses for being concerned for you.'

Suddenly, before she could say another word a rush of activity outside the cubicle alerted them to another unwanted intruder. The curtain was swept aside and out of the corner of his eye, Baxter spotted a hand which reached for the table and grabbed his spring file.

He jumped up and swung open the curtain in time to see a man fleeing out of the pub door. Baxter returned to his seat.

'Well aren't you going to go after him?' Magali said

'No' he replied shaking his head.

'But he has stolen your papers.'

'Yes but they're of no value to anyone and what's more they were only photocopies, I have the originals at home.'

'So you're not going after him then.'

'You see Magali, if I was to chase after him I would have to stop talking to you and I don't want to do that, not even for one solitary moment.'

'Do you know Baxter, I do believe that's the nicest thing anyone has ever said to me,' she said.

Baxter by now realised he was under her spell, he found her so easy to talk to although he contritely realized he had interrogated her. She was not only a stunning woman, but her personality warmed him also. She had an endearing look of innocence, although he suspected there was a darker side to Magali. Inwardly he knew his heart was ruling his head, warning flashes kept invading his desire to know her better, in fact he was aware that he desperately wanted to make love to her and he thought he had received signals which suggested she might possibly feel the same.

'What's on your mind?' she asked

'Nothing really,' he said lying. 'So tell me Magali, where do you live?'

'Where do I live?' she paused as though balancing her reply.

'Sometimes I live with my grandmother in the Chateau de Couvegne near Bourge-Vilaine, and occasionally in my Montmartre apartment in Paris. And quite often in London hotels,' she added.

'And so what do you do for a living? Or is that a silly question.'

'Come, come, Baxter, allow a girl some secrets.'

Baxter knew she was dancing around something, but then with a pedigree and address like that, she most likely didn't have to earn a living.

As they left the public house and she opened her car door, Baxter took hold of her arm. 'How can I contact you again? Do you have a telephone number?'

'Do you really want to see me again, Mr. Baxter?'

Before he could reply a black car screeched to a halt outside the pub. He turned in time to see two men jump out. They ignored him and grabbed Magali, pulling her towards their vehicle.

Baxter swung a punch at the first man catching him squarely on the jaw followed rapidly by another into his groin and was most surprised to see him crumple to the ground. The second one continued to try to force Magali into the black Citroen car. Baxter grabbed the assailant around the neck, pushing his knee into the man's back. The man turned and with a profanity, swung a blow, but Baxter ducked and hammered a clenched fist into the chap's stomach. He keeled over, but quickly scrambled to his feet and pulled Magali closer to the car. Baxter grabbed his arm, desperately tugging him. In the struggle Baxter ripped away part of the thug's jacket. It was then he noticed on the assailants arm part of a tattoo, which looked like flying batwings. Baxter punched him hard in the back which made him half-turn, and then Magali brought her knee up and thrust it into his groin, the man screamed and Magali struggled free.

'Come on.' He yelled to her as they ran back into the pub.

'What on earth was that all about?' he asked the dishevelled Magali.

She was suddenly taciturn and did no more than shake her head.

'Well somebody doesn't like you and I can tell you now, I've seen a similar black Citroen before and it spells trouble. 'Where are you staying? I'll follow you home.'

'I'm staying nowhere; I was intending to travel back to France tonight, so goodbye and thank you for saving my life Mr. Baxter.'

'I don't think that's a very good idea, do you,' he said raising his eyebrows in an attempt to assert some degree of common sense.

She didn't reply but looked down at the floor.

'Would you like me to find you a hotel for tonight?' he offered, 'there are some fairly decent ones nearby.'

'Damn you, Baxter,' she said punching him on the chest with both hands, 'of course I don't want to stay on my own in a lonely hotel room.'

He held his arms out at full length. 'So what do you want to do?'

'You know I want to stay the night with you.' The look she gave him was one which was impossible to ignore, it was a blatant invitation, engineered in such a way she knew he couldn't possibly refuse her. His body was reacting and he was rapidly losing control, and he knew it.

'Well if you're certain, you're welcome to sleep on my settee.' he offered, thinking that was probably all she really meant, even though he hoped perhaps she did want more from him.

'Thank you,' she replied coyly, 'I'll be much safer with you looking after me and I promise I won't outstay my welcome.'

'Okay, follow me in your car; it's only fifteen minutes at this time of night.'

CHAPTER 10

AN INTIMATE COALITION

His Chelsea mews cottage seemed so much smaller with one other person there, something he wasn't really used to, or at least rarely.

'Now this is nice,' Magali said as she walked from room to room with a beatific smile on her face.

'And the bedrooms are where?'

'Only one I'm afraid and that's through there,' he said pointing to the end of the passageway.

Magali looked exhausted, so he suggested she put her feet up and have a sleep on his settee. He spread a throw over her, then planted a gentle kiss on her forehead.

He busied himself in the open plan kitchen where he cooked pecorino and chili enchiladas with a feta and oregano Cretan salad, accompanied by olive focaccia. And for dessert he lovingly prepared vacherin aux fraises. While she continued to sleep, he laid the round table with his best antique Imari pattern Royal Derby porcelain, heavy French silver cutlery with its opulent moulded cherubs and a Chelsea porcelain figural candlestick.

He kept questioning why he had brought her home to his cottage. His only defence was that she was terrified after the attack, so how could he possibly turn his back on her now. Inwardly he didn't want to *not* bring her home, he was desperate to know her better, but that involved asking questions and maybe they were questions she didn't have answers for, or questions she wasn't prepared to divulge answers to.

By the time she stirred the meal was almost ready.

'Do you like red or white?' he asked, holding up two bottles.

'Are you still working?' She asked.

'What do you mean? 'he replied dryly.

'What I mean is, are you allowed to drink now or are you still working?' She flashed him a cheeky grin.

'Of course I'm not working. Now red or white, or do you want a Campari?'

'Red will be fine.' Her gaze shifted and she surveyed the room with apparent approval.

'Dinner will be ready in exactly fifteen minutes, he said.

She roused herself and went into the bathroom to powder her nose.

He shouted after her 'Don't be long will you.'

She just turned and smiled.

He put the last touches to the table, checked the oven, turned the regulator down a notch and waited. Normally, in such circumstances, he would be impatient. Strangely enough this evening he wasn't, despite the fact that for much of his life he had waited for women to appear and been frustrated when they didn't or turned up late. Magali was different, she could take as long as she wished; he would wait like a puppy dog for as long as was necessary.

When she returned twenty five minutes later she had somehow performed a revitalizing trick, for once again she looked fabulous.

'You're late,' He said half joking, quickly turning the heat back on under his dishes.

'But it is good manners to be late.' She replied glibly.

'Really,' he turned from his cooking, 'tell me, how do you explain that one?'

'Arriving on time for dinner is a cardinal sin in France, if one should be punctual, one is likely to be welcomed by someone without make-up and met with an uncooked dinner, so it's polite to be ten minutes late.'

He didn't respond, but beckoned her over to the table. As she sat, her thin cotton blouse rippled, the curves of her breasts were most apparent and Baxter fought hard not to focus his eyes on them.

'You know Baxter, you're a very fine cook. Where did you learn to prepare food like this? '

That momentarily diverted his attention.

'My parents were both killed when I was quite young and so I was brought up by my two aunts. They were quite wealthy at that time and had an Italian cook called Antonio and he used to let me help him in the kitchen. A few years later times were getting harder for my aunts and so they had to let Antonio go. He joined up with his brother and opened a small bistro in Dean Street.'

'Soho?'

'Yes that's right. It was nothing grand, but it served good traditional Italian food. Then while I was on vacation from Oxford.'

'Oxford!' she cut him short. 'You're not only an excellent cook and good looking, but a very clever man as well, I do believe.'

'As I was about to say,' he said, side-stepping her remarks, 'I used to help in the kitchens during term breaks to earn a little cash, so I guess I learnt a good deal from Antonio.'

'What I don't understand, is why aren't you married? I would have thought some woman would have snapped you up long ago, you're not gay are you.'

'Certainly not.' The very suggestion riled him and even though he was telling the truth, he still felt a flush on his face.

'So tell me, are you married Magali and if not, why not?'

Magali hesitated for a protracted moment. 'All right, I take your point,' she said.

Baxter continued to wait for her answer.

'The answer is no, I'm not married and by the way what *is* your first name; I can't keep calling you Baxter?'

'Baxter, just call me Baxter, everyone else does.'

'Am I only another everyone else to you?'

'I sincerely hope not, but it's up to you to make that particular decision. Now eat up before your food gets cold,' he said tucking into his own meal.

'You still haven't told me where you are staying whilst here in London' he paused to ask.

Her reply was not spontaneous and Baxter suspected she was forming an answer in her mind.

'I spend a lot of time in hotels and friend's houses.'

'By the way, do you know who those men outside the pub were, because I've seen a similar car more than once before?'

'Really,' she said. A look of puzzlement flashed across her face.

'Yes in Bourge-Vilaine, but it's not the same car though, just the same model but interestingly, that was also driven by Chinese gentlemen. Quite a coincidence, don't you think?'

'Yes it is,' she said softly

'But that's not the only sinister car I've seen around here.'

'So tell me more?' she urged.

He then went on to tell her about the underground car park in Bedford Square and the Daimler which had picked up two more Chinese characters and taken them into the car park. When he told her about his suspicions about Gallery Twenty One, far from wanting to change the subject she pressed him to tell her more. Before continuing he considered his position carefully, because he always liked to have the advantage of keeping a degree of caution, and besides, he realised she had turned things around. Instead of him asking the questions, it was Magali who was asking them.

'I don't really know any more than that,' he concluded.

She eyed Baxter in such a way that he could see she was weighing up all her options before uttering another word. 'You didn't tell me who you were supposed to be buying my grandmothers letters for,' she said in a matter of fact way, 'surely it's no big secret.'

'Well if you must know, I haven't a clue; all I can tell you is that a contact in the trade told me to meet up with Didier, make the purchase and then wait to be contacted again.'

'That sounds a very odd way to conduct business I must say,' she screwed up her forehead making it very clear she didn't believe his story.

'Actually, in my line of business that's a very common way of doing things, 'he said in a matter of fact way.

She looked intrigued 'And exactly what line of business are you in Baxter?' She had asked the question, but in fact she knew the answer and she knew he would expect her to ask that type of question; he would be suspicious if she didn't.

'Antiques' he replied 'just boring old antiques.'

'So what exciting things did you buy at the auction room then?'

He wasn't expecting that particular question and it left him with a problem. If Magali was at the auction the whole time, then she would have seen him buy the Chinese vase. If he kept quiet about it she would wonder why and that might provoke suspicion and he still didn't know very much about her. He could see she was still waiting for his answer, yet he felt certain she knew it without him confessing.

'Which auction room is that?' he wore an innocent expression

'Bourge-Vilaine,' she replied

'Why don't *you* tell me what I bought?' he said

'How on earth would I know what you purchased?' she snapped, shaking her head slowly from side to side.

'Look,' he said 'I don't believe I've told you a single thing you don't already know.'

She didn't respond but hid behind a cloak of indignant coyness.

'Well I did buy a Chinese vase, nothing special, just one of those pieces which interior decorators like.'

'An antique one I expect.' She enquired cynically

'Yes it was probably antique.'

'Let me see it, let me see it,' she squealed, bubbling with excitement.

'I've sold it on, sorry,' he said

The look on her face made it clear she once again didn't believe him, but he wasn't prepared to risk telling her the whole truth just yet. Something was still not quite right about Magali; he didn't know her or entirely believe her motives for being there.

'May I?' she said holding up a cigarette packet.

'Yes that's fine, please feel free, I'll find you an ashtray,' he said slightly unnerved. Baxter dived into his sideboard and produced a blue glass Whitefriers bowl; not exactly the most suitable receptacle for cigarette ash, but that was all he possessed. Baxter had once smoked but had kicked the habit a few years back and whilst his nostrils easily reacted to tobacco smoke, he had grown to be quite tolerant of its effects, but those same old urges still fought to tempt him once again.

She lit a cigarette, the smell was familiar. He immediately recognised it was a French cigarette, it had that darker brown smell to the smoke, the distinctive blend of Samsun and Izmir Turkish tobacco. This brought home a renewed concern about her true identity. He considered asking if she had followed him on that dark night in Bourge-Vilaine, but decided better of it; perhaps it was better *not* to know if she had been his stalker. Baxter had long learnt the valuable lesson of keeping something back in reserve, a weapon which might prove useful at some time in the future, and he was convinced *she* had done just that to him.

The meal finished, washed down with copious quantities of wine. He picked up his Ming dynasty bronze censor, removed the dragon encrusted lid and lit it. Gradually the burning incense released aromatic fragrances of Juniper and Patchouli. The hallucinatory effect was cumulative combined with the wine. He was by now well aware how his testosterone levels dramatically rose whenever he was close to her, his defences were feeble—his feelings had no protection against her. The agony of all the emotional pain she was inflicting upon him drew him ever closer, yet a warning signal was telling him to resist the temptation to take things further. Despite fighting these feelings, deep inside he knew his resolve was quickly weakening and he was powerless to do anything about it.

'You think of everything, when most men think of nothing,' she said. He noticed a smile emerging from deep inside, slowly breaking into a beacon of happiness and contentment.

He was sitting on the leather settee, she sat opposite, both not taking their eyes off each other. He yawned, an involuntary deep breath and certainly not a prompt to imply he was waiting to fall asleep.

'This is stupid.' Magali declared, rising to her feet. If you think I'm sleeping in *your* bed on *my* own, then you are either very shy or gay and I hope it's not the latter.

'I just thought.'

'Well don't think, she said grabbing his arm,' just take me to bed.'

Looking out of his mews window he watched as streaks of light slowly lit up the beginning of a new day and gradually the limits of his bedroom came into view. He turned over, Magali was still sleeping soundly. She groaned quietly as he moved and then snuggled into his chest. His heart began pounding as it reacted to the warmth of the wonderful body next to him. The smell of her long hair and the sweet aroma of her soft tanned skin were intoxicating, stimulating every fibre of his body. Perhaps these scents were imaginary and it was her sensuality he was savouring, but whatever it was, Baxter was well and truly hooked. He was desperate to wake her, hoping they might repeat last night's performance, but at the same time he was happy to be close to her, content to watch her sleep and savour every movement of her face. He wondered if she was dreaming, and if so, what she was dreaming about, hoping he was in just the smallest part of one of those dreams. He was now fully aware he had unintentionally strayed into a territory without boundaries. Now he needed to define the limits if he was to keep in control. She opened her eyes and smiled. 'So how is my archer this morning?' she said rubbing her eyes.

'Archer? I don't understand,' he said thoroughly confused.

'My Sagittarian lover.'

'How on earth did you know I was a Sagittarian?'

'Lots of things give you away. For a start I think you're

intellectually and spiritually advanced and you clearly have high aspirations for success but like all Sagittarians you lack a certain tact when it comes to seeking out the pot of gold that you so desperately pursue.'

'You make me sound like a pathetic, money grabbing individual,' he said, offended at her criticism.

'No don't get me wrong,' she said. 'Sagittarians are the most big-hearted, generous and fun-loving companions of all, and when it comes to matters of the heart they are loyal and successful lovers.'

'So what about you Magali?'

'Aries,' She said.

'And?' he looked at her for her own self-assessment.

'Aries are complicated people, often not quite who they appear to be, but always assertive. But on the downside we are trusting, at times innocently walking into the lion's den. So am I walking into the lion's den with you Baxter?'

'I do hope so,' he said putting his arm around her. But I wish you weren't going back to France today.'

Without a word, she put her finger to his lips, put her hand between his groins, and pulled him towards her.

CHAPTER 11

PARIS

By far the quickest and easiest way to travel to Paris is by Eurostar, a train ride under the channel which takes just two hours thirty five minutes city centre to city centre, a journey that couldn't be rivalled by any other means. Magali wanted to spend a couple of days in her Montmartre apartment in the eighteenth arrondissement. She didn't particularly need her car; in fact she found taxis much more convenient for travelling around the crowded roads of the French capital. Baxter took the opportunity to accompany her, partly because he was keen to visit the Musée d'Orsay so he could look through the Henri de Montaigne documents, but perhaps more so because he wanted to be with her, to continue the special togetherness they had begun less than twenty four hours earlier.

At St.Pancras station they had forty five minutes or so to kill before the ten thirty departed, so while Magali browsed in a perfumery in the undercroft arcade he ducked into the bookshop for something to read on the journey. Frustratingly the books were arranged alphabetically by author name so it was difficult to pick out the desired genre. Eventually he selected The Lost Crystal, an historical novel set in late Roman Britain. The review suggested it was an interesting read, so he emptied his pockets for the right money and paid the sour-looking girl at the till.

Leaving the bookstore he scoured the concourse for a refreshment place, spotted a coffee shop and sat at a round table outside. When the waiter approached he ordered himself a coffee, he would get a chocolate for Magali when she arrived. The waiter quickly returned, clearly hoping Baxter would order rather more than a mere beverage.

'Sir,' he said with pencil and pad in hand.

'Oh I'll have two Danish pastries and when the lady arrives she'll have a chocolate, but she might be a few minutes so wait until she gets here please.'

He flipped through a few pages of the novel, stopping a couple of times to read the odd line. Looking up he still couldn't see any sign of Magali, he drew his gaze upwards to check the time on the big station clock, no problem there. As he dropped his eyes he noted below the clock, a man leaning on the large bronze statue of the couple in an embrace known as The Meeting Place. In normal circumstances Baxter wouldn't have taken too much, if any, notice of just another person leaning against a natural resting point. But the man was Oriental and after recent events, he suddenly felt uneasy. He also observed the large man was drawing heavily on a cigarette and this brought back memories of Bourge-Vilaine.

He chewed over the situation as he bit into his pastry. Suddenly, he spotted Magali emerge from the shop in which she had been browsing.

He wasn't the only person to notice her walking towards him. The Chinese gentleman visibly clocked Magali, quickly folded his newspaper in half, flicked his cigarette end to the floor and crushed it with his shoe. As Magali passed him, he stood upright, straightened his jacket and then paced smartly behind her.

Baxter folded a ten pound note in half, slipped it in the paper bill and left it in the small round dish. He jumped to his feet, grabbed his holdall and rushed across the crowded terminal. In his haste he narrowly avoided colliding into people as he side-stepped and hopped over their luggage in his attempt to reach her. He grabbed Magali's arm, pulling her along.

'What on earth are you doing Baxter?' she asked.

'Just keep up with me, we've a tail, or at least you have.'

He quickened his pace, as much as was possible in the busy concourse. He took a fleeting glance backwards and the Oriental was running, his long legs striding, as he maintained a gauged distance, just a few yards behind.

Baxter spotted the bookshop he had been in a little earlier; he had noticed it had another exit which gave access to the southern side of the station. Rushing past the sour-faced girl at the till, he made his exit through the other door, emerging in the open courtyard where there was an area reserved for parked taxis awaiting customers. He spotted over the far side the distinctive red circle with blue bar and the words underground blazoned across it. He didn't look back, but made for the stairs which led to Kings Cross, St.Pancras underground station.

As they arrived at the top of the steps, Magali went to turn around, he pulled her forward. 'Don't look back, just keep moving.'

As they travelled down the escalator Baxter half turned and spotted the tall Asian at the top, hovering behind a group of women. The man registered Baxter and immediately tucked his head in his coat and looked the other way.

When they reached the bottom Baxter felt the rush of wind as another train made entry into the station and guessed correctly that it was coming from the northbound tunnel.

The destination on the front glass panel of the train told him it was heading for Moorgate. He certainly had no intention of going to Moorgate or any stops in between, but jumped on the train nevertheless. He watched through the open door as their pursuer stepped smartly into the next carriage. Baxter timed his move perfectly. As the automated message announced 'mind the doors' he waited for the first few seconds of movement and then with Magali in tow, jumped off the train just as the doors closed behind them. As the carriages pulled away they waved to the Oriental, who, peering through the window was clearly agitated.

'Who was that man?' Magali asked.

'I don't know.' He confessed.

'He didn't look as though he could catch a cold, let alone a moving tail,' she remarked sarcastically.

'Don't be fooled by the Asian expression of inscrutability, they can be lethal opponents, and I know that from first-hand experience.'

They ran hand in hand up the stairs, surfacing once again in the main station concourse. He looked up at the large station clock and was alarmed to see it read ten twenty; they had just ten minutes before their train departed and gate six and passport control was over the other side of the concourse, so a nifty run was needed if they were going to catch it in time.

The man at the gate tutted at their late dash, but fortunately French immigration control did not even glance at their passports, the officer merely ushered them into the holding area where they boarded the Eurostar train.

The journey on Eurostar past Ashford International and through the tunnel at Folkestone went by very quickly, as they tucked into a hearty breakfast of bacon and eggs, washed down with strong black coffee. By the time they emerged from the darkness of the channel tunnel bursting into brilliant sunlight, they'd finished breakfast and were now sitting back enjoying the ride as the train raced through the French countryside. At speeds of up to three hundred kilomètres an hour, the icons of tiny villages flashed by, church spires peeping above rooftops were framed in the train windows as passing images.

The Gare Du Nord in Paris is the terminus for Eurostar trains from London. This great cathedral-like building designed in the Gothic style with its distinctive rows of tall iron columns supporting a vast glass roof, is the largest and busiest train station in Europe. The thirty six platforms were like honey to a bee with swarms of people rushing to and fro. Baxter scanned the concourse; the scene before him was reminiscent of William Powell Frith's famous painting of eighteen sixty two titled 'The Railway Station'. The terminus was crowded with people dashing in every direction with groups of figures dragging small children, crisscrossed by businessmen with briefcases and macs over shoulders and elderly couples pulling suitcases along behind them. He imagined people were eyeing him, he looked for watching, preying eyes, but he quickly came to the conclusion it would be impossible to spot any tail that might be waiting for them here. He made straight for the south exit where they waited behind a small queue in the grey austere street.

The trick with Paris taxis is to watch out for those showing a green light, the signal that they alone are available for hire. Even in a queue, if you mistakenly hail a red light taxi, someone behind you will step off the pavement with hand outstretched and nab that vacant one following; you've then missed your turn.

In less than fifteen minutes they were in the heart of the Montmartre quarter or butte Montmartre as it was originally known.

Dominated by the Sacre Coeur Basilica, Montmartre is the highest Paris hill at one hundred and thirty metres and impossible to miss for miles around. They had arrived in a graceful old square with courtyards and passages that burrow unpredictably between the narrow streets.

'Let's take a drink here before we go home.' Magali suggested.

Sitting at a typical French wrought iron table under a spreading plane tree Baxter suddenly felt totally relaxed. He had never yearned for rural escapism, that was something other people did, not him, but he had to admit that for the first time in recent months he felt free from the stresses of everyday life, the hustle and bustle of the twenty first century was suddenly somewhere else, not here.

As he sat soaking up the street scene, the smells and sounds of the day slowly wafted in. The Place de Terte in the centre of this inimitably picturesque part of Paris was made up of a few restaurants, bars and the odd shop and all very expensive if the price boards were anything to go by. However, Baxter soon realised that there was more to this unique place than price. As a patron here you were buying not just a coffee, glass of wine or a galette, but everyone here was buying an experience.

Artists under colourful umbrellas sat at their easels in the centre of the square. Some waiting for business and others already engaged in painting portraits of tourists in gauche, pencil or chalks, a tradition which went back a century or more. This was a painter's paradise and had been, uninterrupted for all those long years. Montmartre became famous in the late eighteen hundreds with the arrival of painters such as Renoir, Van Gogh, and Picasso, and despite the influx of summer tourists, or perhaps because of them, Montmartre still retains its village-like feel, an ambience which sets it apart from the hustle and bustle of the rest of Paris. This effervescent atmosphere excited Baxter and he wasn't in a hurry to leave.

An artist sitting by his empty easel spotted them and came over. With a cheeky grin hidden behind a bushy beard he looked at Magali and gasped. 'Ah, mon ami, the lady is most beautiful.' he framed her face with his hands, gauging the final composition. Would you like for me to paint the beautiful lady for you?' This was a carefully and well-rehearsed question, which was intended to make life hard for any man who considered refusing in front of his wife or loved one. Magali wasn't keen and faltered with feeble excuses, but after continued attempts by the artist and some egging on by Baxter she conceded and followed the painter to the centre of the square. Baxter sat back in his chair thoroughly enjoying the loveliness of the place. The streets with their stone setts were more rural than city thoroughfares. They were never in straight lines, but always curving away from the centre. Street lights were lanterns on elegant columns, perhaps not old, but made to compliment the other street furniture. Across the road people were photographing the curious *Man In The Wall*. The bronze sculpture that famously consisted of a head and bust and a solitary leg had been erected as a tribute to the writer Marcel Ayme.

With the portrait finished, Baxter realised he hadn't asked the price beforehand and so was at a distinct disadvantage when it came to haggling. The painter initially demanded eighty euros but after Baxter took him to one side and made it clear he would only pay fifty, the artist grudgingly agreed. It was still not cheap for a ten minute sitting but it was a good likeness and Baxter was pleased to have it as a memento of their visit.

Leaving the square behind they entered Boulevard de Clichy whose crowded pavements were lined with endless bars, fast food outlets and more than a few sex shops. Baxter didn't care for this change of environment; the people were edgier and faster. Neon signs constantly flashed and pimps and prostitutes leant in doorways. The windows of sex shops were never discreet and made it clear that they sold everything you had *never* thought of and so much more. He was embarrassed for Magali, but probably shouldn't have been. This entire area was, in his opinion, an assault on any decent person's senses and not somewhere he wished to be with someone as refined as Magali.

Turning the next corner and the street scene was different again. Here dominating the end of the street was the famous Moulin de la Galette. The fine wooden windmill with its four long sails in mid-flight was dominated by grand apartment blocks each side of the road.

Magali stopped in front of a magnificent building.

'This is my little pied de terre' she announced coltishly.

Baxter looked up at the cut stone seven floor apartment block. This was a classic Haussmann façade typically designed around horizontal lines. These lines were continuous from one building to another and formed by balconies and cornices perfectly aligned. It was on the balconies where the only ornamentation had been applied and in typical Art Nouveau style.

'Which floor do you live on?' he asked fully expecting it to be one of the little attic ones which looked out from the mass of grey slate roof.

'The étage noble of course,' she replied with a look of satisfaction.

'The second floor!' he *was* impressed because it was here on this level where traditionally the wealthiest families lived, those who could afford to live high enough from the street and avoid noise and pollution, but at the same time without too many stairs to climb.

Although these days there was a modern passenger lift to service the seven floors, Magali took the vast stone stairwell. She skipped merrily up the wide limestone steps, constantly turning round and egging him on, but he couldn't help himself as he stopped on every turn to examine the fine marble busts set into niches around the curving walls. The second floor was quickly reached and once through the entrance vestibule Magali marched down the red-carpeted corridor and stopped at apartment fifteen. She inserted one key after the other and the bolts shot home.

'Come,' she said as she flung open the large mahogany doors, 'this is my Paris bolt hole.'

'Bolt hole!' He muttered to himself as his eyes surveyed the grand salon. Here was a large spacious room, the likes of which he had only ever seen in glossy magazines like Marie Claire.

The silk window dressings were huge and luxurious and gave the room an instant air of opulence. The large pair of french windows ascended vertically from floor to ceiling and outside he could clearly see elaborate wrought iron balconies. The high ceiling was lavishly adorned with magnificent plaster mouldings embellished with running vine leaves and berries and the large moulded centre rose boasted a very large Italian cut crystal chandelier. Below his feet his eyes feasted on the rich Hungarian parquet floor which was dressed with a long and sumptuous Savonnerie carpet.

'This is truly stunning and so façon de France,' He exclaimed bending down and feeling the rich pile.

'Facon de France,' she repeated looking for clarification.

'In the French manner,' he said with authority, 'but is it really eighteenth century?'

'I believe it is,' she said casually, 'I believe there's a label under that far corner.'

True enough as he turned the carpet back a Paris auction label had been preserved underneath. Pierre-Josse Perrot, circa 1740-50. The striking feature of the hand-woven design was the Royal Arms of France ringed by a collar of the order of Saint Esprit. A border of floral swags and shell cartouches paid fitting tribute to the royal declaration of allegiance. The Napoleon III armchairs looked perfectly at home in this regal setting, although they did not look particularly comfortable; they rarely were.

'So what do you think of my Paris pad then?' she asked

Baxter blew a short breath between his lips. 'Impressive. I'm amazed you have an apartment like this. You do own it I presume?'

'Of course I do,' she replied indignantly, 'okay I confess I didn't buy it. It was originally the Couvegne family apartment; my grandmother gave it to me a few years ago.'

'Quite some present,' Baxter remarked

'You haven't seen it all yet, the best room is yet to come,' she giggled with a wicked seductive twinkle in her eye.

The other rooms were similarly lavish. The dining room and library were also behind the main facade, as was the principal bedroom, while the two guest rooms, the stunning modern kitchen and the bathrooms, all faced the courtyard to the rear.

'Sit and relax while I change,' Magali said with a casual wave of the hand.

He wandered over to the fine Sienna marble fireplace to look at a spectacular clock. His eyes lingered at an extremely rare Louis XVI gilt bronze mounted blue, gold and enamel astronomical skeleton clock signed Lamiral à Paris, and the case by the celebrated enamellist Joseph Coteau.

Looking back at the magnificent interior he was struck by the brilliant white walls, panelled horizontally from the floor upwards, then large square ones, all with moulded plaster frames. Each contained either a double ormolu bronze wall light or a picture with strip light above. Baxter was curious about the selection of pictures for he would have expected a type of painting more associated with the grandness of a chateau owner. But these were all broadly speaking Impressionist works, dating from the mid to late nineteenth century. The likes of Charles Francois Daubigny's Washerwomen at the Oise River, brushed shoulders with Eugene Boudin's Festival in the Harbour of Honfleur, and the celebrated Parisian artist Berthe Morisot and her wonderful large oil of a girl in a boat with geese. Without exception, every picture in the room was associated with water; none were of a pastoral or portrait genre and that surprised him.

He walked past the glass topped coffee table with its large breasted ormolu caryatid supports and sunk deeply into the long settee. Leaning back with his right hand resting on the arm, he inadvertently flicked a switch prompting two doors to slowly open and a very large Sony Bravia HD flat screen television appeared, a strange intrusion in this otherwise very eighteenth century interior.

Then he spotted a problem, and a serious one at that. Each side of the magnificent clock on the mantelpiece was a matching candelabrum, but they were not equi-distant, the one on the left was several centimetres closer to the clock than the one on the right. He tried to ignore this imbalance, but his arrangement and symmetry disorder kicked in and he was compelled to rush over and make the necessary adjustments.

It was some half an hour later when Magali returned, fresh from a shower or bath, or perhaps both.

'There are clean towels in the bathroom,' she said, 'and a glass of champagne by the mirror, but don't be too long, a girl doesn't like to be kept waiting.' she winked.

That night they made love and she quickly fell asleep. He lay thinking about the events of the day, from the strange incident in the station concourse in England where, once again, someone attempted to grab Magali, to the amazing apartment here in Paris. Just who was Magali? He was certain he didn't know just yet, but he had a feeling he was sooner or later going to find out, and a gut reaction told him he wasn't going to find the truth very palatable.

Baxter woke to the soft early morning light with a feeling of happiness; he couldn't remember ever waking with such elation and total contentment. He looked at his watch, it was seven thirty, but it took his fussy-headed brain a few seconds to work out whether he was an hour ahead or behind U.K time. Luxuriating in the silk canopied bed he lay admiring the grand room with the chandelier sparkling as the early morning sun played on its many crystal facets. He had noticed the clever use of mirrors the previous night and the way the chandelier played on the mirror glass sending light to every corner of the room making it appear far larger than it was, not that the room was in any way modest. The chalky white louvered doors flanking the long suite of wardrobes with their ormolu fingerplates and handles were clearly designed with the privileged and well-to-do in mind.

The window frame outlined the Paris roofline from a vantage point he had never seen before. He gazed out on the building opposite, fascinated by the oeil de boeuf windows. Each was set in a carved stone surround with a head of Medusa below a moulded triangular pediment. The sides were adorned with oak leaf and berry ornament. The small round windows resembled a wheel with glazing bars much like spokes radiating out from an empty hub. The one immediately opposite was not alone, but part of a symmetrical row peeping out of the grey slate roof across the street. Fine lace curtains prompted him to wonder what sweet little room was hidden up there, surely it couldn't possibly be as opulent as the one he was in. Baxter had always been noted for his powers of observation. While most people walk around cities like Paris with their heads, at best, one floor above street level, he always had his nose in the air looking for roof furniture for it was here where some of the best architectural detail lie hidden from most people's gaze..

'Come on,' she said, 'there's a lot to do today.'

'I'll be up shortly.'

'What are you doing in there?' she enquired mockingly.

'Just thinking.'

'Thinking!' she exclaimed, 'I've never heard of a man *thinking* in bed before. They might dream up fantasies, but from my experience men never *think* in bed, especially not in my bed. Anyway I'm off to buy some croissants from across the road, so finish that thinking and put some coffee on.'

She seemed to be rather longer than he had expected. Baxter had washed and dressed and the coffee had been ready for over ten minutes and would be starting to stew. He drained the last of his second cup and went back to the sitting room and pulled aside the net curtains. He could see Magali on the street below, her arms waving in an irate manner; her voice though low pitched had a distinct tone of aggravation as she conversed with someone who was leaning out of his car window. Baxter felt she was giving the man orders. He suddenly retaliated by swinging open his car door, reaching to get out, and then angry shouts, female barks. Baxter was about to rush down when the man slammed his car door and sped off, his tyres screeching into the distance. Magali looked up and saw Baxter watching, she shrugged at him and returned to the entrance portal.

'Who was that you were talking to?' he asked before she had barely entered the room.

'Just a passing motorist who was looking for the cemetery.'

'But you seemed to be arguing with the man, which seems odd, if he was no more than a stranger.'

'I told him he was in the wrong place, he wouldn't have it though and got angry and so I told him to go and get lost again.'

Baxter so wanted to believe her, but he knew she was lying through her teeth. He was convinced she knew the man in the car. What he had seen had been a personal heated exchange, an argument between two people who shared some common ground. He was saddened that she didn't have enough faith in him to tell the truth. Whatever that incident had been about, she chose to conceal it and that upset him.

CHAPTER 12

GENERAL HENRI DE MONTAIGNE

Magali was preparing to set off to see the family notaire, or so she claimed. Baxter wasn't particularly surprised and neither had he questioned her need, as it wasn't unusual for well-to-do French families to have a Parisian solicitor; someone trusted who had served them and probably their forebears for decades.

'I'll be off then,' she said pausing in the doorway.

He patted her on the shoulder. 'Be careful, won't you,' he said hoping she might change her mind and allow him to escort her.

'Stop worrying,' she said, 'this is Paris, I feel safe here.'

He was unable to accept that Paris was likely to be any safer than London, although he had no reason to back such a supposition. She gave him a kiss and then skipped down the stairs to meet her waiting taxi.

Baxter had his own plans and that didn't include traipsing off to a dreary solicitor's office, so in many ways he was pleased to be free to do his own thing.

Unlike Magali, Baxter had not ordered a taxi beforehand and so had a frustrating wait of a good ten minutes before he spotted a vacant taxi heading in his direction. He stepped off the pavement and hailed it.

As the cab pulled away from the kerb and nosed its way between the long rows of tall elegant buildings, he sat back and contemplated his plans for the day. His first trip would take him to the Musée D'Orsay where he would examine the Henri de Montaigne archive and perhaps finally unravel the origins of his Chinese vase.

The Musée D'Orsay situated on the left bank of the Seine is housed in the former Beaux Arts railway station of the same name and is one of Paris's best-loved museums.

Walking briskly past the long queue of tourists which turned back on itself several times between crowd control bollards, Baxter went through entrance C with Magali's pass. Once inside he made his unhurried way through the middle of the airy and impressive building, dodging the sea of white marble statuary which punctuated the main concourse. Built in steel and glass the former railway station has an enormous domed roof which begins at ground level and gently curves towards the top. No matter where you stand, the dominant feature is the main station clock designed by Victor Laloux, but the best view is from the far end. A trail of lights leading up to the clock and the silhouettes of people walking behind the wall of glass, gives a sense of the size of this ormolu encrusted timepiece.

Although he had more important things to do today, Baxter couldn't possibly walk blindly past one of the greatest impressionist art collections in the world. Here he could gaze lovingly at works by Cezanne, Renoir, Degas and Monet, and not forgetting the magical works of Van Gough.

With his fix of art firmly in his veins, Baxter headed for the modern extension which housed the thematic documentation centre.

Here he found the official military records for the second opium war in China which included Brizay's *Le Sac du Palais* and the extensive account *Souvenirs de Campagne de Peking* by Armand Lucy. Baxter's eyes really lit up when he was handed Henri de Montaigne's, *L'Expédition de Chine*. Of even more importance were the personal diaries the Count had written describing the battles and subsequent looting of the Summer Palace and other buildings.

He quickly became engrossed in the account, written with such clarity that he really felt as though he was physically there in the midst of the battle, he digested the words as he read them.

Peking October 1860
General Henri de Montaigne looked out from the summer gate opposite Nanhu Island across Kunming Lake to Longevity Hill, then over towards the Summer Palace where it nestled amongst a complex of opulent buildings. The General, like every other person

who saw it for the first time, was in awe at the great Imperial marble boat, motionless on the water's edge. It looked as though it could float away, but of course it couldn't.

Henri de Montaigne, in his diaries, described how further afield he could see the gleaming white marble steps leading up to the magnificent four-storied pagoda-capped temple. 'Suddenly' he wrote, 'I was brought back to my senses by the awesome sight growing in the far distance where an inordinate carriageway of dust was rising, moving slowly from the Black Lake. I could see a great Chinese mass on its way to engage my army in what I knew would be the final act of this momentous opium war.'

Henri de Montaigne had come a long way since he was first appointed Divisional General, and then sent to China to command French troops in the joint Anglo-French expedition. His brief, with the help of British forces was to enforce the Treaty of Tientsin.

Baxter cross-referenced with Armand Lucy's account *Campagne de Peking* which outlined how the problems had begun a hundred years earlier when the addiction to opium had become a major concern to the Chinese authorities. As the habit spread in the country's coastal regions from the idle rich to ninety per cent of Chinese males under the age of forty, the authorities closed all the Canton warehouses and prohibited the opium trade. However, these measures fell far short of their intended outcome and were further expounded by the British who jumped at the opportunity to cash in on this lucrative commodity.

For more than a hundred years the Chinese government had imposed severe restrictions on foreign trade. At Canton, the only port open to foreign commerce with the exclusive right to deal with the west was held by a group of licensed merchants known as the Shāqi. The East India Company operating out of Britain had a monopoly of trade with India and China and purchased silks and tea from the Chinese in return for opium and silver bullion.

The Lucy account went on to explain how British merchants soon began smuggling opium into China in order to balance their purchases of tea for export, a commodity which was in great demand in England and its territories.

The sale of opium had been illégal in China since 1800, but the black-market trade continued to flourish in defiance of the Law. However, things started to go wrong after the crew of the British ship, Arrow were charged by the Canton authorities of smuggling Opium. This and other problems led to the Treaty of Tientsin in eighteen fifty eight. The Chinese refused point blank to ratify the treaty and this is why the French and British armies were there to enforce it.

Baxter went back to Henri de Montaigne's account. The General related how the Chinese opposition was not insubstantial. Three weeks earlier his men had engaged a large Chinese army at Palikao known as the Battle of the Eight Mile Bridge and although he suffered two thousand casualties, the Chinese opposition of more than twice that number had been entirely wiped out. Following this momentous victory he was awarded the title of Count of Palikao by none other than Napoleon the third.

The next entry in Henri de Montaigne's diary had the perplexing title- The Battle of Yuan Ming Yuan. Baxter translated this as 'The Garden of Perfect Brightness.' He realised the use here of the word yuan, or garden was a description of the Imperial Summer Palace complex as a whole, but interestingly, it implied that the landscape setting was far more important than any of the elaborate buildings. It was a well-known fact that the landscape around the complex was not natural scenery, but rather designed, shaped, and constructed. Hills and lakes had been planned in ensembles with buildings playing a subordinate role.

Montaigne began describing the battle scene first relating how a tall elegant officer rode up to him, waiting for the final orders.

'Lieutenant Fabriante tells me they are ready to enter battle positions,' announced the Compte d' Herisson, the long standing military attaché acting as secretary to the General.

The General checked the battle composition. The British land forces commanded by Sir James Hope Grant were stationed on the right supporting wing where they waited instructions.

Suddenly the convoy of dust in the distance materialized into a great moving mass as a vast Chinese army swarmed down the high slopes in the direction of the French and British positions.

The Chinese were lined up in large numbers, several thousand at a time, waiting to employ their usual tactic of human wave attack. They were ready to manoeuvre as many men as possible into close range of Henri de Montaigne's army in the expectation that the shock from such a hefty mass of attackers would force the enemy to disintegrate or fall back. This type of warfare relied on large numbers of soldiers engaged in melee combat, but didn't require the skills of individual soldiers. What it did call for was physical courage and coercion. The attackers began to charge into the enemy fire power at great speed attempting to cover the distance in the shortest possible time so that a sufficient mass could be preserved when the attackers reached melee range.

Henri de Montaigne denied the first wave of the Chinese army any opportunity to make a close quarters attack. He gave the signal and one hundred cannon opened up followed by a thousand carbines. Another wave followed with the same consequences.

It was a further hour before the main body of the Chinese opposition moved into position. The Chinese army under their Commander Sengge Rinchen included the elite Mongolian cavalry who made the next frontal attack. It was a fast and courageous move, but suicidal in its brazenness. Within a matter of minutes they were all but annihilated by the superior fire-power from the allied forces.

Baxter cross-referenced with Henri de Montaigne's account in *L'Expédition de Chine* in which he noted that the Mongolians were facing the unlucky omen of the intercalary month the 紫微斗數 or Zi Wei Dou Shu which was unfortunately falling in this the tenth month of the year. Montaigne described in some detail how the intercalary months were part of the Chinese lunar-solar calendars and came about as a result of twelve lunar months being shorter than one solar year, and so every few years an extra month, a leap month uruu-tsuki was inserted to keep the lunar calendar in line with the solar calendar. This unlucky omen was apparently quite a blow to warriors who held a belief that through their martial arts, they were impervious to foreign bullets, but that was in all but the leap month.

Baxter shifted his focus back to the battle account.

'There followed an unexpected thunder of drums,' Montaigne wrote, 'the booms echoed all around the hillside in such a way it was impossible for the French and British armies to tell where the sound was coming from. Suddenly the battle din was joined by the resonance of gongs and horns of the disparate elements of the main Chinese Imperial Army. For the first time I could see individual faces as a sea of red and white standards emerged from the Yinshui valley accompanied by a great furore as they pounded their feet in step with the mighty drums.'

Henri de Montaigne's men waited with bated breath; to a man they were a coiled spring waiting to be released. 'In front of us,' he wrote, 'a little more than a hundred yards away, the battle roar of two thousand warriors erupted as the great Chinese army waved their terrifying hooked swords. As they began their charge, a sea of yellow tunics with red emblems came into focus, some with red turbans, others with sashes over blue costumes.' Henri de Montaigne's French regiments remained dug in and waited.

'When the Chinese were only twenty yards away I gave the order and four thousand carbines opened fire, more than half the opposing army fell to the ground in front of us in this first wave.'

The British on the west wing followed with a second and third barrage wiping out all but a few stragglers who managed to flee back to the hills. In less than four hours the battle was over, leaving just the clearing up to be done.

Baxter noticed there was some discrepancy in the reports, one stating the battle only lasted two hours, but Henri de Montaigne's own account seemed the most realistic at four.

He continued reading. According to the diary it was eight o 'clock the following morning, the sixth of October when General Henri de Montaigne arrived at the doors of the Royal Summer Palace. Yixin, the Prince Gong was long departed along with his dignitaries and nobles.

Henri de Montaigne went on to describe how he toured the Emperor's Palace and many of its ruined temples accompanied by a group of French and British officers. 'I was dismayed to see several empty pedestals where items had already been taken by Chinese brigands. The British generals Grant and Elgin didn't arrive until three hours later and showed little interest in the battle that had taken place the previous day, but set about selecting the most precious objects to send back to their sovereigns.'

Baxter went back to the diary and unfolded a letter addressed to the French minister of war. It read 'It would be impossible, Monsieur le Maréchal, for me to convey to you the magnificence of the many buildings which are known as the Emperor's Summer Palace. There are successions of pagodas all containing gods of gigantic size in gold and silver or in bronze, including one which we estimate to reach seventy feet from the ground. In one grand temple we found a marvellously sculpted throne framed by two huge cloisonné enamel vases. The wall behind was covered by an enormous silk painting depicting views of the imperial palaces, while shelves around the room were stacked with piles of delicately painted albums and books written by the Emperor himself, all contained in beautiful boxes. There were even greater quantities of Nanjing porcelain, old cloisonné enamels, rare red lacquer boxes from Peking, a thousand kinds of jade sculpture, lace, ivory, agate, coral, sandalwood carvings, bronzes from Canton, and pearls the size of hazelnuts. Outside, there are gardens and lakes as far as the eye can see and white marble buildings covered with dazzling shiny tiles of every colour imaginable; add to that views of a beautiful man-made countryside and Your Excellence will have but a feeble idea of what we have seen here today.'

In his diary Henri de Montaigne noted details of vases of porcelain and enamel which he had personally put his name on. Some were of a small and portable size, while two very fine ones from the throne room were more than four feet high. He then went on to say how British officers began pocketing things, setting off a general frenzy among officers and soldiers alike, including many from his own ranks who allowed their men to loot freely, loading wagons with enormous sacks of goods .

When Henri de Montaigne returned the following day, he describes a terrible scene of destruction. 'French and English soldiers are still in a frenzy, rushing from room to room grabbing what they want, but it's the wanton destruction which alarmed me the most,' he said. 'Men with clubs are smashing every piece of porcelain not yet claimed. I witnessed others throwing bronzes at mirrors and shooting chandeliers into thousands of shards.'

General Henri de Montaigne explained how he had acted on orders from Lord Elgin to lay siege on the Royal Chinese temples that sprawl on the southern slopes. He lamented on the wanton destruction saying 'Every temple and edifice has been thoroughly ransacked. Even now many are still fiercely burning, others already in a state of ruin. The paths and gardens are a vast depository for tons of broken porcelain, enamels and other unwanted treasure. Great statues of dogs of foe, emperors and dragons lay smashed where they have fallen, too large for anyone to take away and wagons are lined up ready to make the journey back to the port of Canton.'

In the meantime his men were clearing away the remaining Chinese guerrillas on the summit around the dominant tower of Fo Xiang Ge; he said 'The war was over and the spoils are for the taking.' Baxter ruminated how the General would never know how the controversy over his government's actions would still be raging one hundred years later.

Baxter sat back in his seat reeling from the history of Henri de Montaigne, the amazing story swirling around in his head. He scanned through his pages of scribbling's, *Wow* he said to himself *these accounts are a story in themselves.* He closed his notebook and decided he had to visit the Generals grave which was apparently located in the great Parisian cemetery of Montmartre; a ten minute taxi ride.

Nestling in the hollow of an ancient gypsum quarry, a sign at the entrance explained how the cemetery had been constructed below street level beginning in the early eighteen hundreds. It went on to explain how the graveyard catered mainly for the wealthier or more famous elements of society, simply because at that time, as now, all land in central Paris commanded high prices. The middle and poorer classes were usually buried in the suburbs, where land was far cheaper.

As he began his journey through the quiet and ordered world of the dead, Baxter was immediately taken by this great Metropolis of limestone and marble, a city of the departed which rose up in peaks of architectural splendour and then subsided elsewhere with more modest crumbling tombstones with rusty iron fences.

Here in Montmartre he came across so many monuments of famous people, names synonymous with Paris's illustrious past. Painters, musicians, inventors and the wealthy; all were reflecting a testimony to their greatness, their prosperity, or were there as a result of public gratitude.

As he walked around he was struck by the quietness, a solitude which was only occasionally broken by the rustling of leaves or the quiet padding of a widow bent double, scurrying along clutching flowers. The sound of running water as a tap was turned on and then an old man lugging a watering can towards a grave with plants neatly arranged around it. Young couples were characteristically giggling, always holding hands and sometimes kissing under trees. The young reminded him that in this domain of the dead, it was them who aptly represented the life cycle.

He read so many familiar names carved in marble and filled in with gold as he wandered between the graves. Offenbach, Edgar Degas and long before he reached it he could see Alexander Dumas lying resplendent on his marble tomb with its four great Romanesque columns. In contrast Hector Berlioz was in sombre black marble.

Turning the corner he was suddenly faced with the amazing sculpture of Emile Zola. The chiselled hair appeared to be blowing in the wind, his bronze bust looking out of a pink porphyry tomb shadowed by bay trees. *What a wonderful place to be interred*, he thought to himself and then read the accompanying plaque which explained that Zola's body was no longer residing here in peace, having been transferred elsewhere. Baxter stopped at the next bench and sat back admiring the overall splendour of the place. The massive bronze figure of Osiris looked out over the tomb of Daniel Iffla, an expensive and opulent monumental piece of sculpture which rubbed shoulders with others of far less magnificence. Angels abounded, their wings mostly folded, offering protection within their feathered sanctuary and no less common were statues representing the Virgin Mary. But no matter how impressive individual mausoleums and statues might be, the really dominant feature of which it was impossible to lose sight, was the amazing lattice metal viaduct supported boldly on columnar stanchions which carried the main road over the cemetery; it is said that many tramps sleep under here, a dry if draughty dormitory for those who have nothing but hunger and despair.

He soon discovered the tramps were not the only living residents here.

A small elderly man stopped him and asked if he was English. Baxter confirmed he was, then the man proudly announced he had studied at Cambridge University, albeit many years ago. The wizened gent opened the bag he was carrying and showed Baxter a selection of cat food, some in tins and other as biscuits.

'There are one hundred and one cats living here in this cemetery, but not a single rat or mouse,' the old man said.

'I've seen one or two feline characters, but surely one hundred and one is a very precise number,' Baxter remarked.

'I know every single one of them,' the old man said, 'each has a name and a unique personality.' He bent down to stroke a black cat who was brushing itself against his leg. 'This is Katrine, only three years old, aren't you? She's had nine kittens you know.'

'So how long have you been feeding the cats here?'

'Forty two years now, but it's an expensive task, it takes most of my small pension,' he said raising his head in expectation.

Baxter had never met anyone who was more deserving of a hand-out and so he happily slipped a ten euro note into the man's hand.

Walking between the long rows of gravestones and monuments, it took Baxter nearly an hour to find the last resting place of General Henri de Montaigne. Here the graves were not of the rich and famous but those of Generals, Politicians and Government officials, and their sepulchres reflected their more modest means. He had arrived at a tree-lined circular avenue consisting principally of tall upright mausoleums, often with the name of the owner above a locked iron gate. Occasionally a few flowers could be glimpsed inside, often artificial and if not, invariably long past their life expectancy.

Henri de Montaigne's grave was in one of these tall upright sepulchres. There were no flowers here and the long grass growing in front was ample evidence that the gate had not been opened for many years. Inside on the far wall, a bronze plaque made perfunctory reference to his military background, the date October 26 . 1900, aged seventy four. Below an open book carved in marble with the words.

Ma volonté est que mes dessins, mes etamps mes bibelots, mes livres et mai potterie enfin les choses d'art qui ont fait le bonheur de ma vie n'aient pas la froide tombe d'un musée et le regard bête du passant indifférent et je demande qu'elles soient toutes éparpillées

*sous les coups de marteau des commissaires-priseurs et que la
jouissance que m'a procurée l'acquisition de chacune d'elles, soit
redonnée pour chacune d'elles à un héritier de mes gouts. Edmund
de Goncourt. C.de C.*

'Wow that's some epitaph, Henri de Montaigne' Baxter read it
once more this time translating it into English.

'My desire is that my drawings, my prints, my books and my
porcelains, and all the things which made my life so happy do not
end up in the coldness of a Museum where the reckless passerby will
look at them with indifference. I ask that they are all scattered under
the hammer blows of auctioneers and all the enjoyment I received
from their acquisition be restored to persons with my own tastes.'

Baxter was in no doubt the obituary was addressing the Countess
de Couvegne, who most likely paid for and included the Count's last
wishes. He wondered if she was there with him but there was no
mention of her. He surmised her family would have demanded a
much grander monument; in fact there was probably a family
mausoleum somewhere in France, a place where all the de
Couvegne's would be interred.

He heard a rustle behind, and then crunching on gravel. It didn't
alarm him unduly as he was not alone, other people were wandering
around the cemetery. Suddenly he felt rough hands gripping his
arms; he half turned and was rewarded with a punch in the side. A
large arm circled his neck, forcing him to the ground; A knee
pressed hard against his back and his arm was jerked up behind his
back. Another pair of hands gripped him tightly around his chest
and dragged him backwards across the gravel path. He attempted to
rise onto his haunches but was jerked violently; he shouted out for
help but no one came. Large muscular arms hauled him onto his
feet, turned him around and pushed him inside a tall stone-built
mausoleum. He heard the gate slam shut and the lock engage. This
was the final resting place of Emile Favrier; the green patinated
bronze plaque in front of his face said so.

It was a small shrine, no more than two metres square with a
bronze door bearing a crucifix, sealing the bones which had long
been placed in a recess at the rear.

He half-turned to see his attackers were both Chinese, heavily built and with faces lacking any sign of expression. One of the men pulled the large bronze crucifix in a downward motion. A slow grinding sound followed as the tomb door slowly opened revealing an empty interior. Baxter made another attempt to fight his way out. The man keeping watch had his back to him, so he tapped him on the shoulder and as he turned Baxter punched him hard catching him squarely on the jaw. He had to be fast and follow it up with another strike. As the man recoiled Baxter pounded his clenched fist into the Asians stomach causing him to slump to the ground. Baxter grabbed the gate rattling it loudly but it refused to open, a searing pain shot through his back as he took the full force of a punch from the first assailant. A barrage of strikes followed, he struggled to defend himself, but the blows from both men were impossible to anticipate and before he could recover, large hands fell on his shoulders, turned him around and pushed him head first through the open tomb door. He tried to grab the sides of the opening, but the Oriental used his foot to thrust him through the aperture where he landed on a hard stone floor. The first assailant quickly clambered through the opening, lifted him up and forced him down a flight of stone steps. This allowed room for the second man to follow them into the small chamber. At the bottom of the short flight of steps he picked himself up, but as he struggled to his feet, his arms were immediately grabbed and he was frog marched in a dark and uncertain direction.

With torch beams bouncing off the low hewn rock roof he could see a long passage ahead, an excavation which had been laboriously cut from the local bedrock.

Baxter was regretting his decision to visit the cemetery; after all, what was Henri de Montaigne's grave going to tell him anyway? His fate had lain in the balance at that very moment when he decided to come here, a decision which might result in his death.

CHAPTER 13

THE GHOST TUNNELS OF MONTMARTRE

'Where are we going?' he turned and asked, but got no reply, just a grunt and a tightening of the hands gripping his arms.

The tunnel suddenly opened up into a cavernous chamber; a cathedral-like cave with high roof and natural vertical protrusions rising like pinnacles and turrets.

He was pushed down into a chair and his arms jerked behind the seat back, where they were tightly lashed together with fibrous string.

His captors still said nothing to him but whispered something to each other before returning the way they had come. Their torch light continued to bounce off the walls for several seconds until it disappeared altogether, leaving him in complete darkness.

'Help,' he shouted, 'is there anybody here?' but even as he yelled he knew nobody was going to hear him, not down here several metres below ground level. Destiny had set a trap for him that day and he had fallen into it headfirst.

Gradually his eyes adjusted to the lack of light and a twilight world of shadows and eerie shapes took over. He wriggled attempting to dislodge the knots in the string holding his hands together but they were firmly tied and if anything, the knots tightened the more he struggled. He looked around for something to cut the string but in the darkness he could see nothing. His fingers felt around the edges of the chair and touched a metal tab, a maker's name, not particularly sharp and probably zinc but then the string wasn't rope. He moved his bound hands against the metal tab, sawing the string in a vertical motion, within minutes he could smell the heat conducted from the smouldering binding. While he was cutting the cord around his hands, he scanned the cavern looking for anything which might help him to escape. He spotted a form which had a texture that was different from the surrounding darkness. Baxter had always been fascinated by the fact that even in total blackness, if there was a break in the expanse of darkness caused by matter and the eyes look long enough at the same mass it can be seen. He flexed against the binding and suddenly the string gave way and he released his arms from the chair back. Rubbing his sore wrists, he blindly stumbled towards the form of matter his eyes had previously registered. He held his hands out circling them in front feeling for any obstacle, any unseen hurdle into which he might blindly collide. Despite his fumbling he still missed a crate which sent him crashing heavily to the ground. Back on his feet he moved slowly forward taking care to sweep the floor with his foot in search of any further obstacles. His groin made contact with a hard immoveable substance and then his fingers touched a metal surface. It was cold and flat as he palmed across it pausing to feel between his fingers the characteristic shape of a pen or pencil. His arm struck a vertical object which rolled across the table and smashed loudly on the ground sending the eerie echo of shattering glass bouncing around the chamber. He repeated the search and was rewarded with a very familiar shape, with a flick of a catch a tubular torch flashed into life.

His spirit revived a little as he was suddenly freed from the world of darkness, a place where humans feel insecure, where uncertainty takes over from any ability to cope with the enforced blindness. With this restoration of visibility he was now able to scan his surroundings. This was unquestionably one of the many secret caverns and underground passageways which were rumoured to honeycomb the underbelly of Paris. He knew a little of the history of these quarries having read Claude Reniers great detective novel set in the famous catacombs. This great underground quarry was first excavated by the Gallo Romans in the first and second century A.D and then re-opened and considerably enlarged in the fifteenth century.

The Lutecian limestone was used to build Paris in its early days when it was the burgeoning capital of France.

The cave was clearly totally anthropogenic and certainly not natural in any way. All around this great cavern he could see evidence of the quarry men, the systematic hacking away with crude tools had left individual striations on the rock face and as his torch beam swept across the roof, the Lutetium stone returned a metallic reflection. Lower down a sand-coloured maze of galleries encircled the cavern. He had to decide what action to take next, he didn't imagine he was going to have many more second chances like this, but if he made the wrong decision now, the odds of survival might be poor.

He quickly came to the decision that blindly going down endless tunnels which led to who-knows-where, was suicidal and so he hastily made for the tunnel which he had just been dragged down. At least he knew it led back to the mausoleum. He clambered up the stone steps and arrived back in the small burial chamber. The tomb door was bronze, sounded thick when he tapped on it and obviously not designed to be opened from this side. Just then a funny thought amused him. *They probably didn't want corpses to escape in the middle of the night.* He giggled at the thought, but was rapidly brought back to his senses when a loud grinding sound indicated that the tomb door was once again being opened from the other side. He stumbled down the steps in haste and as there was nowhere else to hide, made for the tunnel once again. Foot falls sounded behind him as he ran bent double down the passageway. Despite the darkness, he covered the distance quickly, suddenly arriving back in the cavern once again, but in marked contrast it was now adequately lit.

'Ah, Mr Baxter, there you are, we thought we had lost you.'

A man in a brown suit stood with hands clutched tightly together in front of him. 'It is so good you could join us,' he said turning to glare at the Chinese who arrived sporting a look of panic on their ordinarily stoical faces.

The cave was well-lit by a string of electric light bulbs, which he guessed would have been switched on from elsewhere.

The man in the suit was impeccably dressed and clearly not Oriental, his words were sometimes rounded and often clipped and contained flattened vowel sounds. His English, although good, was clearly accented in the Afrikaner manner. Although short in stature his neatly trimmed goatee and his discernible gait sent out the clear message that he was firmly in control and demanded respect from his subordinates. Despite that, he was the type of man who could be simply visually dismissed were it not for his bald head which was amazingly shiny, making his head look like a globe on a stand.

The white South African tilted his horn-rimmed glasses, pausing to view his guest and then raised his hand, motioning the two Chinese hulks. They quickly moved forward and pushed Baxter once again into the chair.

The suited man walked over towards him, his feet crunching loudly on the broken glass. He pulled out a stool, sat down and dropped a blue file on the table. He began flicking through some papers, taking note of certain details, and then glanced at Baxter with a terse and thoughtful expression.

Baxter realised there must have been another way out, one of the little galleries would have led to… well he didn't know where, but the man couldn't have arrived here otherwise.

'What do you want with me?' he demanded to know

'I will explain all in good time Mr. Baxter,' he said in a calm and reassuring manner, 'but first,' he said standing up, 'I'll have my torch back.' He held out his hand. Baxter hesitated, desperate to hang on to the torch, but when he received a sharp dig in his back from behind; he decided to do as he had been told and placed it in the man's hand.

The man in the suit sat back down again, straightened his stack of papers, placed them on the table and sat facing him.

Baxter said 'Who are you and how do you know my name?'

'I am your very own worse nightmare Mr. Baxter.'

'Thank goodness for that, I thought for one moment you were a low life that had crawled out from under a stone.'

'Ah, Mr. Baxter, you have a sense of humour, I like that, but you have upset a few people of late.'

'Not half as much as those who've upset me,' he retaliated.

'Now you must be wondering what this is all about.'

'You could say that.' Baxter shot back.

'Let me tell you a little story. Just imagine if you will, a small auction room in rural France. Let me see, let's call it Bourge-Vilaine; where on a bright summer's afternoon an antique dealer is fortunate enough to buy a very important Chinese vase and for just a few euros. My employer was very keen to acquire this piece and sent representatives to bid for it on his behalf,' he said tipping his head slightly forward. 'Are you still following me Mr. Baxter?

'Oh yes, I have to say it's a very entertaining tale.'

'Well you can imagine how disappointed my employer was when he found out that one hundred lots had been withdrawn and the lot he had intended to win had been sold an hour earlier than it should have been.'

'Yes that must have been a great disappointment for him,' he said, fighting to maintain a curious expression. 'But tell me, what's that got to do with me?'

'Don't treat us as fools Mr. Baxter,' he said raising his voice. He levelled a finger at him. 'We know it was you who purchased the vase, but what we don't know is what you've done with it? When it comes to monetary matters my employer is a most generous man, but his generosity is severely challenged when he has been made to look a fool and that's what you've done.'

Baxter shrugged his shoulders. 'I really don't know what you want me to say; I'm completely in the dark about this.'

The man's face suddenly changed, the muscles around his jaws tightened and his eyes darted. 'Tell me where that vase is?' he shouted clenching his fists tightly. 'You're not going to leave this place until you tell me and tell me you certainly will. Sooner or later, once the hunger pangs tear at your body and thirst cuts your mouth every time you open it, you will answer my questions.'

He lowered his voice. 'So be a sensible chap and tell me what I want to know and then we can all go home.' He beamed.

'For the final time I don't know what you're talking about and you can tell that Max Veerman of yours he can get lost,' Baxter said angrily.

'Max Veerman,' the man said and then laughed, 'so good old Max was after the vase as well was he. Well this has got nothing to do with him; I can promise you that. 'Now I'll ask you again where is the Chinese vase?'

Baxter shrugged nonchalantly; this made his interrogator explode in a fit of rage. His face turned purple and he shot up from his chair and slapped Baxter across the face. 'There, look what you did, you made me lose my temper. I'll ask you one more time and if you don't tell me what I want to know, then I'll let my associates here ask you the same question. But Mr. Baxter,' he said in a bombastic voice, '*they* won't be asking in the same way as I am. Oh no, I can assure you about that.' So?'

Baxter once again shrugged and tried to look disinterested. 'I've had enough of this nonsense,' he said pushing the chair back and standing to get up, but he was unceremoniously pushed back down again.

'It might be a big mistake to try and escape,' his interrogator said 'but then on the other hand it might well be a mistake *not to.*' He sported a derisory expression and then laughed. He nodded to the two Chinese men. They stood Baxter up and the taller one swung a punch into his stomach followed by a second and third in quick succession. After their boss raised the palm of his hand they threw him back into the chair. With the wind taken out of his sails, he held on tightly to the arms of the seat, fighting hard to recover his breath.

'Lock him in there,' the man ordered, pointing to a steel door let into the rock face. 'You can spend the night thinking about what I've been asking you and then in the morning Mr. Baxter, I feel confident you will be only too pleased to remember the answers to my question. Oh and by the way, you'll most certainly have company during the night.'

'Company?' he asked, in shock that it might be Magali.

'Yes Mr. Baxter, you will not be alone. Do you know it has been estimated there are more than eight million rats living under the streets of Paris, four times as many rats as humans and half that number live in these caverns, and before you ask, yes they are the large ones Rattus norvegicus.

He had been thrown into another cavern inside the subterranean world far below the streets of Paris. The heavy metal door meant it was in every way a dungeon, a locked chamber which was dark and putrid. He coughed several times as his lungs took in a pungent stench, a fetid mixture of damp, human excrement and a distinct odour of sulphurous vapour. There was no light in the cavern except for a thin strip, where the iron door butted against the heavy metal frame. Within minutes even this ray of optimism suddenly disappeared leaving him in total and absolute darkness.

He wandered around trying to determine the limits of his prison and was amazed to discover it was surprisingly large, but there appeared to be no human comforts whatsoever; if there was a bed or chair he never found it. The only things in the room were him and a few packing crates stacked along one wall. He looked at his watch, couldn't see the time, but reasoned it would be afternoon by now, far too early to try and sleep, but equally what could he possibly do to while away the long hours if not to sleep. He began going over in his mind what he had learnt that morning about the Opium wars and General Henri de Montaigne but the coldness quickly robbed him of any resolve to think logically.

He was becoming resigned to the fact he might well die down here and that old adage kept repeating itself – *We are all born and at some determined time, we all die.*

He reluctantly decided he would at least attempt to doze, so he sat on the floor with his back against the wall. Within seconds the coldness intensified as it rose from the stone surface sending a painful numbness to his nether regions. He suddenly remembered the packing crates. Searching in the dark he eventually found them; dragged three together and used them as a bed. They were far from comfortable, but at least the wooden lids were not damp or cold.

Baxter did everything he could to try and sleep, but he didn't have either of the two prerequisites which might allow him to doze, tiredness or relaxation. His mind was working overtime, but the over-riding sensation was a nervous energy fuelled by his desperation to escape. Even counting imaginary sheep failed.

He suddenly froze, unable to move as he registered a movement on his chest. As he sat bolt upright something heavy ran down his body and scuttled away; it was a rat he was certain of that. He felt an uncomfortable stab of fear, the horror caused him to panic; he banged the sides of the crate and shouted loudly in an effort to keep it and any others away.

Baxter hated rats, he could put up with most things like mice and spiders and even snakes held no great fear, but rodents of the rat family were quite another thing.

He shouted several more times and banged loudly against the crate, but he knew he was never going to be able to relax sufficiently in order to gain any sleep. He was faced with a relentless vigil of rat scaring; he was too exhausted and frightened to think so the night was going to be a very long one indeed.

'Hey you, come over here,' a French voice called out. Baxter jumped in amazement he could have sworn he was alone in his prison. The voice rang out again. It was an odd croaky vocal sound, apparently somewhere in the room but strangely masked as though in some annexed chamber.

'Hello you over there, come here,' the voice urged.

At first he thought his imagination was working overtime and producing voices, but after the third time he knew the sounds were real; but where on earth were they coming from?

A torch beam flashed around the chamber, the light bouncing off rugged stone walls before it firmly fixed on his face, blinding him and denying him any chance of seeing its owner.

'Yes you, come quickly' the voice sounded even more urgent this time. Now he could see an orange light hovering on the far wall.

Baxter stumbled to the end of the cavern, stopping where the pool of light fell on the ground but he could still see no one.

'Up here,' the voice called. He looked up and spotted a strange head looking out of a small opening in a rock fissure.

A rustling sound was followed by a rope as it uncoiled and slithered down the wall landing with a dull thud at his feet.

'Come on, come on.' An extended hand beckoned him up.

Baxter grabbed hold of the rope, gave it a sharp jerk to satisfy himself it was securely tied at the top. He had never before had the need to master the art of rope climbing but had a fair idea as to how it should be done having watched many an adventure movie.

He jumped up grabbing the rope high, gripping it tightly with both hands and then let the end fall on the outside of his leg.

He used his opposite foot to help wrap it around his right leg. He paused, taking in a deep breath and then proceeded to exchange his hold on the rope between hands in an upward movement.

Baxter found the climb demanding on the muscles in his arms and legs, muscles he rarely deployed these days, but he had the advantage of strength. However, half way up he made the grave mistake of looking down. A surge of vertigo hit him and he froze, unable to move.

'What are you waiting for?' the croaky voice asked.

'I don't like heights,' he replied.

'Well if you stay down there you will never have to dislike heights again,' the voice said sarcastically.

Baxter gritted his teeth and fought his fears as he continued upwards until he was level with a little round bearded face which was peering at him through a small opening in the rock face.

He scrabbled his feet against the rocky surface until he was able to swing his legs into the gap. He had got thus far, but the fissure opening was narrow; far too narrow he thought for someone of his size. 'I'm not going to get through this, 'he said

'Trust me, you can get through. Turn sideways,' the voice said urgently, impatiently.

Baxter strengthened his hold on the rope and edged his feet

further into the entrance hole. He twisted his body sideways and felt a sudden jerk as hands gripped his ankles and pulled.

As his body passed through the opening he let go of the rope.

The natural fissure merged into a tunnel of much smaller dimensions than he would have liked. Baxter wasn't keen on small claustrophobic spaces, but he had no choice but to put all his trust in his new found guide. His rescuer held up his oil lantern to inspect Baxter's face. The man had a normal size head and hands, but a very short stature and Baxter now realised the man was a little person of probably a touch over a metre tall.

'Take this,' he said handing Baxter a torch, 'and follow me.'

The little chap played out the light from his lantern in front of them. He had no problem navigating the tiny passageways, unlike Baxter, who could only keep up with difficulty on account of his height. He desperately tried to avoid hitting his head on outcrops of stone, but several times he felt a decisive bump.

His guide suddenly stopped and waved his lantern so that the light fell on the ground. Baxter looked over his shoulder, the man pointed to a hole in the floor which appeared to descend to the centre of the Earth.

It was now necessary to perform a difficult and what appeared to be a potentially dangerous task. The little man demonstrated how to cross the obstacle by placing his left foot on a tiny outcrop of rock on the left hand side and then quickly springing his right foot forward, propelling him to the far side of the hole.

Baxter had to look down at his feet in order to know exactly where to place them. The drop was horrendously deep, the rugged sides were illuminated by fluorescent coloured rocks. His head started the usual reeling and an involuntary spasm ripped down the back of his legs as vertigo hit home.

'Come on, do it now,' shouted the little chap.

When it came to it the task was easier than he had expected mainly due to his longer leg reach, but he still didn't like it; Baxter had never been easy with heights and never would be.

They continued like this for several minutes, jumping across the holes which became more numerous, until they reached what looked like a dead end. The passageway snaked to the left through a narrow crevice. The man looked back at him, giving a reassuring grin as he slid down on his backside into another subterranean chamber. Following his guide he sat on the ground and slithered down the funnel-like chute until his feet made contact with terra firma.

'Come on, this way,' the little man said, pointing to a long corridor which snaked ahead. Baxter followed closely behind and straightaway understood what this new place really was.

The walls were lined continuously on both sides with neatly stacked bones from floor to ceiling. He didn't need to ask if they were human, the way they were consistently stacked in six rows of leg and arm bones punctuated by a row of skulls was evidence enough. It wasn't so much the gruesome show of ossuary which unnerved him but the bones appeared to be alive and moving as rats slipped in between them, tipping the bones and moving the skulls.

Their journey along the passageway continued for a good five minutes with no variation to the ossuary arrangement until they arrived in a large cavern, much like others he had seen but with a marked difference.

'Where are we now? Baxter asked.

'The ossuary of Saint Mere Eglise,' he replied, lighting another lantern and handing it to Baxter. His new found friend told him to wait while he went to make further arrangements.

'Do not stray from this cavern,' the little man said, 'there are many dangers around here, so take heed.'

The strange cavern was certainly very different from anything he had ever seen before, except perhaps in the little crypt in Hythe, Kent, but that was on a much smaller scale. He was looking at a spectacle which consisted of tens of thousands of bones neatly stacked in this, the main part of the ossuary catacomb; a place where many years ago, human remains were stored once the city cemeteries could take no more burials? The neat rows of bones paralleling the walls were punctuated by niches with their contents arranged in a more decorative fashion. He stopped to look at a larger than normal sepulchre which had an inscribed stone- OSSEMENTS-DU-CIMETIERE-DES-INNOCENTS-DEPOSES. EN AVRIL 1786.

'Who *are* you?' a voice echoed eerily, the sound bouncing around the chamber until it finally faded away.

Baxter looked around, startled. A slightly taller 'little man' with a much longer, pointed beard, strode towards him with the first little chap waddling from side to side behind. Baxter explained how he had been bundled into the mausoleum by two thugs and then forced into the underground cavern, interrogated and then locked up in a rat-ridden dungeon.

'The two thugs were Chinese,' he said,' but there was also a white South African man who was a very dangerous character.'

'The Shāqi,' the taller man said.

'Yes, you are one of the lucky ones my friend,' the first little chap said with a nod of his head.

'It's most fortunate,' the taller man interrupted 'that Claude here, found you because you were in the hands of the Shāqi and few come out of their hands alive.'

'They gas people in there you know,' the little lad Claude said.

Baxter realised what the sulphurous smell in his dungeon had been; it was obviously gas which had been absorbed into the rock walls. He shuddered at the thought of what his fate might have been.

'But how did you know I was in there?' Baxter asked them.

'We have spyholes everywhere; look there's one just here,' he said, pointing to a pipe-like hole in the rock. Baxter peered inside.

'You won't see anything unless there is someone at the other end with torches or lanterns, then the pinpricks of light will shine on the ceiling here,' the taller chap said pointing at the rock roof.

Seeing Baxter was still confused Claude added 'I heard you shouting, you see sound also travels up these pipes, they increase the sound and if you listen carefully you'll hear the rats. Baxter put his ear to the tube and could hear soft squealing sounds, far away but quite distinct. In contrast, he realised his shouts must have been practically ear busting! It also occurred to him that without the presence of rats in his dungeon, he wouldn't have shouted out in the first place and therefore no one would have known he was there. Thank goodness for the rats he thought to himself.

'We steal things from them you know.' said the taller man with a marked pride in his voice. 'Like that torch you're holding.'

'We like torches,' the little lad Claude said, 'but they go out and die very quickly.'

Of course, the batteries! Baxter realised that would be a problem for them down here.

'They bring things in to these caves and we steal them from under their noses and they think it's one of them.' They both chuckled as they clapped their hands together.

'We must hurry before they come looking for you,' interrupted the taller man. 'There is only one safe way out of here, so come follow us and be very careful, for it's a dangerous path that we must take.'

They now entered a long winding passageway which had a distinct incline and very soon Baxter's legs were under muscular strain. With every step the muscles in the back of his legs contracted, sending spasms down to his feet. The path started to level off, much to Baxter's relief and then they crossed to another trail.

'Be careful now,' the taller man said, 'hold onto Claude's shoulders and don't let go.'

'And don't look down,' Claude added knowingly.

Baxter now found himself in a very strange world; a world he never knew existed far below the streets of Paris and one which had long been forgotten by all except a little person or two.

They had reached the start of a long open gallery, in geological terms it was a shelf or ledge of rock which spanned across an enormous cavern which plunged hundreds of feet below. Although the shelf was a couple of metres wide, when Baxter, against his guides advice, looked down, he reeled. He had spent his whole life in fear of heights; they even invaded his dreams, often waking him up in a state of perspiration.

The floor of the cavern below was in total darkness and not visible, but the rugged sides glittered with a luminescence which reflected every hue of colour imaginable. Puffs of steam rose up from geothermal activity, the result of gas from aqueous solutions deep inside the earth's crust.

Holding on desperately to his guide he was sweating profusely; he had a strange familiar feeling, that uncontrollable urge to throw himself over the edge, a common side-effect for people who suffer from vertigo.

He continued behind Claude, holding on to his shoulders and praying the man had a steady step and knew what he was doing. Baxter stumbled on a loose rock sending it rolling over the edge. He steadied himself by tightening his grip on Claude's shoulders; it was several seconds until he heard the sound of the rock landing many feet below.

Suddenly a burst of activity rose up from the deep accompanied by a crescendo of screams.

'What on earth is that?' Baxter said in alarm, as a fluttering of wings flapped around his head.

'The stone you kicked over the edge disturbed a colony of big-eared bats,' Claude said.

'Seems like a funny place for them to live.'

'Not at all,' the taller man said, 'they like the geothermal heat.'

Over the top of the little chap's head he could see a row of dark objects which appeared to partially block the way ahead. As he got closer he realised they were rusted iron trucks once used to transport rock out of the quarry. He guessed the ledge had at one time been a railway track built on a natural spit of rock.

They inched past the wheeled trucks and entered a passageway, a winding tunnel hewn out of the solid rock. They had only gone a few yards when the little men once again stopped and quickly extinguished their lamps.

Claude put his finger to his lips. 'Keep quiet and don't make a sound. Oh and turn that torch off.'

The two lads suddenly knelt and peered through a narrow opening in the rock face into a dimly lit area below, Baxter knelt down beside them.

The cavern, some five or six metres down, was in marked contrast to all those he had previously seen that day; It was not so much a cave but a room which was carpeted and furnished with comfortable chairs and tables and at one end where the source of light was at its strongest, he could see a projection screen.

All of a sudden the room below was flooded in brilliant light from lamps strung along the roof, live with what he presumed was pirated electricity followed by a very loud hullabaloo. The unmistakable angry sound of dogs filled the cavern, barking and snarling in a menacing way, yet where were they? The dogs appeared to be invisible. Baxter's heart pounded as he looked down in stunned silence.

'Don't fear.' The taller man explained that the noise was from an electric machine, 'it is not real.'

Baxter guessed it must be a P.A.system, with guard–dog yowls burned onto a CD.

'All this is to keep strangers away, anyone who might accidentally stumble into these caverns, and I can tell you it works as they usually flee in terror.'

The noise suddenly stopped and Baxter noticed an ingress of people entering casually through the far doorway. Although some were Oriental, many weren't. The latter tended to group in conversation whilst the others made their way to the chairs and sat down.

He looked at his guide for an explanation.

'Shāqi training school,' the little man said.

And then he saw it. A large square recess was evidently the focal point of the room as all the tables and chairs faced it. A neat wooden frame enclosed a pictorial image, it was one he had seen before and it immediately brought home the reality of exactly where he was and the sort of people who came here.

The carefully painted ensign consisted of four batwings enclosing familiar Chinese letters in the middle, the very same image Hadley had believed to be the sign of the secret organisation called the Shāqi and identical to the notes pinned on Didier and Hadley's backs.

'The sign of the Shāqi?' Baxter enquired. The man nodded confirming it was.

'This is a most dangerous place,' he said softy.

Next to the batwing emblem a blackboard had been chalked on ready for a lecture or meeting. Baxter screwed his eyes to read the Chinese characters.

故曰：知彼知己，百戰不殆；不知彼而知己，一勝一負；不知彼，不知己，每戰必殆。

'You understand that?' the little man Claude asked.

'I do,' Baxter replied smugly, 'I think it must be a statement of their philosophy of life. It's set out as three proverbs and reads'

It is said that if you know your enemies and know yourself, you can win a hundred battles without a single loss.

If you only know yourself, but not your opponent, you may win or may lose.

If you know neither yourself nor your enemy, you will always lose.

'But come, we must go,' urged the taller man, 'it's not safe here.'

Turning another corner and Baxter was rewarded with a sight so surreal that it seemed impossible. He blinked expecting the mirage would go away but it didn't. The passage ahead snaked steeply down to a lake of emerald green water sitting in a natural rock-formed basin just below the city water table.

The steep path ended on a rocky shoreline where gentle waves rippled against its edge, lapping from natural vortex draughts which brushed lightly against his cheeks as they fanned in from the far end of the cavern. It was raining, creating a strange sensation as water droplets sprinkled from the great rocky roof above, softly pinging as they hit the surface of the water.

'What now?' he asked

'We must make passage over to the far end,' the taller man replied as he ushered Baxter into the gondola-style boat which was gently bobbing up and down on the water's edge. The rope was lifted from the jetty stanchion and the two guides slowly rowed the heavy craft away from the bank. Baxter sat at the front holding the lanterns. Their light picked out green and yellow flashes twinkling on the walls and roof, a reflection of the slow moving water.

After about five minutes the pinging sound of water droplets stopped and Baxter noticed his lanterns were now illuminating the cavern roof, creating moving shadows across its span. The covering was now considerably lower and had a smooth concrete-like nature.

Gradually Baxter began to make out a strange melodic sound, at first barely discernible and far away but as they progressed across the lake it gradually became harmonious and full of orchestral depth. He couldn't determine where it was coming from, it sounded like amplified surround sound as the musical tones bounced around the enclosed space.

'Is that music I can hear?' Baxter looked for an answer.

'It's the Opera Haussmann,' the little chap replied. 'Many years ago that roof could be opened with hydraulic rams; you see it is the floor of the theatre above. It's said they used the lake as a setting for great opera's like.....' he was cut short by a sudden loud rattling sound followed seconds later by multiple pings on the surface of the water. And now the distinctive sound of splitting wood as bullets hit the side of the boat.

'Put those lanterns out.' urged the little men. He dropped them below the water line and all three of them were immediately cast into darkness. The bullets continued to hit the boat, water was collecting in the bottom and it quickly began to list.

'Over the side quick,' the little chaps said in unison.

'What about these lanterns?'

'Leave them,' both men shouted as they dived into the water.

He launched himself into the depths and as the icy coldness hit his body it took his breath away. He reached out and swam after the others. He caught them up quickly, he was a strong swimmer and he paced them for several minutes but soon began to leave them behind. He stopped, treading water, as he looked back towards them. The gloom at the far end of the underground lake was suddenly lit by tiny flashes as another round of bullets raked the lake. This brought home a renewed sense of urgency, also, numbness was beginning to cause the early spasms of cramp, a condition to which he was prone and so he resumed his pace. Within a few minutes he was aware that he was beginning to falter; he was becoming breathless and the muscles in his legs and arms were contracting, painfully, but ahead he could see a slight incline where the waves lapped the shore. He took a deep breath and with every last ounce of energy, reached for the small beach. The others climbed up the scarp a few minutes later.

Standing once again on dry land they were now out of reach of the Shāqi guns. From that distance and in the darkness which now shrouded the cavern, the gunmen couldn't see Baxter and the little men on the far shore, nor the boat they had been in, but despite that they continued blindly strafing the water where the gondola had previously been and where they expected Baxter and the other two were floundering.

'The Shāqi again ?' Baxter enquired.

'The Shāqi?' they both replied. Claude said 'they have cameras everywhere and must have seen us, but we're safe now, they can't follow us across the lake.'

Baxter turned to the taller guide. 'I don't quite understand, do you actually live down here or what?'

'Of course we live here. Our families have lived in these caves for two hundred years, ever since they first mined the stone.'

'I see, so your forefathers were miners digging out the rock, but why did they stay here in the caves and not go home at the end of each day?'

'Because after a fifteen hour day, who wants to make a long and difficult one hour journey back to the outside slums. It was easier to live here in the cavern, in the warm and dry.

Noticing a look of amazement on Baxter's face, he added.' We do have proper cabins made of re-used oak, with fires and running water. I'll show you in a minute.'

'So how many are there of you down here?'

'I can only tell you about our commune, we have eighty four at the moment, lost two last week in a fight with the Shāqi. But if you mean how many live in all the secret caverns under Paris, then no one knows it's thought there could be more than a thousand, but who knows, it could be many more than that.'

'And are you all….'

'Little people,' he cut in, 'no, but most are. You see two hundred years ago the mining company advertised over the whole of France and beyond for little people. The reason for this was that it was much cheaper to use the old tiny Roman tunnels and entry chutes, rather than dig new larger passageways, and so as a result, we, the descendants, have inherited our small stature from them. Mind you,' he added with a twinkle in his eye, 'Lofty here didn't come out quite right, did he?'

Baxter thought that last comment hilarious, as the taller little man called Lofty was barely over one and a half metres tall.

From the shore of the lake they took a meandering path up to a ridge of rock where the little men proudly pointed to their commune in the dip below. It was impossible to make any tangible plan of the layout, as every house appeared to be haphazardly built against its neighbour, but the one thing that did stand out was the universal use of moss green tarpaulins, a flimsy type of roof covering, but presumably adequate for the incessant dripping of percolated water. Claude ducked into a small building and came out seconds later clutching two lanterns.

Moving on, they soon arrived at the entrance to a tunnel with round brick-arched roof and simply paved floor. This was at last evidence of a proper man-made structure and reassuringly an indication of more recent civilization. The little men once again called for caution as they lined up, one in front of Baxter and the other behind. Claude told him to place his hands on the lad in front and follow his every step.

He suddenly realised they were walking alongside a railway line; the silver glint of the track ahead was bending away to the right.

Then a distant hum was quickly followed by a rush of air, cold and foul as it blew his hair backwards.

A fervent conversation took place between his guides and they steered him into a rounded recess. The sound got louder and the guides extinguished their lanterns just before a beam of light hit the end of the tunnel. The cold wind intensified, hitting him at great force and sparks much like a firework display lit up the ancient brickwork.

'Hold on tight,' shouted his guides.

Seconds later, a train screamed past at alarming speed.

To his horror Baxter realised he was inside an operational Metro tunnel and had just been walking inches away from electrified lines.

His guides led him on further until the subway suddenly met a large expanse. He followed them up several stone steps which terminated in a flat wide surface. Another distant roar and rush of wind marked the imminent arrival of yet another train. As it slammed past from the opposite direction, the carriage lights illuminated the deserted station platform. Of course! He realised this was one of the fabled secret ghost stations of the Paris Metro. He had once read somewhere how some had been closed down during the Second World War and never re-opened, whereas others had simply never been completed. With a shortage of funds towards the end of the vast Metro project, a number of linking stations were never finished and so their entrances were bricked-up. Passengers in the train passing by at great speed would never catch so much as a glimpse of these ghost stations, their platforms shrouded in total darkness.

At the end of the platform the guides pointed to an iron spiral staircase, handed him the precious torch, wished him good luck and then they were gone.

The climb up the twisting stairs was long and in places worrying. He could see ample signs of metal fatigue, in fact he felt quite certain it was only the rust which was holding the whole thing together.

At the top he pushed hard on a circular iron manhole cover, but of course it refused to move. Examining it with his torch he noticed two large iron securing bolts. He pushed and pulled but they were well and truly bonded by rust.

He decided there was nothing else for it but go back down to the station platform and look for an alternative way out. He turned to descend the stairs and as he lowered his left foot the step suddenly gave way tearing itself from the side rail. He grabbed for the handrail, desperately holding on. He brought his foot back up to the step where his right foot rested and regained his composure. He began to weigh up his options, as he shone his torch down the staircase. The broken iron step was dangling, hanging loose but still attached. He had renewed doubts about the rest of the staircase as it all looked very precarious from this angle. If he was to attempt to climb back down he would have to bypass the broken step and that would be difficult, probably suicidal.

It occurred to him that the hanging step might make a good implement to hammer over the securing bolts on the hatch, the ones he had previously been unable to budge.

He bent down and tried to reach the hanging step but it was both difficult and dangerous and required a certain dexterity, something which Baxter didn't naturally possess. Holding onto the handrail he dropped to his knees and extended his left arm as far as he dare. He inched his hand closer, his fingers made contact with the dangling step, brushing it but not yet able to make a grip. He lowered his hold on the handrail stretching downwards even further until his fingers finally gripped the step. He twisted the partially severed end several times and after a few minutes it came away in his hand, suddenly and with surprising weight. His arm swayed as he fought to hold it in his fingers, almost dropping it at one stage, but he finally managed to grasp it fully in his hand.

He returned his attention to the hatch above his head. Using the iron step section he tapped the first securing bolt, but soon realised he was going to have to use much more force.

He raised his arm over his shoulder and hit it full power. His action caused a tearing sound followed by a slow groan and then he felt the staircase move backwards. He grabbed the hatch bolt and steadied both himself and the iron stairs. He remained like this for several minutes, not daring to move, terrified the entire spiral staircase was going to fall outwards and collapse in a heap on the station platform some thirty feet or more below.

Gradually he recovered his composure. He continued to steady himself and the staircase by holding on to one of the bolts. With his other hand he gently tapped the second pin with the broken step. Eventually both bolts were driven back and with every ounce of his strength he slowly lifted the rusty cover and then slid it to one side. He placed the palms of his hands on the edge of the iron frame and flexed to pull himself up. As his feet raised clear of the top step, the staircase moved away, seconds later crashing to the ground with a deafening clatter accompanied by clouds of dust, which rose up partially blocking out the light.

The brightness dazzled him as he emerged into daylight, back in civilization, wherever that was. The distinctive sounds of traffic and shouting tradesmen brought him to his senses. Startled, he looked around and realised he was in a busy Paris market place. Several traders looked at him with suspicion, or curiosity or perhaps both. One declared to his customer 'Some people find very strange ways of coming here, but our veg is so good they come all the way from Australia.' That caused a roar of laughter from his assembled group of customers.

Baxter asked a scurrying little old lady where he was.

She stopped and stared at him with an expression of irritation. 'Lamarck Caulaincourt market!' she replied giving him a very suspicious look.

Lamarck Caulaincourt market he said to himself, utterly amazed because as the crow flies, he had travelled barely one kilometre from the cemetery where he was first grabbed, even though his circuitous journey down there had been considerably longer.

He spotted a taxi with its green light showing, put his hand out and jumped in. After instructing the driver to take him the short distance back to Magali's apartment, he fell into the soft leather seat exhausted.

Arriving back at Magali's flat Baxter was wet, exhausted and bewildered by his experiences, but he still had to spend time relating the whole story before she let him bath and change.

The water was comfortingly warm as he abandoned himself to its depths, the bath salts gently easing away his aches and pains, maladies both physical and mental which were the result of his enforced incarceration in the Montmartre caverns. He closed his eyes and tried to extinguish everything from his mind, casting away the fatigue of the day; but he still couldn't get his head around the experiences he had been forced to endure. Here in Magali's apartment it strangely felt as though it had all been a dream but the reality was that he'd been held captive and had witnessed first-hand how ruthless the Shāqi could be. But what he really wanted to know was who was behind this secret Chinese organisation, was it the mysterious Veerman, the man who's name continually cropped up every time there was an incident involving his Chinese vase?

Recalling the blackness and stench he had been forced to endure in the lock-up cave, he shuddered to think what might have happened had it not been for his new friends the little people; he was in no doubt it was thanks to them that he was here luxuriating in Magali's bath.

The warm scented waters of the bath eased away most of Baxter's aches and pains. Even his levels of stress were gently put to sleep, but he was to be denied the opportunity to quietly relax for the rest of the evening.

He found himself reluctantly agreeing to take Magali to the Montmartre wine harvest festival, the one event she attended every year. It was a spectacle she was desperate not to miss.

This famous festival was five days of celebration with one

hundred and twenty exhibitors spread over one thousand square metres. Tonight was the final act, the culmination of so many carefully orchestrated presentations.

Set in medieval-style tents the exhibitors offered tastings of wines from France, culinary demonstrations and workshops, along with mouthwatering artisanal delicacies.

It was early evening by the time they arrived, but there were still parades of musicians, dancers, giant papier-mâché puppets and masked harlequins. The marquees were laden with local produce from cheeses to bread kneaded into fantastic shapes, and shoulders of lamb and golden-skinned chickens sizzling on barbeques.

They wandered around the tents tasting the wines and very soon Baxter realised the vin rouge was going down far too easily; he would have to take it easy or he wouldn't last the night.

As darkness fell the concerts began. Jazz, classical and of course the Follies Bergere all performed in separate marquees.

The evening eventually ended with a spectacular firework display, loud and varied with shooting coloured explosions which lit up the night sky, a pyrotechnic spectacle which left everyone gasping with admiration.

'I don't believe it.' Baxter cried at the sight of Magali's turned-over flat. Clothes were strewn across the bedroom floor, rugs upended and furniture overturned. Cupboards and drawers had been partially emptied of their contents. '*The bastards*' he growled to himself, yet he found it odd that they had made such a mess. The time his flat in Chelsea had been searched, those doing it had taken considerable care to hide the fact, they went to great efforts to conceal that they had even been there. So just who was behind this? It just didn't make any sense. He wondered if it was perhaps a botched robbery, but quickly dismissed that idea as nothing appeared broken, no sign of anything missing, and there was certainly much of value here. In fact the more he thought about it he realised this was a carefully orchestrated act. Everything had been placed, not violently thrown or carelessly rifled, but placed in position to suggest the property had been violently turned over.

This had to be a declaration of warning, but to Magali or him, or perhaps even both of them, but from whom? The only players in the frame seemed to be those whose clutches he had escaped from earlier that day, but without any clues he was at a loss to know. One thing that did occur to him however, the likelihood was that someone had been watching her apartment and took the opportunity to break in after seeing them go out for the evening.

It took them almost two hours to clear up the mess and by that time it was two o'clock in the morning and both had lost any appetite for sleep. The cleaner would be in later in the day to fine tune the housekeeping.

So with bags packed, they headed for the station with the intention of making an earlier than planned return to England.

CHAPTER 14

WINDSOR AND PARK OF MAYFAIR

The clock on the mantelpiece struck seven times in a high-pitched metallic tone as Baxter turned the key in the front door of his Chelsea mews cottage. Magali had a shower whilst Baxter made hot chocolate. When she finished he went into the bathroom stripped off and turned on the shower, but decided to have a quick shave first. He suddenly realised he could hear talking. He opened the door slightly and listened.

'I'm back in England now, in a friend's flat in London.' Magali explained on her mobile phone. 'No, not yet, but I will fill you in tomorrow.' Can't speak further.' After ending the call Baxter noticed she appeared to continue tapping the menu for a few further minutes.

Baxter finished showering and exhausted, the two of them jumped straight into bed and grabbed four hours sleep.

Magali woke first, it was still morning, but only just, as she initiated a mid-day bout of love making. Baxter rose to the occasion, but inwardly wanted to do no more than slip back under the covers and sleep.

Magali always seemed to bounce back no matter what life threw at her. She had a knack of burying what had happened in the past, it was an innocence which defined her very character and one of the things Baxter loved about her, although it also irritated him at times.

With a song on her lips she happily skipped into the bathroom to shower leaving Baxter in a thoughtful state.

Baxter leaped into the sitting room and delved into her handbag, taking out her mobile phone. Checking the memory, he found no phone number recorded for last night which meant she had deleted it, but why? He desperately wanted to question her about her call of the previous night, but caution told him not to. He was about to explore her handbag further, but the sound of the shower suggested she would be returning any minute.

He did his upmost to persuade her to change her mind about going out today. He didn't know why but he had a niggling feeling this might not be just another day, it was probably only the aftermath of yesterday's events, but even so he was concerned for her safety. To make matters worse she wouldn't say where she was going and held steadfast when he insisted he was going to accompany her. She insisted her mission was a girly thing, important but quite safe, and assured him she and her car would be back outside his cottage before he knew it.

Without fully realizing it, Baxter had fallen into the couple category. Like Darwin's finches, he was slowly adapting to a shared life, rather than that of the bachelor. In the past Baxter's romances had rarely lasted very long. He didn't think it was because he was a lousy lover, nor was it down to poor temperament or lack of attention. Somehow his lifestyle which was at best busy and at worst hectic, manic even at times, did not gel at all well with having a successful couple relationship.

With Magali off for the afternoon he decided he had enough time to do something about his Chinese vase, so set about cutting open the hot water cylinder and retrieving it from its hiding place. Even though he had confidence in the knowledge that porcelain couldn't or at least shouldn't come to any harm, even in mildly hot water, he was nonetheless relieved when he pulled it out of its hiding place and found it was still as perfect as the day he had concealed it there.

It was twelve thirty so he decided to sort the copper cylinder out later that afternoon. Baxter rang for a cab asking for driver two one six whom he had used on so many occasions and trusted as though he were a brother. Within minutes a rap on his front door told him his cab had arrived.

'Good afternoon Mr. Baxter, where to?' Steve asked as Baxter carefully placed the packaged vase in the boot.

'Bond Street please Steve.'

He jumped into the cab and leaned back stretching his legs as the taxi pulled smartly away from the curb. The hackney cab slowly threaded its way through rain-darkened busy London streets, negotiating the lunch hour rush as it competed with cars, white vans and crazy couriers on motorbikes. Heavy rain drummed noisily on the cab roof and the driver's windscreen wipers worked hard to retain a clear field of vision.

The journey gave Baxter the opportunity to clear his mind of all the individual facts which were gelling together forming a disparate picture, and go through them one at a time crossing off those which didn't fit. But to his dismay, he couldn't find a single event which arrived at a sum total, and neither could he find a single one which could be dismissed.

They arrived twenty minutes later outside the auction house. With rain lancing down in oblique torrents, he pulled up his collar and skipped smartly, but carefully onto the pavement.

Windsor and Park was a multi-national corporation with a long and illustrious history and one of only a handful of prestige auction houses still operating in London. The up market Bond Street offices were its flagship, although it had auction rooms in most major capitals throughout the world. Windsor's had gained the respect from a large and influential international clientele, and were noted for their selective lists of only the choicest antiques. Baxter had often brought in pieces of art, optimistically hoping they would be up to the standard demanded by Windsor's, but his offerings were mostly rejected on the grounds that they were not of the quality or rarity those rooms specialized in, and so he had invariably fallen back on the minor rooms. However, in this instance he felt reasonably confident they would like what he'd brought along with him today.

The fine neo-classical façade in fashionable Mayfair sported a large flag with the initials W.P. which clearly conveyed wealth and exclusivity. He entered under the blue awning carrying his precious parcel and passed through doors which were opened for him by a liveried doorman.

In the marble vestibule he let the front desk know he was there and then sat on one of the long leather benches waiting for David Salisbury to arrive to take him up to his office.

He casually flicked through the pages of Country Life, but found it impossible to focus his attention on such mundane matters as who Lady Marietta was now engaged to; *who bloody well wants to know that* he mumbled to himself. Not even the article by a well-known historian on the trials and tribulations of owning a listed building aroused more than a passing interest.

Despite his considerable knowledge of Chinese porcelain, there was still that niggling doubt that it might not be all he thought it was. After all no one else had seen his vase, even Professor Hadley had only seen photographs of it.

'Anyone sitting here?' a squeaky voice asked.

Before Baxter could reply, a man of small stature wearing a pale blue plastic mac and a peak cap sat next to him. He kept looking at Baxter, irritatingly so. He tried to ignore the man but he knew no matter what he did, the chap was going to engage him in mundane conversation.

'It's a bit grand in here int it?' the man commented.

Baxter nodded, noting with irritation the puddle which was forming around the man's feet.

'It's the cat's whiskers, this place,' he said, Baxter nodded again. He had never quite understood what that meant.

'I've brought in a valuable painting, it were my aunties; she left it me, you know. Do you want to see it? It's one of those Constables, worth a small fortune, I bet.'

Baxter now curious, nodded and the man removed the newspaper to reveal a mediocre modern copy, probably worth little more than a pint or two of beer.

'So what you got in there then?' he demanded, pointing to Baxter's neatly bubble-wrapped and brown-papered parcel.

'Oh nothing as exciting as your painting, I can assure you.'

He had initially been suspicious of the little man who suddenly befriended him. Over the last few weeks Baxter had been wary of almost everyone who invaded his privacy, but this time he was certain this character was quite harmless, in fact if anything he appeared to be a few cupcakes shy of a picnic so to speak, and just an irritant that wasn't going to give him any peace.

Up in the second floor office, David Salisbury studied the vase for several minutes taking note of the brilliance of the blue and the way the tone very softly melted into the glaze when viewed at a raking angle.

'Well what do you think?' Baxter meekly enquired unable to hold back the suspense any longer; he had to know one way or another.

'I don't really know how to tell you this.' Salisbury sat back in his chair sporting a look which was difficult to gauge. Baxter couldn't decide if it was good or bad news, but suspected the latter.

'You're going to tell me it's a very clever fake, aren't you?'

'A fake!' Salisbury laughed then coughed into his fist.

'Do you know this is the finest piece of Imperial porcelain I've had the pleasure to handle in thirty years? It's fantastic, where on earth did you find it?'

'It came out of the back of a van a couple of months ago at the Kempton antiques fair,' he said lying through his teeth, deliberately not mentioning the auction house in Bourge-Vilaine and hoping they didn't post auction results. He somehow doubted they did even though they had some limited internet access.

The reason for the blatant lie was in response to what Professor Hadley had told him concerning the French authorities, who would demand application for a French passport if they knew he had imported it into the United Kingdom.

'Oh I know, over at Sunbury,' Salisbury said. 'We've had a few good pieces from there over the years. That place is such a cosmopolitan fair, with sellers coming from all over Europe bringing everything from church fittings, to french scruffy chic iron tables and chairs. I suppose you don't know anything about its provenance?'

'Well, I believe I do David, but not from the seller.'

'Go on,' he prompted.

'I take it you knew the late Professor Adrian Hadley?'

'My word yes, everyone knew Hadley and what a dreadful tragedy that was. Our rooms here often used his expertise.'

'Well before he was killed I showed him photographs I'd taken of the vase and he was convinced it was the missing Henri de Montaigne vessel; do you follow me?'

'I certainly do. Go on Baxter, I'm all ears.'

'Well, I'm not certain if I can add much more, except to say I understand, like its partner, it was taken from the Summer Palace in Peking during the opium wars in 1860.'

'That's the all-important and slightly concerning part.' Salisbury sighed. 'We might have problems with the Chinese with this one.'

'But I thought....'

Salisbury cut in, with a raised hand, 'You thought the hundred year rule protected you from a claim from the country from where it was stolen. Well up to a point you're right, but the Chinese could put pressure on the British Government to return it under the UNESCO nineteen seventy repatriation of Chinese relic convention. They will say it is cultural property as it has scholarly value, historical meaning and... artistic merit. The Chinese call it *'keeping the dragon in the box'.*

Seeing a look of concern on Baxter's face he quickly added, 'Don't worry too much, I doubt they will do any more than make representations to the British Government and although diplomatic relations are high at the moment, your vase left China years ago as part of the spoils of war, so they don't really have a leg to stand on, so to speak.'

Baxter gave a sigh of relief.

'But,' Salisbury continued, 'ideally it needs an export license to encourage bidders from abroad, so we will apply to the E.L.U and hope the Waverley criterion doesn't apply.'

'The Waverley criterion?' Baxter repeated.

'That's the benchmark set by the Department for Culture, Media and Sport to regulate export controls on objects of cultural interest;

but I can't see any outstanding significance in relation to the U.K.'

Salisbury scratched his chin, his eyes suddenly opened wide as a broad grin filled his face. 'The British Government will appease the Chinese by issuing an export license so *they* can buy it, and judging by recent auction results they are highly likely to be successful.'

'That's precisely what I would like to happen to my piece; I believe it should be back in China where it belongs.'

'An excellent sentiment Baxter, but I don't think you need worry. The Chinese are buying up every piece of cultural property on offer, not just here in the U.K, but throughout the world and they have the economic resources to do it. Mind you' he added as an afterthought, 'there are those in this country who are giving the Chinese a run for their money.'

'Like Max Veerman?' Baxter asked.

'Ah you know about our friend Veerman do you?'

'Professor Hadley told me he was a shrewd collector.'

'Amongst other pursuits,' Salisbury said raising his eyebrows.

'Other pursuits?'

'Yes, Mr. Veerman is a somewhat illusive and tricky customer. You see, no one ever knows whether he's bidding on behalf of his Chinese clients or for himself. The clever part is he never bids personally, that's always carried out by his company. We suspect he often bids on his own behalf and at the same time for his Chinese clients. If that's the case, then what he's doing is illegal.'

'One way and another he seems to be a thorny character then,' Baxter said.

'I think thorny is not quite the right word I would personally use to describe Mr Max Veerman, but one thing I will say to you is, if you're ever unfortunate enough to meet the man, make sure you remember to forget you've met him.'

'So what's your conclusion about my vase then?' he asked nervously.

'I can't confirm yours is the Henri de Montaigne vase without further research, although I must confess that if Professor Hadley thought so then it's most likely to be the case.'

'And if it is, what sort of money are we talking about?'

Salisbury snatched off his glasses and scratched his head. 'I don't really think I could even give you a reasonable estimate at this stage, but I can tell you it will certainly be edging towards a seven figure sum.'

At last Baxter felt he could relax in the knowledge that his vase was finally in safe hands, and would hopefully set him up with a nice little windfall. This wouldn't be happening tomorrow or the day after, but Salisbury said he would like to get it into the late autumn sale which would be in a little over two months' time.

When Baxter emerged from the auction rooms it had stopped raining and the remains of the afternoon were quite pleasant, so on his way home he stopped at Rumbold Street Antiques to take a quick look in case his contact Nigel had bought in anything worth considering.

In the window, sitting on a chest of drawers Baxter spotted a Tunbridge ware box. It looked as though it was something he would definitely want to buy, but he had to play his cards right if he was to get it for the right price, the price which would give him a profit, and that was what the game was all about.

As was his usual way, Baxter casually browsed through the shop picking up items and dismissing them, and totally ignoring the box in the window.

'See you then Nigel,' he called out as he made for the shop door.

'By the way Baxter,' Nigel shouted 'have you noticed that fabulous quality box in the window?'

Baxter turned 'Box, no I haven't, but I suppose I could have a quick look, just in case I can do something with it,' he said dismissively.

Nigel scurried towards him, leant into the window display and handed him the wooden box.

'What is it then?' Baxter furrowed his brow feigning ignorance.

'Now you know exactly what it is, it's a Tunbridge ware sewing box. You think I've just come up the river on me bike, don't you?'

He always says that thought Baxter 'Well,' Baxter paused, 'I might be able to do something with it, what's the trade on it?'

While Nigel checked in his stock book Baxter looked it over carefully. It was a handsome Victorian sewing box with a fine scene of the Pantiles in Tunbridge Wells set within a floral border, and in unusually excellent condition. The decoration was produced by cutting different coloured wood in bundles in such a way that the ends formed a mosaic-like pattern. The inside was well stocked with sewing utensils. The little trays contained scissors, needle cases, bone bodkins and a whole host of accessories for the busy Victorian housewife.

'It's yours for a bag o' sand governor.' The cockney voice shouted across the room.

'Where did it come from?' asked Baxter.

'Where did it come from you ask,' he said pausing, 'it only came in today, a little old Lady from some posh Knightsbridge mansion brought it in, said it belonged to a famous Baroness, but wouldn't say who that was. It cost me a few quid I can tell you.'

Baxter knew that was a made up reply and didn't contain any degree of truth whatsoever.

'A bag o' sand?' Baxter repeated, trying to remember what that was in cockney slang.

'A grand,' he reiterated, 'and that's giving it away.'

'A thousand! you've got to be kidding,' Baxter said under his breath.

'It looks more like a monkey to me,' he shouted back to the shopkeeper. *I'm not paying more than five hundred for that,* he said to himself.

'A monkey, a bleedin monkey for that, you've gotta be joking, me old mucka.' Nigel shook his head in disgust.

'Look' said Baxter 'I've one last offer on the table, if you don't shake my hand I walk out of the shop empty-handed.'

'And if I don't like your offer, I'll kick your *bottle and glass* outer my gaff.' They both laughed.

Baxter had known Nigel the Knocker for years. He was a well-known scoundrel, got his name from knocking on people's doors, asking if they had anything to sell and then ripping them off. The man had also done time in Pentonville for selling stolen goods, so although they had a kind of rapport, Baxter was always on his guard when in his shop.

'I tell you what Nigel, I'll give you a monkey plus a ton, and that's it,' said Baxter emphatically.

'Throw in a pony and it's yours,' He said handing the box to Baxter, who shook his head.

'No sorry not today.' Baxter unrolled the notes and counted out his offer. The dealer took Baxter's six hundred pounds, taking care to count the notes carefully, holding several up to the light to check the metal strip.

Baxter thanked him and promptly took the box around the corner to Auntie Wainwright's Collectables. She specialised in sewing memorabilia, souvenirs and boxes, the three vital ingredients which categorized Baxter's purchase.

'Let's see.' Auntie Wainwright said folding her hands together and smiling a fixed grin. She put on her glasses and checked the box meticulously, scanning the veneers to make certain not a single piece was damaged or missing. Auntie Wainwright was no pushover; she would always spot any sign of repair no matter how expertly done, and where others might miss a tiny bit of damage, auntie would never fail to spot it. She gave a very approving grunt when she went through the contents.

'Nine hundred,' she said.

There was never any room for negotiation with Auntie Wainwright, the price she offered was the only one she would pay and that was final.

'And a cup of tea from the cafe around the corner,' she added with a cheeky grin. Baxter didn't mind as he had made an easy three hundred pound profit for just twenty minutes work.

He loved this business, wheeling and dealing in antiques constantly kept him on his toes. It was the hunt he adored, the satisfaction of finding something in one place which would be worth more in another. It was down to a good nose and knowing who specialised in what and how much they were likely to pay. Yes, he just loved making a good hit.

At Mario's next door he bought himself a hamburger and two plastic cups of tea and after dropping one off at Auntie Wainwright's, headed to Bedford Square Gardens to consume his takeaway.

CHAPTER 15

THE BLACK DAIMLER

Sitting in Bedford Square Gardens Baxter mulled over the meeting he had had with David Salisbury and was congratulating himself heartily at the thought that Windsor and Park, no less, were going to sell his Chinese vase. His mind went back to Magali and he wondered if she had returned to his Chelsea mews cottage yet.

A jogger approached, puffing, as he negotiated the slight rise in the tarmac path. As he drew level the man threw a small tube at Baxter and then accelerated away.

'Hey, Hey you,' Baxter shouted after him, but got no response as the man continued to sprint out of the gardens.

The cardboard tube contained a neatly rolled piece of paper.

'Mr. Baxter', a handwritten note began, 'I have some information regarding your friend Magali. She's in serious trouble and needs your help. If you want to see her again, and I'm certain you do, then be on the corner of Ross Street and Mayfield Road in thirty minutes. And Mr. Baxter do not even think about going to the police, we will know if you do and the consequences for your friend will be fatal.'

The strange and menacing letter was not signed and was in blue ink on un-headed notepaper. The contents though brief and to the point, shook Baxter; he was in no doubt whoever was behind the message meant every word of it.

Past events had made it clear someone was desperate to get their hands on Magali and now it seemed they had got her, but he felt certain it was him they were really after. Were sinister parties still after the vase even though it was no longer in his possession? How could he possibly ignore their threats? He would never be able to live with himself if anything happened to Magali.

Baxter had been on the corner of Ross Street for at least ten minutes but so far there'd been no sign of anyone who might be looking for him. The light was fading fast and it was raining, droplets bouncing on the stone-flagged pavement, not heavily but enough to make him pull his collar up. On any other occasion Baxter would enjoy being out on the London streets at night, and especially in the rain. He often took a nocturnal stroll just to soak up that unique sensation of trepidation the city streets evoked.

An elderly lady passed by, her umbrella up, her small black and white dog insisted on sniffing around his ankles. He looked at the woman and she gave the hound a tug.

Two teenage girls giggled as they crossed to the other side of the road, probably thinking his motives might be seedy. *It's alright, I'm not a pervert or someone looking to pick up a young girl,* he said to himself. *Mind you...* He was suddenly distracted by a man with his coat collar up and walking quickly as he made his way towards him. Baxter gave a sigh of relief as the man walked past, but he abruptly stopped a couple of yards away, turned on his heels and returned.

'Have you got a light, mate,' he asked with a distinctly laboured accent. Baxter looked up ready to say he didn't smoke, but paused when he saw the man was Chinese.

'Sorry I... don't smoke;' He looked around uncertain if this was the contact he was supposed to meet, his instincts told him it was. Precipitously the situation was about to unfold, he had no idea how it was going to pan out, but he would test the waters.

He turned his back and began to walk away. *Just keep calm,* he told himself. Suddenly the man thrust his hands against his shoulders pushing his face against the wall and holding it there. He heard the brakes of a fast moving car screeching to a halt, doors opening and the sound of men jumping out, then a hood was thrown over his head and he was in darkness. He struggled, attempting to punch his assailants but his enforced blindness made it quite impossible to achieve anything that would help him defend himself.

Large hands grabbed him around his stomach, lifted him off his feet and bundled him into a car.

The journey to wherever they were going only lasted a few minutes and when Baxter heard the whirring of an electric door opening, he knew straight away where he was.

The car doors opened and he was once again manhandled. He tried to anchor his legs in the front seat well, but when a second pair of hands grabbed his waist, he was dragged forcibly out of the car. They jostled him into a lift which ascended a floor or two and then pinged as it came to a halt.

Still hooded and denied any chance to observe his surroundings he was frog-marched a short distance until he heard a door open, and then close. He was pushed into a chair and the hood was finally removed. His first impulse was to rush to his feet, but as he moved, an iron grip tightened around his arms; he changed his mind very quickly.

The room was a small office, little used or so it appeared as it was too tidy and lacked the usual work related debris one would expect to see in a daily working environment. He turned to look at his guards but was gripped violently on the shoulders and forced to look forward.

After several minutes the door opened and a moderately built man entered. He was nattily dressed and although quite compact he had a manner which left little doubt that he was physically fit and unquestionably tough. He paused in front of Baxter, tilted his glasses and then smiled an unconvincing grimace, an expression which had disappeared by the time he settled himself at the table.

'Ah… Mr Baxter, it's so good to see you again.'

'I don't know why because we've never met, have we?' Baxter quipped.

'Not formally no, but we've been in close contact on several occasions. Of course you may not have been aware of it.'

Baxter didn't recognise him unless… as he studied his face it dawned on him he could be the man who accompanied the Chinese down at the Bourge-Vilaine auction room. If that was the case he had put his money on him being the buyer for the legendary Max Veerman, or perhaps even the man himself.

'You seem nervous Mr. Baxter, I do hope you don't think we are going to harm you in any way?'

Baxter didn't immediately reply, instead he raised his eyebrows.

'You are joking!' he said after a few seconds. 'That threatening note you sent and the way your goons just treated me, I think anyone would be nervous, but you don't frighten me I can assure you of that. In fact, quite frankly I'm getting bored with this whole business,' he said heroically.

'That's good news as I don't wish to frighten you, but I'm so sorry you're bored. And by the way, be very careful calling my associates goons, they don't like that sort of label.' Baxter felt the grip tighten on his shoulder as though the thug was reinforcing the point, 'anyway it's so nice you could pop in for a chat today.'

'I don't think I exactly had very much choice about that, do you?'

'Oh, come, come Mr. Baxter, I can assure you we only want a tête-à-tête with you, after all we are all friends here,' he said rubbing his hands together.

'So what do you want then? And where's Magali?'

'Ah yes, your friend Magali.' He interlocked his fingers together, 'Well, I'm afraid to say she's in a bit of a predicament. You see Mr. Baxter, you have something we want, but not for nothing I hasten to add. 'We wouldn't expect you to just give it to us; oh no, we are prepared to buy it from you. Now let me see,' he said scratching the back of his ear and then closing two fingers across his pursed lips, 'I wonder what we can offer you? Money; no I don't think you would part with it for a few pound notes. I wonder what else? Ah now, what about your friend Magali? Yes, her life would make a very fair exchange, don't you think.'

'Look whoever you are, I have nothing that would interest you, and I don't have a clue what you're talking about.'

The man leant forward in his chair. 'Do I really have to spell it out for you word for word? '

'I think that would be a very good idea, don't you?' Baxter retaliated, still trying to act the brave but innocent.

The man shot him a piqued glare. 'Alright Mr. Baxter, you obviously like to play games so we'll play it your way. A month ago you bought a large Chinese blue and white vase in the Bourge-Vilaine auction rooms in France. Unfortunately, I and my representatives arrived too late to buy it on account of one hundred lots being withdrawn. Now that wasn't your fault, it was a one in a million chance and the auctioneer should have compensated by delaying the following lots. Anyway, my agents tried to stop you on your way home.'

'Yes they certainly did.' Baxter cut in.

'They were merely attempting to politely ask to buy it from you, no more than that.'

'Hang on,' Baxter intervened, 'they were trying to force me to stop, in fact they tried to run me over the side of the Cameau ravine bridge.'

'Wait a minute,' the man said, 'I think it was you who was doing the pushing over the bridge, so let's put the record straight shall we? You killed my men Mr. Baxter; we found them still in their car several hundred metres at the bottom of the ravine, and where is your car, in a scrap yard?'

'I suppose firing shots at me was their way of offering a polite expression of friendly interchange, was it?'

'Firing at you; he chuckled, 'no you're imagining things.'

Baxter nodded. 'I didn't imagine that, I can assure you.'

The man's face changed dramatically, he looked across at the Chinese agents and they shrugged. 'Are you certain they shot at you?' he said with a look of doubt.

'My car has bullet holes in it you can go and see for yourself if you like, it's still in Ravens Road Garage. In fact, the insurance company have already made enquiries with the police concerning my claim. They might well come knocking on your door.'

'Well I can assure you that was nothing to do with me or Mr... '

he suddenly stopped.' 'Or my employer, he quickly added.' He bent down and scribbled something on a notepad. 'But I admit I did arrange for you to be apprehended in Avranches so another associate of ours could search your car in order to make you a fair offer, but we failed to find the vase. I can't imagine how you managed to smuggle it out of the country and into Britain, but we know you did Mr. Baxter, unless of course it's still in France, but I somehow doubt that.'

'You searched my cottage, didn't you?'

He didn't reply 'Why did you visit Adrian Hadley, Mr. Baxter?'

'Of course you would know about that because you copied the files from my computer, but it was just for a chat. You see we're old friends or were, nothing more.'

'You see we have a problem here, because when we went to speak with the Professor.'

'Speak with him, that's a laugh isn't it?'

'Yes, speak with him Mr. Baxter. Anyway, he had a large folio open on his desk and guess what the picture was?' Baxter didn't reply, he shrugged his shoulders, but he knew what the man was going to say.

'It was an illustration of the vase you bought at Bourge-Vilaine, or at least a very similar one, so I can't help thinking that the Professor had seen your piece and was researching it for you.'

'So you had him killed.'

'My word Mr. Baxter you do have a very vivid imagination, I can't possibly imagine why you would think we would do such a terrible thing; after all we are a very respectable organisation here you know.'

'And where is here?' he enquired

'It wouldn't help you to know that, in fact you'll be much safer if you don't. Now the problem I'm faced with is simply this, my superior needs your Chinese vase and I can assure you Mr Baxter that sooner or later he will get it. But I regret he is not as understanding as I am and will resort to any methods he deems necessary and that might well include unfortunate measures.

'I take it we are talking about more killings and the illustrious Max Veerman,' Baxter said.

'I think your imagination is working overtime.' The man's darting eyes made it clear that Baxter's supposition regarding Veerman had unnerved him, perhaps even caught him on the hop.

'Look,' he said calmly 'I want to help you but I can only do so much. I don't know where you've hidden the vase, but you must hand it over to me for your own and your friend Magali's sake.' Baxter could see the man was studying his face looking for any signs of compliance, but Baxter was determined he find none.

The man rose from his chair and walked to the window. 'My superior has been very understanding and just in case you need to retrieve it from some depository or other hiding place, he has authorized me to give you forty eight hours. Within that time you will return the vase to your cottage where we will collect it. If you don't comply, or if you contact the police, your friend Magali will have a nasty accident and I have little doubt, so will you.'

Baxter was speechless, it appeared they had him cornered. He could quite easily get the vase back from Windsor and Parks, but did he have any guarantee they wouldn't still kill Magali and himself anyway. He had witnessed the brutal way these people conducted business and so he very much doubted they would honour their words and let them free, free to blow the whistle on their nefarious activities.

The man rose to his feet and stood in front of him. 'If I were you I would take this threat very seriously Mr. Baxter because my superior doesn't fool around, he's not like me I can assure you.'

'How do I know you have Magali or if she's even still alive?'

'We would be very stupid to kill her at this stage of the negotiations. You never throw your bait overboard until you have caught your fish; she is the bait and you and your vase Mr. Baxter are the catch.

'So what happens to the bait when the catch is landed?'

The man didn't answer but walked over to a monitor screen and switched it on. Baxter moved closer to look and the guards grabbed his arms.

'It's alright' the man motioned to the two men, who let go of him.

He was concerned at the sight of Magali tied to a chair, gagged and clearly distressed, but relieved she was at least alive. Then he noticed a telephone on a table close to her, perhaps with a number, but he couldn't quite make it out from that distance.

'You say that's my friend Magali but I can't see her face very well,' he said squinting, 'don't have my glasses with me, is it alright…'

'Yes.' He nodded to the guards and Baxter got up and walked over to the screen, bent down and could see every detail. The telephone had a card set in a recess and various extension numbers, but at the top it had an eleven digit number which he took great lengths to memorise.

'Take note Mr. Baxter, you are punching above your weight and that can be a very dangerous thing to do, so heed my warning and do the sensible thing. That is, if you want to see your friend again and I'm certain you do.'

The return car journey was once again in blackness and like before lasted no more than five or so minutes, but this time Baxter took careful note of the changes in direction. However, he quickly realised the driver had taken several deliberately confusing circles and U-turns which made it quite impossible for him to keep track.

Even though the vehicle was still moving, the car door by his side of him suddenly opened, a fist hammered home into his stomach, forcing him to slump over and then a mighty shove propelled him out of the car. His body hit the road hard, the momentum made him roll over several times, bouncing along the kerb, before his head made contact with a lamp post. He instinctively clasped his arms around his head to try and cushion the blow, but by now the damage had been done. He whipped off the hood and immediately felt a warm trickle of blood make its way down his face.

'You could have at least stopped before dropping me off,' he shouted after the car which was rapidly disappearing in the distance. He hadn't once had the opportunity to see the vehicle, but would have bet a small ransom it was the black Daimler he'd seen so many times in Bedford Square. And, despite the driver's subterfuge, he was in little doubt where he had just been taken.

Baxter collected his car from where he had left it nearby, and headed back home. If he needed any validation that Magali really had been kidnapped, then the absence of her car outside his cottage confirmed it. Back inside he bathed his bloodied head, studied with dismay the black bruises forming on his arms and legs and had a shower. Afterwards he scanned the contents of his refrigerator, found nothing which would provide him with an instant meal and so slumped onto his settee, closed his eyes and mulled over his predicament.

There was no way of getting around the fact that he was now faced with quite a dilemma. Should he give them his valuable vase to save the life of poor Magali and perhaps his own life as well?

If he didn't, he had few doubts they would keep to their word and kill her. He could go to the police, but his interrogator had said he would know if Baxter did that, which probably meant Inspector Monroe was mixed up with them, so he couldn't take that risk.

He felt certain there was another way around the problem, if only he could find it?

In a flash it came to him. He did his 'subtraction from ten' trick to bring back the telephone number he had memorized from the phone close to Magali, and dialled the digits.

'This is Gallery Twenty One,' the recorded message said, 'I am sorry but the office is closed for the evening. If you would like to leave a message, please do so after the beeps and we will get back to you.'

'Thank you very much' he said under his breath and put the receiver back.

He was now satisfied she was being held in Gallery Twenty One and the telephone number confirmed that was also where he had been taken, but how to get her out?

He needed a plan and needed it fast. Baxter's favourite maxim was 'never limit your challenges, but better instead challenge your limits'. He knew only too well the depth of his limits; he needed to extend them so he decided to ring his friend Keith, an architect who might just have some ideas about the building in Jermyn Street.

'Come in Keith, it was good of you to come so quickly.'

'No problem, I take it you've seen the car opposite with its two suspicious occupants?' Keith said in a rolling Brythonic Welsh accent.

'Yes, watching me I would say.'

He gave Baxter a long narrow look. 'So if they *are* watching out for you, what have you been up to then?'

'It's a long story and you might not want to get involved, and I'd understand fully if you didn't.'

'Shut up and just tell me how I can help?' he said with an uneasy smile.

'Well,' Baxter paused. 'What I really need is a miracle.'

'No such thing,' declared Keith positively and without a sign of hesitation.

Baxter shrugged his shoulders. 'I'm not so certain about that.'

'Miracles,' Keith said, 'are impossible because they don't respect any of the laws of nature.'

'But surely the laws of nature are only based on the events scientists have observed in the natural world.' Said Baxter.

'Maybe,' replied Keith, 'but I still say miracles are impossible.'

'I don't agree, I believe there is an exception to every rule. After all it only takes one black swan to undo the rule which says all swans are white.'

Keith managed a weak smile 'True,' he said slowly.

'But this doesn't help us with my problem,' said Baxter changing the subject. He explained the predicament he was in, only the most recent developments, choosing to keep it brief as by now it was touching close to midnight.

Keith chewed over the problem for several minutes but confessed he couldn't summon any great brainwave. He did however, suggest Baxter could go to the Borough Council department in the morning and look at the original building planning application.

'That sounds an excellent idea. Yes I'll do that tomorrow.' Baxter felt a ray of hope, a weak one, but at least it was a possibility.

'Slow down Baxter, I don't think you fully realize the complexities of carrying out a planning search especially one that goes back that far.'

Suddenly Baxter shouldered a feeling of deflation, 'No... I didn't think about that,' he said lamely. The revelation might have seemed far worse had it not been for a softening around the edges by Keith's Welsh accent.

'Don't worry.' Keith said noticing Baxter's flattened expression.

'I'll meet you at the planning offices at ten tomorrow morning and guide you through the process.'

The following morning Baxter wasn't at all surprised when he looked out of his window and saw two goons sitting in a car opposite. Veerman was evidently not intending to let Baxter out of his sight, not that he was in the car personally but those men were obviously his eyes and ears on the street. But this left him with a problem as he certainly didn't want them following him around all day. He rang the taxi rank asking for driver two one six and ten minutes later the cab pulled up in front of his house.

Steve was a seasoned expert when it came to shaking off a tail, he had done it many times before and with his knowledge of London, knew exactly how to lure a stubborn follower into a trap.

With Baxter behind in the passenger seat, he drove off down the Broadway at a sedate pace with the tail one car behind. At the Horseferry junction Steve took a right then left and left again rejoining the main road, the tail continued to follow. All this did was confirm the fact that he really did have a tail.

Steve phoned in to his control and asked for a 'piggyback' to be broadcast and the message was flashed to more than fifty other drivers all over London.

Baxter said 'what was that all about then Steve?'

'A 'piggyback' is a call for assistance and a nearby driver has offered to rendezvous,' Steve said, craning his neck to look through the rear mirror.

Steve soon spotted his fellow driver, they exchanged a few words over the radio receiver and the other cabbie overtook the tail and followed closely behind. They entered Kingsway where Steve turned off abruptly taking a side road and then down a narrow slipway. The two taxis and their tail sped into the old tramway tunnel which runs under the length of Kingsway, which many years ago took trams down to the Victoria Embankment.

The second taxi dropped its speed allowing Steve to gain some distance, which meant on the bends he would be out of visibility from the tail.

Halfway through the tunnel the track divided where it entered the long lost tram station of Aldwych. Steve put his foot down and veered left leaving the deserted platforms in the middle. By the time the second taxi arrived, Baxter's cab was out of view and the following taxi with its tail still closely behind, took the right hand fork. In the dark confines of the station approach it was highly likely the tail hadn't even noticed there was a fork in the track at this point.

Steve carried on until he emerged in daylight, many miles to the east of the second taxi and tail, who eventually exited the tunnel close to Waterloo Bridge.

"You've lost them,' Max Veerman screamed down the phone.

'They disappear in old tram tunnel,' the Chinese agent said. 'They just disappear and we not find,' he jabbered excitedly on the other end of the telephone line.

'You did put a tracking devise on his car didn't you?'

'That no good Mr. Veerman, no good at all.'

'What do you mean no good, they work perfectly.'

'He take taxi, the man replied.

'A taxi! So would it be a stupid question to enquire if you took the cabs registration number?'

'Ah yes we take, it P7 YCO

Veerman was furious, he couldn't stand incompetence. The Chinese Shāqi agents were good at their job up to a point, especially where violence was required, but were incapable of any logical reasoning. He picked up the yellow phone and rang his contact at the Metropolitan police cab law enforcement section.

'Michaels, Veerman here. I need to find the whereabouts of one of your black cabs registration no P7 YCO.'

'Shouldn't be a problem as long as he is currently active.' came the reply, 'I'll get back to you shortly Mr. Veerman.'

When the man from the Met returned Veerman's call all he could tell him was the driver's number, but driver two one six had clocked off, so was temporarily no longer contactable. But he added there had been an incident of some kind, what they call a piggyback had been requested, but whatever the problem had been, it was now resolved.

'Get me this driver's full name and address,' Veerman barked.

'Sorry, no can do,' the Met man replied. Taxi companies never give out individual names and addresses, even to us, unless we get a Court order. Veerman snatched up his telephone and rang the Chinese Shāqi headquarters. 'How many men do you have located in London at the present time?'

'One hundred and eight,' came the reply

'I want every one of them out looking for a taxi with the registration plate P7 YCO.'

'But there are twenty two thousand taxi cabs in London,' the man protested.

'Just do it, shouted Veerman.

The clerk looked perplexed when Keith requested the planning application for the Gallery Twenty One building in Jermyn Street.

'Nineteen sixty five' he whistled; It'll probably only be on microfiche by now,' he said in an officious manner.

'No it won't,' interrupted Keith 'the building is in a conservation area so there will be paper copies on file.'

'Right' replied the clerk, clearly irritated by this apparent know-all who was trying to tell him his job.

'There will also be building regs, so we'd like those as well.'

'Building regs, I see.' The clerk made a brief note.

'So are there likely to be any other submissions?'

The clerk shook his head, 'Doubt it, although there may be Ministry of Defence mine clearance documentation, but that's about it. There certainly won't be a lawful development certificate, too early for one of those. Anyway, if I were you I would go and get yourselves a cup of coffee, as this may take quite a while. By the way there's a good café around the corner.' he announced, as he walked away to search the archives in the basement.

Over a cup of exceptionally good coffee Baxter related the rest of his tale to Keith who sat open-mouthed, displaying an expression of incredulity, clearly amazed by Baxter's story. He agreed it was probably wise to find a solution which didn't involve the police or handing over the vase to the Cartel, and said he would certainly help if he could.

Thirty minutes later they returned to the planning office and as Keith had rightly predicted, the clerk had found the application and it was indeed the original paper submission.

Inside the folder he removed the outline planning schedule complete with preliminary architect's drawings of the exterior, but no sign of the detailed building control plans.

'Excuse me.'

The clerk made his way back to them.

'Where are the building control plans and detailed architect submissions? Keith asked, raising his eyebrows.

The clerk checked the enclosure's list, and it did indeed include all eight detailed architect submissions, but they were no longer in the file.

He scratched his balding head. 'Looks like someone's taken them away and not returned them,' he said, 'it happens now and then but one things for certain, Mr. Abbott's not going to be very happy if he finds out.'

'Well I won't tell him if you don't,' Keith quipped.

Before they departed Keith noted the name of the firm of architects who had been responsible for the original plans.

'Well I suppose that's it,' Baxter said as they left the council offices, 'I think we can guess who lifted those files, but I tell you what Keith, we're not going to find a way into that building without them.'

'Not so fast my friend.' Keith paused, deep in thought. Then he slapped his leg. 'Of course, what an idiot I am, they won't be the only blue prints.'

'That might well be true but who else would have copies?'

'The architect who designed the building of course'

'Yes, but that was a long while ago so you're losing me here.'

'We might be in luck because the architects were Lowther and Jennings and would you believe it, they're still in business and you may depend they'll have the original blueprints. Architects never throw any of their commissions away, I can assure you of that.'

'But are they likely to let us see them.' Baxter was sceptical.

As an architect himself, Keith knew only too well those in his profession could be very cagey in regard to their records.

'Ah now that's the best part, you see I play golf with Mike Jennings every Wednesday afternoon, so it shouldn't be a problem. I'll pop over now and have a word with him, just leave it to me.'

That afternoon, in the safety of Keith's flat, they poured over copies of the original blueprints for Gallery Twenty One and other plans of the later extension to the rear of the property, showing its relationship with the underground car park.

The plans which formed the original building control submission included materials, structural safety schedule, fire safety provision, ventilation, electrical installation, drainage, access and usage of the various elements.

There were certainly plenty of opportunities to examine here, especially the drainage and ventilation systems.

Both men fleshed out various ideas, each one getting more daring, but one by one they melted into impossible dead ends.

It quickly became obvious that if there was a weak point, then it was going to be found in the main construction details of the building.

The plans were certainly very comprehensive and showed how the lowest floor was designed to contain vaults. The massive foundation below ground level had reinforced concrete walls of staggering thickness. Above this the plans showed the showrooms at pavement level and then offices above. Workshops had been planned for the next level and finally a penthouse suite occupying the entire fifth floor.

'Now' said Keith, 'the interesting points are the access corridors and the way the floors are laid out, and that shaft there, the small one, do you see it?'

'Yes, I see it Keith, but what is it then?'

Keith's eyes widened. 'I know what it is, it's a lift shaft. Yes, just a small one, I'd say to house a six hundred kilo capacity lift and no more. Enough for six people and the way it has exits on every floor means it gives access to the showroom, offices, workshops, and the penthouse suite.'

'Now let's see,' he unfolded the copy of the later plans. 'When the underground car park was built in Bedford square a few years later, Gallery Twenty One had a large five storey rear extension constructed at the same time.'

'I can see that, but what's it for, it's not clear on the plans?'

'Well there are a few clues and I think I know how that space is used. You know you told me about the black Daimler which did its disappearing act in the underground car park?'

'Yes, but I still can't quite fathom that one out.'

'Well if we look at the electrical amendment plans, there is provision for a new three phase supply, so why and what did they need it for?'

'I don't know, it seems strange to me.'

'Well perhaps not that strange, you see the new extension is in essence a tall vertical chamber with one access point on the level of the vaults, and another at the penthouse suite, but no others. There is also a large void at the top.'

'I'm still not with you,' Baxter said, baffled.

Keith continued to pour over the plans, then sat bolt upright 'I think what we have here is a lift shaft, and for no ordinary elevator, but a vehicles lift. Look its big enough to hold a car and more importantly it lines up with where you saw the black Daimler disappear in the underground car park.'

Baxter considered the point for a few moments. 'Now that's interesting.' He rubbed his chin, mulling over the possibilities. 'I'll tell you what Keith, I think there might just be some mileage in that.'

'Ah now, look here.' Keith said pointing to the plans. 'See that chamber at the bottom there.'

Baxter confirmed he could.

'That's housing for hydraulic pistons, it's got to be and there's a rope pulley stanchion built into the roof.'

'Which means precisely what Keith?'

'That means it's got to be a lift, and what's more it's a traction-hydraulic elevator, so it's a big one and for something pretty special. You see it would have overhead traction cables and a counterweight, but it's driven by hydraulic power instead of an overhead traction motor. The weight of the elevator and its load, plus an advantageous roping ratio reduces the demand from the pump to raise the counterweight, thereby reducing the size of the required machinery.'

Baxter decided to stop him right there. He knew from bitter experience once his friend got going on a subject, he didn't stop until he had done a full dissertation.

'Well done Keith, I think I've worked out how to get in to the building.' A plan was beginning to form in his mind. 'There are just a few more details to iron out,' he added hesitantly.

'You're going in through the lift shaft aren't you?' he said with a guarded half smile.

'Yep, now what are your acting skills like?'

'Acting!' Keith exclaimed with a quizzical look. 'I should imagine they wouldn't earn me an Oscar, but I've done the odd amateur routine.'

'Good, because if I'm to pull this one off I'm going to need you to put on the performance of your life.

'Well, if you want my opinion, I think the whole idea of yours is crazy, utterly crazy.' He slowly shook his head.

'Maybe not,' Baxter replied dragging out his words.

'Well, all I can say is be careful, all entrances into that building will be heavily alarmed and with the latest technology, take my word for it,' he said, rolling up the plans.

'Perhaps the building is alarmed, but I'm not planning to enter the building per se.'

Baxter had formulated a plan that he considered could work, but that didn't mean it would necessarily work, but he conceded it should work if nothing went wrong. Optimism was a key ingredient in Baxter's make-up, he knew without it he could never attain the confidence to win in life, and this was ever more acute as he grew older and he hoped wiser.

CHAPTER 16

THE ASSAULT ON GALLERY TWENTY ONE

All was set for Baxter's expedition; on Keith's dining table he made a rudimentary sketch of the layout of Gallery Twenty One,

the Jermyn Street building and spent some time familiarizing himself with its plan. He knew the risks he was taking and to that end, he handed Keith a note outlining what he was intending to do, where and why. He also included details about Hadley's murder and the incident on the bridge in Brittany.

'If by any chance you haven't heard from me after twenty four hours,' Baxter said, 'please ring New Scotland Yard for me and inform assistant commissioner Atterbury at Specialist Crime & Operations Directorate, and give him the note, he'll know what to do.'

'Are you certain you want to go ahead with this?' Keith looked even more anxious than he had before.

'I've no choice, I have to do it for Magali's sake, they'll kill her otherwise.'

'Why don't you ring your friend at Scotland Yard first and seek his help, he's bound to have experience in these situations.'

'No Keith, definitely not, these people have contacts all over the place I can't risk it. And that applies to the Paddington Green station and Inspector Monroe as well.'

Baxter made an almost exact copy of the letter, but added a fictitious statement which mentioned the existence of evidence regarding Gallery Twenty One and murder on a grand scale, this was his own personal insurance policy, should he need it.

During his visits to Bedford Square Baxter had noted one recurring event and that was the arrival every afternoon of the black Daimler and always at precisely seventeen hundred hours. True it often turned up at other times, but at five o'clock sharp it always arrived en route to the underground car park.

It was four thirty five when Baxter and Keith arrived by taxi in Bedford Square Gardens. There were very few people about as they casually made their way to the underground car park entrance. The notice clearly stated 'Strictly no access to pedestrians, entrance one hundred yards.' A bold arrow pointed to the other end of the square. Baxter ignored the sign, as he led the way down into the dark tunnel. He was immediately rewarded with the sound of a hooter as a car roared into the dark entrance behind them.

'Can't you two read?' the driver shouted as he swerved around them, his wheels bumping against the nearside kerb. Baxter continued on regardless, Keith following behind. They made their unhurried way along the pillared aisles until they reached bay sixty one B.

'This is it.' Baxter announced. He flashed on his torch and checked his watch. 'Five minutes to go,' he said.

This was to be one of the longest five minutes he had ever known. Baxter hated waiting and especially when it involved clock-watching, even waiting for a kettle to boil irritated him.

He continually glanced at his watch, three minutes, one and then at precisely five o'clock he heard the distinctive growl of the Daimler. With its lights bouncing off the concrete roof it entered the car park and stopped in front of the steel panel, the same one from where it disappeared the previous time.

As soon as the steel door began to slowly drone into life, Keith began his act. He moved quickly towards the car singing and then stumbled against the driver's door, clumsily, jolting the vehicle.

The front driver's window opened and a head peered out. 'Get out of here you drunken sod, before I give you a good hiding.'

Baxter was amazed, for he had never in his life seen a better or more convincing drunk act, he didn't realize Keith had that ability or bravado in him. His act was certainly as good as the one last week where the drunk made himself a nuisance just before the baseball bat thugs turned up. He still wasn't certain if that had been a coincidence or an orchestrated act, he suspected the latter.

Keith waved his right arm in front of the car windscreen, the neck of a bottle in his hand. 'You bloody stuck up posh git,' he drawled.

While Keith was drawing the driver's attention Baxter gently opened the Daimler's luggage compartment, flashed him a signal from behind and on cue Keith bumped clumsily in to the front of the car causing it to rock from side to side, at the same time Baxter nimbly climbed into the boot.

Huddled awkwardly in the pitch black luggage compartment, Baxter held the boot open a few centimetres with the tips of his fingers. Seconds later he felt the vehicle roll slightly and then heard the car door click shut followed by footsteps and then another door slamming. He immediately sensed an aggregate mass of movement and realised Keith had been right because he was travelling upwards in a car lift.

A sudden jolt marked the end of the ascent. He was certain the car had gone up without its driver, but had no way of checking without breaking out of his hiding place. He decided he couldn't risk waiting any longer so he cautiously raised the boot and crawled out taking care not to rock the vehicle; a quick crane of his neck confirmed he was indeed on his own.

The lift had no physical sides; it was an open platform raised and lowered by means of large steel cables. It was dimly lit, but he could see the car occupied ninety percent of the area. The lift shaft walls were concrete except for the one to the right which had laminated faux wood panels. He paced across towards the panelled wall and a light sprang to life, illuminating a door with small screen and keypad. The door had no handle and neither did it have a traditional lock, so it was immediately obvious he wasn't going to gain access to the rest of the building from here.

Looking around he spotted a dark recess and a sign 'DANGER

LIFT GEAR.' Immediately above he spotted an access panel to a lift mechanism. This was not for the large vehicle lift he was standing on, it was more likely for the passenger lift which he knew from the plans ran parallel to this one.

He heard a voice speaking on an intercom below. 'Okay Mr. Veerman, I'll bring it down when you're ready.'

Now the sound of footfalls and a door opening close by.

He ducked into the darkened recess just in time to see a tall well-dressed man exit and get into the back seat of the car.

'I'm ready to come down now,' he said on his in-car intercom.

'Right you are Mr. Veerman,' the voice below replied.

Baxter realised the floor he was now standing on was an integral part of the lift platform and would be descending any minute.

He had the option of making a dash for the section of floor which abutted the panelled wall and penthouse suite door, but it was brightly lit and so he would be lucky not to be seen by the man sitting in the car. At that moment it became a desperate race against time, the clock was ticking and he knew minutes could be vital in this crazy escapade.

Suddenly the lift jolted and then started to descend; Baxter struggled, but then thought quickly, he only had seconds in which to act. He sprung his body upwards, gripping hold of the iron girder above his head which formed the cross brace of the roof truss. He hung precariously, as the distance between him and the disappearing lift increased.

Baxter had never been particularly agile or athletic but he was strong, yet it took him several attempts before he managed to haul his body onto the girder. By this time the lift had reached the basement and from his position high above, Baxter watched as a second man appeared from an anti-chamber, got in the driving seat and started the engine. All of a sudden an ear shattering roar came from above, followed by a blast of wind which gyrated around him like a giant vortex. Baxter held on desperately, totally unable to move, as the current lashed his body sideways. The effects of vertigo were sending familiar spasms down the backs of his legs. He knew it would only take a momentary loss of concentration and he would plunge to his death on the basement floor.

With the car gone and the exhaust dispersal fan silenced, all was quiet once again in the shaft, but the lift was still at the bottom and so Baxter's troubles were not over just yet. He could hardly stay where he was perilously balancing on a steel girder and for how long? Perhaps the rest of the night! He was equally aware that when the car eventually returned, someone was quite likely to look up and see him squatting there. True, the darkness would provide some degree of invisibility from down below but that would diminish once the lift returned to its position here on the top floor.

With nothing below him he looked around the roof cavity searching for a solution. It gradually dawned on him that his only option was the inspection hatch, which housed the small passenger lift mechanism.

Keeping one hand on the girder he reached up for the trapdoor, but it was still several feet away from his grasp. The terrifying reality was that he was going to have to get off his backside and somehow stand up, but even he knew there was no way he could possibly do that, not in a million years.

Another plan came to him, it wasn't ideal and might still be dangerous, but it was perhaps the last resort.

He shuffled his way the couple of yards back to where the A-frame roof truss met the wall of the small passenger lift shaft. Here he was able to hold on to the wall and walk back along the girder to the trapdoor.

He reached for the clasp that held the lift inspection door shut and turned it, the door swung open. He still had to pull his body up into the opening. He grabbed the ledge and pulled with all his strength, his body rose and his legs dangled precariously in mid air. One final desperate heave and he managed to haul his frame into the inspection cubicle, partially closing the hatch behind him.

The waiting was not an easy or comfortable experience in the cramped confines of the inspection chamber which was mostly taken up with the mechanism for the passenger lift. A large wheel with steel ropes was connected to numerous gears and cogs. This was a dangerous place to be in if the lift was ever activated.

He continued to wait in darkness, huddled and uncomfortable, every minute developing a new ache as a result of being unable to stretch his legs, or alter his position.

Eventually, after some thirty minutes or so, he heard the familiar whirring as the steel door far below opened. He froze, watching the door slowly rising and then the black Daimler glide into the lift.

The familiar hum followed as the lift started to rise, getting louder by the second, whipping up his anxiety to a point where his body was physically shaking.

Keith, having done his part went home full of concern for his friend, and in some ways wishing he had been able to play a bigger part in the adventure. Even now he didn't quite know how Baxter was going to find Magali in that large and only partly understood building.

After studying the blueprints they had come to the conclusion that the car lift was the only way into the structure, and the general layout suggested there would be links between the various parts.

Keith voiced his concerns about intruder alarms, although he said he somehow doubted there would be any in the car lift. The showroom would naturally be heavily alarmed and as for the vaults, well the level of security there would be most formidable.

Baxter's plan was to reach the penthouse apartment, then take the emergency stairway down to the workrooms and offices, which was where he suspected Magali was being held. Another concern was the possibility of patrolling security men, but would they be watching offices and workrooms? The assumption was that they would likely be glued to monitors showing the vaults, showroom, front vestibule and car lift entrance.

Through a crack in the hatch opening Baxter watched as the car lift ascended the last few yards and then came to a halt. When it stopped the driver opened the rear door and the same well dressed man stepped out. *Max Veerman,* Baxter said to himself, it had to be.

The man and his driver walked over to the door which was immediately below him and a sudden beam of light once again lit up the keypad. Baxter strained to watch as the driver first tapped in a seven digit code 5 0 8 3 3 1 4; the man then held his face close to a small screen until a flash recorded his eye retinas. The door soundlessly opened and both men stepped into an ante-room.

Baxter could hear them talking, remarkably the apartment door had been left slightly ajar and the conversation suggested the driver would only be there for a few minutes.

Baxter crept out of his hiding place and dropped silently to the ground. He peered through the partially open door where he could see an ante-room and a little further on another door, which he presumed led to the penthouse suite.

Suddenly footsteps sounded, loud and purposeful and getting closer by the second. He felt his pulse quickening as he watched the moving shadow of a man coming his way from the apartment. Baxter shrank further back into the shadows as the driver passed by his hiding place. To his relief, the man merely opened the car door, took a large envelope from out of the glove compartment, mumbled something incoherent and then returned back to the penthouse suite.

Baxter looked closely at his sketch of the building layout and homed in on two further exits which were drawn as being on the right-hand side, just inside the ante-chamber. He nervously crept through the partly open doorway. The penthouse suite door was immediately ahead and now closed. To his right, partially hidden in the corner, he spotted the two exits he was looking for. These doors were not panelled in fancy imitation teak, but utilitarian plain timber fire doors and neither had a courtesy light above, which if anything was a relief. He could see from the outset they were far less security protected than the main penthouse suite door, even though they still had a key pad lock. Baxter discreetly held the lens of his penlight in his fist to narrow the field of light as he checked the plans. It was the second door he was after, he prayed the code used by the men a few minutes ago would be the same as he tapped in the numbers five, zero, eight, double three, one and finally four. Nothing happened; he swore to himself and gave the door a perfunctory push and to his amazement it opened.

The stairs were concrete and the walls the same with no effort to add any decoration. The handrail was iron and of the plainest design one could possibly imagine. But this was, after all, no more than an emergency fire escape, or on rare occasions, a means to gain access if the lift happened to be out of order.

One floor down and once again Baxter tapped in the seven digit code five zero, eight, double three, one four. The control panel flashed to life '*Incorrect combination.*' He realised he had made a wrong assumption. Because both doors on the floor above had activated with the same code, he presumed this would apply to all doors in the building. *Think logically* he told himself, there had to be a rational reason why the door on this level was different. Of course level! That was perhaps the common denominator. The floor above was the fifth floor though, so why would the last digit be four? He then remembered the building was a five storey structure and therefore, the basement was likely zero, so he repeated the code adding three as the last number and to his relief the door swung open.

He had already noted on the plans that this floor was designated as workshops and he could see straight away that the large expanse of workstations were clearly no prison, Magali wasn't going to be here on this level.

The next floor down was the prime contender; it was here where he thought he would most likely find the woman. Again he modified the code, this time ending it with two for the third floor. The door opened into a long corridor which gave access to a row of offices. One by one he searched them. They were uniform in size and layout. Each had a single desk and adjustable chair, computer monitor and telephone as well as the usual in and out trays, empty of course. Often a few books or ledgers were neatly arranged on shelves and a filing cabinet completed these tidy and organized workplaces.

In marked contrast, office number seven was very different. For a start it was considerably larger than those he had already searched and although it had the same desk, unlike the fastidious nature of the others, it was piled high with books and paperwork which all but hid the computer monitor and a telephone couldn't be seen at all. On a nearby shelf he flicked through folders containing photographs of Asian art. One wall was completely set aside as a library with hundreds or perhaps even thousands of reference books.

A leather settee in front of the shelves was similarly a depository for reading or research matter. He then spotted a large folio open on the settee, but it was not so much the size of the book which caught his eye, but the coloured plate showing the Henri de Montaigne vase. He was intrigued, because it was the same book Hadley had shown him, or at least another copy of it. He turned the pages back to the frontispiece and the words jumped out at him. *To my friend Adrian Hadley signed Grandidier,* He realised the significance of his discovery. There was no doubt about it, this book had been stolen from the Professor, its presence in this office was clear evidence that the organisation who worked here were in some way responsible for Hadley's death. He couldn't, of course be certain that Veerman or his cohorts had carried out the killing themselves, but he was convinced they must have ordered his death and the only logical reason for that would have been because Hadley had refused to reveal details of Baxter's vase.

Baxter took several pictures of the book with the camera on his mobile telephone, taking care to show details of the room in which it resided. He felt certain the presence of Hadley's signed book on these premises linked the Professor's death with this shady organisation, a corporate body which he now suspected was the cartel mentioned by Hadley. If this was the case, then he hoped the police would use the snaps as evidence.

There were four of them in the control room that night, an ordinary shift of fourteen hours from four thirty to six thirty am. The evening shift was always the longest and certainly the most challenging in terms of keeping awake and occupied. At least on the day shifts there was always plenty of activity, but night times were deadly.

Contrary to regulations, all four would have at least two hours sleep, at different times during the night. Some occupied their time reading magazines, others playing cards, every one of them would silently count down the hours until they were relieved.

Once the staff had left the building for the night and Max Veerman had returned after collecting his early evening take- away, the bank of flickering monitors was barely glanced at.

They couldn't even stretch their legs and patrol the building, due to the sensitive levels of the surveillance systems; that at least would have provided some variance to a shift which was at best well paid, but otherwise long and tedious.

Often tempers flared at the slightest grievance, but humans will always bond when necessity forces them to spend long hours in isolation from the outside world.

Baxter continued his search but so far no sign of Magali. At the far end of the corridor an office spanning the width of the passage was locked. All the others had been either open or unlocked, so he guessed this one was different, quite possibly a secure lock-up, the sort of place where she might well be held.

There was only one problem, there was no sign of a keypad to open the door. He knocked, no response. He knocked once more, this time a little louder but again no response. He whispered 'Are you in there Magali?' Immediately the whole building came to life as amber lights pulsated and alarms sounded, creating a din which resonated off the concrete walls. He realised what he had done. Keith had warned him not to speak, or even cough as there could be a voice waveform recognition system in the building. His friend had said it would be an effective security precaution and he was right.

A message came over the tannoy *'This building is in lock down, I repeat this building is in lock down. All doors and windows are charged with two hundred and forty volts electrical current. Do not go near main access points and do not move until instructed, I repeat do not move until instructed.'* The automated message continually repeated the grim warning and the pulsating lights carried on rotating.

In the control room on the ground floor the security guards jumped to life as the alarms sounded. Scanning the monitors they watched the massive steel shutters came down in the basement, sealing it off from the lift shaft. Other shutters slowly closed off the main corridors to the vaults and showroom. None of the cameras showed any signs of an intruder, but then the video cameras were only filming the basement vaults, interior of the passenger lift, showroom and rear car park entrance. One of the security guards switched on the auxiliary heat detector system which was capable of scanning every square centimetre of the building.

Baxter knew he was in trouble now; in desperation he threw a metal ruler at the door to test whether it really was charged with electricity. The instantaneous flash and loud crack that followed left him in no doubt that it was alive. This meant he no longer had the option of leaving by the back stairs in an attempt to make his escape.

Realizing his choices were negligible he ran back down the corridor and ducked into office number seven, the untidy one. The leather settee with the bookcase behind looked a perfect hiding place. He crawled underneath, removed a line of books from the shelves behind and then squeezed into the empty cavity and lined the books up in front. Now, he was surely invisible.

In the control room the security guards continued to scan the flickering monitors. The thermal heat locator had not yet detected any target, there were no obvious signs of human activity in the open areas, but to make certain the guard turned up the sensitivity level to ten millibars, its fullest extent.

'There.' The security officer pointed to the screen where an orange glow shimmered from under a settee. 'We have an intruder in the second floor offices,' he said jubilantly, 'number seven, under that desk, see him?' he asked his comrade, who nodded in agreement.

The man beamed. This was what he had been waiting for for so long, a bit of action, a chance to show how heroic he was, and an opportunity to show off his new role to his colleagues. He had long daydreamed of being involved in deadly conflict, usually in the guise of an SAS combatant, in action, fighting against all odds.

He had recently been appointed night duty 'special precautions control officer' and was already stepping into his Faraday suit ready to tackle his very first emergency operation.

From his hiding place Baxter suddenly heard loud squelchy footsteps slow and heavy and getting closer by the second, then they stopped. Peering between the cracks in the books he could see a looming darkness and then a body mass blocking out the light.

He held his breath, desperately fighting the irritable cough, that nervous expelling of air which always surfaces from nowhere on such occasions when it was critical it shouldn't.

The footsteps moved away, stoping, he thought, at the other end of the room.

'This is special precautions unit. Target is no longer under the settee, I repeat target is no longer under the settee in room seven. Please confirm the present target position.'

The guards in the control room checked their monitor once

again. The special precautions guard was throwing out too large an expanse of orange from the thermal heat locator, so they told him to leave the room. Straightaway the glow from Baxter's body heat showed his continued presence under the settee.

Baxter blew a whistle of relief when he heard the footsteps leave the room but it was to be a short-lived reprieve. The footfalls returned, the settee lifted and put aside, the books removed and his hiding place was laid bare.

Baxter looked up in dismay taking in the large figure who stared down at him, an oddity who looked as though he had climbed out of a science fiction novel. Dressed in a highly conductive stainless steel Faraday suit with built-in gloves and boots, he was quite alarming. He took out his phone. 'Control I have the target, you can turn off the electrical charge now.'

Then over the tannoy '*This building is now out of lock down, I repeat this building is out of lock down.*'

Baxter considered making a dash for it, after all this strange chap could hardly run after him, but the hum of the passenger lift suggested help was only minutes away.

'Sit on that chair and don't move,' ordered one of the two security guards who had just arrived from the lift. Suddenly the man's phone came to life.

'Have you found the intruder?' enquired the voice on the other end.

'Yes, we have him here in office seven,' the guard replied.

'Good, take him to the interview room, I'll be down shortly.

When Baxter was ushered into the previously locked room at the end of the corridor he could see straightaway it was different from the rest. Sure enough it was a very secure, cell-like room but it wasn't Magali's cell, or at least she wasn't there now. He straightaway recognised the familiar surroundings as those, where hooded, he had been brought only twenty four hours earlier.

It was to be a further ten minutes before the door opened and in stepped a tall impeccably dressed man, the same figure he had seen getting out of the car and going into the penthouse suite.

The man had a presence which was immediately noticeable. He was distinguishably aged, his hair white, but his face looked younger than his likely tally of years. He was elegant to the extent that his looks commanded respect and his expression suggested a lean towards gentry.

Baxter had expected the presence of yesterday's bespectacled compact man; instead it was the big boss himself, Mr. Max Veerman.

The man walked past Baxter without so much as a glance and proceeded to the small barred window, placed both hands on the sill and looked out. He remained like this for several minutes before he turned, with an expression of annoyance and cleared his throat.

'So, Mr. Baxter, you chose not to heed our instructions, instead you have broken into my property and put us to a great deal of inconvenience,' he said in an educated yet matter-of-fact way.

'I didn't exactly break in,' Baxter retaliated, 'I was in the back of your Daimler when the car lift took me up to the top floor.'

'And pray tell me what were you doing in the boot of my car?'

Now he had a problem, as there was clearly no explanation that would mitigate his presence in the man's vehicle. He decided he might as well state the obvious, whatever he said it was unlikely to make much difference now.

'I got into your car in order to break into your property so I could search for my friend Magali whom you have kidnapped.'

'I see,' he said slowly, 'but tell me who gave you the key codes to gain access into my property?'

'No one, no one at all,' he said, 'the truth of the matter is I simply watched your driver punch in the code when he opened the door which leads to your apartment floor and then used the same code several times but with the last digit changed to correspond with the floor.'

'Very clever Mr. Baxter, but I'm intrigued as to how you knew to change the last digit and what the numbers would be.'

'A guess that's all, just a guess, no more than that.'

'A lucky guess, 'Veerman said raising his eyebrows, 'I will have that little loophole in our security sorted out, yes very clever. Do you know I actually respect ingenuity, but I never tolerate it when it infringes my integrity?'

Even though Veerman continually turned away to glance out the window, Baxter couldn't tear his eyes away from him. It was not just his voice which exerted power and conviction, but when you faced him and met his gaze it conveyed the same crystal clear physiognomies.

The man appeared to come to a decision. He turned sharply and glared across at the security guards. There was no doubting he was flashing them a look of annoyance, a look which demanded action over the locks. He cleared his throat and made his unhurried way to the desk.

'So tell me who is taxi driver two one six?'

'I haven't a clue what you're talking about,' he lied.

'I'm referring to your accomplice, the taxi driver who is in this with you and who is no doubt hiding the Chinese vase for you. We will find him sooner or later, take my word for it.'

Baxter wasn't happy his friend Steve was thought to be involved, but relieved Keith had not been mentioned. He needed to do or say something quickly to deflect the situation. 'I think you should read this letter before you do anything else,' Baxter said handing Veerman the copy of the letter he had given to Keith.

The man read the letter twice, then tutted, shaking his head slowly.

'My, my, Mr. Baxter, you do have a very bad impression of us don't you? I really can't think why. You see we wish you no harm, and as for your ludicrous suggestion that our organisation might have something to do with the unfortunate killing of this Professor… who was it?'

'Hadley,' Baxter said

'Yes quite, well I really do wonder what evidence you think you might have.' He shook his head again. 'You really should be more careful about making such accusations; you know it could get you into serious trouble one of these days.'

'I think you might just be surprised at the evidence I have and I can tell you now that if anything untoward happens to me or Magali, that evidence will be in police hands.'

Veerman clapped. 'A very commendable and brave speech Mr. Baxter, but it's late, so we'll talk further in the morning.' He rose to leave, reached for the door handle and then turned on his heels. 'If on reflection, you think of anything you wish to tell us, you will find a notepad in your room. Good night Mr. Baxter, oh and by the way don't try and wander around my building in the night, it might be fatal next time, in fact I can guarantee it will.'

Baxter was taken down in the lift to a lower level and led past the vaults into what was most certainly a cell.

The room was no more than four metres square with a solitary tiny barred window, just fifteen centimetres across. The walls, ceiling and floor were bare concrete, lightened with a coat of white paint, thickly applied but failing to hide tell-tale signs of wooden shuttering. In the far corner a stainless steel sink was provided, with a bar of soap and towel; below a metallic bowl was the sole toilet facility.

Baxter sat on the single bed, bouncing to test its level of comfort. The mattress was not particularly well stuffed, but the duvet seemed adequate enough. The only other furnishings were a metal framed canvas chair and x-frame table with a notepad and pencil placed on top. He walked over and sat at the table and idly doodled, drawing concentric circles which decreased in size until they ended up with a solitary dot. He wrote the word Magali several times, on each occasion adding more and more outrageous scrolls and flourishes. He filled in the gaps with cherubs and foliate motifs. He didn't know why he had written her name and certainly it wasn't a conscious scribble, more a subconscious reaction to boredom.

On the wall he spotted some very faint graffiti. It had been erased, but a pen had scored the paint surface. He ran the pencil obliquely across the scarred paint and a familiar image slowly came into view. It was the batwing symbol with the usual Chinese letters, but something else he hadn't seen on the other examples, the initials M.V. He decided they had to be the initials for Max Veerman.

Had some unfortunate soul left a last message, an accusing finger at Veerman, naming him as being behind the batwing symbol?

It suddenly dawned on him that Veerman wasn't that clever after all, for he had forgotten to have Baxter searched and what was still in his pocket, his mobile phone.

He tapped in several numbers but soon realised there was no dialling tone, the concrete shell was obviously too thick.

He went over to the tiny window and tried it again, but still no signal. He turned up the volume and reached into the deep window embrasure and held it against the pane of glass. He had a signal but he couldn't put the mobile next to his face to make a call. Wait a minute, he smiled to himself. 'I can send a text message.'

He wrote out an urgent message. Keith's telephone number was in the menu so he tapped in the number then held the mobile against the glass. He nervously waited for the numbers to engage and then a loud screech deafened him and continued until he turned his mobile off.

He now knew why they hadn't bothered to search him. The building obviously had an internal telecommunications blocking screen, but why? That in itself was sinister for a supposedly innocent import and export antiques business.

The light in the cell automatically went out shortly after ten, so he submitted to settling down for the night.

Baxter had no idea how long he had slept, but a sound was invading his slumber. It was a strange irregular tapping, and he quickly realised it was coming from the radiator. He felt for his penlight and checked his wristwatch, it was twelve thirty five.

He listened, fascinated as the rhythmic sound continued in short regular bursts for about a minute, then a gap and once again a paced tapping resumed for about the same time. After the third performance he came to the conclusion that it was a coded message with the number of taps representing letters of the alphabet. He picked up the pencil and pad and waited, he was beginning to think he had left it too late as he drummed the pencil against his teeth.

The tapping once again resumed. He counted nine taps. *That would be I if it was meant to be the ninth letter of the alphabet,* he said to himself as he wrote down the letter I. A short gap was followed by nineteen which by his reckoning was S. Within a couple of minutes he had the message clearly written down on his note pad.

IS- T H A T- Y O U- B A X T E R? He wrote down his reply on the pad and converted the letters into numbers and then tapped back Y E S -I S- T H A T- MA G A L I. The reply confirmed it was Magali who was in the room next door.

The coded messages became longer. She went on to say 'You've got to rescue me Baxter.'

'I know, and that's why I'm here, but how? I happen to be locked up like you.'

'You must overpower the guard when he comes in with your breakfast at nine o clock and then get me out of here.'

'Sounds possible, but we will need to find a way out of the building.'

'Don't worry about that, we'll find a way out,' she replied, still in radiator-tapped code.

This was a tall order for Baxter, breaking in was one thing, but overpowering a guard, that was something else! By now any chance of further sleep had gone. His adrenalin began rising as he strung together a plan, a line of attack which came to him surprisingly quickly, but then perhaps that was because only one scenario existed in this situation.

Baxter's strategy was simple enough, but it was going to require more luck than dexterity or strength alone. It was certainly no great feat of his imagination, but a classic setup which had been played out in countless stories and films for more than a century. His plan required deception, some agility, surprise and strength and not forgetting split second timing.

Magali was spot on with her forecast. It was precisely nine o'clock when, from his crouched position perched on a ventilation box-section pipe above the door, he heard footsteps approaching. Keys rattled loudly in the lock and the lever handle slammed over. The guard entered with the tray of food in both hands. He spotted what appeared to be Baxter's body lying in the bed, but what he didn't know was this was a very careful piece of dressing which had taken Baxter some time to arrange. He had finished it off by placing the toilet bowl upside down with the sheet covering it.

The guard suspected nothing as he stepped through the doorway.

Baxter timed his jump perfectly, landing squarely on the man's back and sending him plummeting to the ground. The tray shot out of his hands and clattered noisily across the concrete floor.

Baxter grabbed the heavy tray and crashed it down on the guards head. A quick search of the unconscious man's pockets produced his bunch of keys along with a card of key codes. He locked the cell door behind him leaving the guard groaning inside.

It took Baxter several frustrating minutes to find the right key to the room next door, but eventually he did and as he flung the cell door open he was rewarded with a passionate kiss.

'I knew you would rescue me, my clever hero,' she said, her long arms frantically clinging to his neck.

'We're not quite out of the woods yet,' he said unwrapping her embrace. He was surprised how stoic she seemed to be, considering her two days of incarceration. But there was no time for further niceties, he had to get them out of there quickly before the alarm was raised. He suspected the one major factor in their favour was the time of day, as he imagined staff would be arriving for work at nine o'clock, which meant most of the alarm systems would be turned off.

The only security issue they might have to avoid was the voice waveform system which was probably left on continuously, as all staff would be logged into its recognition data.

He explained how his blunder calling her had led to his capture and urged that she take great care to remember not to say a word once they were out of the cell.

They took to the concrete stairs, running up as fast as their legs would permit until they reached the second landing. He tapped in the code he had used the night before, five zero eight double three one four, but to his horror it didn't work, the screen flashed the message '*Incorrect combination.*' He was momentarily stunned, suddenly the cards had changed and they were no longer in his favour. The logical explanation could only be that a different code was required to open doors from opposite sides. He had to think quickly and was about to suggest they return down the stairs again when he remembered the guard's code card. It had five sets of numbers all with seven digits, the first ending with 0, the last with 4, precisely as he expected it to be. With that in mind he reasoned how he must have tapped in the wrong number last time so he tapped out the digits again adding the number four at the end.

A message appeared '*- Incorrect combination. Beware one more incorrect attempt will activate the central alarm system.*'

He looked at Magali and held out his hands, unable to know what to do next. He suddenly grasped the likelihood that Max Veerman had already changed the key codes; he shouldn't have been surprised because he must have been furious that Baxter had used them to break into his property.

Seeing his perplexed expression Magali pointed to the fourth set of digits. He couldn't understand why she thought they might work. She wet her finger and drew the number three and then pointed to the door. The realization hit him like a sledgehammer. He suddenly felt very foolish because he had counted the floors thinking this was the top one forgetting the basement was number 0 and so this was only the fourth level and therefore the third floor. He tapped in the numbers this time ending with 3 and the click of the lock confirmed the numbers had worked.

They darted up the next flight of stairs and within minutes reached the door leading to the top floor, opened it and he was once again in the lobby opposite Veerman's penthouse suite. The door opposite led to the car lift and although he knew the combination would end in the number four as it too was part of the fifth floor, there was one little matter he had completely forgotten about. Previously the door had been left partly open, but now to his horror, facing him squarely in the face was an eye laser screen.

Magali noticing his hesitation, started to tap in the code numbers once again, ending with the number four.

Baxter put his hand on her arm to stop her. He pointed to the retina eye laser screen, she huffed her shoulders. He shook his head warning her not to proceed. She raised her eyebrows in a motion which asked what else should they do.

He shrugged. She continued tapping in the last digits but delayed pressing the final green validation button.

She looked at him, pushing him to make the final decision. He reasoned to himself *Oh well you never know the screen might be just a bluff.* He didn't believe that for one minute but he knew this was their final and only chance to escape. If the alarms did go off, they were really in trouble with nowhere to hide, but equally there was no other exit to head for, or at least not without being spotted.

He nodded. With the digits tapped into the keypad she hit the validation button and astonishingly the door opened and in the dim light he saw the Daimler waiting motionless for them.

He pointed to the car and she understood he wanted her to get in. Meanwhile he made for the control panel, quickly scanning the options before pressing home the green button.

The lift mechanism groaned to life as he jumped into the driving seat beside her.

The minutes dragged painfully as the lift made its slow descent.

Baxter felt certain someone was going to hear it, the noise was far too distinctive to be ignored. He half expected to see Veerman peering over the side from above, but so far he wasn't.

The next bit was always going to be difficult as he wasn't certain how the car park doors opened; he hoped the car sent a remote control signal automatically, but he really didn't know.

The lift came to a halt, but it came as no surprise when the exit doors failed to open. He got out and looked for a control panel, Magali followed. 'I think you' she started to say as Baxter thrust his hand over her mouth, she had forgotten she mustn't speak, but remarkably the alarm didn't sound.

'That was…' he went to say but before he could finish, alarms sounded, a loud wailing which was deafening and continuous.

'The system must be on a time delay,' he shouted, 'come on let's get out of here fast,' he yelled diving back into the car. He pressed the electric starter button and the mighty V6 engine growled into life. The loud roar of the air circulation fan competed with the siren and at the same time the familiar whirring sound confirmed an automatic devise in the car had turned on the exit door mechanism.

He could only go backwards so thrust the automatic transmission into reverse. The car shot backwards faster than he had expected, loudly ramming the slowly rising metal door and causing it to judder to a halt.

He thrust the Daimler into first and moved away from the groaning door, allowing it to continue a now uneasy upward ascent. Baxter knew it was only a matter of minutes before the guards would arrive and he was suddenly proved right.

Shouts sounded, two or three he guessed and then gun shots, loud and agonizingly close followed immediately by the noise of metal being punctured. The front of the car was peppered with bullets, triboluminescent flashes lit up the darkness and then the windscreen shattered around a small hole where a shot had impacted.

'Get down.' He yelled to Magali as he put the car into reverse and then slammed his foot on the accelerator as hard as he could. The Daimler lurched backwards hitting the last few centimetres of rising door shutter, noisily slicing off the top of the car roof as it careered into the underground car park. He spun the car round in time to see two men with guns in outstretched hands emerging from under the crumpled exit door. He put his foot down hard on the accelerator as another round of gunshots hit the rear bumper. With his foot hard on the gas and with a relentless squeal of tyres, he careered the wrong way round the car bays, narrowly missing oncoming vehicles, until they finally emerged into bright sunshine.

He slowed to a sedate pace as he circled Bedford Square Garden's trying hard to ignore the curious faces watching the roofless car make its noisy way past them. A sudden juddering towards the back of the vehicle told him one of the tyres had been punctured by a bullet. They wouldn't be going far, but then he wasn't intending to go any further than the nearest quiet backstreet.

Baxter stopped the wrecked car in a cul-de-sac some distance from the main road and they hotfooted away before anyone saw them.

'Where is your car Magali?' he asked, hoping she would say it was nearby.

'Outside Twenty One Jermyn Street.'

Baxter sighed. 'That doesn't help us then; they are bound to be keeping a watch on it.'

A few minutes later while walking along the Broadway, Baxter spotted a taxi and asked the driver to take them to the centre of Piccadilly.

Opposite the statue of Eros he telephoned his friend Keith, hoping he was working from home today and not out on a job.

'Of course you can come round,' he said in a relieved but nervous voice, 'but cut across the back alley and through the rear garden, just in case anyone is keeping a watch on me.'

They hovered on the edge of the pavement waiting for a break in the traffic, when it came they dashed across the road and headed off towards Keith's place.

Baxter related the tale to the stunned architect with the occasional note of heroics from Magali.

Keith urged Baxter go straight to the police, but he said he needed to think very carefully before rushing into anything, and Magali wholeheartedly agreed on that point.

Keith insisted they stay with him for the time being, as Baxter's cottage would certainly be under surveillance by now.

Keith chuckled. 'I still can't believe you actually pulled it off, that Max Veerman must be furious you managed to snatch Magali from under his nose, and in spite of all his so-called security measures.' He flashed a broad grin, an infectious sentiment Baxter had never before witnessed from the normally staid Keith.

'Not only that,' Magali interrupted. 'Baxter has also destroyed his precious Daimler,' she said leaving to use the bathroom.

'Yes, well that will be covered by his insurance policy,' Baxter shouted after her.

Keith said 'I bet he'll still take it to heart though, those sort of people always do, they see it as a personal violation. He shook his head. 'I wouldn't want to be in your shoes, mate.'

'Actually,' Baxter began 'you're sharing them because you helped us.' He didn't respond to that statement of involvement.

'Magali seems a nice woman.' Keith said changing the subject. 'She's a plucky little thing and very pretty as well.'

'Now you know why I like her so much.'

'You must do, after all the effort you put into rescuing her.'

Magali returned and they changed the subject from boy's talk to the matter of the future.

Baxter decided now was the time to explain all to Magali. He was only really filling in the gaps, because she was well aware of much of the story, but she doggedly maintained her pretence at total ignorance. She praised him on his idea for hiding the vase in the copper water cylinder; she wasn't surprised Veerman's men didn't find it, 'They couldn't find a drunk in a brewery,' she said laughing.

Baxter related how enthused David Salisbury had been with the Chinese vase and his expectations for a good result in the forthcoming auction.

Then with a little apprehension, he explained why the vase was so important to Veerman and his fellow cartel members.

He said it wasn't just the pot itself they were after, although it was an important piece, but it was one of a pair, each with a Sanskrit inscription and it was the meaning behind these inscriptions which was the important factor.

'Where is the other one Baxter?'

'Veerman has it; he's been sitting on it for nearly forty years.'

'So what are these inscriptions then, what do they say?' she asked casually

'Well my friend Professor Hadley translated both of them for me.'

'And that's why they killed him.'

'Was it. That's awful' Magali interrupted.

'Yes it is. You see he discovered the inscription read 'the rock of Batuta is in porcelain made for the Imperial court.'

'Rock of Batuta,' she said furrowing her brow.

'The rock of Batuta is probably the diamond of Batuta; a legendary gem which was presented by the Arabian dignitary Ibn Batuta to the Muslim eunuchs at the Chinese court in the mid-fourteenth century.'

'Wow' she exclaimed 'and do you know where this diamond is hidden?'

'I believe I do now.'

She looked at him coyly, he now knew he needed her help if he was going to crack the last strands of this mystery.

'Magali I'm going to trust you with something,' he said, choosing his words with care. 'The diamond is in a piece of porcelain which was shipped to France by a certain General Henri de Montaigne; does that strike a note with you?'

He was surprised when she appeared not to know the name, even though her grandmother had been buying letters written by him.

He went on 'I don't know what shape it will be, but I'll know it when I see it, I'm certain of that.'

'Well that doesn't tell us very much, does it?' she rebuked him in an irritated manner.

'I haven't finished yet. I believe the porcelain which contains the diamond is in your grandmother's chateau down in Bourge-Vilaine.'

The look on Magali's face was difficult to gauge; Baxter wasn't certain if it was shock of indifference, or stunned silence.

'I don't think we can wait much longer,' Baxter said 'After the events of the last few days, it's clear Veerman and his cartel are after the same thing as us, it's only a matter of time before someone else gets hurt or worse.'

'You're right about that,' Keith said smiling through clenched teeth, 'and I think they'll only stop their threats once the diamond had been publicly declared found and in a safe and secure place.'

'Look,' said Baxter suddenly reaching a conclusion, 'I'm going to France first thing tomorrow morning. I intend to pay a visit to the Countess de Couvegne at Bourge-Vilaine. If either of you want to come along you're most welcome.' He looked hopefully at Magali.

'Count me in,' she said. I'll speak with grandmother, that should help, and besides she might possibly know where the diamond is hidden.'

'I somehow doubt that.' He shook his head. 'No it's going to be very well concealed, but possibly right under her very nose and probably always has been.'

Keith was disappointed he couldn't go with them due to work commitments, but offered them the use of his flat for as long as they needed it.

The following day Baxter looked out of Keith's front window and to his horror noticed a car opposite. He knew he was being paranoid, but after recent developments that wasn't surprising. The only thing which made him think maybe it was a coincidence, was the fact the driver was the only occupant, whereas previously there had always been two.

He decided to be cautious so slipped quietly out the back door, crossed the small neatly manicured gardens and jumped on a number twelve bus.

He was off to collect his new car, or at least not exactly a brand new one, as the insurance policy had taken into account the age of his written-off vehicle. Although his old car was only six years old, the pay-out would only buy him one of a similar vintage.

The red Celica shone like a button, it was obvious it had been nurtured every bit as much as his old car, and was of a similar age and model and so would be familiar to drive, something he considered sensible and appealed to his symmetry disorder condition.

Mike the mechanic agreed to collect the loan car from Baxter's place in the morning and was happy for him to leave his new Celica in his workshop overnight. He gave him a key and told him to lock up when he left next morning and drop the key in the letterbox.

Chapter 17

Bourge-Vilaine Re-Visited

The road was familiar as he breezed along the narrow winding tarmac, framed by high hedges either side. Occasionally a break in the hedgerow revealed a network of fields, a palette of greens as far as the eye could see. It was just after ten thirty French time and already the sun had climbed high enough to direct its heat through the open sunroof. He was deliberately avoiding the faster motorways which cut straight lines through the undulating countryside. This was partly to avoid the incessant tolls, which not only added to the journey cost, but also often led to long tailbacks at this time of the year. Despite being used to driving in car- locked London, Baxter had never liked travelling in fast moving multiple lanes of vehicles whose traffic flow was dictated by lorries of a size which was often intimidating, especially for someone in a small sports car.

Along the way Magali telephoned her grandmother on her mobile, explaining that they were on their way to see her. She told her what they were looking for and asked if she had any ideas to help them in their search.

'So how was she about our ideas and plans?'

'Fine, no problem,' Magali said. 'Actually she knew all about the diamond story, but not where it was hidden.'

'Did she really,' Baxter was stunned by the revelation that the Countess knew about the diamond, he couldn't for the life of him imagine how.

'But,' Magali added 'what she did say was that the only place where there was any Chinese porcelain remaining in the house was in the Oriental collection room in the Countess de Couvegne tower.'

'That makes sense, wow that's really thrilling.' Baxter was suddenly extremely excited. He realised he was going to be looking at objects which had been handled by Henri de Montaigne, the man he had been researching, the person who was behind this whole riddle. It also dawned on him that the same treasures had come from the Chinese Summer Palace and so had been venerated by the great Ming and even earlier Emperors.

'So she is expecting us then?' he enquired

'Not exactly, well yes she is, but grandmother won't be there herself, she's got to go out. She might be back before we leave.'

She noticed a look of apprehension on Baxter's face and was quick to add. 'Don't look so worried, I have my own key to the tower,' she said riffling through her handbag and producing a large key.

'Grandmother said we can let ourselves in, besides Jacque her butler will be around if we need any help.'

'So tell me about your grandparents; you've never talked about a grandfather.'

'Grandfather died before I was born, and so I didn't know him. He was in the resistance and was apparently shot in the final year of the war.'

'Tragic just tragic, but it's interesting because it means your father inherited the title of Count and your mother became Countess, so how did that affect your grandmother?'

'French lineage is quite complicated, but it meant my grandmother retained the hereditary appendages of the family name. Whereas my late Mother, who was the sixth Countess retained the title.'

'So in that case are you now the seventh Countess?'

'No no.' she was quick to add. 'Descendancy never runs down the female line, or at least it hasn't since the early seventeen hundreds, so I'm just plain old Magali de Couvegne.'

He turned to her. 'One thing we must agree on before we get there; the diamond, if we discover it, does belong to your grandmother and so there's no question of keeping it for ourselves or anything like that.'

'Of course, I couldn't agree more, and that's why I'm keen to find it. But tell me, what are *your* motives Baxter?'

240

'Perhaps it's because of you,' he said squeezing her hand, holding it for a few minutes until he had to let go to change gear.

'Oh I don't know,' he said thoughtfully. 'I suppose it's all down to the challenge, and because my very good friend Adrian Hadley lost his life because of it. I feel I owe it to him to finish what he started.'

'That's really nice. You know you are a kind man Baxter, I think I've made a very good choice with you.'

'You've only known me for a short while,' he said

'Maybe,' she replied, 'but it's the best while I've had up until now.'

'There's a lot better to come if you hang around,' he said chuckling. He noticed a sudden change in her face which showed what could only be described as a look of regret.

'You *are* going to hang around aren't you?'

'Look Baxter, whatever happens in the future, please believe me when I say that what we've had is the best, anything in the future will be a bonus.'

Magali was one of those people whose face is the window of their spirit, when all was well there was a light within. Since he had known her, he had, on several occasions, noticed the light had slightly dimmed; but in that split moment the light had disappeared entirely and that worried him.

It was now four hours later and Bourge-Vilaine was in the distance, easily recognisable by its castle perched on the hilltop and the town nestling below. Just before the town outskirts, about a kilometre away, he spotted the familiar signs of massed tourism-coaches, lots of them, parked in a large car park in front of the Chateau de Couvegne.

He chose a spot well away from the coaches. The last thing he wanted now was one of them carelessly backing into his new, shiny red car.

'Wow.' Exclaimed Baxter, 'your grandmother certainly has a magnificent house, it's truly wonderful, you're so fortunate.'

She nodded in agreement, but said nothing in response.

The honey-coloured chateau stood proud and resplendent, seemingly untouched by modernity yet still dominating the countryside which fell away on three sides. The long symmetrical frontage was finely proportioned, typical of most French Chateaux yet appearing to be different, as indeed all are in their own distinctive way. The wings embraced a façade punctuated by two round towers complimented by a matching pair at the rear. All had high conical slate roofs with internal staircases. In the centre a turreted Gothic style entrance porch had long welcomed the good and wealthy in their carriages. Above, nestling in the middle of the building, were the tops of belvederes with their copper-covered cupolas green with the patina of time and weather.

The walls of weathered stone had intricate string courses and turrets. Roofs were no less decorated, the slates hung in ornamental courses, which were particularly striking on the conical tower roofs.

At the entrance a tourism board set out a brief history of the chateau. 'This magnificent seventeenth century masterpiece' it claimed 'was first constructed in the sixteen forties and is a superb example of Louis XIII style architecture designed for residential use, as opposed to military defence.' It went on to explain how some historians considered it was designed for a combination of the two.

Unlike the hordes of tourists, Magali didn't make entrance through the grand central porch, but paralleled the building with Baxter in toe until they reached the right hand corner where a tower snuggled between the main front façade and a west wing. Magali reached inside her handbag, removed the large key and turned it in the enormous Renaissance lock plate. The oak door studded with iron bolts opened unsteadily, noisily as the ancient hinges moved against their working parts.

Entering the tower they left behind the bright sunshine which irradiated the courtyard and were cast into a dark void whose walls and floors emitted a smell of damp and decay. It was immediately obvious the tower was rarely used these days, it lacked the regular airing a building of this nature needed in order to maintain a healthy condition. Magali closed the door explaining the need to keep nosey tourists out. 'They'll wander into any place which is not securely closed off to them and that infuriates grandmother.'

She explained that this was the Countess de Couvegne's grandmother's private room, a place in the tower where the third Countess, almost a hundred years ago, had sat and written her now infamous letters, a place of solitude where she had the quiet and solace which allowed her to read without being disturbed by family or servants. She explained that the Countess had loved to while away the hours admiring her favourite pieces of Oriental porcelain, and in the tower above, she had a bed where she could retire, alone and at peace with her beloved letters.

'So I take it the third Countess lived here during the late eighteen hundreds then,' he said trying to orientate the facts he already knew, with the family tree.

'Yes and lived here until nineteen eleven.'

Baxter walked around the room in a state of wonderment, finding it hard to believe he was actually here amongst the memories of General Henri de Montaigne and of course the infamous third Countess. Between the large tapestries were glimpses of hewn stone walls; the colourful wall hangings depicting mainly Mediaeval chivalric scenes, did much to hide the austerity and coldness of their construction.

Two large Chinese vases stood to attention either side of the door. Impressive for their size and construction, they lacked the refinement necessary for them to be classified as Imperial wares. They were typical of the porcelain made in the many potteries around the harbour of Canton and produced solely for the export market and definitely not what Baxter was looking for.

He wandered over to peer in a large mahogany and glass cabinet. He could see some nice pieces, bowls of various shapes and sizes, the dishes, mostly blue and white, he guessed they were probably all from the Ming Dynasty. One shelf was devoted to small porcelain brush rests with peaks between the grooves. However, it was a particular tone of blue that he was looking for and as yet he hadn't spotted it and was starting to worry.

Magali wasn't exactly helping either, she seemed to be preoccupied, looking through some books. It was as though the business in hand was of little importance to her and he was getting a bit irritated at her apparent disinterest.

The room had not been properly tidied for many years and some of the furniture had been added later, hiding various items.

Baxter was beginning to think maybe he had got it wrong. There was no sign of anything which was early blue and white porcelain and certainly nothing which even vaguely matched his vase.

'I think this is all going to be a waste of time,' he said resolutely

'Do you know Baxter,' she said wryly, 'this is the first time I have known you to give up so easily; I really am surprised at you.'

'Well, look around this place,' he said scanning the chamber, 'tell me where could something as big as a pedestal for two vases be hiding?'

Magali seemed to consider for a few minutes and then pointed to the far wall. 'Have you looked under that table over there?'

'No... I suppose not' he said dragging out his words. He went over to the other side of the room, half-heartedly, as he doubted very much it would produce anything other than run of the mill clutter, but as she had pointed it out he had to show some sign of interest. A long paduk wood table stood against the wall, practically unrecognizable as it was piled high with packing crates and part of a garniture of Imari vases with ormolu mounts and more than the occasional string of cobwebs.

Removing the lids of several packing crates he found they contained some pottery and lots of straw, but were clearly far too small to contain what he was searching for.

'There's not.' he started to say, but was interrupted.

'Why don't you try underneath?' she suggested.

'Alright,' he said resignedly, 'but it's going to be a waste of time.'

'Just shut up and look,' She said.

He dropped to his knees and looked below the table; it was

certainly crammed with all manner of stored away oddments including several rolled-up Persian carpets and three leather suitcases with Peninsular and Orient travel labels still attached to the sides.

He tugged at the larger of the trunks pulling it free and then on looking inside found it was disappointingly empty. He reached for one of the rolled up Persians and with some effort managed to heave it out. He rolled it to the centre of the room which stirred up a cloud of one hundred year old dust, triggering a bout of coughing which didn't subside for several minutes. He ducked down again and continued to move things around, and then in the gloomy confines he caught a sight of a slab of blue and white porcelain hiding partly behind the other carpet and leather suitcases.

In mounting excitement he grabbed the remaining cases by their handles, sliding them across the floor. The other carpet was next and suddenly he was staring at something even *he* hadn't really expected to find.

With Magali's help they started to drag the large piece of porcelain from under the table. Baxter winced every time it became snagged by an uneven flag stone and the scraping sounds, produced when the porcelain protested about the rough surface, were almost unbearable. Eventually the piece emerged from its hiding place under the table.

It was certainly the right shade of blue and its decoration mirrored his Chinese vase exactly. He instinctively knew this was the original base for the pair of Henri de Montaigne vases, long redundant since the companion pieces had been sold, but unmistakeably that was precisely what it was.

'That's our piece,' he said to Magali, his heart pounding wildly in excitement. 'I knew I'd find it here, I just knew it.'

'Excuse me, but who found it,' she demanded with a look of indignant umbrage.

'Alright, you spotted the paduk table which I hadn't noticed, but...'

She cut him short, 'Of course you didn't see it, men's eyes do not connect with their brains like women's do.'

'What a load of old rubbish,' he said chuckling.

'Actually it's not,' she said brusquely, 'don't you know that females begin studying faces as babies, and this shapes their brain development.'

'But surely no different from baby boys though.'

'Well that's where you're wrong. It's a known fact that facial gazing skills in boys are much less acute than girls and that's why boys don't look for connection in the same way as girls do.

'But wait a minute, I'm not saying it is, but even if that's true, you surely can't claim the same applies to adults.'

'Actually,' she said getting on her *high horse,* 'the brain-based behavioural patterns in children continue to influence men and women throughout adulthood.'

Baxter decided he had been out-manoeuvred on this one and so chose to let it drop.

'Anyway, how do you know this is the base you're looking for?' she exclaimed, raising her eyes anticipating his reply.

'I just know, trust me. Now do you think your grandmother would mind us looking at it a bit closer?'

'No, go ahead' she replied in a matter of fact way.

Between them they carried the heavy two metre long base across the room, finally lowering it gently onto a side table.

This was, in essence a finely moulded plinth decorated with lotus leaves and stylized flame motifs and two leaping dragons with four – clawed feet outstretched ready to grasp a finely modelled flaming pearl. Each end terminated with a large circular inset, now vacant but evidently once housing very substantial vases. With Magali's help he carefully turned it over, exposing its unglazed base.

'What on earth's that,' Baxter pointed to a strange patch in the centre. 'That's very strange, it looks as though someone has made a large oval hole and then filled it up with soft grey plaster, and definitely after it was taken out of the kiln.'

With excitement rising in her voice she urged him to go further.

'Find something to scrape the plaster out, come on quick.'

'But what about…'

'Don't worry about grandmother, she said confidently, cutting him short.' 'She'll be okay with this, just trust me.'

Baxter did trust her now; she had at last proved her fidelity so he felt he had no reason *not* to accept what she was telling him.

He took out his pen knife and gently pared away the plaster of Paris filling. Within minutes a sparkle of light danced on the facets of a crystalline object. The blade of his knife pinged as it made contact with the hard transparent ball which effortlessly slipped out of its five hundred year old hiding place.

'Let me see it, let me see it.' Magali was jumping with excitement, swaying from side to side, peering over Baxter's shoulder. He was dumbfounded, for here in his hands was the largest diamond he had ever seen, perhaps the largest diamond that anybody had ever set eyes upon. He was finding it difficult to comprehend the fact that it really was a gem and not a large ball of cleverly cut glass. Its size and enormous weight challenged his acceptance that this really could be a genuine diamond.

'I want to hold it' Magali pouted.

As he handed it to her he heard the oak door open.

'What the hell are you doing here in my house?' A tall figure stood motionless in the open doorway, a silhouette against the brightness outside. A tall lady of gracious posture entered the room, pausing just inside the entrance. Her porcelain white face sported a look of consternation, an expression which made it abundantly clear she was very upset, very upset indeed, but she didn't appear intimidated or frightened.

Baxter looked towards Magali. 'I think you'd better explain all this to your grandmother, she doesn't look too happy.'

'Grandmother!' the woman bellowed at the top of her voice. 'I am no one's grandmother,' she declared. 'Just who are you and what are you doing in my house? I'm going to call the police.'

Baxter looked at Magali once again. 'What's all this about Magali?' he said waiting for an explanation.

She didn't reply, but sheepishly looked away from him.

The woman suddenly spotted the porcelain stand on the side table. She walked over to it and pinched the neat pile of plaster dust between her fingers. 'What on earth have you been doing here? How dare you violate my property?'

'I think madam, there has been a misunderstanding.' Baxter began. 'You're going to have to help me out here,' he said turning to Magali, 'perhaps you should show the Countess what you've got behind your back,' he suggested, hoping this might alleviate the situation.

'So tell me, you,' she pointed to Magali, 'yes, you, the woman who claims to be my granddaughter, what exactly *have* you got hidden behind your back?' Without a reply Magali spun on her heels and narrowly avoiding the Countess, dashed out through the open door. Baxter was stunned, and he suspected the Countess was equally astounded by Magali's unexpected behaviour.

He went to dash after her, but tripped clumsily on a rolled up carpet, his feet sliding out of control until he steadied himself. He spun around and almost collided with the bewildered woman.

'Sorry,' he said as he raced out through the doorway.

Outside, in the bright sunlight the courtyard was thronging with tourists, but he quickly spotted Magali running through the front gates. He sprinted after her, but as he neared the car park he watched her jump into her car, loudly grate the gears and disappear from view.

Her car, he thought to himself! How had she managed to get that here when she had travelled to France with him in his vehicle? In fact, come to think of it, she had left it in Jermyn Street. The Healey was surely still there.

He jumped in his car, the tyres spun on gravel, spitting it out over the flowerbeds as he followed in pursuit. He rapidly left the suburbs of Bourge-Vilaine behind and was soon on the open road heading north. As he accelerated harder he began catching sight of the rear of Magali's car as it careered around corners at far greater speeds than he could achieve. During the short time he had known her she had demonstrated that she could turn her hands to most things, but drive at speeds like that, he was frankly surprised.

The high-hedged lanes had now imperceptibly merged into an ascending mountain road. Although supposedly a main route into northern Brittany, the road at this point was only just wide enough for two cars to pass one another and in places where there was an overhanging rock, a layby was the only way two vehicles could possibly negotiate passage.

Baxter was trying to put the various pieces together as he sped after her. His mind kept working, desperately trying to understand what had just taken place, and more to the point, who was Magali? As a result of the intimacy they had shared together, he thought he knew who she was, but after this latest incident he realised he didn't. He had been completely fooled by the 'my grandmother' claim and obviously she did not after all have any aristocratic blood, but she did have the diamond.

What he couldn't understand was how she came to have the key to the chateau tower, and come to that, how did she know about the tower and what it contained?

He realised her telephone conversation in the car was also phoney; she was obviously talking to no-one at all. But she was taking a big risk just turning up and blatantly going into the tower. He guessed she thought with all the tourists milling about, two more wouldn't stand out. It was also quite a reasonable assumption that the Countess was unlikely to be wandering around, the aristocracy rarely do when the public are invading their property. But Magali had been wrong about that supposition.

He was suddenly brought back to his senses as he turned a sharp right, meeting another oncoming vehicle in the middle of the road. Baxter slammed on his breaks, the other car did not appear to spot him until the last moment when the driver veered violently right; he bounced against the rock face, crumpling the side of his car which slowed him significantly. Baxter stopped a few yards away, and looked back, but the other driver carried on.

He had lost vital minutes, and despite the near miss, he accelerated even more aggressively in his desperation to catch Magali up. A loud crunch up ahead was followed by the whining of an engine and then an explosion, loud and protracted. By the time he reached the broken fence, her car was a burning ball of flames, still bouncing nose over tail down the steep incline.

There was nothing he could do as he watched the vehicle burning on the lower section of snaking road two hundred feet below.

Baxter was speechless. He felt he should be doing something. A car passed by at speed, perhaps not noticing the broken fence, whether the driver did or not, he didn't stop.

The last thing Baxter wanted now was to get caught up with the local Gendarmes, so he jumped back in his car with the intention of turning it around. He hadn't done any more than switch on the ignition, when he realised the road back to Bourge-Vilaine would now be blocked by Magali's burning vehicle. That other car wouldn't be going much further either, once it reached the lower section of road.

He thumbed through his map book and discovered if he carried on up the hill there was an alternative way back to Bourge-Vilaine by heading first towards Rennes.

Baxter could have carried on back to Cherbourg and caught a late ferry home, but he suddenly had no appetite for making the long journey back to England. He had previously booked a hotel for the night for himself and Magali and so decided he needed to sort his head out before he could move on from this dramatic day.

After a much longer journey than anticipated, he arrived back in the mediaeval town shortly after five thirty. He bought a bottle of whisky from the bar, and lay on the large double bed trying to come to terms with the loss of his beloved Magali and all the things that had happened during that eventful day, a diurnal which had ended in such tragedy.

He only stopped the one night in the hotel, and despite a cracking hangover, the following day he made an early start for home.

Ten miles from Bourge-Vilaine he arrived at the spot where

Magali's car had impacted after careering off the road higher up and plummeting down the steep hillside. The sight before him was awesome, terrifying in fact. Her car had been pulled off the highway and left on the wide verge awaiting collection by a breakdown company. The Austin Healey was a blackened shell, it was down to bare metal with barely a trace of paintwork remaining. The chassis was twisted brutally out of shape and the roof had been crushed flat against the remains of the seats. Equipment had been used to forcibly open the front of the car which looked like a half opened tin can. There was no uncertainty that anyone could have survived such total destruction. Her body, or at least what remained of it would have obviously been removed. He only hoped her death had been a quick one, he fought hard, but couldn't stop the tears forming and then running down his face.

'Why Magali, why did you have to do this? I love you, I always will and I thought you loved me too, but you didn't, did you?' He pulled out his handkerchief to wipe his eyes. 'Please tell me I was wrong, because I couldn't bear to think it was all an act.' He placed a bunch of flowers by the car. 'Good bye Magali, God bless you, wherever you are.'

Baxter hadn't bothered to search her car or even the immediate area around the crash scene, the diamond was most likely to have been in her handbag which would have been burnt, exposing the non-combustible contents inside. The police would have found the stone as it was too large not to have gone un-noticed.

It was strange, but Baxter no longer cared about the diamond, and in a funny sort of way he was relieved his quest was over, he just hoped Veerman and the cartel saw it that way.

With a heavy heart he made his unhurried way home, but over-riding all the emotions her death were inflicting on his mind, he couldn't shake off the uneasiness that told him something wasn't quite right, in fact, a few things were positively wrong. Something had happened in that room in the chateau tower, that just didn't make any sense. Was it the way Magali had pointed the way to the hidden base, that had certainly been very fortuitous; or was it the sudden appearance of the Countess? And, how did Magali manage to drive away in her car, which he knew without any doubt, had been in London the day before?

He kept going over the events in slow motion; the images flashed by like an old film, faded and partly missing a few of the frames.

The realisation gradually dawned on him that the gap between perception and reality had grown to the extent that he was never going to tie all the loose ends together, not now, following Magali's death; she had taken with her, too many vital clues. There would always be far more questions than any answers that might reveal themselves in the future; of that he felt certain.

CHAPTER 18

DOUBLE CROSS

It had been a fortnight since he had returned home to his cottage, but Baxter was still struggling to come to terms with the loss of Magali.

With the help of a glass or two of whisky, sleep should have come easily, but his sleep pattern had been dreadful ever since her death and was fuel for two different dreams. The most common was seeing Magali desperately trying to escape from the burning car, it often woke him in the middle of the night and he would be sweating profusely.

The other dream always seemed to kick in just before waking up. It was a more graphic vision which portrayed Magali running towards him with her arms open wide. This dream always brought the bleakest of torments when he realised his mind had once again been tricked by the short-lived moments of happiness, before shattering his illusions the moment he woke.

He turned the radio on and the evocative lyrics of Katie Melua filled the room. *'This is the closest thing to crazy I have ever been, how can I have got in so deep? Why did I fall in love with you?'* He quickly changed channels, unable to come to terms with those poignant words. The Richard Allinson late night show provided a more sedate music selection with light chat and humorous banter. It was so much easier to listen to and contained no thought evoking sentiments, so he was able to mull over the situation as it stood.

Baxter at last felt quite safe in the belief that he was unlikely to be bothered any more over the diamond. Veerman's Chinese agents would have kept him up to speed in regards to the recent events in Bourge-Vilaine so he would know all about Magali's tragic death.

But what had changed in Baxter's reckoning was the irrefutable fact that she had been working for Veerman all the time and he,

Baxter, had been merely a pawn in her plans. Veerman would have guessed Magali had found the diamond; in fact she had probably telephoned him and told him so. His agents would have searched the scene, but did they find the stone? Or did the police discover it; if so was it secreted away by a dodgy inspector. He concluded that he would probably never know any of the answers to these questions.

The only point which still puzzled him was why had there been no mention of the robbery on the national news. Surely the Countess de Couvegne would have been furious after they ran off, Magali with the stone and him on her heels. A diamond of that size would have been priceless, but there had been no knocking on his door, no inquisitive police questions. Something was not quite right, but he couldn't quite put his finger on it. He knew he should let these last unsolved strands go, but that wasn't in his nature, it was going to be a very long time before that was going to happen

Max Veerman was a happy man today, he had worked tirelessly to achieve success, but his latest coup had eclipsed everything else he had ever done. He picked up the large diamond sitting in pride of place on his desk and awarded himself a wide grin. At last he had the rock of Batuta, the largest diamond the world had ever known and one day it was going to make him very rich.

From the latter part of January, the twenty third to be precise, he'd had the feeling this was going to be his lucky year for it was the Chinese year of the dragon, considered the luckiest of all twelve in the Chinese zodiac.

'Ah there you are Magali, come here.' He put his arm around her, landing a perfunctory kiss on her forehead.

Most people would think them an unlikely couple, those knowing they were not father and daughter would guess it was her beauty and his money rather than age related compatibility.

Veerman was thirty years her senior, true he had looked after his figure but these days his white hair was rapidly receding around the edges cancelling his faltering attempts to look younger than he hoped to appear to others. Naturally he felt good when out in her company, it flattered his ego like nothing else. He was used to other men looking at her, wondering if he was her father. But he would make a point of shattering their illusions and perhaps hopes, by giving her a lingering kiss in front of them. He felt no particular feelings for her, except when she pleased him in bed, and she did that very well.

Equally he felt certain her feelings towards him were motivated by greed, not just for his money, although she liked what it could buy. But he knew she also loved to soak up the power he emitted to all those around him.

Magali picked up the heavy rock. As she slowly turned it over, a brilliant light of many colours bounced off its facets. 'I suppose it is real?' she asked, flashing a look of considered doubt.

'Real.' Veerman chuckled 'of course it's real, I checked it myself with my thermal conductivity tester, it's certainly not zirconium dioxide, I can tell you that.'

'I see,' she said softly; then smiled to herself.

He noticed a look of uncertainty on her face. His ego demanded that he clarify why, as usual, he was right. 'You see cubic zirconia is a thermal insulator while diamond is one of the most efficient thermal conductors of any mineral and this stone is a first class thermal conductor.'

'That's alright Max, I believe you,' she said dismissively. As usual he had impressed her with his diverse knowledge. He was rarely lost for words or unacquainted with any aspect of what was under discussion. He made a point of doing his homework before showing his hand, and was always one step ahead of the rest, no matter how technical the conversation might be.

'Mind you,' he said thoughtfully, 'it's mostly down to you, you're the one who managed to snatch it for me.'

'I hope you remember that Max, it wasn't an easy thing to achieve, believe me.'

'Oh I most certainly will,' he stressed. 'You are such a clever woman. I knew you would pull it off and you did.'

'But never again Max, don't ever ask me to do cloak and dagger work like that again, get your goons to do it next time.'

'Magali, you know the Shāqi can't be trusted to carry out sensitive tasks like that, it requires someone with… well, someone like you,' he said with a half-smile. He went on. 'They're fine when it comes to supporting roles, but they always go in heavy handed and more often than not kill someone and that can be very irritating and inconvenient at times.'

'Yes I suppose you're right,' she said, 'but that's it, I've done my bit now, haven't I?'

'Besides,' Veerman began, 'it can't have been that bad, you must have had many tricky situations when you were a Revenue and Customs investigator, I mean that's why I wanted you to work for me in the first place.'

'Is that what I am, another of your workers.' Alarm bells were beginning to ring. Was she anything other than another of Max's crowbars? She had prised the diamond from its rightful owner and dropped it in his lap, but was that all she was to him?

'Of course you're not just one of my workers.' he put his hand on her shoulder but she shrugged it off.

'Look,' he said 'I promise I won't ask you to do anything like that again.' *Or at least not for the time being,* he said to himself.

'That's alright then Max. 'She believed him and immediately sighed with relief. 'Mind you' she added as an afterthought, 'it *was* quite an adventure really.'

'Yes I'm sure it was,' said Veerman, 'pity we had to lose a Chinese agent in the process, but it was the only way we were going to shake off that chap Baxter. Luckily agents like that are easily replaceable.'

'Yes, but what a great idea to swop cars. Baxter had no idea he was chasing a Shāqi agent in my car, rather than me. But how did you know the man would go over the edge, surely you couldn't have planned that.'

'Quite simple really, a tiny hole in the break-fluid pipe allowed him to use his breaks quite normally for ten miles or so. But once the fluid ran out completely, he was suddenly and without any warning, left with no breaking pressure and at the sort of speeds I expected him to reach, sooner or later he was going to come a cropper on one of those treacherous bends.

'You think of everything Max.'

'Of course I do and that's why I'm successful and the likes of that Baxter chap are not.'

'I wouldn't mind betting he thinks the diamond is now in the hands of the local Gendarmerie,' she said. They both laughed, but inwardly she was crying.

'What about my car, are you going to get me another one to replace it?'

'I take it you took the hire car back?'

'Of course. So….' she said eyeing him.

'All in good time,' he said smiling.

'What happens about Baxter now Max, you're not going to chase after him anymore are you?'

'Do I detect a little spark of ardour between the two of you?'

'Well you did tell me to sleep with him, didn't you?'

'Fair point, but I didn't give you permission to enjoy it, did I?'

She didn't reply, but suddenly familiar feelings released dreadful pangs of longing, craving for his body nestling next to hers, rather than the old man sitting in front of her. Baxter was a lovely man, they had shared a wonderful experience together, but she had a serious agenda to consider. Life, she reflected, could be so cruel at times and sadly this was one of those times.

'I also told you to get him talking,' Veerman said brusquely, 'and use that transmitter to send back the recording, but you didn't record a thing did you.'

'He never mentioned anything about the vase,' Magali said 'or for that matter anything else of interest to us.'

'Well, I can tell you now that when Baxter sells his vase at Windsor and Park in a couple of weeks' time, I'll buy it to add to mine.'

'You're going to buy it!' she interrupted 'why, surely you don't need it now you have the diamond?'

'A pair is always far more valuable than a single specimen and this pair will be priceless when I take them back to China.'

'So what about Baxter?'

'Don't worry about him.'

'You are not going to....'

'Kill him, no of course not, but I'm disturbed by your obvious concern for him.' He dropped his lip to show he was irritated by her apparent betrayal of loyalty.

'How on earth are we going to sell the diamond though Max?'

'We,' he said giving her one of his dark looks, 'we... are not going to sell it, but when things have quietened down, perhaps in a year's time, I will sell *them*.'

'Them' she repeated puzzled at the sudden pluralism.

'Yes my dear, them. I could never sell a seven hundred and sixty five carat diamond, the largest polished stone in the world without proof of ownership. That Countess de Couvegne would dispute it straight away. No, next year I'll have it cut up and I'll be very wealthy, very wealthy indeed.'

'How wealthy Max?'

Veerman puffed, looked up at the ceiling. 'I suppose if it's cut into individual stones, then say ten million pounds, give or take a few hundred thousand.'

'That's very nice for you,' she said

Veerman noticed the look of disappointment on Magali's face. 'Don't worry there will be something in it for you,' he said and then quickly added, 'as long as you do as I ask and without question.'

That's exactly what I was worried about, she said to herself and somehow his last remarks confirmed her suspicions regarding his real motives towards her. Already she was putting into place contingency plans, plans which had to take into account the rapidly unravelling nature of her assignment. She was surrounded by wealth, but that wasn't the real reason why she was here acting the role of an ex-customs officer. She was going to have to come up with a tactic which would allow her to leave Veerman without compromising her goal. She didn't have a clue how she was going to achieve it, but she knew sooner or later the opportunity would present itself. In the meantime she would play her cards very close to her chest.

CHAPTER 19

LOT 52

It was now four weeks since the events at Bourge-Vilaine and Baxter had made a little progress towards putting the tragic consequences behind him.

He had received good news from David Salisbury, the Bond Street specialist who confirmed his vase was indeed the missing Henri de Montaigne piece and Salisbury suggested a pre-auction estimate of eight hundred thousand to one million two hundred thousand pounds.

His specialists had carried out extensive research and established beyond all doubt that this was the missing vase, the one removed from the Imperial Summer Palace in eighteen sixty and sent to France by Henri de Montaigne.

The Chinese Government, as expected, had sent a representative over from Beijing to examine the piece. This was followed by a diplomatic request for repatriation from the Chinese cultural representative, but their request had been respectfully rejected.

The catalogue description described lot fifty two as;

The Henri de Montaigne vase.

An exceptionally rare temple vase with ovoid body and expanding neck with two elephant-head handles complete with horns, decorated in ch'ing-pai under- glaze cobalt blue. Round the body a four clawed dragon among clouds with waves below, above flying phoenix amid cloud scrolls. The neck with overlapping leaves. On one side it is reserved by a Sanskrit inscription.

Yuan period circa 1350. 85.5cm.

Note; X-ray spectrographic analysis produced 0.1 Mn/Co. counts cobalt to manganese ratio. Research laboratory for Archaeology, Oxford.

Provenance:
1) Removed from Hall of Benevolence and Longevity, Summer Palace, Peking China 1860.
2) In possession of General Henri de Montaigne, Brittany France.
3) Possibly Mr. Pope London 1908 sold to Unknown buyer.
4) Sunbury bought by the vendor from unknown seller 2010.

The lot details were accompanied by no fewer than twelve full-colour photographs and a few references to similar pieces world-wide.

The auction room in Bond Street fell silent when lot fifty two was announced. There had been considerable publicity for this impending sale, and this particular lot had been heralded as a once in a lifetime opportunity to acquire one of the finest examples of Imperial porcelain from outside China.

Because of its value, it had been designated as a Premium lot, which meant only bids from registered buyers who had left a substantial deposit, would be allowed to place bids.

Baxter sat discreetly in the office watching the large one hundred and fifty centimetre television screen which was split in two. One half, recording the proceedings on the rostrum and the other simultaneously recording the bidding public, in such a way it gave him a bird's eye view of the entire proceedings.

The auctioneer on his round pulpit-like rostrum began.

'Lot fifty two is next, Ladies and Gentlemen.' He pointed to the video screen, waiting while the twelve images rotated on the slide show. Baxter felt a pang of pride mixed with a dread of failure as he watched the slide show from the comfort of a leather settee in the auctioneer's office.

The auctioneer continued 'This lot is illustrated and described in your catalogue and eight hundred thousand starts it.' He scanned the room then pointed with outstretched hand. 'Eight hundred thousand, thank you.' The maiden bid came from the centre of the room. The auctioneer standing with arms apart, hands resting on the rostrum, continually surveyed those gathered in front.

'Nine hundred thousand,' rang out from his assistant manning one of the lines of telephones on his right.

'One million, it's this side of the room now, one million pounds, do I see one million two hundred and fifty?'

'Yes sir,' came the response from the assistant taking a telephone bid.

Baxter was beside himself, he could barely handle the excitement. His journey over the last few months was coming to a satisfying and happy ending. The adventure had been long and at times arduous, like a roller coaster gaining momentum or a small snowflake rolling downhill until it becomes as large as a boulder.

'It's one million two hundred and fifty thousand pounds on the telephone,' said the auctioneer. 'Do I have one million five hundred?' The two assistants assembled at a table on his left, scanned the room for any sign of another bid. One spotted a discreet bid and pointed. These bids could often be little more than a wink or a nod, and until an interested buyer began bidding, they could be difficult to spot. However, once the auctioneer had his bidders in sight, he knew exactly where to look each time.

'It's against you Nigel.' The auctioneer told the assistant taking the telephone bids. Then the internet came into play.

'I now have two million. It's against you in the room at two million pounds. Do I see two million five hundred anywhere?'

The pace was now slowing, despite a few telephone and internet bids still coming in.

'Thank you sir, two million five hundred. It's against you on the telephones and the internet at two million five hundred thousand pounds.'

He looked towards the telephones 'Do I see three million?'

'One more here Sir, two million seven hundred and fifty,' said his assistant watching the internet monitor.

He turned back to the room 'It's against you in the room at two million seven hundred and fifty thousand pounds.' The auctioneer caught the eye of the bidder in the centre of the room. 'It's not yours, one more sir?' he asked. The flicker of an eye took the bid to three million pounds.

'Do I see three million two hundred and fifty?'

The auctioneer eyed the telephone assistants who one after the other shook their heads.

'Fair warning now, I'm selling at three million pounds.' He waited for what seemed ages, although it was only seconds.

'One more Sir,' his telephone assistant shouted. And that was the end; the hammer came down at three million two hundred and fifty thousand pounds. It was followed by congratulatory applause.

At three times the estimate, the vase was acquired by an anonymous telephone bidder. Annoyingly Baxter was refused any information regarding the successful buyer, although he suspected it was probably a Chinese purchaser, or perhaps Veerman and the cartel. One way or another, he didn't expect to ever see it again.

From now on Baxter hoped his life was set to be rather more comfortable. Within three or four weeks he would receive a cheque from Windsor and Park and even after their commission, he would still have a tidy sum to put away.

He found himself considering different options, some money orientated, but others closer to his heart and on the top of his list was a determination to encourage the police to delve further into Hadley's death. He knew Max Veerman and the cartel were behind it but did he have enough proof, in fact did he have any shred of evidence save for the photograph of Hadley's book in their offices. Despite having absolutely nothing incriminating to take to the police, he wasn't intending to rest until the death of his friend Adrian Hadley had been explained and the culprits behind bars.

Back in his Chelsea cottage he sat back and as he sipped his malt whisky he pondered. There were good days, not very many, but a few, and Baxter thought today had been one of the best in his life so far and certainly the most profitable. The only thing that darkened the edges of the day was that Magali wasn't here with him; that would have been the icing on the cake. He found it difficult to accept she would never know how successful the sale had been. Even good old Keith was on his way home following a holiday in the Maldives, so he had no one to share his celebration. As he raised his glass to absent friends he felt certain she was up there somewhere looking down on him, perhaps even regretting what she had done. Philosophising, he tried to put the last parts of the jigsaw together. There was little doubt she had used him in order to procure the diamond, but for herself or was it for Veerman?

It hurt when he remembered how Magali had betrayed his trust, but even so he refused to believe what they shared had been anything other than genuine. He found it easy to convince himself that Max Veerman must have had some sort of hold over her, after all the man had kidnapped Magali in an effort to force Baxter to hand over the vase. Perhaps, he pondered, she was the innocent party after all and what she did had been merely to protect him.

Tiredness and the effects of the alcohol were rapidly closing in and would shortly deny him the opportunity to come to any logical conclusions that evening. Perhaps, he considered there were after all no logical explanations to be found and if there were, maybe he was passed caring anymore.

CHAPTER 20

TRUE COLOURS

Max Veerman was jubilant, he had successfully outbid all interested parties at the London auction house and bought the second Henri de Montaigne vase for a touch under three million four hundred thousand pounds including buyer's premium.

The hammer price was probably half a million over its true value, and that was why the other bidders dropped out, but he now had a pair which would be worth nearer ten million pounds to the right people and he knew exactly where to find the right people and it was not here in the United Kingdom, but on the other side of the World in China.

This hadn't been a cartel purchase, in fact he had taken pains to keep quiet about his intentions to buy, knowing full well the cartel representatives in Hong Kong had red flagged it. This meant he was forbidden to bid against them, but he had, and beaten their internet increments.

He knew he was going to have to be smart when the time came to sell the vases as a pair, because they would need provenance which would then expose him as the buyer of this particular one.

The cartel was unlikely to be impressed so he wasn't entirely certain how he was going to reinvent them, but that would be a few years down the line. In the meantime he was going to enjoy them.

In his top floor luxury penthouse apartment Max Veerman relaxed in his leather armchair, gazing at the vases, luxuriating in their beauty.

As a pair they were a sight he thought he would never see. He couldn't take his eyes off them; he bent down and kissed them as though they were animate objects. He laughed, he had never been happier before in his whole life. He couldn't believe it, but standing in front of him were both the Henri de Montaigne vases.

He had acquired the first one some forty years earlier and spent every day during that time searching worldwide auction details for the missing one. Max had even dreamt of stumbling onto it in a small English antique shop tucked away in rural Sussex, but after all those heart-wrenching years, here it was side-by-side with its pair.

'So that's it, is it?' Magali scoffed as she entered the room. 'That's the vase you paid over three million pounds for.'

'Yes it is and isn't it a beautiful sight, don't you think I'm clever?'

'Clever! You're crazy Max. Three million pounds for that... I think Baxter's the one who's clever.' She laughed mockingly.

'What...' bellowed Veerman 'how dare you question what I buy, or how much I've paid for it, or for that matter, what it's worth. And I can tell you now, Baxter might think he's clever, but we will see.'

'Was it worth the lives of five people though Max?'

Veerman sprung from his chair and with rage in his eyes lurched at Magali striking her across the face with the back of his hand. She didn't shy away, but turned her head at the impact and laughed.

'You bitch, you're laughing at me,' he screamed clenching his fists into tight balls.

'Yes I am, you pathetic old man,' she said with as much venom as she could gather.

Suddenly, he completely lost his composure and punched her in the face first with his left fist followed rapidly by his right. His second blow landed with such force that it spun her around sending her plunging backwards straight into the first Chinese vase which fell heavily against the second one.

Veerman froze, staring as she lay sprawled on the ground amidst the shattered fragments of his two prized Chinese vases.

He screamed, 'what have you done, my vases, my beautiful vases.'

She had never heard a grown man scream like that before.

'You're going to pay for that and dearly. How could you do that to me? They were worth a fortune and look at them now.'

'You did it yourself Max,' she said straightening her legs, 'you broke the vases when you punched me.'

She thought he was going to cry but then his face changed and once again he became like a wild animal.

As she struggled to her feet he punched her in the stomach and then as she stooped, he lifted her head and when she looked up, his fist struck her face yet again. She could have fought back, she was certainly more than capable of taking care of herself, but she knew she had to grin and bear it. Retaliation at this stage would blow her cover. She took a breath and swallowed 'You bastard, I'm leaving you Max, you've hit me one time too many.' She reached in her jeans pocket and switched on her R.240 audio transmitter, a tiny flat device only four centimetres square which could detect a whisper up to thirty five feet away.

This was a very clever device. When Max first gave it to her in order that she could secretly record Baxter, he placed a sim card into it, sent a text message from her cell phone to the sim in the device, and that provided a unique link. Now she was going to use it against him.

'I suppose you're going to your fancy man now, are you?' he goaded her, 'Well make the most of it because I have a contract out on him already. I can promise you this, he'll be dead by this time tomorrow, if not sooner.'

'You like killing people don't you Max.'

'I don't kill them, I get my agents to do it, but yes, I do enjoy removing anyone who gets in my way.' He made a slashing motion across his neck and laughed, it was a sickening gesture which sent shivers down her spine.

'I wonder how many people you've had killed Max. Is it just the five I know about or is it six or maybe ten?'

'A lot more than that, I can assure you and I haven't finished yet, not by a long chalk.'

'Like Professor Hadley and that chap Didier, not to mention several Chinese agents and goodness knows how many others I don't even know about.'

'You don't know half of it. You don't think I got where I am now by being Mr. Nice Guy, do you?'

'No, I know that now, but why are you so determined to add another innocent life to your list?'

'It's all arranged, Baxter will meet his maker and that's all there is to it. I couldn't stop it now even if I wanted to, and I don't.'

'You bastard, and will you kill me as well, now I'm no longer of any use to you?'

'Probably.'

'Just who do you think you are, come on tell me?' she screamed.

'Who am I? I'm Max Veerman and you of all people should know by now, no one crosses me and that includes you.'

Veerman dropped to his knees and scooped up a handful of porcelain shards. 'Look what you've done to my beautiful vases, my beautiful Henri de Montaigne vases.'

His words fell on deaf ears because Magali had by now, fled the room and was in the lift, on her way out of the building.

CHAPTER 21

A CHANGE OF ALLEGIANCE.

It was shortly after eleven o'clock on just another day, or so he thought, when he had first jumped out of bed a couple of hours earlier. Baxter was wiping away the foam after his usual early morning shave, when his peace was shattered by a loud and persistent banging. He pulled on his dressing gown, tying the cords as he made his hurried way to the front door.

Baxter was speechless, he couldn't believe what his eyes were telling him, he blinked but the image standing before him didn't change or go away. This was impossible he told himself, it just wasn't happening, how could it possibly be?

'Hello Baxter.' The voice was hesitant and nervous.

'Magali, I…. I thought you were dead,' he uttered in surprise. He placed his hands on her shoulders and sure enough she was real. He shook her gently.

'What the hell's going on?' he stared at her, finding it difficult to find anything else to say, such was his state of shock.

There was a feral look in her eyes, eyes which were wide with fear and despair. This was the same fear he had seen on Didier's face that night in the bar Rat de Cave.

A car passed by and she put her right foot forward onto the doorstep. 'Please Baxter, let me in quick, I'm in big trouble, please help me.' She shook off an involuntary shiver. He read her body language which clearly expressed a state of urgency, heightened by the way she changed the weight from one leg to the other as she shuffled from side-to-side in the poorly lit doorway.

Baxter remained in a state of bewilderment; he neither welcomed her in nor slammed the door in her face. In desperation she pushed past him, pausing in the hallway, panting as she tried to regain her composure.

Baxter closed the front door and walked past her. She followed him into the sitting room.

He spun her around to face him. 'Who did this to you Magali, I want to know what's going on?' he demanded.

Her face was as white as chalk and her eyes were ringed with swelling, dark and ugly. He could see emotion rising in her pitiable face and then she lurched forward flinging her arms around him. He tried to push her away but she clung onto him desperately, her arms embracing him with every ounce of her summoned strength. His heart melted and he quickly gave in and put his arms around her, holding her tightly, she winced and gave a tiny shout.

'You're hurt, what on earth has happened to you?' he cocked his head curious, waiting for an explanation, transfixing her eyes, his own holding her gaze, denying her any opportunity to look away.

'I'm alright,' she replied unconvincingly dropping her eyes from his gaze. He noticed her fingers nervously playing with the pearls on her necklace. He detected an unfamiliar shyness in her manner, her body language was declaring a reluctance to open up in front of him, a disinclination to explain how and why she was standing there in his sitting room all those weeks after her supposed death.

'I'm afraid to ask but...'

'Well don't then,' she said petulantly through her tears.

Baxter was still bristling 'I must Magali, I have to know what this is all about and what sort of game you're playing. I'm confused and I need answers.' He closely watched her every reaction, but her face was blank as she continued to stare at the floor.

'Look you can't expect me to just accept that you've returned, I think you owe me a little more than that, don't you?'

She opened her mouth as though to say something, but seemed to think the better of it and closed it again.

Magali knew she had to curb her emotions and be very careful what she told him. The truth could only be divulged in part, she so longed to tell him everything, but couldn't. Her mind was working overtime trying to find words to change the subject, but they didn't arrive quickly enough.

'Well, what's the story then and I don't want a pack of lies this time?' he stood with hands on hips waiting.

Magali's face gave little away. Baxter could see she was deciding whether to answer his question, or perhaps more likely how to answer it, with or without lies.

'Can I sit down and I'll tell you everything I promise and then you can tell me to leave if you want to, and I expect you will.'

Baxter eyed her closely 'I think that would be a very good idea, telling the truth, that is, so sit down then.'

'You're not making this very easy for me, Baxter.'

'Easy!' he said, 'I don't think you have the slightest idea what you've put me through?'

'Sorry,' she said, looking passively back at the floor.

Baxter still couldn't come to terms with what was going on here. *I can't believe you're still alive,* he said to himself, *if only you knew how I've cried for you,* he wanted to tell her but his male pride made such an admission quite impossible.

'Look at me,' he said

She slowly raised her head.

'My God, your poor face, Magali.' In the lightness of his sitting room he saw for the first time just how badly hurt she was. Suddenly all feelings of hostility and self-hurt were extinguished and he only felt compassion. He knelt and looked closely at her face. It was a different face from the one he knew, a pale complexion distorted by tears and re-shaped by several black bruises around her eyes which were no longer sparkling and green, but slowly closing to a narrow darkened slit. Her lips were swollen and bore traces of dried blood. He went to the bathroom and returned with a basin of warm soapy water and gently bathed her face and then went off and came back with two ice packs.

'Hold these tightly against the bruises; it should take down the swelling. I think I should call you a doctor?'

'No, please don't do that.' she replied quickly, 'I don't need a doctor.'

'Okay, but I can't do any more in the way of first aid.'

'Thank you, Baxter. I don't deserve you,' she said softly.

'Well to be honest with you, at the present time, I have to agree with that.'

Once again her face crumpled and she burst into tears, an uncontrollable emotion which was difficult to question.

If this is an act he said to himself, *then it's a bloody good one.*

He raised her head and cupped her face in his hands and planted a kiss on her lips. It was intended to be no more than a calming gesture, but her arms encircled his neck once again and denied him the opportunity to pull away.

She was still shaking when he handed her a crystal tumbler generously filled with single malt Scotch whisky.

'I don't really like whisky' she protested.

'I'm not giving you something to like, it's medicinal so drink it, all of it,' he ordered. As she gingerly sipped the drink she smiled and appeared to brighten slightly.

He crossed the room, poured himself a dram and then returned and sat in front of her, swirling the amber liquor around in his tumbler. 'Drink it,' he said taking a mouthful himself.

Magali screwed up her face as she obediently took a sip, and then choked a little.

'It's very strong.' She gasped.

'It will make you feel a lot better in a minute or two, now just drink it, all of it.'

She forced the last of the Scotch down and asked for some water. As he sat back in his armchair he noticed the colour was gradually returning to her cheeks as the alcohol brought upon the desired calming effect, but with her eyes now glazed, he realised the drink might have gone straight to her head.

He downed the last of his drink and leant forward and raised his eyebrows in an attempt to coax her into making some sort of explanation.

Even though he knew he might not like what Magali had to say, he needed to hear her excuses, if she had any, and her reasons for betraying him the way she had.

'So are you feeling a bit better now?'

'Thank you,' she replied holding his stare. There was now a strange calmness on her face and she almost managed a smile.

'So first of all, tell me who did that to you?'

She didn't respond but disengaged his gaze, looking once more at the floor.

'Was it those Shāqi agents who were after you before?

She looked up, knowing full well the reaction she would invoke when she told him the truth. 'It,' she paused, took a deep breath, 'it was Max Veerman.'

'Veerman,' he shouted, 'Veerman did that to you.' He stood up 'I'm going to kill that bastard, he's gone too far this time.'

'Sit down Baxter,' she pleaded, 'I will try and explain, but I have to tell you the whole story right from the beginning or otherwise it won't make any sense.'

'I'm all ears,' he said waiting for what he expected would be a string of feeble excuses. Baxter felt he should be more sympathetic, but was anxious to hear her explanation.

Magali took a deep breath, hesitated and then sighed. 'You might not like what I'm going to tell you and you probably won't like me either by the time I get to the end, but I'm going to tell you the truth this time.' *But not the whole truth,* she said to herself.

'Just tell me, and then I'll tell you what *I* think.'

She sat back deciding how much she needed to tell him. She lit a cigarette using the brief interval to decide on a tactical approach. She realised her explanation would have to be comprehensive, but she still had to take great care what she did reveal, she couldn't possibly compromise her position, which was tenuous at best.

'This is right from the beginning,' she said grabbing the last few seconds of thinking time before committing herself to what she was going to say and what she was not.

'Right.'

'Well, as you know I was born in nineteen seventy five in Brittany where I had quite an unremarkable childhood, living with my French parents. At the age of seventeen they sent me off to the Catholic University of Paris where I studied at the Institut de Langue et de Cultures Anglaise.'

Baxter raised his eyebrows. 'Impressive,' he said. ''no wonder your English is so good; sorry, do go on.'

'While I was there I managed to get a Baccalaureate in English language. After that I went on to the American Business School in Paris.' She suddenly looked upset as though the story was coming to a sad episode.

'Go on.' Baxter urged.

She pulled herself together. 'It was tragic really, because a few days after arriving at the University my father who worked for the French Government in Northern Spain was tragically killed in a car accident in the Pyrenees.'

'I'm so sorry,' he said butting in, 'that must have been heart-breaking for you.'

'It was a difficult time I must admit.' She composed herself but the sadness remained in her eyes. 'After three years of study I obtained a degree in humanities and as there was nothing to keep me in France, I moved to London.'

'I'm sorry to interrupt, you say there was nothing to keep you in France, but what about your mother?'

'Now things at home were a bit tricky after my father died, you see my mother never forgave him for making her a widow. She blamed him as though he had done it deliberately, poor dad.

Anyway, six months later I had a telephone call saying she had died overnight from a heart attack.'

'Poor you.' Baxter was genuinely sympathetic as he took her hand and gripped it tightly. 'So what did you do in London?'

'I applied for a civil service position and I think because of my good English, they offered me a post with Revenue and Customs.

'Revenue and Customs, wow,' he exclaimed.

'It wasn't that remarkable really, I can assure you. As a probationer I spent nine months back behind a school desk learning the legal and admin aspects of R & C followed by a year of tactical training in Sussex. At the end of all that and much to my amazement they offered me a job as a fraud investigation officer.'

'I can see now why you're so gritty.'

'Gritty!' she said shooting him a look.

'Well you know what I mean, let's say tenacious.'

She didn't reply, but gave him a dogged stare.

'So are you telling me you're still with Revenue and Customs?'

'No.' she was quick to reply. 'I spent three months as part of a team investigating one of Max Veerman's off-shore companies. I suppose I got too close and when he turned on the charm,' she shrugged, 'I fell under his spell.'

'What, romantically?' he said in amazement.

'I thought so at the time, but I made a serious mistake as that liaison compromised my position, and of course I now realize Veerman orchestrated events so that it would do just that.'

'Sounds about right,' he said.

'Anyway, I had no choice but to hand in my resignation to Revenue and Customs and after that I moved in with him in his penthouse apartment above Gallery Twenty One.'

Baxter said 'Do you know, it crossed my mind at one stage that there might be more to you than met the eye.'

She didn't respond, but went on 'I made the mistake of thinking I was there by virtue of my attraction, but I kept being asked, no told, to carry out the odd covert job for him and because of my previous training, it was difficult to say no. It was at that time when I started to question his true feelings towards me.'

Baxter was beginning to fear the worst as he chewed over what she was telling him.

'So I take it, I was one of your covert jobs, was I?'

She agonized over the question, but knew she was going to have to answer it sooner or later. She looked at his face to try and gauge his reaction, but he gave nothing away. She held her breath. 'Yes you were, but please believe me when I say it was against my better judgement. Even though I didn't know you then, I knew the kind of things Max got up to and the ruthless way he carried out his business. So yes, I agreed to go down to Bourge-Vilaine to keep an eye on you.'

'Just a minute.' He interrupted. 'I can't imagine how on earth Veerman knew I was going to Bourge-Vilaine in the first place, I told no one, not a soul.'

'It was a Mr. Fresne.'

'Fresne,' he repeated, I can't believe it.'

'You of all people should know the antiques world in London is a small close-knit community, you've got a reputation, so when word got out that you were off to France, people like Max took note. He knew a potentially interesting vase was due to be auctioned and put two and two together and presumed you were there to bid on it as well; you see even though he wasn't certain if he even wanted the piece, he needed to make certain no one else got their hands on it, and especially not a small face like you. They were his words not mine.' She added quickly.

'So you weren't there for the Couvegne letters then?' Baxter asked.

This was a tricky point of contention and one she couldn't answer entirely truthfully. 'No, I didn't know anything about them, we didn't even know they existed,' she lied, 'but then we had no reason to. The ironic part is that without them, the link to the diamond would have been lost forever.'

She went on to explain how Marcel Didier was questioned by their agents down in Bourge-Vilaine.

'Question him, that's a joke,' Baxter said cynically.

'No, actually they were only trying to find out exactly what he had been telling you. You see they thought he knew about the Chinese vase, and maybe he did, but we now know it was details about the letters which he was selling you.'

'Yes and what a waste of time and money that turned out to be,' he said raising his brow.

She went on, 'Didier was very drunk when he left that bar and stupidly went to swing a punch at one of our men, when he tripped and fell down a long flight of steps.'

'Sounds very convenient to me, especially as the steps where they found his body were some fifty metres away from the bar.'

'Actually, I agree. I think there was more to it than that, because apparently he ended up with a knife in his chest.'

'And a Shāqi note pinned to his back,' Baxter added.

'I didn't know about that,' she said frowning, 'Max never mentioned anything about notes.'

'He probably didn't even know,' Baxter added 'The Shāqi are a law unto themselves if you ask me.'

Magali said 'They searched his pockets and found a key with a tag which was labelled 'Chateau de Couvegne tour Ouest'. They also found a copy of a letter he had written to a Philippe Fresne in London telling him about some documents. The letter went on to describe a room in the west tower at the chateau, saying how, as gardener there, he could lay his hands on wonderful Chinese treasures.'

'So that's how Fresne got involved,' Baxter said, 'of course, and that's how the information found its way to my door.'

These revelations suddenly answered a lot of questions for which he had hitherto been unable to find a satisfactory explanation, in fact to a large extent, any explanations whatsoever.

'So am I correct in thinking it was you who followed me to the Rat de Cave bar that night?'

'Yes it was,' She said hesitantly. 'You see at that time we didn't know where you were going or who you were intending to meet, but we suspected you might have an accomplice or local informant and so it was vital we knew who that was.'

Suddenly another unexplained event required clarification and he felt certain she was going to have the answer he was looking for.

'Tell me Magali,' he hesitated for a moment, uncertain whether the answer he suspected might follow was one he even wanted to hear. 'Do you know who fired a shot outside the bar Rat de Cave the night I was mugged?'

She was slow to respond but after a moment or two said quietly, 'Yes I do.'

'So…' he looked at her, waiting for a reply.

'Do you really need to know, because after all, whoever it was, they were looking out for you, possibly even saved your life.'

'Yes I do, because I think I know exactly who it was, but I can't quite convince myself that I'm right.'

'So… who do you think it was then?' she said deliberately attempting to be dismissive.

'I think it was you Magali, but I hope you're going to tell me it wasn't, because I'm finding it very difficult to accept you were walking around with a gun in your handbag. I mean, what sort of woman does that?'

'The sort of woman who is frightened carries a gun for her own protection. Max suggested I take it, even though I didn't have a clue how to use it. Just flick the safety catch and pull the trigger,' he said and that's just what I did when I saw you being attacked.'

'You certainly are quite a girl aren't you?'

'I don't know, am I?' she questioned coyly

'What about Avranches?' he asked.

'Well, when you managed to buy the vase from under everyone's noses, all hell broke loose. Max ordered an e-notice.'

'An e-notice?' he stopped her in mid-sentence and gave her a puzzled look, one which demanded an explanation.

'That's the second highest alert for assistance. It would have been circulated by e-mail and telephone firstly to Shāqi agents, then to various people in high places like police chiefs and others.'

'Police chiefs and others?' he queried. 'That man certainly has a lot of clout to have people like that under his control.'

'You don't know the half of it and even I don't really know who he has under his cloak, but I believe there are even representatives from the British Government in his circle.'

'Did he ever mention an Inspector Monroe?'

'No, not that I can remember, but he certainly knew a number of faces in the police force. Anyway, then you disappeared from under our noses; I don't know how you managed that, but I got a good shouting at over it.'

Baxter told her how he had taken his car to a tyre and exhaust centre and asked them to deliver it back to his hotel. He explained how he ordered a taxi and took the vase to Rennes, where a shipping company arranged for its safe passage to England.

'Clever,' she said, 'that fooled us. Anyway after you disappeared from our radar I got a message to say our Shāqi agent had spotted you and was on your trail. Half an hour later we heard our agents were dead. We were then informed that you had been taken to Avranches police station. That caused real panic because there were no agents left in Brittany, so Max told me to go straight to Avranches. Well I can tell you that really frightened me, to be told to track down a killer.'

'I didn't actually kill those Chinese agents you know; they tried to force me off the road and even fired shots at me.'

'They shot at you!' she said with a baffled look.

'Yes, or at least at my car, but they came off the worse for wear when the two of them went over the side of the bridge and ended up at the bottom of a ravine. But why were you ordered to rush to Avranches?'

'Max needed someone to check your car to see if the vase was still in it, although I think he suspected it would probably be with you in police custody by that time. Anyway, when I telephoned Max to tell him it wasn't in your car, he said the police mustn't be allowed to take any action against you for Didier's death or the bridge accident.'

'Why on earth not, surely that would've been exactly what he would have wanted.'

'No, quite the opposite, because you see, he was frightened we might never find the vase if you remained in police custody.'

'So how did you fix it for me to be released?'

'It was Max not me, as I said before, he has friends in many high places, and the French Inspector's superior was one of those *friendly faces*, as he liked to call them.'

'And the incident outside the pub in London when those heavies tried to grab you, what was that all about?'

'That was nothing to do with Max. It was another rival Chinese gang, who it seems, thought they could get at you by kidnapping me in order to force you to hand over the vase, and before you ask, the incident at the railway station was also a kidnap attempt by the same rival gang, I'm certain of that.'

'And Montmartre cemetery?' he asked

That again was nothing to do with Max or at least I don't think it was.'

'Well no, I know that was the Shāqi, but were they working in conjunction with that other gang or with Veerman or perhaps they are all in cahoots.'

'I know Max has close associations with the Paris Shāqi organisation, but I'm convinced he didn't know anything about what they did to you in those underground caverns, and besides, it wasn't going to produce the vase was it, in fact the very opposite.'

'Sh....,' he stopped her in mid-sentence and put his finger to his lips and listened. He could hear a curious sound, a clicking and scuffling. At first he couldn't decide where it was coming from so went to the door and listened in the hallway. The strange noises were coming from his front door and then he heard a jingle, like door keys rattling. At that moment he knew exactly what was going on.

'Someone's trying to pick my front door lock,' he whispered.

Suddenly a loud frantic banging interrupted the tranquillity of the cottage. The pounding was intense and accompanied by what sounded like someone putting their shoulder to his door; his new security door, which he had recently had installed at great expense.

'Down on the floor quick,' he whispered to Magali hitting the deck himself. He crawled over to the front window and looked out. The car parked opposite, although empty, looked ominous; he knew they were once again under surveillance.

'They must be surprised they can't gain entry like they did last time,' he said crawling back to where she sat.

Thank goodness he had invested in a new front door and high security deadbolt with the latest spring less mechanical locking technology; it had been expensive, but appeared to be already proving its worth.

There had been silence for several minutes. Baxter shuffled back across the room to the window. Peering cautiously behind the opened curtain he could see two Chinamen lounging in the front seats of the car parked opposite, and clearly not intending to go anywhere. He sidled over to the sideboard and poured himself another drink.

'I think we can safely say Veerman has men out there watching us, but I don't think they know we are here, I'm certain of that.'

'I didn't believe for one minute he would give in just like that,' she said.

'You can sit back on the settee now, but keep away from the window,' he said. 'Now going back to what you were telling me. I take it the time I was picked up and thrown in your friend Max's Daimler, that wasn't another rival gang was it?'

'No, you're right and this is the bit you're not going to like.'

'I don't like the way you say that.'

'Can't say it in any other way really, you see the note you were dropped and the kidnap operation on you, *was* carried out by Max's men.'

'I knew that, saw a telephone number on the screen next to the recording of you tied up and guess what? It was Gallery Twenty One who answered, or at least an automated recording.'

'But it was no more than a bluff and all part of a plot to force you to hand over the vase. Max was confident you would want to save my life and given the gravity of the situation he thought you would give in and do as he demanded.'

'Of course he did, and I admit I did fall for the phoney image of you trussed up and looking distraught, but I also doubted he would free you once he got his hands on the vase, that's not his style, or at least according to his track record it isn't.'

'Where Max went wrong,' she said smugly, 'he never dreamt for one moment you would find a way to break into Gallery Twenty One and try and rescue me. Max has always maintained his fortress was impregnable.'

'Nowhere,' he said, 'is completely invulnerable, there is always a weak spot somewhere, it's just that it's not always possible to identify, or for that matter, use it successfully. But in Veerman's case he didn't look beyond the obvious, his walls and doors were secure enough, but his car wasn't and that was his one big mistake.'

Magali went on 'When they discovered you hiding in his offices they suddenly had a big and unforeseen problem. There was no way you could supply them with the Chinese vase if you were detained in Gallery Twenty One and so it was decided you had to be allowed to escape with me, in fact to add credibility, the plan was for you to rescue me.'

'A clever piece of psychology that. Veerman obviously knows me better than I know myself. Anyway, go on.'

'After they locked you up in the basement room, Max told me I must help you to help me escape.'

'I think I get the gist,' he said.

'Actually I was furious at having to leave the comfort of the penthouse suite to spend the night sitting in a cold cell next to you. No one told me how I was supposed to communicate with you, but I remembered the radiator trick.'

'Remembered it from where?' He looked at her curiously.

She looked flustered, momentarily. 'Oh from my customs training course, we often used to listen to messages like that.'

'Did you?' he said. Baxter didn't believe that explanation for one moment. 'Still that was a clever idea all the same.'

She went on 'When the guard entered your cell he had already been instructed to accidentally leave the door open, but he wasn't expecting you to bash the daylights out of him. Max had instructed all his day shift security men to let you, or rather us, escape.'

'Obviously there were those who didn't listen to his instructions' Baxter added.

'How do you mean?'

'The ones who opened fire on us, or was that also a clever trick as well?'

'No it wasn't, those bullets were real enough, it seems no one informed the night shift guards down at the underground car park exit who were getting ready to go home, and that's why they opened fire on us.'

'What about that business of faking your death on the road from Bourge-Vilaine,' he asked 'and who did die in that accident?'

She once again found herself having to balance her reply and this time the equilibrium would be an imbalance of the true facts. She explained in detail how they switched cars in the car park after snatching the diamond from the Chateau de Couvegne. She went on to say that it had been one of Veerman's Chinese agents who went over the side to his death. 'Max never did replace my car though, so again I lost out.'

'You know.' he began 'losing you meant nothing,' he lied, his pride denied him any opportunity to express the desolation she caused by faking her death. 'But meeting you meant everything to me, it was the most marvellous thing that ever happened in my life.'

She lowered her head and simply said 'Sorry.'

'And what about the diamond?' he asked 'Where is that now?' As if he didn't know, but he thought he would ask anyway.

'Max, of course, has it, he was delighted with it.'

'I bet he was, and at my expense,' said Baxter.

'Don't be too disappointed; things might not be quite as you may think.'

'What do you mean by that?'

She suddenly realised she had said rather more than she should have, so back tracking she said 'Of course Max has it, but I can't say anymore, besides, you did quite well with your Chinese vase didn't you?'

'Yes I did, or at least I will once I get paid.'

'Now don't get upset.' She began. 'But do you know who bought your vase?'

'I didn't, but I think I do now and I daresay if it was Veerman and if, by chance he does have the other one to the pair, he'll make a tidy packet when he sells them on.'

'Oh no he won't,' she said with a giggle.

'What's so funny Magali?'

'Max lost over three million pounds buying your vase because it's now on his sitting room floor lying in a hundred fragments, alongside the other shattered vase.'

'What... how on earth, I don't believe it.'

She then went on to explain how Veerman had hit her and sent her hurling into them and in doing so destroyed both vases.

'I daresay he will have them insured, people like him never lose that kind of money,' he said.

'Actually I know for a fact he won't have either of them insured.'

'Why on earth not, surely he's not that stupid?'

'Because he bid against his cartel superiors, and that's a very serious misdemeanour. To insure them he would need to outlay large sums on an insurance policy, in fact potentially enormous sums unless he could cite the vaults as the secure depository.'

'Well surely that's what he would do,' he said.

'Well no, it's not quite as simple as that. You see if he claimed they were in the cartel's vaults, he would also have to pay the insurance policy out of cartel funds and the annual audit would expose the fact and they would crucify him.'

'I see and that's obviously why he's so fanatical about having the best security systems.'

'Quite.'

'So... what about your luxury apartment in Paris?'

She dropped her head and stared at the floor, 'Sorry' she said softly.

'I take it that was Veerman's as well?'

'Of course it was, I could never afford a place like that. It was his hospitality apartment, his place in the centre of Paris where he could entertain rich clients and demonstrate his power and financial standing. I don't have anything. What you see before you is a lie, a through and through body of deceit and I don't blame you if you never want to see me again.'

Baxter refilled his glass and offered the bottle to Magali, who shook her head and then proceeded to light a cigarette.

'Do you know, I thought I knew you Magali,' he said regretfully, 'but I've come to realize that I didn't know you at all? I can't believe you told me all those lies and what an act you put on for me; you deserve an Oscar for those performances.'

His only weapon now was to walk away, but could he ever do that; he liked to think he could, but in reality Baxter couldn't, not now.'

She stared at him long and hard 'What are you thinking?' she asked.

'I'll tell you what I'm thinking,' he said relieving the tension that had built up between them. 'You were using me to satisfy your own ends. Do you know, I was completely fooled by your act?'

She sniffed, and then anger suddenly suffused her face. 'I wasn't acting,' she replied sharply, 'I didn't know I was going to fall in love with you, that wasn't supposed to happen, it was unprofessional I know, but it happened the first time we met.'

Baxter reflected on what she had said.

She looked up and whispered in a quiet reflective voice, 'Do you honestly think all those times we shared together were part of an act? Okay, I admit I was caught up in a conspiracy to help Max get his hands on your Chinese vase, but underlying my inability to escape his clutches was a love, so intense it incessantly tore me apart. I've never loved anybody in my life as I love you Baxter.'

He looked at her thoughtfully. He really didn't know what to think, he felt he just couldn't take the wounds her lies had inflicted upon him. He was determined not to take the bait, if that's what it was. He still wasn't one hundred percent convinced of her sincerity and he suspected she might be falling back on him as a last resort. She knew he was now wealthy, or at least soon would be, and she herself had admitted her loyalty to Veerman had been monetary led. Also he wasn't at all certain if she would fit into his world, a world of antiques and research, museums and stuffy auction rooms. And for that matter, he into hers, because she had enjoyed a very glamorous lifestyle of late, and whilst he would soon be able to match it, he wasn't intending to try.

He sat back in his chair and chewed over Magali's explanations.

He was aware that a certain familiar awkwardness had returned, one which he had experienced the first time he'd been close to her and despite their previous period of closeness, he felt as though they were starting all over again. Not from a point where they had left off, but fresh at the starting blocks, as strangers new to each other.

'You don't believe me do you?' she said breaking the silence, 'you think I'm still playing the part. Well I'm not, I love you, I loved you from the very start and that's all there is to it. I admit I've made a few mistakes'

'Wake up Magali, you've told me lie upon lie and you say you've made a few mistakes.'

'And I suppose you haven't, Mr. Squeaky Clean,' she said defensively, 'and besides I haven't lied to you, I've just kept some of the truth under wraps.'

'Point taken,' he grudgingly conceded, 'but what still worries me is what you might *not* be telling me now and what other skeletons you've got hanging in your wardrobe?'

'There's nothing else, that's everything,' she said. But she knew there was so much more she was holding back from him. She had only told him what she considered he need know, the bare minimum to support her account. The explanations she had come up with had been the best she could do on the spur of the moment and she knew Baxter didn't believe half of them.

Baxter on the other hand had decided he was going to reserve his judgment for the time being and play things carefully; she had deceived him once, so he was finding it difficult to trust her now. However, inwardly he knew he was going to falter, sooner or later. The thought of her warm body next to his was already raising his temperature, in the same familiar way it had so many times in the past.

Magali stubbed her cigarette out and indicated she wanted to use the bathroom. He nodded 'Help yourself, you should know where it is,' he said, slightly sarcastically.

While she was gone he quickly opened her handbag, riffled through the usual feminine necessities and then felt the outline of something heavy and unusual, it was a pistol. He heard the toilet flush and so clipped the bag shut and returned to his chair.

When she returned her eyes straightaway fell on her handbag. Her expression said she realised her mistake in leaving it there and the look she flashed him, Baxter thought, was reproachful.

'I only wish I had some proof that Veerman was behind all those murders,' Baxter said as she made herself comfortable.

'I have,' she replied looking up with an expression of relief.

'I very much doubt if your word would hold up against the class of legal team Veerman could muster. No Magali, we need something tangible, something which cannot be ignored or conveniently pushed under the carpet.'

'But I think *this* might be the sort of evidence you're looking for,' she said taking the cell phone out of her handbag.

'A mobile phone?' he laughed, 'I don't think so.'

'Just shut up and listen,' she said irritated by his flippancy. She tapped on the menu bar then played back the message which had been automatically sent from the tiny transmitter to her cell phone.

'I suppose you're going to your fancy man now are you?'

'Well, make the most of it because I have a contract out on him already. I can promise you this, he will be dead by this time tomorrow, if not sooner.'

'You like killing people, don't you, Max.'

'I don't kill them, I get my agents to do it, but yes I do enjoy removing anyone who gets in my way.'

'I wonder how many people you've had killed, Max. Is it just the five I know about, or is it six or maybe ten?'

'A lot more than that I can assure you and I haven't finished yet, not by a long chalk.'

'Like Professor Hadley and that chap Didier, not to mention several Chinese agents and goodness knows how many others I don't even know about.'

'You don't know the half of it. You don't think I got where I am now by being Mr. nice guy, do you?'

'No I know that now, but why are you so determined to add another innocent life to your list?'

'It's arranged, Baxter will meet his maker and that's all there is to it. I couldn't stop it now even if I wanted to, and I don't.'

'You bastard, and will you kill me as well now, I'm no longer of any use to you?'

'Probably.'

'Just who do you think you are, come on tell me?'

'Who am I? I'm Max Veerman and you of all people should know by now, no one crosses me and that includes you.'

'That's it, we've got him, this is more than enough to make certain he's locked away for life.' Baxter jumped to his feet and poured himself another drink.

'Be careful.' Magali warned. 'You don't know these people.'

'And you do?' He looked at her quizzically. 'Yes of course you do, don't you. By the way, where did you get that clever little device from?'

'Max gave it to me. I was supposed to record anything and everything you told me.'

He glared at her, then slammed his hand down hard on the coffee table and stood up, 'Oh that's charming, you really do know how to put the knife in, don't you? And here I was beginning to believe you were sincere after all, how wrong I was.'

She gave him a long wounded look. 'No Baxter, you've got it all wrong,' she said with soft dignity, 'I never once even turned it on. I wasn't going to put you at risk, you have to believe me.' She looked up at him with tears trickling down her cheeks.

Between the gentle sobbing he could see remorse in her eyes; eyes which had transformed into shades of warm sage brown, eyes which were saying she cared, and for the first time he believed those tearful eyes were conveying the truth. He walked over and took her hand, he felt her shudder at his touch. She responded by standing up and pressing her body close to his. Suddenly the familiarity of her sensuality hit him hard, he wished their clothes were not denying him the feel of her soft skin and despite fighting against them, those same old feelings had returned, sending a rush of blood through his veins.

Her anxiety and trauma had somehow only added to her sexuality. He put his arms around her and held her tightly and as she looked up he kissed her passionately. Sexual tension finally prevailed; he lifted her up and carried her into the bedroom.

CHAPTER 22

TIMELY RETREAT

'We must make a copy of that recording,' Baxter said suddenly, sitting up in bed. 'What's the best way?'

'There must be something here.' She paused, got out of bed and skipped into the sitting room. Magali returned a few minutes later and stuck her head round the bedroom door. 'I've got it,' she announced jubilantly. 'Can I use your computer?'

'Of course, help yourself,' he said, climbing out of bed, grabbing his clothes and putting them on as he hobbled after her. Magali walked over to Baxter's laptop and tapped it on. She plugged a tiny converter into the usb port and placed the cell phone sim card in the slot.

'Here you are, one copy, recorded and stored in your video library,' she declared proudly.

Baxter made two copies on compact discs and put a user password onto his windows log-in page, to make certain no one else had privy to its contents. He put one CD in his pocket and tucked the other inside his collection of musical discs.

'Is there any other evidence we could pass on to the legal authorities?' He asked.

Magali thought for a few seconds 'Veerman has a tiny tattoo on his arm, it's the Shāqi emblem.'

'What, with the four bats?'

'That's the one; all the members of the Cartel have it, they have to reveal the tattoo before meetings. It was devised over a century ago as a form of insurance to guarantee the member was genuine Shāqi. Mind you, all London members are registered with Veerman's voice waveform recognition system now, it's something he swears by, and it's standard security procedure.'

Something had just dawned on him. 'I suppose you are registered on his system as well then?'

'Of course,' she said, 'I would activate every alarm in the building if I wasn't, and before you ask, yes that's why the alarm didn't go off when I spoke in the car lift the night we escaped from Max's clutches.'

That answered yet another of the many mysteries surrounding her.

'Baxter.'

'Yes,' he turned to face her.

'Can I ask you the obvious question?'

'You can, but I can't guarantee an obvious answer.'

'Why don't you just go to the police?'

'Because I still don't know who to trust. I'm certainly not convinced Inspector Monroe is as squeaky clean as he may appear.' He thought for a minute. 'I definitely think we need to keep quiet about the recording for the time being. In the meantime I'll write a letter to Atterbury, the Assistant Chief Commissioner at Scotland Yard, outlining the situation and let him know I have an incriminating recording which firmly puts Veerman in the frame for murder. In fact I'll send him one of the CD's.'

'As insurance?'

'Yes exactly.'

'Is he likely to take notice of you, he sounds like a man of rather senior rank?' she looked at him sceptically.

'He certainly is, and what's more I believe he heads the Specialist Crime & Operations Directorate.'

'Well, there you go then,' she said.

'No wait a minute, I know him, not on an old pal's basis or anything like that, but we are both members of the Oriental Society. In fact I was talking to him only a few days ago at the British Library. He gave me his calling card and told me to contact him should the occasion arise. I must admit that was a curious thing for him to say, but yes, I think he might well be very interested in Max Veerman and the cartel.'

Magali gave him a doubtful look. He thought she was about to say something, but seemed to change her mind at the last minute.

Baxter went back to his laptop, typed a short note to Atterbury and then sent the order to print to his wireless printer.

Nothing happened, so he checked the w–i fi connection and pressed print once more. Again no response.

'Damn, the paper's jammed,' he said spotting the message on the front panel screen.' 'It's always doing that lately.' He cleared the jam and pressed print again.

'I think something's happening out there Baxter,' Magali said from the top of the stairs.

'Just coming,' he said whipping the letter out of the printer and turning it off.

When he reached the bedroom Magali was looking out between the undrawn curtain and the window.

'You'd better take a look out here, I don't like it.'

The two men were walking around the front of his cottage. They stopped and framed the sides of their faces with their hands as they peered in the downstairs windows. When they reached his garage, they rattled the doors and then slowly returned to their car.

'Look Baxter, we need to get out of here and fast.'

'Right,' he said thoughtfully.

'Are you listening to me? She shook him.

'Yes, I'm just trying to think,' he said quietly.

'Baxter,' she said with voice raised. You've got to take Veerman's threats seriously, he never makes idle promises. You might think you're clever and the bravest man on the planet, but I can tell you now you wouldn't stand a chance against those Shāqi agents down there, and neither would I.

Baxter could see she was genuinely terrified and finally agreed that his cottage might not, after all, be a safe haven for either of them.

As he threw a few things into a holdall he realised her state of terror was catching. He wasn't afraid as such, but certainly apprehensive. He had been alert ever since this escapade started, but his vigilance was now cranked to the highest notch and for the first time in a very long while, he felt vulnerable. His emotions had long been painfully stretched, but now he was threatened with physical harm.

He peered once again out of the corner of the curtain; the black saloon was still parked opposite, an elbow perched on the edge of the open car window and wisps of blue smoke wafted out of the vehicle. A square Oriental face looked across towards his cottage, motionless, and strangely harmless looking, but he knew that expression could change in a split second from one of apathy to murder.

Baxter realised the situation was now changing, not by the week or even by the day but by the hour. Any thoughts of leading a normal life without threats from Veerman or the Shāqi had been well and truly dashed by today's events. Magali was right, he had to get them out of there and fast.

Baxter's home was a mews cottage, a former stable to the big house but the one big drawback was it had no rear entrance. He racked his brains for a solution. He paced from room to room and then in the bathroom his eyes registered on the small wooden door which once served as a hay loft entrance. The other side of the wall was his garage, but the little loft door hadn't been opened for years; in fact he wasn't even certain if there was still an opening behind. It could have been blocked up when the property was renovated and placed back as a decorative feature.

It took him less than ten minutes to dig around the old plaster loosening the hold between the wooden frame and wall. He levered the framework with a large screwdriver and the hatch door flew open sending a sudden rush of air against his face.

He peered into the dark garage and smiled at the sight of his car. 'Perfect,' he said.

'That doesn't really help us very much,' Magali commented as she joined him by the opening.

'I don't know about that,' he said deep in thought.

'You're not trying to tell me you think you can simply drive out through the garage doors and off down the street without being seen by Veerman's agents sitting in their car. They will gun you down before you hit the tarmac.

He didn't reply, but rushed back to the sitting room and picked up his phone.

'Keith, its Baxter here, glad you are home; how was the holiday mate?'

Keith began to talk about his recent trip to the Maldives, but Baxter quickly stopped him.

'Sorry to butt in, but we are in a bit of a pickle. Can you help us my friend?'

'Yes Keith, we *are* at my cottage. Ah, I have Magali here as well, I'll explain all tomorrow. Look mate, there are two of Veerman's thugs sitting in a car opposite, can you do another piece of acting for me and stall your engine so it stops in front of them, very close and do it at exactly twelve thirty?'

Keith agreed and promised to be there on time.

Baxter got on the phone again. 'I'd like to speak with driver two one six please,' he said to the taxi control operator.

'Steve, here'

'Hi Steve, this is Baxter. I need a taxi and I need you and no one else, is that possible?'

'I was just about to clock off for lunch mate, but as it's you, how can I refuse.'

'Well you could, I expect I could find someone else if necessary,' he said tongue-in-cheek.

'What, and miss another car chase or getting myself gunned down in the street. Do you know Mr. Baxter, taking you around London is the only excitement I ever get these days?'

'Yes... well this time it's different. You see, I want you to pull up opposite my cottage, in fact behind the black car which is parked there, as close as possible, and at exactly twelve thirty five. Then walk over and knock on my door and wait at least a couple of minutes. I'll have to square up with you tomorrow, will explain all then.'

Baxter waited with Magali in the darkness of the garage, all the time peering between the cracks in the large wooden doors.

Keith arrived first, driving slowly and then stalling his engine so that his car stopped on the road, but in front of the black car. Keith jumped out, cursed loudly as he raised the bonnet and peered inside.

Minutes later Steve pulled up in his taxi and parked behind the black vehicle. He leisurely got out, stretched and then proceeded across the road, whistling as he went.

'Oi, you can't leave that cab there,' one of the Chinamen shouted.

'I'll be two minutes,' Steve replied, as he calmly walked across the road and knocked on Baxter's front door.

The Chinese driver learnt out of his car window and began remonstrating with Keith, obviously unhappy about being blocked in, but he continued to examine his engine with his head tucked under the bonnet.

This was the cue. Baxter started his engine while Magali threw open the garage doors. She hopped in the passenger's seat and he put his foot down hard on the accelerator, swinging the car out onto the road.

As he sped past Keith and the Chinese, the agents jumped out of their car and pulled out their guns firing several shots in quick succession. Baxter glanced in the rear view mirror and saw the men running after him with arms outstretched and then he noticed a flash of white leave one of the men's pistols. At that very moment a bullet pinged against a lamp post to Baxter's right and another tore into the tarmac just ahead of them. Suddenly the windscreen of a car coming towards him shattered. Magali put her hands in front of her eyes as the vehicle veered dangerously into their path. Baxter swung his steering wheel to the left, sending his car onto the pavement, hitting dustbins and narrowly avoiding a street lamp before arriving at the end of the road.

At the junction he turned left, entering a line of slow moving traffic which became heavier as he made his way out of Central London. The density of the traffic was a relief, as it shielded him from any other cars which might be summoned to take up the pursuit.

A few minutes were all Baxter had needed, and that's what he got. Keith had already jumped into his car and sped off by the time the agents had returned to their vehicle and Steve had done the same, but unknown to him, his number plate had been noted.

The Regent was not a top-notch hotel, but the three star rating reflected its reasonable level of comfort and general facilities, but more to the point, it was tucked away down a nondescript side street on the outskirts of Stratford, some four miles from the city centre.

Baxter rang Keith from the bedside telephone, and he confirmed that he and Steve had left the scene without any problems.

In the safety of the hotel their intimacy continued as though it had never been interrupted, although in Baxter's mind lingered a nagging doubt; he felt certain there was more to Magali's story beneath the superficiality of her account.

It appeared the mystery of General Henri de Montaigne and the rock of Batuta was finally over. It irritated him immensely to concede that Veerman had won and was going to cash in on the diamond in a very big way.

He desperately wanted to go to the police, but doubted they would act against someone as powerful as Max Veerman and if, as he suspected, the man had the police in his pocket, then that would further endanger not only him but also Magali.

He was just coming out of the hotel bar, having decided to post the incriminating evidence to Atterbury the Assistant Chief Commissioner, when the bell boy stopped him as he passed the front desk.

'A message for you Mr. Baxter,' he said handing him a sealed envelope. He noticed the small brown parcel in Baxter's hand.

'Do you want me to post that one for you sir?'

'Thank you, but no, it's got to be sent by recorded delivery.'

'Not a word to anyone now,' he told the youngster as he took the message and then eased a ten pound note into the bell boy's hand. 'That should cover it.' He winked at the youngster who nodded appreciatively.

The message was from Detective Chief Inspector Monroe of Paddington Green police station saying he wanted an urgent word with him, and if at all possible, sometime tomorrow. Would he please telephone and let them know when he could call in.

At first, Baxter didn't question the fact that Monroe had left him a message here at the Regent Hotel, but then his brain kicked in and he suddenly wondered how on earth the Inspector knew he was staying there? He had told no one and was pretty certain Magali hadn't, there was no reason why she would.

He had been put on hold after ringing the taxi company and was curious as to the reason why.

'Mr. Watson will speak with you now,' the receptionist said.

'You were asking for Steve, are you a relative?' the uncompromising voice enquired.

'No just a friend. I need a taxi, just for a short journey. I always ask for Steve, but what's happened, I don't understand?'

'I regret to inform you sir, that operative two one six is no longer with us.'

'No longer with you, I don't understand, where's he gone?'

'Yesterday afternoon the brakes on his taxi failed and he was tragically killed when his vehicle collided with a bridge support.'

'You mean murdered.'

The supervisor was slow to answer. 'I don't know about that sir, but the police are looking into it.'

'The police you say are investigating, which station is that?'

'Paddington Green, I believe.'

'That wouldn't be an Inspector Monroe by any chance, would it?'

'I believe that was his name sir. As for your taxi, things are rather busy at the moment so it might be twenty minutes or so.'

'Don't worry, I'll get one from here,' he said, still struggling to come to terms with the sad news.

At the hotel foyer Baxter said he needed a taxi and the receptionist pointed to the doorman.

'A taxi Sir, yes, no problem,' the doorman said galvanizing himself into action. 'What is your destination Sir?'

'The nearest post office, wherever that is?'

The doorman stopped for a minute, considered the matter and

then stepped smartly to the pavement, hailed a passing cab and leant in and instructed the driver to take Baxter to Stratford High Street Post Office.

As he sat back in the comfortable rear seat of the taxi, Baxter went over the recent revelations. He guessed Monroe would be involved in some way; he had a knack of being one step ahead of Baxter, but always one step behind Veerman. He, or the cartel had obviously tracked down Steve the taxi driver, and had him killed for his part in helping him the day before and perhaps also the incident last week. The journey to the post office took less than five minutes and Baxter could have easily taken his own car or walked there, but he didn't know the area at all well, and now Monroe knew where he was staying, the chances were that he was being watched.

With the package safely in the hands of the Postmaster, he jumped back in the cab and returned to the Regent.

As he paid the cabbie, Baxter noticed the familiar sight of two individuals sitting in a car opposite. He couldn't be certain that they were watching him, but even from that distance, he felt certain they had the look of Asians.

As requested, Baxter telephoned Monroe and agreed to meet him at eleven a.m. the following day.

During the long restless night, he had come to the decision that they needed to move location yet again. He didn't know how, but Monroe had tracked him down and if the two sitting in the car across the road were Asians, then the Shāqi also knew where the two of them were, and that was a situation he couldn't leave unresolved. He realised that whatever they did the following day, whether travelling in a taxi, or in his own car, they were going to be followed and as he was intending to move to another hotel, he couldn't leave his vehicle behind at the Regent.

The next day they showered early, dressed and were packed ready to go before eight a.m. On the way down to breakfast, Baxter glanced out of the double glass doors; the two men, or perhaps a different pair, were sitting in a black car opposite, the driver smoking with his elbow on the open window.

Baxter had failed to come up with a plan, there was no plan that he could think of which would provide them with the opportunity to leave the hotel without being observed. He wasn't so much concerned about the first part of their journey which was to Paddington Green police station; it was the second leg to the new hotel that was going to present the greater challenge. One way or another, it was vital he get rid of the tail, if he was to stand any chance of securing a safe sanctuary for the two of them.

As they left the hotel, Baxter kept his rear view mirror in sight, and, not surprisingly, the black car pulled away from the kerb and followed at a lazy pace.

'I take it we are being followed,' Magali said, after noticing Baxter's preoccupation with his rear view mirror.

'Yes, I'm afraid so.'

'Shāqi?' she asked.

'Yep, your friend Veerman hasn't given up yet.'

'He's not my friend,' she snapped.

'Who are you going to ring?' he asked, noticing her switching on her mobile.

'No one, no one at all. Just checking the time.'

'There's a clock there,' he pointed to the dashboard.

The traffic in Mile End Road was heavy and at times he wasn't certain if his tail was still behind, but when he turned on to Whitechapel Road, his fears were confirmed. After a short while they took the City Road; a ring way which was faster and provided at least a slim chance of out-running the tail, but Baxter quickly realised this was not going to happen.

Passing Regents Park, he looked to his right and wondered if any of the side roads would give him the opportunity to disappear, and then in his rear view mirror he clearly saw two cars overtake the tail and forced it to stop.

'Watch out!' shouted Magali.

He was just in time to see the cars ahead had stopped at traffic lights. He slammed on his breaks, sending the two of them careering forward. Magali's holdall hurtled into the foot well spilling its contents. While they waited he helped her pick up the scattered items and then noticed her mobile. The screen had the message 'Track and Trace.' 'What's that all about?' he asked, pointing to the message.

She shook her head. 'I haven't a clue, it must have happened when the phone hit the floor.' She quickly turned the mobile off.

As he craned his neck to look through the rear windscreen, he watched as the two Orientals were escorted out of their car and with a hand pushed down on their heads, they were guided into one of the un-marked cars.

'Well, well, well, it seems our Asian friends have been picked up. But by whom I wonder?'

Magali didn't respond, merely nudging his arm to encourage him to take notice of what was going on ahead, as the light had now changed to green. The traffic was on the move again and five minutes later he turned into the car park of Paddington Green Police Station. Magali took a seat in the front waiting area, while he checked in at the front desk.

Detective Chief Inspector Monroe stretched and then leaned back in his chair flexing his long fingers together. 'I do appreciate you coming in like this, I think we have a few things further to discuss, don't you?' he said leaning forward.

'I nearly didn't get here, I can tell you.'

'Oh, and why was that Mr Baxter?'

'I was followed, don't ask me how, but I think someone with nasty intentions was tracking our every move, until they were mysteriously apprehended.'

'Now, that's interesting,' Monroe said thoughtfully, as he rose from his chair and left the room. Returning a few minutes later he said, 'I've got one of our technicians checking over your car, so we'll see what they come up with.'

'So, it wasn't your lot who detained those men who were following us?'

'Certainly not.'

'Tell me Inspector, how did you know we were staying at the Regent Hotel?'

'We have our ways,' he said, with a casual wave of the hand. 'Ah....,' he exclaimed, suddenly realising Baxter's innuendo

'We certainly do not put tracking devices on people's cars, if that's what you're thinking. Anyway, it is supposed to be me who is asking the questions Mr. Baxter.'

It seemed Baxter had finally caught the attention of Inspector Monroe. Magali had earlier confided that she had never come across the policeman's name in connection with Veerman and hadn't seen him in the offices of the cartel, but that was little confirmation that the Inspector was straight, or for that matter, to be trusted.

Baxter knew his back was against the wall and therefore had no other option but to take his chances with the police but he would make sure they knew he had adequate insurance.

Before coming here he'd thought long and hard and reluctantly came to the decision that the time had arrived when he would have to come clean and lay at least most of his cards on the table. However, he decided at the outset to keep one piece of evidence to himself, that was his insurance.

'I'm waiting Mr. Baxter,' Monroe said tapping his pen on the desk. 'I think there's quite a lot you haven't told us, so let's go over what you know about Professor Hadley's death.'

Baxter related the whole story from the death of Marcel Didier and the Bourge-Vilaine auction room where he bought the Chinese vase, also the reaction it caused at the time which resulted in the crash on the bridge, when the Chinese tried to force him off the road. He told the strange tale of his arrest in Avranches and sudden release following an apparent intervention by Assistant Commissioner Atterbury.

Baxter noticed the Inspector's ears prick at the mention of the name Atterbury. He then went into considerable detail about Professor Hadley, and explained why he was so certain Veerman had ordered the professor's death. He left out all the events which were, according to Magali, not connected to Veerman including the Montmartre business.

Neither did Baxter reveal the fact that he had Veerman recorded on his laptop; he was keeping that piece of evidence under wraps for the time being.

Monroe looked thoughtful as he leaned back in his chair, popped a sweet in his mouth and rolled it around for a few seconds. 'Tell me Mr. Baxter why should we believe what you're telling us now, where's your evidence? You do realize Mr. Max Veerman is a very well respected member of our community.'

'What about the taxi driver Steve?'

'Do you mean operative two one six?'

'Yes, he was murdered by your very well respected member of the community Max Veerman, or at least he ordered the killing.'

'Come, come, Mr. Baxter, the man's brakes failed, it happens.'

Baxter was riled; the Inspector was obviously an intelligent man, so why on earth couldn't he grasp the absurdity of what he was saying? Or was he conveniently being obtuse. 'I've given you enough evidence for God's sake, so tell me, why did you agree to listen to what I had to say if you had no intention of taking me seriously?'

'But I am taking you seriously Mr. Baxter; I'm always interested in people who break the law, believe me.'

'Excuse me but I don't think you are,' Baxter said. 'I don't think you fully appreciate that men like Max Veerman are not mere domestic lawbreakers, but international criminals who use subversion to escape from justice.'

'Perhaps,' Monroe said.

Baxter sighed and then banged the desk with his fist in exasperation. He felt like he was banging his head against a brick wall, as every step he took, he seemed to step back even further.

Monroe rose from his chair. 'Calm down Mr. Baxter, we *are* taking what you've told us seriously and we'll be paying Mr. Veerman a visit within the next few days. Believe me, we'll get to the bottom of this.' His face flashed a wrinkled grin, a half-hearted gesture at best.

'The next few days!' Baxter shouted in disbelief, 'why not today? He could be gone in twenty four hours and then you will never get him; but then, perhaps that's precisely what you want,' he said sarcastically.

The look Monroe exchanged wasn't in any way satirical, but now contained a mix of irritation and acquiescence.

'So tell me, where is he likely to go?' Monroe said softly.

Baxter couldn't answer that, although he suspected Paris was a likely contender.

'Besides, it's all down to a simple matter of a search warrant and that has to come from a Magistrate,' Monroe pointed out, 'but be assured Mr. Baxter, we'll be looking very carefully at Max Veerman and his affairs.

There were two raps on the door.

'Yes,' Monroe bawled.

A Sergeant walked smartly in, placing a small rectangular object on the desk. 'Engineering unit found this Geo-fence GPS tracking device strapped to the gentleman's car Sir.'

Monroe picked the device up, turning it over in his hand.

'That's typical, made in China,' he said.

'Of course it was made in China,' Baxter said vitriolically. 'Veerman's associates are Chinese.'

'Quite,' Monroe said thoughtfully. 'Now go home and leave it to us here at Borough Operational Command, there's a good chap.' He held out his hand, beckoning him out of the door.

Before checking into The Wayside Hotel, just off the Ruislip Road at Greenford, Baxter tapped Keith's telephone number on his mobile.

'Keith here.'

'It's Baxter. Look, do you know anything about tracking devices and any way to block them?'

'You're being followed again are you?'

'Yes, and not only by Veerman's heavies, but I'm certain Inspector Monroe is also tracking our every move.'

'You always said he was dodgy.'

'So, is there anything we can do to avoid being tracked?'

'No problem, all you need is a GPS Anti-Tracking Unit.'

'Right, okay Keith and what is that precisely and where can I get one from?'

'An ECM tracker transmits countermeasure at an incredible 1575 MHz,' he said, obviously enjoying the opportunity to show off his insatiable appetite for scientific fact.

'Yes, but what does it actually do?'

'It is spectrally matched to L1 C/A satellite signals and as a

result it will disable all standard GPS locating units. I have one here if you would care to pop in and collect it.'

With the small anti tracking device plugged into his cigarette lighter, Baxter and Magali headed for their new hotel, confident, they would no longer have to keep looking over their shoulders.

CHAPTER 23

COUNTESS DE COUVEGNE AND THE ROCK OF BATUTA

Summer had moved on since he last visited Bourge-Vilaine, a momentous experience thanks to Magali snatching the diamond, and then heartbreak after she faked her own death.

Much to his surprise the Countess de Couvegne had contacted him by email, although he couldn't for one moment imagine how she had procured his internet address, although he suspected it was probably via her solicitor. The message requested he pay her a visit as she had a proposition to put to him. To say Baxter was hesitant would be an understatement. He had made a great deal of money from the sale of the Chinese vase, a piece which once belonged to the celebrated Henri de Montaigne. The General had been closely connected with the Chateau de Couvegne and the third Countess, so the present aristocratic lady would have more than a passing interest in an item which was once part of her family history.

Baxter simply ignored the e-mail hoping that would be an end to the matter, but the following day another one arrived at his in-box.

'You must go,' Magali urged, 'she wouldn't be inviting you down there unless it was for something rather special.'

'Like, where is my diamond, or do you know that Chinese vase you bought was stolen from me, so where's my money?'

'I think you're wrong Baxter,' she said thoughtfully. 'The Countess mentions a proposition she wishes to put to you. I think you owe her the courtesy of at least listening to what she has to say, don't you?'

'You're a good one to talk about courtesy to the Countess.'

'You won't let that go, will you?' she flashed him an uncomfortable look.

As usual Magali talked him round; she had a knack of making him feel conscious of his actions as well as his inactions. He could procrastinate until the cows came home, but she would always win.

'Okay, I give in, I'll email back and agree to listen to what she has to say, but obviously I'll be going on my own.'

'No you're not, I'm coming with you,' she said adamantly.

'What after the way you behaved, stealing her diamond like that, I don't think so.'

'I should have told you before,' she said meekly, 'but I've been in contact with the Countess and apologised for my behaviour and she has accepted my apology in full.'

Baxter shook his head in amazement. 'Do you know Magali you never cease to amaze me, you have depths which I cannot begin to fathom and within those depths are mysteries, which even now you keep secret from me.'

'Don't we all have secrets which we keep close to our hearts, isn't that what makes us who we are and does it not define our unique personality.'

Baxter decided not to engage in a philosophical argument, he had long learnt the futility of trying to out theorise Magali, she was an expert in such matters.

When he made the appointment to visit, the Countess said she hoped Baxter would bring his young lady along as well.

Even if he had been able to dissuade Magali from going, which was unlikely, this invitation made it clear the Countess expected her presence by his side.

It was a Monday morning in France and they were just passing the little Mediaeval town of Bourge-Vilaine en route for the Chateau de Couvegne. As they passed through the entrance with its miniature turreted towers either side, it was immediately apparent the house and grounds were today closed to the general public. This time Baxter drove across the gravel forecourt, pulled up inside the main covered entrance and skipped up the marble steps with Magali close on his heels.

As he pulled the bronze ring he heard the bell resonate inside the hallway. The heavy ornate doors opened almost immediately and a slim well-dressed middle-aged man stood subserviently. Bonjour Monsieur et Madam, est-ce que je peux vous aider? ' he asked in a sombre and staid tone.'

'The name's Baxter.' He announced with his best French accent. 'The Countess *is* expecting us.' The man nodded and ushered them in.

They entered the grand hall, a masterpiece of Baroque craftsmanship from the early years of the seventeenth century. A white stone staircase dominated the large airy space, its stairs rising easily between great marble columns before turning back on themselves. A balcony overlooked the entrance, not a real one but a clever piece of tromp-l'oeil paintwork.

Baxter looked up and gasped. He touched Magali's shoulder and pointed to the ceiling where a large roundel contained a magnificent painted depiction of cherubs casting a Baron's coronet, flying amid blue skies swirling with great billowing clouds.

They followed the manservant silently along a red-carpeted corridor lined each side with rooms. Along the way Baxter dawdled, admiring the gilt-framed images of the long line of Couvegne's and their relatives confronting each other across the corridor, a portrait gallery which charted the personal history of the previous occupants of the house. Several times Magali had to tear him away from a portrait he had stopped to gaze at.

Where doors were open Baxter saw wonderful things. Furniture, porcelain and silver and huge cut glass crystal chandeliers. There were smaller chandeliers at regular intervals along the corridor, deployed to give maximum light to the otherwise dark passageway.

The servant knocked on the end door and waited respectfully.

'Entrée,' came the muffled reply from within. The servant opened the double doors and stood courteously as they entered. He closed the magnificent panelled doors behind them, the mahogany discharged a hollow echo, rich in tone, yet distant as it resonated down the passageway.

The Countess looked so very different from the previous time they had met. In these opulent surroundings she came across as a striking lady, tall and most elegant. Although now in her late sixties she possessed the shadow of a once beautiful woman, only the grey in her hair suggested she was perhaps older than her looks might imply.

'Thank you for coming,' she said genially, holding out her hand. They shook hands, something they had definitely not done the last time he had met her.

The Countess spoke slowly in perfect, eloquent English. 'Sit down, Mr. Baxter and you, madam.' She pointed to one of two matching chaise longue in the centre of the room.

Baxter could barely contain himself as he surveyed the enormous room. This was the grand lounge, the elegant day salon with high ornate ceilings and walls decorated with plaster-moulded panels filled with gesso and gilt trophies and great floral swags. It was filled with sunlight by large floor to ceiling french windows which led out to a terrace. The opulent furniture, he felt certain, wouldn't have been out of place in the Palace of Versailles. Baxter experienced a sudden spasm of envy at the thought that, despite his modest sum from the sale of the vase, he could never afford to live in such splendour.

The Countess starred at him thoughtfully, noticing his interest she said quietly. 'So Mr. Baxter, do you like what you see?'

'It's simply magnificent, so elegant and yet refined. I just love the stucco female figures languishing over those door pediments.'

'The plasterwork was designed by Bagutti and done by the Artari brothers,' she said beaming broadly.

'Interesting, they don't sound very French to me,' Baxter remarked, but immediately wished he hadn't.

'Indeed no, you're perfectly correct, French workman couldn't achieve work of this quality. All the plasterwork was carried out by immigrant Italian-Swiss artists brought over especially to create this type of intricate workmanship. They were mainly employed in Paris, but also here in the provinces.

'Impressive,' he said unable to find a more suitable expression.

'Now please make yourself comfortable with the cushions,' the Countess said, acknowledging the nature of her beautiful, but rather uncomfortable couches.

She walked across to the French windows and then turned. 'I expect you are wondering what this is all about, Mr. Baxter.' her impassive face gave nothing away.

'I must admit I am intrigued Countess.'

'I will try and explain, but first of all, congratulations on your success with the Henri de Montaigne vase. I hear it did very well in the London auction rooms, very well indeed'.

'Thank you,' he replied humbly, nodding slightly. He had no wish to add any further details unless pressed to do so, especially if that was why he was here.

She walked back and settled herself in an armchair. 'Now I would like to tell you a story.'

Sounds promising Baxter said to himself.

'Where to begin,' she said thoughtfully, nudging her back into the deep cushions. She cleared her throat softly and took a long sip from the glass of water by her side.

'It all started in 1860 during what is known as the Second Opium Wars, but then knowing your background, Mr Baxter, I imagine you know the history of the Chinese wars.'

'Well yes, I do reasonably well, especially the looting of the Chinese Summer Palace and the wanton destruction of much of the most important porcelain that was ever produced in China,' he said, eager to show he had done his research.

'Yes, that was most unfortunate, and I should point out that it also included destruction of the jades, bronzes and silks, not to mention some very fine, early calligraphy and paintings.'

'Those soldiers have a lot to answer for, eradicating history on that sort of scale, it was disgraceful,' he said.

'On any sort of scale it's disgraceful, Mr. Baxter,' she corrected him. 'You are, of course, quite right though, but I have to admit it was mainly our French troops who were responsible. You see they didn't want the local peasants to take those treasures away and trade them for drugs, so they were loaded on to wagons and dumped outside and then smashed to pieces and spread on the trackways. Do you know that the Chinese government was forced to hand over twenty one million ounces of silver to Britain, along with the sovereignty of Hong Kong?'

'I knew about Hong Kong,' he said,' and that's why we handed it back in nineteen ninety seven, but not about the silver.'

'The third Countess de Couvegne was at that time very close to the French commander General Henri de Montaigne and when he was not on some military campaign, he lived with her, here at the Chateau, I think you understand what I mean.'

Baxter confirmed he did.

She went on 'The General was powerless to stop the needless destruction in the summer palace, and even sided with the English commander whose troops had mostly watched in dismay.

Anyway, rightly or wrongly, the General brought back the two vases as trophies for the Countess and they were placed in the main hall here at the Chateau. Now Henri de Montaigne was no fool and he quickly realised each of the vases had an inscription, but he was unable to translate them, so he had the text deciphered in Paris. To his amazement he discovered these inscriptions related to a large diamond called the rock of Batuta. A little more investigative work and he predicted the stone was still concealed in the base which had once housed the vases when they were in the summer palace. And of course the base was still in China, so all hopes of finding the diamond were at that time lost. That was until the year nineteen hundred when a second French expedition was being planned, with the objective of going back to China to quell another much smaller uprising.'

'The Boxer Rebellion.'

'Yes Mr. Baxter. The Boxer Rebellion. However, General Henri de Montaigne was in retirement. Undaunted, he saw this as an opportunity to look for the base which he was convinced contained the diamond and so joined the French force as an advisor. The Countess' diaries relate why he was going and what he hoped to find. They also tell us that he did find the base for the two vases, and amazingly it was still in situ in the sacred Hall of Benevolence and Longevity. He immediately sent the base to the port of Canton, ready for shipment back to Bourge-Vilaine.'

'And that was the base we found in your tower, with the diamond still in it,' Baxter said humbly.

She didn't comment on his last remark, choosing to merely give a soft 'Hmm'. She went on, 'He wrote several letters to the Countess explaining in some detail the importance of this and the other vases, and how it would bring them good fortune. Henri de Montaigne unfortunately contracted a severe infection on his journey to Canton and, as soon as he arrived back in France, he was immediately taken to Paris where he died a few days later. He never had the chance to see his beloved Countess again, and the porcelain base remained in a warehouse in Canton.'

'That really is a tragic story, I never realised that part of it.'

'No, Mr. Baxter, few people do. Now the Countess was so devastated that she never opened his last letters to her and with a broken heart, she died twelve months later. That might have been the end of the story had the Countess not passed on the account to her son, who related the saga down the line of inheritance until it reached my late husband, who, fortunately passed the story on to me.'

'So that was what the letters were all about,' Baxter said with a quick glance at Magali.

'No, Mr. Baxter,' the old lady countered, 'there was rather more to the letters than that. You see going back even further, the Countess was born Marie de L'Anchanteron. Her father was Baron de L'Anchanteron and her mother the French aristocrat Marie de Chalenois. At the age of just seventeen she married Henri de Couvegne and they had one son. Tragically, the Count was killed a year later in a duel. As a result she inherited much wealth. After that the third Countess led a, well shall we say a disreputable way of life despite her youth. In fact some commentators at the time described the house here as 'a monument to aristocratic misbehaviour'. She now spent much of her time in Paris where she mixed with people in the French high Court, but she also hosted lavish parties here at Couvegne and entertained the cream of Parisian aristocracy, including royalty.

At the age of nineteen she had a secret relationship with Le Compt de L'Avegnet and shortly afterwards the French statesman Emile Cellovier and she had a daughter by him, although that was kept a secret.'

Baxter asked 'How on earth do you know all this?'

'Why, the letters of course,' she said, 'that's the reason why they were so explosive in their content, but there is more to come.'

She reached into a small cupboard and flicked through a bundle of letters then unfolded one. 'A letter dated 1858 mentions, and I will quote from it,' she said unfolding it and then putting on her spectacles. 'I had a most wonderful flirtation with Badinguet. He came down to Couvegne for the weekend on the pretext of taking some country air. I must say he was every bit as romantic as has been written of him.'

'Napoleon the third, how wonderful,' Magali exclaimed. This was the first time she had spoken.

'Yes, that's perfectly correct, Badinguet was his nickname but make no mistake, this was a dangerous liaison and one which would have blown the entire Parisian aristocracy apart had it got out, and even today it would have serious historical implications.'

'No wonder you were so desperate to buy the letters,' Baxter said.

'Yes, Mr. Baxter, I was determined to have them safely back where they belong, here in the chateau and prepared to pay whatever was necessary to procure them.'

She continued. 'This, of course, was all before the third Countess met Henri de Montaigne a few years later, although I wonder whether they were perhaps acquainted before, but there is no mention of it. Now the real problems arose as a result of the Countess being a prolific letter writer, often composing up to four each day and I can tell you they were very graphic in their detail. Some she sent to friends, a few to her son, but most she sent to her youngest daughter who was married to a Monsieur Jacques Ferrande the Mayor of St.Briac in Brittany.

The years went past and over good and bad times the Countess struggled to maintain the property. Much of the Chinese collection was sold off, I think, for relatively modest sums and this included the two Henri de Montaigne vases. What we do know is that one went to her daughter's husband Jacques Ferrande who was an avid collector of all things Oriental. Whether it was a gift or not, we don't know, but the other was sold to the mysterious English dealer, Mr. Pope, for nine hundred francs.

'Why was he mysterious?' interrupted Baxter.

'Because it's rumoured that not a single item he was known to have purchased was ever seen again and when he died in nineteen twenty one, he had not a penny to his name.'

'Do you know which of the two vases went to England, and which one stayed in France?' he enquired, even though he was fairly certain of the answer.

'Ah now, this is where the story comes up-to-date. You see five years ago the Countess's daughter's great grandson Fabien Ferrande died without leaving any heirs. He had inherited the big house in St.Briac and all its contents, although by that time the remnants were little more than a sad reminder of his great grandfather's collection. Being the nearest relative I was left the estate and its contents, which I had stored in the old west tower.'

'I see,' said Baxter. 'Wow, that must have been fascinating to sort through all those treasures.'

'Well actually it wasn't. You see I have a very well stocked house here and so I didn't for one moment think there would be anything I needed amongst that jumble of tea chests. I'm ashamed to admit that I never even bothered to look in those trunks, although I always intended to, one day. But what I can tell you is that someone else quietly went through the contents, and that person I now know, was my gardener Didier.'

'Didier! I met a Marcel Didier in a bar called Rat de Cave,' Baxter said.

'Your voice makes a statement Mr. Baxter,' she said frowning deeply, 'but your face wears a question.'

'I was just wondering...'

She cut him short, 'yes, it was the very same man you met in the bar, Rat de Cave.'

'I knew he was a shady character,' said Baxter

She tipped her head sideways in agreement. 'Unknown to me,' she went on, 'he had spotted something or things which he thought he could quietly sell in our Bourge-Vilaine auction rooms, and to be quite honest it was only by sheer chance that I found out about his nefarious activity.'

Baxter butted in 'So when did you find out about the letters then?'

'You see, Mr. Baxter, Didier thought he was being rather clever by selling details of the letters to a number of antique dealers.'

'Mugs like me.' Baxter interrupted. 'He must have made a mint.'

'Indeed he did make, what to him, was a handsome bounty, but where he went wrong was by selling the information to a good friend of mine, and it was he who tipped me off.'

'So why didn't you claim them back from the auction room as stolen property?'

'Because Mr Baxter, I didn't know for certain they *had* been taken from my house, even though the likelihood was that that had been the case. But also, at that time, I didn't have the benefit of knowing the identity of the man who was selling the information; it never even crossed my mind that it could have been my gardener.' She shook her head 'Do you know, he was the most unintelligent man I've ever known; a good gardener yes, but I still can't believe he had the nous to recognise the value of those items. Had I known it was Didier, I might have put two and two together and realised sooner, rather than later, that it was him who was selling the letters in our auction rooms?'

Baxter said, 'Didier may have been a scoundrel and on the surface not too intelligent, but the more I learn about him the more I realize he was a crafty little character.'

'You mean a crafty big character,' the Countess corrected.

'Yes, that's true, he certainly was a big man.'

'Anyway, on the morning of the sale I prepared myself to do battle with the auction, and then a police officer called here. He told me my gardener had been killed.

I have to admit that I was not particularly saddened by the news. That might sound a bit cold to you Mr. Baxter but what he told me next put everything that had happened recently into context. The policeman told me they found a burnt fragment of the Bourge-Vilaine auctioneer's estimate for a chest with various papers. That in itself wasn't of any great significance, even though he had apparently tried to destroy it in his fire grate, but the sergeant also found a bundle of Couvegne letters which Didier had obviously kept aside. It was this evidence which aroused the officer's suspicions. They also found over two thousand euros hidden away in a drawer, so where did that come from? Certainly not from the wages I was paying him.'

'I should imagine it was from all those gullible people like me,' Baxter said. 'Did you know his real name was Andre Poisson?'

'I didn't at the time, but the police delved deeper into his background and discovered his real identity and I might add, a whole host of crimes associated with the name Poisson came to light. You see Mr. Baxter, old crimes have long shadows, and I believe they finally caught up with him the night he was killed.

'And you've no idea who killed him.'

'No, Mr. Baxter, but I suspect he had many enemies. Anyway, going back to the letters; I can tell you I was sickened by what had been going on behind my back, so much so that I decided to ask my solicitor to bid on the letters for me. What's more I was so desperate to secure them that I told him not to come back here without them.'

'So it was you or rather your representative who put in that high bid in the auction rooms.'

'Yes it was, and just as well, because someone else was desperate to get them.'

Even though Baxter had accidentally bid on them, he realised someone other than him had been pushing the bid price up and he wondered who that might have been. 'Do you know who the other bidder was?' he asked, hoping she didn't know he had contributed to the high result.

'I have my theories, but let's just say it was someone who appreciated their content and therefore their monetary or political value and I suspect the latter. So you see, I had to have those letters at any cost.

'I can see that now,' he said sympathetically.

'Apart from the shame they would have brought on my late husband's family, I knew they included a large batch dated from eighteen sixty to nineteen hundred and ten.'

It all made sense now; Baxter realised the letters had a secondary importance. 'Am I right in thinking you now have correspondence from General Henri de Montaigne concerning the vase inscriptions and his belief about the diamond?'

'Yes, I most certainly have, and before you ask, the last ones by the Count had never been opened.'

Baxter said 'And after you bought them you opened the letters dated nineteen hundred and discovered the truth about the diamond.'

'No, not exactly,' she said. 'Now going back to the third Countess' day, here is the strange part. Reading her diary, which I hasten to add came with the batch of letters, I now know that in nineteen hundred and ten a large crate was delivered here. The diary states that it bore the original labels put on it by the General and further stickers for Canton harbour, which means it had for some strange reason, been lost for ten years before someone sent it the rest of the way home. When the base arrived the Countess was at a loss to know what to do with it as the accompanying vases by that time had been sold, so she stored it away in her room in the tower.

'Now I have been trying to solve the mystery of the diamond for most of my life, but when those letters surfaced I thought I would finally crack the mystery wide open, but sadly that was not to be the case. The stone is never mentioned once and without the family oral tradition, it wouldn't even be known to exist.'

'That would have been a great loss, but the vases would have still talked to us, sooner or later.' Baxter offered.

'Not to me though, because I didn't know a Chinese vase which might have been originally brought to this house by Henri de Montaigne, had surfaced in London. The first I heard about it was when the auction house in Bond Street contacted me to ask if I could supply them with a provenance for it. They sent me wonderful coloured pictures and as soon as I saw them I knew straight away it was the missing vase.'

'So what about the provenance?' Baxter nervously asked.

'Well I couldn't supply them with one. I didn't and still don't know how it got to England, or when.'

Of course Baxter did, because it was him who bought it in Bourge-Vilaine and then took it back to the U.K; but he wasn't intending to own up to that fact.

The Countess cleared her throat. 'What I don't know is whether it was still in the Jacques Ferrande collection when he died five years ago, so I don't have a clue where it had been for the best part of a century.'

Baxter caught a look in her eye which betrayed her suspicions that the vase most likely also came via Didier. Their eyes locked for several seconds and during that time Baxter weighed up whether he should tell her he bought the vase not in London, as he had informed the Bond Street auctioneers, but in the Bourge-Vilaine auction room. That would immediately make it highly likely it was also stolen from her house by her gardener Didier. But as he fought with his conscience, he convinced himself that he didn't actually know the vase had been stolen from her house or for that matter if Didier had sent it there for sale. He argued the whole situation could be a mere coincidence. In the end Baxter decided not to interrupt the brief silence that ensued.

The Countess broke the silence 'I sent the pictures to Paris and had the inscription translated by Andre Ponperrier at the Louvre Museum. It was only then I realised where the stone was.'

'So you knew the stone was hidden in the Chinese base?'

'Oh yes, Mr. Baxter,' she said with a distant smile on her lips. 'So tell me, would you like to see it now.'

'See it, I don't follow,' he said mystified.

'The diamond of course,' she said pertly, as she walked across to the fireplace and tugged a bell pull.

A few minutes later her servant came into the room. 'Madame.'

'The rock please, Jacque,' she said softly.

He walked over to an Italian marquetry cabinet, opened the two doors, reached around the flank and slid a panel side-ways. Baxter heard the click as a lock turned somewhere within the inner part of the cabinet. The man lifted up the forward-facing decorative strip and the whole front façade opened, revealing a secret spacious compartment. He removed a pair of white cotton gloves from his jacket pocket, put them on and then reached inside the cabinet and cautiously removed something wrapped in a velvet cloth.

Jacques walked sedately across the room and placed the mystery object carefully on the table in front of them. He glanced at the Countess who returned a small nod and at that command he slowly unravelled the material, exposing a brilliant diamond. The countess picked it up and a fusillade of colours bounced off of its many facets.

'Heavens,' Baxter exclaimed.

'Surprised you, did it? I thought perhaps it might.' The Countess smiled.

'But how?' Baxter asked, as he bent forward to look at it closely.

'I just don't understand, I thought...'

'You thought,' she cut him short, 'your friend here stole the diamond when the two of you raided my home.'

'Well yes, precisely, and I do apologize for what we did that day, but I really did think she was your granddaughter,' he said.

He looked at Magali imagining how rotten she must feel, but was surprised to see no sign of remorse or embarrassment, or come to that, surprise of any sort. She merely shuffled her bottom on the seat of the chair, something she often did when bored.

Despite this he felt he had to go to her rescue. 'Magali was being driven by an evil man,' he explained 'but she has turned over a new leaf. You can trust her now,' he said supportively.

'It's alright,' the Countess said 'I knew full well it was only a matter of time before someone came to my door looking for the stone, but I had a problem. You see the base with the diamond was taken out of China in nineteen hundred and ten, and although we know the Count removed it some ten years earlier, as I said, he died in Paris before completing the cargo consignment docket and so the shipping record is dated October fifteenth nineteen hundred and ten.'

'Now if you know anything about the pillage of war treaty, you will know all about the one hundred year rule.

'Vaguely, but I still don't quite understand.'

'Let me explain,' she said. 'The one hundred years are not up until October of this year and that's still a few months away. That being the case I couldn't risk offering it for sale before that date. What made things worse, following the sale of the second Henri de Montaigne vase, the one you sold, I was convinced someone would discover the meaning of the inscription and come looking for the diamond, and I was right wasn't I?' she said, raising her eyebrows at him, but not at Magali.

Baxter nodded.

'So I decided to have a copy made by my jeweller in Paris, and a jolly good one it was too don't you agree?'

'Well I didn't really see the other one that closely.' Baxter confided, 'so to be honest with you I wouldn't know the difference. But you saw it close up, didn't you Magali?'

'I saw it reasonably well,' she said, 'and it looked real enough to me, and so it did to someone else.'

'That someone else would of course be Mr. Maximillian Veerman,' the Countess said.

Magali nodded.

'So you see, Mr. Baxter, few people would doubt it was genuine, even an expert would have to carry out tests to determine its authenticity. The diamond simulant it was made from was strontium titanate, a very costly but at the same time difficult material to detect from a real diamond, even for a gemologist. Most, if not all, would be looking for the tell-tale signs of cubic zirconia. And they do that by testing for thermal insulation, but of course strontium titanate which the copy is made of, like diamond, is a thermal conductor. Even a close examination under a powerful lens will show some flaws, and this is the clever part, because you see the real gem also has minute flaws, but cubic zirconium will have no flaws whatsoever.'

'But what I don't understand is, why didn't you just bury it in the garden or something like that, why go to all the trouble and expense of having a copy made?'

'You clearly don't know the ways of the cartel, Mr. Baxter. If your friend here hadn't stolen it and presented it in the lap of Max Veerman, do you think he would have given up just like that?'

'No, I take your point, I guess they would have likely given you some very nasty treatment. Yes, on reflection it was a good idea to make them think they had the real thing.'

'I think so Mr. Baxter.'

'Hang on.' A sudden realization hit home base. 'So you knew all along that Magali was working for Veerman and the cartel. I see now it was all part of an act, you catching us finding the diamond and pretending to be angry when Magali ran off with it.'

The Countess flashed a look at Magali who suddenly looked uncomfortable. The Countess didn't respond, but quickly moved the conversation along.

'Tell me, Mr. Baxter, what happened after the sale when they arrested you at Avranches?'

'You know about that!' he exclaimed.

'Oh yes indeed, I was interviewed by the police after my gardener was found dead and they told me they had a suspect in custody, but I gather they decided it had not been you after all.'

'They actually accused me of murdering your gardener Marcel Didier?' he said.

'That's strange,' she said 'someone must have tipped them off, do you know I can't imagine who that might have been.' She fell into a silent line of thought.

'Besides, I wasn't exactly impressed with the level of respect or competence in the local police,' he remarked.

'Well Mr. Baxter, you know what it's like over here; mediocrity very much rules in this country and nowhere more so than here in Brittany.'

Just then the french windows slowly opened and her manservant reappeared.

'Ah, tea is served if you would like to come this way,' the Countess extended her arm.

The terrace looked out over extensive countryside. The view was broken by two belvederes, identical and with their corresponding balustrade wall they framed the view perfectly. The table was laid with dainty antique porcelain cups and saucers, silver tea pot and a plate with small fancy cakes, neatly arranged.

As the servant went to close the doors, she raised her hand and stopped him. 'Jacque, please put the stone back in the cabinet.'

He nodded, but didn't answer.

'Now you must be wondering why I *really* asked you to come down here to see me.'

'Yes, Magali and I have been mulling that one over ever since you contacted me. We certainly didn't expect you to produce the real diamond.'

'It was not to gloat, Mr. Baxter, I can assure you. In fact the reverse, as I need your help.'

Baxter looked at Magali and raised his eyebrows, confused. She shrugged back.

'Over the past few months I've heard all about the killings here and in London, I take it you know all about them.'

Here it comes thought Baxter, she is going to say she wants the proceeds from the vase. He balanced his reply 'Things have been a little tricky of late, I must admit.'

'Yes, well I fear there may be more to come unless I do the right thing about the diamond now.'

'The diamond!' he said, that was a respite from his immediate concerns, 'and the right thing is?'

'I want you, Mr. Baxter, to tell me how I can contact the Chinese authorities.'

'The Chinese authorities!' he repeated

'Yes Mr. Baxter, I wish to hand the diamond back to them.'

Baxter exhaled. 'Wow, that's some gesture, Countess.'

'Not really,' she replied, 'you see I don't need the money, I have more than enough to last me until the Lord calls me in. I've come to realize that the rock of Batuta is something very special. I now recognise that it is part of the diminishing cultural property of the Chinese people, but it's also an instrument of death and will continue to be so until it is finally out of circulation. So what do you say, can you help me Mr. Baxter?'

'I believe I can, but why me? I don't understand why you should feel you can trust me.'

'An apple doesn't fall far from the tree, Mr. Baxter, and I happen to know your background has roots of decency and you have strength of backbone, and I believe a wide canopy of wisdom. What's more you have taken on the cartel single-handed and beaten them, or so I'm informed. In other words, I'm a good judge of character, Mr. Baxter and would value your assistance. '

'Thank you,' was all he could muster.

There was a pause in the conversation as the two women exchanged looks. The Countess very suddenly broke her gaze and looked back towards him. 'Good for you, Mr. Baxter. Now as I was saying, I can think of no one more able or trustworthy to carry out this task for me. Also' she added as an afterthought. 'Since selling the other Henri de Montaigne vase you're now very comfortably off, so I doubt you would need to risk double- crossing me for the money. You might even feel it apposite given the circumstances.' The look she gave him said more than a thousand words.

The cunning old Countess, he said to himself, she's got me sized up exactly; she knows where that Chinese vase came from and as a result she's kept her cards covered right until the last minute.

Baxter mulled the problem over in his mind. He had to play this carefully because he didn't know for certain if Veerman, wherever he was, knew he had a fake diamond.

He swallowed, and then cleared his throat. 'It will need an export licence which could be tricky with the French authorities here.'

'So what do you suggest, Mr. Baxter?'

'Magali stood up and walked over to the wrought iron terrace balcony. She looked out over the glorious vista of fields and wooded hilltops. Baxter could see she was deep in thought and then remembered she had been a Revenue and Customs officer. If anyone knew how to go about this, she would.

'We could apply to the E.L.U.' Baxter suggested.

Magali turned, a broad smile lit up her face. 'I've got it. We can seek asylum for it, under the UNESCO 1970 Repatriation of Chinese Relic's Convention.'

'Sorry,' said Baxter shaking his head. 'I'm afraid, in order to qualify as cultural property, it has to meet certain criteria.'

'Which is?' Magali asked.

'Well, the diamond would have to possess scholarly value, historical meaning or have important artistic merit and I can't really see how a diamond has any of those attributes?'

Magali was waiting for him to say those words. 'That's perfectly correct,' she said.

'So how can a diamond fall into that category?' he asked

'It's quite simple really.' She rose and walked slowly back to the table and put her hands on the back rail of a chair.

'Well?' He asked waiting for her to make her point.

'You know, Baxter, for someone who believes they are the smartest card in the pack you can be very slow sometimes.' Magali had led him into a verbal trap and was now going to enjoy watching the look on Baxter's face when she took him apart. 'We simply put the diamond back in the porcelain stand and then it will have artistic and cultural value.'

Baxter clapped and the Countess joined in.

'Well done Magali,' he said, 'I always said you weren't just a pretty face.'

'You have never *ever* said my face was pretty.' She elbowed him lightly in the stomach.

The Countess stood up and walked towards the fireplace. 'One last thing, Mr. Baxter, I would be most cautious about mentioning anything concerning what we've discussed here today, even to the police. I happen to know there are dark forces in that institution, particularly in London.'

Baxter said, 'Does the name Inspector Monroe mean anything to you Countess?'

She thought for a minute. 'I don't believe it does. The only thing I can tell you is that I happen to know there is someone in the city police force that can pull strings, and very suspect ones at that.'

'So do you have a name?'

'Oh no, Mr. Baxter, but I believe he is known as 'M'. I'm afraid that's all I can tell you.'

'*Monroe,*' he said under his breath.

Baxter said he would do the necessary to get the ball rolling as far as the diamond was concerned, and would make haste for Paris. He would speak to the people in UNESCO tomorrow afternoon. This, he told her, was the starting point and he hoped they would take it from there and liaise with her directly.

The Countess smiled in relief as she wished the two of them luck, but as they turned to leave, Baxter noticed a change of expression on both the Countesses face and a similar look on Magali's. It was as though they were secretly conveying something which was privy only to them. What's more, there had been something elusive, perhaps even guarded about Magali's attitude since they had arrived here in the Chateau de Couvegne, something which unnerved him, yet inside, he was fighting to shrug it off as merely his imagination working overtime.

That night they booked into a small hotel near the Champs-Elysees, it was nothing special but adequate for a one night impromptu stay in the French capital and conveniently located for the next day's planned excursions.

CHAPTER 24

ST-OUEN DE CLIGNANCOURT

A noise had woken Baxter; not a sudden one, but a steady hum was building up outside his window. He turned over and listened to the gentle puffs of breath next to him. He lightly stroked her hair but she didn't stir.

When Baxter threw back the curtains and looked out on Place de Concorde, he checked the weather and discovered another glorious morning outside. It was barely six am but already Paris was coming to life. People scurried back and forth, snapping up the freshly cooked croissants and baguettes, later baking's wouldn't be as good as this. Typical Parisian men, sometimes with a lady on the arm, sauntered into bars where they sat outside drinking coffee, or in some cases Pernod; the men always dunking their baguette in their black coffee, in the classic French manner.

Everyone, no matter what their objective seemed to be galvanized into getting the day kick-started.

The traffic around the Place de Concorde was building up to the normal rush-hour momentum. A gendarme with small baton stood in the middle of the roundabout waving his arms and pointing in an aggressive manner, an archaic means of traffic control which was far from modern technology, but nonetheless seemed to work perfectly well. Every now and then he blew his whistle, as a threatening gesture to a car or bus which wasn't behaving in quite the way he considered appropriate in order to keep the traffic flowing.

The cacophony of car horns would intensify for the next hour or so and then slightly abate as the day progressed until the evening rush-hour when the gendarme would return.

Baxter shook Magali and reminded her they were going to the

flea market this morning and they needed to be there before eight if they wanted to catch the early bargains. The well-known saying 'the early bird catches the worms' was never truer than at the Paris flea markets.

'Go away,' she groaned indolently, 'I just want to go back to sleep,' she retaliated pulling the covers up over her shoulders and tucking her head inside.

'That's alright, I'll go on my own then, but don't say I should have *made* you get up when I return with wonderful treasures.'

He went to the bathroom, showered and when he came out Magali was standing in her dressing gown waiting to go in.

He didn't say a word, just smiled. Baxter knew she would make the effort to get up in order to go to this particular antiques and bric-a-brac market.

The most important flea market in Paris and probably the most famous in Europe is Marché aux Puces St-Ouen de Clignancourt, situated at Saint-Ouen on the northern fringe of Paris. Strictly speaking it isn't a single bazaar but a grouping of more than a dozen flea markets which by all accounts total more than two thousand stalls and shops which sprawl over six hectares of residential suburbs.

Here the bargain hunter could find an eclectic mix of vintage, French country, Paris apartment, cottage, rustic chic and shabby styles, in fact, virtually everything from antiques to junk. Here, less than thirty minutes from the centre of Paris was the favoured haunt of serious antique buyers and the more intrepid collector who was willing to forage through boxes and crates in search of a gem.

Baxter loved it here, he never tired of the mish-mash of beauty that was the Paris flea market, and of course, the jazz on every corner which was invariably Django Reinhard, gipsy style. He was in his element around so many things that were old but new to him. He scanned every stall and table with the anticipation of finding a trophy, no matter how big or small.

Baxter and Magali arrived early while the morning was still

young, at that time when ebullient stallholders, having set up their stalls, were sitting around tables dunking croissants in black coffee and tossing witticisms across the adjoining stalls. They spent the first hour or so scouring the maze of cobbled alleyways at the eastern end. He always started here, the not so attractive part, where one had to get dirty, dig deep and sleuth around.

Baxter soon noticed Magali's obvious disinterest in this ramshackle part of the market, so suggested they head for the favourite haunt of the casual tourist; an area called Venaison. Here, in marked contrast, the cobbled alleys were home to charming, fashionable bric-a-brac shops selling everything from quality mid-price items to expensive top of the range antiques.

After an hour of browsing through stalls of specially selected and overpriced offerings, he had failed to find a single item to tempt him. Magali on the other hand was thrilled with a Hermes scarf, snapped up after lengthy bargaining for forty euros.

They stopped at a leafy spot where red and white checked tablecloths on round iron tables gently rippled in the breeze. They chose a table under the shade of a spreading chestnut tree and sat and admired her purchase. Within seconds a man in a crisp white apron marched smartly out of the café across the road and stopped, turning on his heels in front of them, hovering with pencil and pad in hand. He was the archetypal Parisian waiter, short, dark-tanned with tightly curled black hair. His face as wrinkled as chamois leather, yet when Baxter looked up to order, the barman's smile was as smooth as a seasoned encyclopaedia rep. Baxter ordered hot chocolate for Magali and café crème for himself, and of course, three croissants. The waiter spun on his heels and was gone in a flash.

Baxter enjoyed people-watching and listening almost as much as buying and this was the perfect place to do it. There were always so many languages being spoken by the crowds of tourists who passed them by. Strangely the native French tongue was often the least encountered, although he would smile at the many clumsy attempts to converse in that language.

A small group of Americans accompanied by a tour guide took a table close by and immediately the decibel level increased.

'Oh my God, you are telling me we have only seen an eighth of this market?' A voice proclaimed loudly, as though he wanted the whole world to hear what he had to say.

'That's all so far.' said the English speaking guide.

'Goddamit, this is gonna take us forever, Mabel. While we are here you might as well take a few more snaps for the folks back home in Utah.'

It wasn't just the diverse assemblage of buyers and browsers that interested Baxter, but also the vendors who could always manage the basic bartering language of English, Italian and often German. Generally speaking there were two kinds of sellers. There were those who practiced the art of display and lovingly curated their collection on tables under brightly coloured canopies. Their presentation painstakingly put together suggested they were not necessarily concerned whether or not you bought anything, in fact you might get the impression that their display would be upset if you did take something away. And there were those who didn't care what their stall looked like, piling it high in a jumble of confusion. Others simply tipped their stock onto blankets on the ground.

'I've often wondered where the term flea market comes from,' said Magali with a look of expectation at Baxter, for he usually had an answer to anything connected with antiques and their history.

'Now that's a good question.' He paused as he dredged his brain for the story he had been told many years ago. ' Well, as you know flea market is English for the French *marché aux puces*, and I believe it originated sometime in the eighteenth century when chiffoniers, or rag-and-bone men, resold goods and clothing found in aristocrats' rubbish bins. The craze soon caught on and very quickly the poorer elements of society were bringing along flea-infested furniture and other household items, which they sold to the public. They set up their stalls here at the present day Porte de Clignancourt, just outside the gates of Paris, in order to avoid fees and taxes incurred within the city walls. Mind you, it's a disputed theory, and has been argued over by historians and linguists for more than half a century, but I think it's likely to be true.'

Magali interrupted him 'Now that's a turn up for the books.'

'What is,' he replied laughing.

'Isn't that your friend over there?' she said, her outstretched finger levelling at a woman who was darting from stall to stall. They watched in amusement as the lady pointed to what she wanted, paid and then moved on to the next stall leaving her lackey to collect what she had bought. Minutes later the little man emerged trotting behind as he pushed an overloaded trolley piled high with textiles.

'For goodness sake do keep up, Mark, 'she snapped.

'Yes, that's Shirley, Shirley, alright,' he confirmed. She spotted him, raised her hand and he waved back. 'She won't have time to stop and chat with us,' he remarked as she disappeared into the clutches of yet another textile merchant.

They paid for their petite dejuner and headed off to finish the last bit of browsing.

Baxter was just straightening after examining a box of oddments on the ground, when he was barged into, sending him reeling sideways.

'Pardon. Excusez-moi, ' a husky voice said. The Oriental man held his hands out apologetically and turned as if to leave and then spun suddenly, reaching into his coat pocket. Baxter caught the glint of a blade as the man retracted his arm, gripping a knife tightly in his hand. The man grabbed Baxter's shoulder and lunged with the knife aimed at his chest.

'Put that down or I'll blast your brains out.'

Magali stood behind the man, legs apart, with a gun clenched in both hands, the barrel pushing hard against the back of his head.

The man dropped the knife, turned and fled. Magali quickly slipped the gun back into her shoulder bag.

'Stop him.' Baxter shouted, as he sprinted after him.

Then a rather wonderful set of events unfolded and they appeared to take place in slow motion. He spotted Shirley coming out of the shop with her man following behind.

'Stop that man.' Baxter shouted once more. Shirley looked over in surprise, grabbed her trolley loaded with textiles and with split second timing, pushed it directly in front of the fleeing thug. The man hit the trolley full on, plunging headfirst over the top of it, then landing spread-eagled on the pavement.

By the time Baxter arrived a small crowd had begun to assemble. Someone was busy ringing the police as another emptied the contents of the Asian's pockets. A piece of folded paper was examined, handed round and Magali took it from the last onlooker.

'What is it?' Baxter asked.

She handed it to him, it was a note handwritten in French but more to the point, the top heading had the conjoined batwing logo. Baxter urged Magali to leave before the police arrived.

'I had no idea you were still carrying a gun,' he said looking at her curiously, but he had felt the distinctive shape of a firearm in her handbag once before.

'It's a dangerous world out there,' is all she said.

'I just can't believe it,' he said as they sat in a bar drinking more coffee and hot chocolate, 'I thought we'd be safe here in France.'

'You're never safe from the likes of Veerman, trust me, he'll never give up, it's against his nature,' said Magali; she managed a weak smile.

Baxter read the note which had been taken from the thug. It was brief and to the point. *'Baxter is in the café Equinox, do it now.'*

'Someone tipped him off,' Magali said 'It wouldn't have been…'

'Shirley, no definitely not,' He interrupted 'There's no way she would be involved in something like this and besides, if it had been Shirley why would she have intervened to stop him. No it wasn't her.'

'What about the other chap you spoke to?' she shot him a glance which was laced with suspicion.

'What Phillips, no, he's just another dealer. I must have bumped into at least half a dozen regulars this morning. I just wonder,' he said pausing to think.

'What?' she asked.

'I booked the hotel on my mobile phone using my internet account, you don't think someone has hacked into it do you?'

'I've just had a horrible thought,' Magali said

'What's that?'

'You left your garage doors open when we made that hurried retreat from your place.'

Of course, he suddenly realised they hadn't had time to close them, should have asked Keith, he thought to himself. Then the realization of what he had done, or rather not done hit him.

'This means someone has been in my cottage and probably hacked into my internet, they did that before you know.'

'They might have even stolen your laptop,' she remarked.

'The recording of Veerman,' they both said at the same time.

'And that's how they knew where to find us minutes after I booked the hotel yesterday,' he added ruefully. 'And they will have followed us here to Clignancourt. Still at least my contact at the Met, Atterbury, has a copy of the recording.

'The trouble is we are still likely to be under observation,' she said. 'Whoever sent the note to the knifeman is going to be out there, following our every move, ready to instruct another killer.

'Hang on, I've got an idea. Wait here Magali.'

Baxter went to the counter and grabbed the waiter's arm.

'Monsieur, I have a big problem. There is a man across the road who is going to kill me.'

'Kill you, Monsieur?' he said raising his dark bushy eyebrows.

'And why would he wish to do that?'

'See the lady sitting over there,' he pointed to Magali and the waiter nodded. 'A very beautiful lady,' the man drawled with a leer.

'Yes, well, that's her husband with the gun.'

'I understand fully, Monsieur.' He flashed a cheeky grin.

Baxter unrolled two brown fifty euro notes and slapped them on the bar 'Do you have a rear exit? I need to get back to my car which is parked in Avenue Dupres Venuve.'

'Wait here,' he said, snatching up the money and stuffing it in his apron pocket.

Baxter glanced back over to Magali who raised her brows in anticipation of a solution. Baxter shrugged his shoulders and she laughed.

The waiter returned with the cook in tow. He was a short man with an incredibly long handlebar moustache. He struggled in the confines of the bar, as he fought to put on an ancient brown leather flying coat with goggles hanging around his neck.

'Renee, here, will take you back to your car in his motor. Quick follow me.'

Baxter waved Magali over and they went out the back, through the kitchens and store room, emerging in a small back yard.

'Not in that,' Magali said surveying the faded yellow Messerschmitt bubble car which resembled an aircraft fuselage.'

'It's a nineteen fifty four KR175,' Baxter announced.

'I didn't think you knew anything about cars, you always claimed you were not remotely interested in makes or models.'

'I don't and I'm not, but my friend Keith had one of those, it was his baby, that is until it blew up and destroyed his garage in a ball of flames.'

'And you expect me to get in that. It looks more like a cockpit without wings to me.'

'Come on,' he said 'we've no choice.'

Renee lifted the front canopy which was one-piece with the windows and doors and the two of them, with some difficulty, scrambled onto the rear tandem seat.

The cook grabbed the tubular handlebars and pushed hard sending the car forward, hurtling through the back alleyway.

Baxter wasn't quite certain what the waiter had told Renee, but the man drove like a madman. With his foot hard on the pedal, he reached and maintained the top speed of thirty miles an hour, keeping in first gear, which suggested that was the only one that was operable.

The mad french cook careered through the back streets of the market, narrowly avoiding stalls and people and shouting 'youpi' back to his passengers every time he avoided some obstacle. The rear wheels left the ground on every bend and with a lack of proper suspension the two of them were catapulted from their seats each time the car encountered a bump in the road.

The road ahead was suddenly blocked by a large delivery lorry whose back was open; two men were walking down the tailgate carrying a commercial refrigerator. They spotted the fast-moving bubble car and stopped and Baxter could see a look of terror on their faces. He braced himself in expectation the mad cook would brake violently, but instead, he veered sharply to the right. Baxter held his hands in front of his eyes as the man careered down a narrow alleyway. Magali screamed in alarm as the car bounced against the gutter on each side. An unattended fruit barrow piled high with produce loomed into view, but the brakes failed to stop the vehicle quickly enough. The Messerschmitt bubble car hit the barrow end on, sending the cart into the air; fruit and vegetables pounded the windscreen, others tumbled over the roof. Baxter was alarmed when, several times, Renee held his hands in front of his face and screamed 'oh mon Dieu'. Amazingly, the man barely slowed, before thrusting his foot back down on the accelerator, sending the car hurtling forward once again. The sound of the noisy gyrating engine was now accompanied by the crunching of the remnants of the wooden barrow jammed under the front bumper, as the car pushed it along until it disintegrated under the wheels.

The cook negotiated a few more side streets, and then Baxter spotted his car. 'Over there, you can drop us just there,' he said with a sudden feeling of relief.

With that Renee braked hard, sending the two of them careering into the back of the front seat and then, a split second later they were thrown back again just as forcibly.

As they scrambled out of the now battered bubble car, Renee pulled away a piece of wood lodged in the radiator, casually throwing it to one side. He shook both their hands and with a look of triumph, jumped back in and sped off shouting 'youpi' until they could hear him no longer.

Back in the heart of Paris they drove into the visitor's car park behind the UNESCO building in Place de Fontenoy.

The large five story building housed the headquarters of United Nations Educational, Scientific, and Cultural Organisation.

Baxter scanned the information board and discovered the culture department was situated on the seventh floor. They took the lift up to that level, alighted and followed the signs pointing to the Movable Heritage and Museums section.

As was usual for large organisations of this nature, the unit was split into several departments. Baxter asked for help at the reception desk and was directed to the department of Illicit Traffic of Cultural Property.

It took Baxter over an hour to relate the 'how's and wherefores' behind the discovery of the rock of Batuta, and Countess de Couvegne's wish that it be repatriated to China. The secretariat was impressed by her generosity and told Baxter and Magali that he didn't for one moment think the French Government would refuse a repatriation passport in this particular case. However, that was not the end of the story, because the repatriation request would require consideration from many other departments and would take some time to implement.

Baxter knew all about cutting through French Bureaucracy. It was usually easier to cut through a piece of string with a cigarette paper than deal with what is, euphemistically called, l'administration.

Finally the officer suggested UNESCO handle the arrangements. They would initiate the French side of things and liaise with the Countess and of course their UNESCO counterparts in Beijing.

CHAPTER 25

DECEPTION

As the port of Calais was much closer to Paris than Cherbourg, Baxter decided to abandon his return ferry ticket and reserved a crossing to Dover, but this time on Magali's mobile phone.

'Your passports please, sir,' the man in the booth at Dover said. Baxter unwound the car window and handed their passports across. The officer took one look at Magali's gold embossed blue *Passeport Francais* and put it down, but Baxter's red and gold United Kingdom wallet appeared to be of rather more interest to him. The border control officer studied Baxter's face for a few seconds and then tapped the details of his passport into the computer. Baxter heard an audible ting and the officer looked at his monitor again and double-checked Baxter's details. Finally he leaned out of his booth and handed both passports back. As Baxter reached through his car window to take them, he noticed the man press a switch and a red light momentarily flashed.

The barrier rose and he proceeded at a sedate pace towards the covered Revenue and Customs building.

A white van ahead was directed into an inspection area. *Probably contraband cigarettes* he thought to himself smugly. Ahead, two yellow-jacketed men were observing vehicles as they passed the Revenue and Customs point. When Baxter reached them, he was quite surprised when one of the men in a high-vis jacket stepped out in front and raised his hand. 'Please drive into that side bay sir.'

The sign above read 'Beware Catsclaw'. Even if he had a reason to make a break for it, the spikes would rise and all four of his tyres would be immediately punctured.

'If you and your passenger would care to step out of the car sir,' he said in a calm but firm way.

They followed another officer up a short flight of steps and entered a reception area, where they were quickly ushered through a doorway just beyond.

The interview room on the first floor was characteristically simply appointed, but nonetheless comfortable enough. If they had any uncertainty as to whether they were being apprehended against their wishes, then the bars on the windows left them in no doubt.

'So have you found contraband tobacco, large quantities of alcohol or perhaps even drugs in my car?' Baxter asked the uniformed officer, as he entered the room and sat down in front of them.

'I'm not Revenue and Customs sir, but harbour board police, and I can tell you now that we have no interest whatsoever in the contents of your car and I can say the same for Customs.'

'So what is it then? Baxter asked angrily.

'Your passport, sir, has been red-flagged by the Metropolitan police.'

'Which means what precisely?'

'Well, I'm afraid we will have to hold you here, until they send someone down to collect you and take you back to London.'

Baxter sprang to his feet. He felt the anger boiling; he paused, fighting to calm the emotion in his voice 'This is preposterous, you're treating us like criminals.'

'Yes, what have we done?' Magali joined in.

'I'm sorry sir, and you madam, but I have my orders. I feel certain it will all be sorted out very quickly; these things usually are.'

'And may I enquire who in London has issued this arrest warrant?'

'I'm sure it's not an arrest warrant, sir; I don't think I can really tell you anymore.'

Baxter said 'Is it, by any chance, a certain detective Chief Inspector Monroe of Paddington Green?'

He thumbed through his papers. 'I shouldn't be telling you this but as you come to mention it, yes, it is a Chief Inspector by that name?'

They exchanged glances. Magali frowned, then was the first to speak 'I'm not happy about this, sergeant; I can't say any more, but this Chief Inspector Monroe may not be who he claims to be.'

'Really, madam, please, I'm certain your accusations are quite unfounded, Inspector Monroe is from the Met.'

'Well, can I make a telephone call?' Baxter asked

'It depends; I have to enquire as to the nature of the call and the recipient please sir.'

'To a friend of mine,' he said assertively, 'it's a Mr Terrence Atterbury, who is the assistant chief commissioner at the Met, or to be precise, he heads the Specialist Crime & Operations Directorate.'

The officer tilted his cap forward and scratched his head. 'The Assistant Chief Commissioner.' He raised his eyebrows, suddenly surprised. 'So do you know his number then?' he said with a look which implied he doubted very much that Baxter would have been privy to such a high-ranking officer's telephone number.

'No, but I have it here,' he reached in his inside pocket and took the business card out of his wallet.

'It's zero three double zero, one two three, one two one two, extension two one three.'

The officer tapped in the digits on the dialling pad and waited for a response. 'Ah, is that the Specialist Crime & Operations Department?' he asked the operator. The reply came in the affirmative. 'This is Dover Harbour Board Police; do you have an assistant chief commissioner there by the name of Mr. Terrence Atterbury on extension two one three?' The reply, once again, came in the affirmative and she said she would put him through as soon as he was free, but that might be a few minutes. Could he hold on?

He confirmed he could.

'Atterbury here.' The voice was uncompromising and intimidating to the lower ranked sergeant.

'Good afternoon, Sir.'

'Yes, get on with it man.' Atterbury snapped

'I have a Mr. Baxter here who says he knows you and wishes to speak with you, Sir.'

'Put him on.' Atterbury barked.

Baxter spilled as much of the story as he could to Atterbury, who said very little. But when Baxter had finished he asked to speak with the police officer.

'I didn't catch your name sergeant.'

'It's Mathews, Simon Mathews, Sir.'

'Right, Mathews, now listen very carefully to what I'm going to tell you.'

'Yes, Sir,' Mathews replied.

'On no account are you to allow Inspector Monroe to collect Mr. Baxter and his companion. He *is* who he claims to be and is from the Met, but we currently have him under surveillance as part of a serious crimes investigation, do you understand what I'm telling you?'

'Yes, sir…, do you want us to arrest him when he gets here?'

'No, most certainly not, we will deal with that. Just tell him they have already been collected by someone from the Met, no more. In the meantime, I'll come down and pick them up personally, shouldn't be more than ninety minutes or so. Oh, and Mathews.'

'Yes, Sir.'

'I'll give your chief superintendent a ring now and explain the situation. In the meantime, it's imperative you don't mention this telephone call to anyone else until I get there, do you understand?'

'Yes, Sir, fully,' he replied stiffly.

'I'm relying on you Mathews and I might add, if you carry this out to the letter there will be a mention about this to your super.'

'Now that's interesting,' the officer said, as he put the receiver back on its stand. 'Your friend, the Commissioner, has instructed us to look after you until he arrives, as he's intending to escort you personally back to London.' Baxter sighed with relief. 'Thank goodness for that,' he said to Magali.

'So what did he say about Monroe?' she asked.

'Not much really. It seems Inspector Monroe is who he claims to be, but there are some issues which may affect your safety, but I can't say any more than that, only that you must wait here for the Assistant Commissioner.'

'I thought so,' she said, 'he didn't come across quite right.'

'How come,' Baxter looked at her quizzically, 'you have never met him, or have you?'

'No it's just what you've told me about him,' she replied shakily.

They were now offered a very different style of hospitality. This new room was a comfortable lounge with leather sofas, a vending machine for coffee and tea, and a plate of biscuits laid on for them. There were no bars on the windows here, but even so they were still in a reserved and secure area.

It had taken him over an hour to drive down from London and Monroe was furious. On arrival at Dover Harbour Board Police Station, he was informed by the desk sergeant that Baxter and Magali had already been collected. There was no one available to offer any explanation. The message the desk sergeant had been left said someone from the Met had over-ridden his instructions.

Monroe didn't need to guess who had stepped in and done that, it was the same person who was always meddling in this investigation. Someone, who owing to rank, was always just outside his reach and that was none other than Assistant Chief Commissioner Atterbury. Due to the officer's senior rank, Monroe was for the time being powerless to do anything about it. What's more, he didn't for one minute believe Atterbury had arrived before him as that would be impossible, unless he was already in the area, and that he very much doubted. No, he was convinced Baxter and Magali were still here waiting to be collected.

With his unmarked car parked in shadow, yet with a clear view of the police headquarters building, Monroe decided to keep his head down and wait. He knew he had to get it right this time; he'd missed his opportunity once before, there wasn't going to be a second chance, this was his final one. He knew full well if he didn't succeed and finish it for once and for all, he would have some very difficult explaining to do.

When Atterbury arrived just over an hour later, he went over the top, greeting Baxter with warm handshakes and a strange overdramatic old pal's act. They were only casually acquainted so Baxter was a little baffled by his show of amity. Sergeant Mathews was congratulated on a good job well done, and promised a mention to his station Superintendent.

Baxter and Magali pulled away in their car, followed closely by Atterbury's sleek silver Jaguar XJ.

Sergeant Mathews was not the only one to see them depart. Monroe, in the shadows of the freight transport building lowered himself in his car seat and watched as they came down the short flight of steps, a warm handshake all round and the unhurried exit out of the compound. He told his driver to follow the two cars, but at a discreet distance. He had a short conversation on his mobile phone and then stretched in the back planning, his next move.

Baxter driving his red Celica, quickly left the sprawling suburbs of Dover in the distance and shortly afterwards the seaside town of Folkestone before heading along the M20 motorway towards London. As they passed the Eurotunnel complex this brought back memories of their trip by Eurostar a couple of months earlier. His mind wandered back to the mysterious caverns below Montmartre, he still didn't have a clue what that was all about, or how it fitted into the larger picture. *I wonder if the little men are still watching the Shāqi through their little spyholes* he mused to himself.

Magali had fallen asleep and purred softly as they sped through the Garden of England.

After some thirty five minutes his mobile beeped. He didn't usually respond to telephone calls while driving; it was, of course, illegal but considering who the caller was he felt in this case he could hardly ignore it. Atterbury said he needed to stop at the next roadside services, the Road chef at Maidstone, which was also conveniently about the halfway point.

The cups of coffee all round went down rather well despite being served in waxed cardboard cups. Atterbury stood up and stretched, then wandered over to the public conveniences.

'What's on your mind?' Baxter asked, noting how Magali had suddenly fallen quiet and bore a look of apprehension.

'Nothing,' she snapped back.

'Liar, I don't believe you.'

She said, 'I simply don't know if we can trust him, that's all.'

'What, Atterbury?' he chuckled.

'I know he heads SCO, but do you really know anything about him?'

'SCO?' Baxter said.

' Specialist Crime & Operations.'

'Yes, of course,' he said, puzzled by her familiarity with the acronym. 'Well I would rather trust him than Chief Inspector Monroe, wouldn't you?'

She reluctantly nodded in agreement, although her acceptance was not totally convincing.

Atterbury returned. 'Right, let's make a move, I'll follow you up to the outskirts of London, then we'll regroup again.' Suddenly the buzz of a mobile phone sounded. Atterbury turned on his heels.

'Yes,' he barked 'Really, are you certain? Right, I see.' He paused in thought. 'I tell you what, I'll bring them back with me; it'll be safer that way. And you say bomb disposal are on their way. Good, I'll leave you to deal with them Constable.'

'Right chaps, it seems we have a problem here. My officers who were following behind spotted two individuals in the car park, tampering with your car.'

'My car?' Baxter exclaimed. He turned to Magali 'I bet that's something to do with Monroe.'

'Well, we don't know that for certain, so don't jump to conclusions,' said Atterbury. 'But if what we suspect is indeed true, then Monroe will be determined to stop you reaching London and is likely to resort to desperate measures.'

'You mentioned a bomb?'

'Possibly,' he said coolly.

'So what do we do now then?' Baxter asked.

'Well we can't take any chances, and I don't want to have to wait for the bomb disposal squad, that could take a couple of hours or more.'

'So it really could be a bomb!' Magali exclaimed in horror.

'I wouldn't put anything past Monroe,' Atterbury said. 'You'd better come back to London in my car; I've instructed my officers to wait until your vehicle is searched by the bomb squad.'

Noticing a look of alarm on Baxter's face he added. 'Don't look so worried; you will have your car back by tomorrow morning and hopefully still in one piece, but I wouldn't say the same for you if you *were* to drive it away right now.'

Crossing the car park, Baxter strained his eyes trying to see his car which was parked a few bays away from Atterbury's Jaguar. He then caught sight of it in the distance with a blue and white tape draped around it. He shuddered at the thought that in two minutes time they could have been scattered across the car park in a thousand pieces.

The doors of the Jaguar closed with a barely audible hollow clunk, a reassuring indication of the luxury this car afforded.

With Atterbury at the wheel they took the non-motorway exit.

'Is this the right way?' Baxter asked, concerned he had taken a wrong turning.

'We've temporarily sealed off the motorway link to make sure our suspects can't leave the scene. Also taking the A road should shake off Monroe, in case he's still trying to tail us.'

The view of the Kentish countryside sped by. The distinctive oasthouses with their conical terracotta roofs stood proud and more often than not, grouped with small hamlets of houses and often a church with pointed spire. In this part of Kent there was no shortage of weather-boarded Kentish barns, typically with long low roofs almost sweeping to the ground, effortlessly blending into the folds of the landscape.

Atterbury maintained a steady pace as the afternoon slowly turned to dusk and, almost imperceptibly, the countryside turned into a silhouette of shapes and forms as darkness enveloped the hills and valleys. Now only the occasional Church spire, black against the darkening sky, gave any indication of civilization.

The phosphor blue halo illumination on the driver's console and impressive iTech platform now irradiated the interior of the car, a high-tech assemblage which looked more like an aircraft cockpit than a car dashboard. The sat-nav displayed the road ahead disappearing from the screen and nondescript blocks of brown which denoted the rapidly disappearing built-up infrastructure.

Along the way Baxter explained a few more details about the cartel, how they had illegally imported Asian art and the way they laundered money for the British criminal fraternity. He firmly pointed the finger at Max Veerman as the organisation head and the Chinese Shāqi agents, who carried out his evil deeds. Atterbury gasped when Baxter disclosed the fact that the diamond in Veerman's possession was after all nothing but a fake.

'The compact disc you sent me with the recording of Veerman was a brilliant piece of detective work,' he said in a congratulatory tone, 'I take it you have a copy or two?' Atterbury looked in his rear view mirror focusing on Baxter.

'Yes of course, don't worry about that.'

'I suppose you've hidden them somewhere safely in your cottage?' he was still watching Baxter intently.

That last sentence sent a chill of suspicion down Baxter's back. Why was Atterbury so interested in his copies of the recording? Something small, yet disquieting, was building in the back of his mind. Something was not quite right, but for the time being he couldn't put his finger on it, so let it drop.

'No, not really,' he replied not wishing to elaborate any further.

Atterbury said there was a drinks decanter in the fold-down tray set located in the back of the seats, and that they might as well sit back and relax with a glass of wine.

That seemed an excellent idea and soon he and Magali snuggled together on the long soft leather rear seat, each with a large glass of wine.

CHAPTER 26

IN THE DARK SHADOW OF EVIL

Atterbury pulled into Springwell Place, a once thriving Kent farm which had ceased agricultural activities some ten years previous. These days it was a holiday let, a familiar haunt to Atterbury who often booked weekend breaks here. Being less than thirty minutes away from central London it was conveniently close, yet isolated and peaceful and provided a relaxed retreat for him and his wife; a welcome escape from the busy city life. Like most weekdays at this time of the year, it was deserted.

The farmhouse wasn't joined to the former business side of the farm, which lay in a separate courtyard nearby.

The three Kentish barns, long stripped of their tractors and farm machinery now lay empty and largely unused.

Atterbury waited patiently, wondering where his men were; they should have been here by now. If they didn't arrive soon, time would override the strength of the sleeping drafts he had plied Baxter and his woman with.

To his relief he spotted lights catching the trees at the far end of the drive and a few minutes later Baxter's car swung into the courtyard, followed by a second car.

'Drive it straight into that barn,' he instructed, pointing to the largest of the three. The agricultural storehouse had full-height hefty ledged and braced doors which were already propped open, casting a pool of light onto the threshold.

Once Baxter's car had been parked inside, the three men lifted Baxter and Magali out of Atterbury's Jaguar and propped them up in the front seats of the vehicle, it was then pushed tightly against the right hand wall of the barn.

Atterbury told the Chinese to wait outside in their car and keep a close look out.

Baxter blinked, but he couldn't seem to be able to move. It took several minutes before it registered in his fog-laden head that his hands were securely tied behind his back. He looked to his left; Magali was slumped sideways still asleep beside him, also bound, but to his amazement they were both sitting in a car, not just any car, but *his* car.

As his head began to clear he looked out the window taking stock of his surroundings.

They and the car were in a high-roofed building which was illuminated by a long row of suspended light bulbs.

It didn't require the brains of Einstein to recognise the building was a typical Kentish barn which meant they were still in the county of Kent, but where?

In front of him there were two continuous rows of timber aisle posts with storage bays on the left hand side, some still containing straw, others with what looked like obsolete farming equipment. The roof was high and lofty with great oak tie beams held together with curving wind braces. A row of clasped purlins were intersected by crown posts which looked far too grand for a mere barn.

Looking around it appeared the only entry and exit points were two pairs of large doors sited opposite each other. Magali murmured and then stirred.

'Are you alright?' he asked, although in the circumstances it did seem rather a silly question.

'Not really, my head feels as though someone hit me with a sledgehammer, what happened to us Baxter?'

'I think it's safe to say I've made a very grave mistake. That wine Atterbury offered us was laced with something which knocked us out.'

'We've been drugged?'

'Yes I think so.'

'But why would he do that, and why are we tied up here in your car, what's going on Baxter?'

'I think we can be fairly certain that dear old Atterbury is in with

Monroe, *and* both are in the pay of Veerman, and no doubt he's behind all this. But I still find it hard to believe the real villain was Atterbury.'

'I don't, he was far too friendly; I had a few reservations right from the beginning,' she said.

'Well, why didn't you say something?'

'I didn't like to, he was your friend, but I just felt something wasn't quite right.'

'Yes, I was a fool in thinking he was being friendly, I now realise he was on my tail, right from the start.'

'So what are we going to do now, Baxter?' she looked forlornly at him.

'I don't know but,' he stopped 'Sh… I think I can hear somebody outside speaking to someone.'

He put his ear to the driver's side window and closed his eyes and listened, but the voice was far too muted to hear anything other than an unscrambled hum.

Baxter thought hard, trying to take stock of their predicament, he was desperately marshaling his options, but in the back of his mind a growing feeling of doom was creeping into his thought processes.

He suddenly came to his senses and told himself he wasn't going to give in just like that, he never surrendered that easily, not him.

He glanced around once again, but now the windows were starting to mist over. He wiped the windscreen with his head.

'I have a bad feeling about this, a really bad feeling.'

'Please don't say that, Baxter, not now, after all we've been through, there must be a way out of this.'

No matter how hard he tried he just couldn't think how they were going to get out of this one, unless...

He turned to Magali 'Swivel round in your seat so I can untie your hands. She did as he asked and his fingers picked at her bound wrists. But after five minutes of picking, tugging and fumbling he came to the conclusion that the nylon twine Atterbury had used was a type which produced incredibly tight knots which required a knife to release. He realised this seemingly obvious solution was not going to work.

He eyed with dismay the empty cigarette lighter portal. He didn't smoke these days and so only used it to plug in his sat nav and before he returned it, Steve's anti tracking device. He needed something sharp, but there was nothing which would cut through the blue nylon cord.

He heard the sound before he realised where it was coming from, a slow laboured screeching of un-oiled iron hinges.

As the large doors to the right slowly opened, a pool of light from a powerful floodlight above illuminated the familiar frame of Atterbury as he walked in carrying their coats.

Baxter swallowed. 'What are you up to Atterbury?' he shouted.

'You will find out very shortly, I promise you that,' he said, in a voice which was now belligerent. He threw their coats on to the bonnet, put on a pair of brown leather gloves and then picked up Magali's shoulder bag and tipped the contents out. A large object slid over the side of the wing landing loudly on the concrete floor. Atterbury bent and picked it up gingerly.

'Now what have we here?' he rocked the gun, with his gloved finger in the trigger loop. 'A Glock seventeen with sixteen rounds still in the chamber. Now that's interesting, I wonder why a lady should have a lightweight pistol in her shoulder bag, and with trijacon night sights front and rear. It looks to me as though there is more to you than meets the eye, my dear,' he said giving her an unpleasant sideways glance.

'To protect myself from people like you,' she retaliated.

He put the gun in his pocket. Quickly dismissing the other contents from her bag, he riffled through her coat pocket. 'Now this is a pretty pink phone,' he said turning it over in his hand.

'Be careful, it's new and I don't want it damaged,' she shouted.

He opened the car door on her side and leant in 'You're a plucky little thing, aren't you? But without your gun you want to watch your tongue.'

She didn't reply

'It's alright, you can have your mobile back, but it won't help you in here, no reception at all.' He laughed as he pushed it purposefully into the top of her bra. 'Oops,' he said, 'careless me' as he fumbled around her breasts. She head-butted him, catching him on the jaw and he let go with a shout.

'You bitch; he snarled, then leant further in and kissed her on the lips before she had the chance to shy away.

'Leave her alone, Atterbury.' Baxter yelled, leaning across.

Atterbury laughed 'Ah how touching, I suppose you're in love and that's why you are blind, Baxter. You think you're invincible and you don't care, you take chances and look where it leads you.'

'And where *has* it led me, Atterbury?'

'It has led you here where you must be stopped from doing any more damage, but I'll add, I never had any intention of causing you any harm until you threatened us.'

'Us?' Baxter said.

'The cartel and all it stands for. That is to say Mr. Veerman and people like myself. But there are far more important reputations than mine to protect. But as I said, I never had any malice towards you until you stirred things up and that's the truth of the matter.'

'Your idea of the truth, Atterbury, is just one of the many lies you believe the most.'

Atterbury scowled, his face suddenly betraying his growing distaste for Baxter. 'You have been just a little bit *too* clever, but not clever enough. You think you have the evidence to implicate Mr. Veerman of conspiracy to murder, you sent me a tape, remember.'

'That was a big mistake sending it to you. But do you really think it's the only copy Atterbury?'

'No I don't, but I find it difficult to believe you were so stupid as to leave a CD copy hidden amongst your discs and the original recording on the laptop in your cottage, now that *was* a very silly thing to do.'

'That's how you knew which Paris hotel we were in, you hacked into my internet account and had us followed and then paid some bumbling idiot to kill me.'

'I admit I was unfortunate in my choice of hit man, but it's not easy to find them at short notice, especially in Paris.'

'There'd better not be any damage to my cottage,' he said boldly.

A fleeting, unpleasant smile crossed Atterbury's face and when he spoke, Baxter witnessed a sudden coldness in his voice. 'Why of course not, my men were very careful, they are experts, they left everything neat and tidy except for your laptop. I'm afraid you'll never see that again, but then where you're going you won't be needing a computer; I can assure you of that.'

'So tell me, Atterbury, where *are* we going?' he asked innocently, but he had a shrewd idea what the answer was likely to be.

'On a one-way trip to meet your maker,' Atterbury said sepulchrally as he tilted a nearby twenty five gallon drum and then began rolling it on its edge across the room towards them.

'That doesn't sound very friendly, in fact it seems to me you're being most unfair to Magali who's done nothing to you.'

'It's not meant to be friendly or fair,' he retorted. 'As one great American statesman once said, *he who believes there is fairness in this life is seriously misinformed.'*

'Tell me one thing, Atterbury. Why did you ever get mixed up with Veerman, what's in it for you?

He righted the drum 'What's in it for me!' he shouted, 'Well if you must know, and it doesn't really matter now if you do, so I'll tell you. You see, I'm one of the original members of the cartel. I first met Veerman in Hong Kong in the late sixties. Then I was just an inspector with the British police force, stationed there for a five year stint. I don't know whether you know how little an Inspector is paid, but I couldn't afford any of the niceties of life in British sovereignty Hong Kong. When Veerman came to me with an offer which far exceeded anything I could earn in the police force, I couldn't say no. You see they needed someone who would turn a blind eye to the smuggling of Asian art out of China and into British controlled Hong Kong and I was their man, and still am and that's why I must now dispose of the two of you.' A thin smile formed on his lips, turning rapidly into a wry pathetic leer.

'You bastard,' Magali yelled in disgust, her face was ashen and distorted by a mixture of fright and anger. Her eyes, that nature had intended to be kind and caring, had an unnatural, angry glare. 'Baxter looked on you as a friend,' she shouted.

'Yes, and Max Veerman looked on *you* as a friend, and you've betrayed him. Well, do you want me to tell you what he told me to do with you?'

She didn't reply.

'Well, I'll tell you anyway. His exact words to me were *burn the bitch, I wish I could be there to hear the two of them scream like a pair of geese.'*

His voice lacked any emotion whatsoever and Baxter now had the tangible measure of the man.

'How can you be so evil, Atterbury? And tell me, how do you sleep at night?'

Atterbury raised his gaunt face and jeered at them. 'How can I be so evil? Don't you realise bad men do what good men only dream of and I wager you dream of doing some unscrupulous things yourself, but you don't have the backbone to carry them out.'

'You are simply a pathetic, narcissistic little man, Atterbury, and I can tell you now, you don't know me at all.'

Atterbury was becoming visibly angry and there were now long regular spaces between his words. Beads of sweat were forming on his brow and deep purple veins throbbed below the surface of his skin. 'Don't try and tell me you've never dreamt of doing something which was just a little bit dishonest, something you knew was bad, but was for the greater good, because I don't believe you Baxter.'

'Maybe, but the difference is I've never acted upon my fantasies. Social Hedonism doesn't mean everyone is entitled to live on Temptation Island. Like Epicurean philosophy, social hedonism means maximizing pleasure and minimizing pain, but it has never implied rampant wickedness or lies.'

'Ah the Calculus of Felicity, so you are indeed an educated man, Baxter.'

'And you're just a wicked, evil little man, I've had better shit on my shoe than you will ever be.'

Atterbury suddenly exploded with fury, his face turned purple with rage. 'Those are the words of someone who has outlived their purpose, so make the most of it, Baxter, because they are the last you are ever going to utter, and do you know what?'

'Tell me.'

'I'm sad I won't be able to hear you scream in agony just before you die.'

'Don't threaten me Atterbury; we're not afraid of you.'

Atterbury smiled coldly 'I'm not threatening you, I'm going to kill you.' He tilted the drum again and rolled it closer to the car.

'You won't get away with this Atterbury.' Baxter yelled, as he realised the drum was full of petrol.

'But I have Baxter, don't you see. I am Assistant Chief Commissioner for the Specialist Crime & Operations Directorate, so I can get away with anything. No one is going to question my judgement, so I *will* get away with it and you will die.'

'There are people who know you took us from Dover; despite your rank, the police there will suspect you.'

Atterbury made a dismissive gesture with his hand. 'I didn't exactly take you from Dover; Sergeant Mathews will confirm that I only followed your car.'

'They won't fall for that one, Atterbury, not once they connect it with this place.'

'What are they going to find here? There will be no fingerprints of mine. The drum will go up a hundred feet in the air when it explodes and the building will burn so fiercely there will be nothing but a few cremated bones scattered around the burnt-out chassis that was once your car.

'Don't you think they are going to wonder why and how it exploded?' Baxter snarled.

'Yes they will, but I'll be telling them you made a run for it at Maidstone services and I never saw you again. Sergeant Johnson will confirm I checked in at the yard at twelve thirty this evening, before telling him I was going home.'

'Very clever, Atterbury, of course, thanks to the drug you slipped in our drink, you had plenty of time to go back to your office and then return here.

'So, what about the other officers who were checking for a bomb under my car at the service station?'

'Actors, paid actors, nothing more.'

'But don't you think the police will wonder why we had been tied up in our car inside a barn. How are you going to explain that one?'

'Well, let me enlighten you, it's perfectly simple really. For a start the fire will destroy all traces of the string and most traces of you and your lady friend. With a little prompting from me the investigating officers will conclude you must have been hiding in this barn for some devious reason. You were certainly in your own car so were you perhaps waiting for someone and haphazardly smoking? When they search outside they will find a carelessly dropped packet of heroine which has your fingerprints on it, so it shouldn't be difficult for them to put two and two together and conclude this was a drug deal gone wrong.'

'But it won't have my prints on it though, will it.'

'Oh, but it already does, your fingers touched the sachet when you were sleeping. They will also find two Chinese drug traffickers dead in a car stuffed with drugs, shot with the gun that has your friend Magali's fingerprints on the butt. I think I can safely say *that* will wrap this little mystery up, don't you.'

It seemed Atterbury had thought of everything. He was going to get away with their murder and that meant Veerman would escape justice as well.

'Don't look so frustrated, Baxter, because I'm inspired by your words, but you're the author of your own destiny. It's now time to say goodbye, so do enjoy the next world, if there is one. You will certainly find out long before I do.'

He slammed the car door, rolled the barrel the last few inches and then righted the drum against the front and back doors on Magali's side. He reached into his holdall and removed a rope fuse, then carefully dropped the end into the top of the barrel. He replaced the lid and secured it with nuts and bolts. Atterbury took care as he laid the fuse across the concrete floor stopping just inside the large wooden doors. He removed the petrol cap on Baxter's car and showed it to them, dropped the keys and filler cap on the ground and then waved goodbye. He walked back towards the large wooden doors, opened just one, flicked his lighter, bent down and held it close to the fuse. The heavy door thundered as it was slammed shut and the external iron bolts were shot home.

Outside, Atterbury, still wearing his leather gloves, removed the bag containing the sachet of heroin from his pocket which had Baxter's fingerprints all over it. At the edge of the drive he selected a spot close to the flower beds. He took the sachet out of the polythene bag and carefully placed it partly under the spreading purple flowers of a verbena. Atterbury knew full well the whole area would be searched, and the sachet of heroin would be quickly discovered.

His Chinese associates watched him from their car which was parked nearby in the drive. He walked over to them and the driver unwound his window expecting to be told to go home. Atterbury removed Magali's gun from his pocket and shot both men through the head, then threw the gun into the nearby bushes.

Magali and Baxter heard two distinct gun shots and then the screech of wheels as Atterbury sped away.

Baxter was now thinking hard, there had to be some way of getting out of there. He had already discovered the impossibility of trying to undo the bindings around their hands and he hadn't found anything sharp enough to cut through nylon twine, so he couldn't afford to waste any more time trying that option.

An icy fear churned in his gut; was this going to be it, was he going to be no more? He shook away his fears and concentrated on exactly what the obstacles were.

All four doors were locked, but more to the point, his were tight up against the wall and Magali's doors were blocked by the big petrol drum. This left just the rear luggage door.

The small ball of flame fizzed as it made its way towards the barrel of petrol. Baxter knew they only had a matter of minutes to get out before the whole place went up. The prospect was so appalling he inwardly laughed and then cried.

Atterbury reached the end of the long drive and was surprised to see a car stopped in the gateway, lights still on and engine running. He approached cautiously, wishing he still had Magali's gun. His powerful headlights exposed what appeared to be an empty vehicle up ahead. He pulled up behind the other car. Suddenly one of his rear doors opened and as he turned he caught sight of a burly Oriental. 'What are you up to?' he shouted.

The man threw something onto his back seat. 'You forget take this present from Mr Veerman,' he said, slamming the door shut. Atterbury turned to see a small brown paper-wrapped parcel, and then heard the car in front roar away.

The blood had drained from Magali's face. 'What are we going to do Baxter, I'm frightened, she said.'

'I'm working on it, don't worry, there's going to be a way out of this, trust me there's always a way,' he said brazenly, camouflaging an underlying unease which he didn't want to share with her.

'What is it then, tell me what can I do?'

'A prayer might help,' he said dismissively.

'I didn't know you were a religious man Baxter.'

'I'm not, but I'm always willing to join the winning side.'

'Wait a minute I've got an idea,' he beamed at her, 'this is what we're going to do. With the back of your ankles lift the bar behind your legs, the one that changes the seat position.'

'Yes I have it,' she said raising the adjustment bar with the back of her feet.

'Lift your body up so I can move your seat.'

As she arched her backside he pushed her seat forward and a

gap opened between them. They repeated the exercise, this time with Magali nudging his seat backwards.

He now had a gap between the two seats, not a large one, but sufficient for an agile person to pass between them. He turned his body sideways placed his legs on the steering wheel, took a sharp intake of breath and pushed against it as hard as he possibly could. His torso plummeted backwards sending him awkwardly onto the rear seat. Next he inched his hands as high up his back as he could and used his finger tips to push down the button which lowered one of the two seat backs. He stopped to regain his breath.

'You are going to have to be quick, Baxter, we haven't got much time left.'

'Right,' was all he said. With the rear luggage compartment exposed, he clambered head first into the boot and pushed the solitary holdall to one side.

'There's just one problem,' he shouted.

'What's that?'

'I can't turn round to undo the rear door. I am going to have to reverse and re-enter backwards, which is going to be tricky.'

'Well don't just talk about it, get that back open quickly.'

Back in the boot his hands fumbled for a catch, but to his dismay there wasn't one.

'There's no bloody door release on this thing. Pull that door lock spike next to you, it should unlock everything.'

She did as he asked, but it made no difference to the rear luggage door, it was quite obviously not designed to open from inside.

'How are you getting on back there?' Magali said, half turning.

'That didn't work,' he shouted back as he wiped the perspiration from his eyes.

He turned round again and with some effort, managed to raise his foot and kicked the window several times, and although his shoes were leather, he was never going to be able to exert anywhere near enough power to break the screen.

He desperately scanned the confines of the dark luggage compartment, and then they stopped at something which gave him a sudden surge of optimism and resolve. Strapped in a side tab he spotted the car jack, a heavy and sizeable object.

He turned and reversed back into the boot and with the jack clasped tightly in both hands he struck the rear window several times. However, the toughened glass combined with the fact that his hands were still tied behind him, meant his awkward feeble blows were having no effect on the glass.

'Baxter,' Magali shouted, 'you've got to hurry, the flame is nearly up to the car.'

'I'm doing my best, but the bloody glass won't break.'

'Hit it harder or we are going to die in this car.'

Magali had inched her body downwards and began kicking the front windscreen with all her might.

Baxter tirelessly thrashed his jack-wielding hands at the rear windscreen. His heart was thumping violently and he was aware of acute pain as a result of the restricted space he was being forced to manoeuvre in. He used a four-letter expletive which he never used, especially, in front of a lady. This fuelled an inner strength, an instinct for survival which sent him into a blinding temper.

Magali could see he had lost control as his rage drove even more ineffectual bombardment on the rear window. 'Leave it Baxter. Atterbury has beaten us,' she said resignedly.

'Not yet he hasn't,' Baxter yelled. He went berserk pounding the glass with animalistic violence. Suddenly an explosion sounded, as the glass shattered into thousands of shards. Baxter cleared the window aperture and rolled out of the boot.

'Take the handbrake off,' he shouted to Magali.

'It's done,' she yelled back.

Baxter put his back to the car and pushed it clear of the barrel.

'Get out of there quick,' he screamed.

He knelt and placed his wrists against the burning fuse. He couldn't see what he was doing and shouted as the flame bit into his skin, but persevered and after a few seconds the nylon twine melted and his hands were free.

He ran back to the barrel and tried to remove the lid from the top of the drum so he could pull the fuse out, but of course Atterbury had bolted it firmly down. Without a spanner or pliers, he knew he stood no chance. He tugged at the fuse, but it was looped inside so it couldn't be pulled out.

'We need a knife,' he shouted 'we've got to find something to cut that fuse.'

'But there's no time left, look,' she screamed pointing to the ball of flame which was about to climb the drum. He stamped on the fuse several times, but it refused to go out. He predicted they had little more than a minute before the whole barn would go up in an enormous explosion.

He ran towards the wooden doors slamming his shoulder at them, but the heavy iron bolts on the other side held them secure.

'We're not going to make it, are we, Baxter?'

'Of course we are, don't be silly.' He tried not to sound concerned, but by this time he was shaking with fear.

Magali joined in, hurling herself at the doors, but quickly crumpled to the ground with a look of helplessness. 'You know, Baxter, you're the best thing that ever happened to me I've only one regret.'

'What's that?' he shouted as his threw his body once again against the heavy doors.

'I would have loved to have grown old with you.'

'Don't worry, you will.'

'Baxter.'

'What,' he shouted back, reeling from his last ramming of the doors.

'There's something I have to tell you before we die.'

'We're not going to die,' he bellowed back.

'But I have to tell you something really important.' Then she screamed.

'What,' he yelled.

She pointed to the ball of flame which had climbed to the top of the barrel.

'Lay on the ground,' he shouted.

A deafening crash followed by a heavy collision against his body sent him hurtling to the ground where he landed on top of her; he wrapped his arm around her head in one last desperate attempt to shelter her from what was happening.

He experienced a sudden draft of fresh air plummeting across his back. *The backdraft from the explosion* he guessed.

'Get them out of here fast' The voice was familiar but cut short by a violent pair of hands which lifted him off his feet, propelled him through the open barn door and then dragged him across a gravel yard, where he was roughly deposited on the edge of a ditch. Magali landed by the side of him just as an ear-shattering explosion sent them and the police tumbling backwards into the cutting. Flames leapt into the night sky, a hundred feet high and more, setting light to the dry reed thatch which immediately turned into an inferno. The sounds were tremendous as the roof sizzled loudly sending up black sooty deposits which floated down softly, sprinkling on their heads. *Those scraps of debris might have been us* Baxter said to himself.

A second smaller explosion sounded from inside, feeding the fire with a renewed energy. The flames refuelled, shot up the three hundred year old dry-oak timbers turning the shell into an inferno.

Monroe came over. 'Are you two alright?'

'I think so,' Baxter replied. 'Are you alright, Magali?' she didn't answer and she didn't react when he put his arm around her and kissed her. There was a steady flow of blood running down her forehead, so he placed his handkerchief on the wound.

'Cut this lady free, Constable,' Monroe ordered.

The tall young policeman whipped out his penknife and gingerly cut the cord which held her hands behind her back.

An ambulance arrived, its sirens competing with the roar of the fire and further police cars pulling into the yard, saturating the area with rotating blue lights.

Monroe held his arm out and Baxter grabbed it and the Inspector pulled him out of the ditch. 'In the car, we can talk on the way.'

'What about Magali?' he said watching her being helped out of the cutting.

'She needs to go in the ambulance, just so they can keep an eye on her. Bit of a nasty crack on the head that, but she'll be alright though. Don't worry, they'll probably take her straight back to your hotel. I take it that's where you're still staying.'

'Too true,' he quickly confirmed. 'Until Veerman's behind bars, I can't risk our lives in that cottage of mine.'

'I'm sorry we can't offer you police protection, but you know how it is? But we've made your place secure and we're carrying out twice nightly observation drive pasts.'

'So is there any sign of anyone in a car watching my place?'

'Yes and no, there doesn't appear to be a constant watch as such, but the same car has been spotted circling the area on a number of occasions. We've done a car plate check and it's come back red flagged.'

'What does that mean Inspector?'

'It means 'hands off'. Someone's telling us to keep our noses out of their investigation, or they have protected identity, I don't know which, but I suspect the former.'

Two fire engines swung loudly into the yard spitting up the gravel as they turned the corner, then breaking sharply as men jumped to the ground and began unrolling hoses.

Baxter climbed into the back of the police car with Monroe

'I'll tell you what Inspector; I never thought in my wildest dreams I would be pleased to see you.'

'No, I gathered that might be the case.' He returned a wry smile.

'Do you know I really thought it was you who was bent and on the payroll of the cartel, I never once thought it was Atterbury?'

'I know you did, and I used that weakness in your judgement to sow the seeds which would finally catch Veerman. But we nearly lost you, we really did.'

'Lost me, how do you mean?'

'Do you know we've been trying to bring the two of you into safe custody for the last twenty four hours; you really gave us the run around?'

'At Dover, of course!'

. 'Yes, we had you tagged at Border Control, but you had to ring Atterbury and that put us in a tight spot I can tell you. Anyway, I didn't believe the harbour board police sergeant, the idiot.'

Baxter said 'I think he was intimidated by Atterbury.'

'Oh yes, he was good at doing that, but in hindsight, it presented us with a unique opportunity to catch Atterbury in the act, but it so very nearly went wrong.'

'What happened over there? he asked as they drove past a car with its front door open.

'Two men inside with a single bullet hole through their head,' he said shrugging his shoulders.

'Chinese?'

'Yes.'

'We heard a couple of gunshots. The work of Atterbury again, I presume?'

'I would imagine so,' was all Monroe said.

'He certainly didn't want to leave any loose ends, did he? Do you think there is any chance of catching him, Atterbury, that is?'

'If you look just up ahead you'll see what's left of his burning car, and I can tell you now there isn't much of it and even less of him.

A fire crew were aiming their hoses on the wreckage, but it was clear no one could have survived an inferno like that.

'What happened to him, that caustic little man?'

'I think someone put a bomb in his car, don't you?'

'Now I wonder who that was,' Baxter said with a grin.

'I would imagine,' said Monroe, 'once it was thought Atterbury had disposed of the two of you he himself was considered to be a liability and so was disposed of.

'The Shāqi?' Baxter suggested.

'I would imagine so, but almost certainly acting on orders from Veerman.'

Monroe fumbled in his pocket and after much pulling and tearing managed to rip open a bag of sweets.

'So tell me, Inspector, I take it you followed us all the way here?'

'Well no not exactly, unfortunately we lost you at the Maidstone services, or at least we didn't know then that we had.'

'Yes that was funny, so what happened there?'

'We followed your car out of the services car park and back onto the motorway.'

'But you couldn't because I left it there,' Baxter said cynically.

'Well someone drove it out and we naturally thought that

someone was you. We followed your car for several miles until we realised the Jaguar was nowhere in sight.'

'Atterbury took the A road, not the motorway.'

'I see. Anyway, your car pulled off at the Hillborough turning, circled the roundabout twice and then all of a sudden disappeared. We turned back and searched a number of country lanes, but by then we'd completely lost you. We spent a further hour searching the dark lanes and laybys, but it soon became evident that we were not going to pick up your trail again. Luckily, Taffy, back at the nick, mentioned a farmhouse that Atterbury occasionally rented for weekends away. Once we had the address it was just a matter of getting to you in time.'

'I have to admit it was a close one,' Baxter said.

'Now it just leaves Veerman. I take it you still have a copy of that incriminating recording of yours?'

Baxter went cold. 'How on earth did you know about that? I've never mentioned it to you.'

'Ah, no, quite so,' he said hesitantly, 'but that was why Atterbury was after your blood, you sent him a copy, didn't you?'

'Yes, but I still don't understand how you knew about it.'

'I'm afraid I must hold my hand up to that one. You see, we were never quite certain about your involvement with the cartel and so you were flagged to every police force. When it was reported to us that your garage doors were wide open, we sent a couple of officers around to your place to check all was well. I went with them and we noted some evidence which suggested your cottage had been searched. We were obviously concerned for your safety at this point, so we investigated further. On your desk I noticed a computer mouse and cables leading to speakers, but no computer, only a printer. Now, fortunately you have a wireless laser printer and these can in certain circumstances retain memory of past jobs. We took your printer away with us and gave it to our boffins to look at. Well, they were delighted because you had created a waiting queue due to a paper jam. You obviously cleared the paper and printed the first copy and then turned your printer off and as a result we found the second copy.

'My letter to Atterbury.'

'Precisely, it was still in the internal hard drive. So we knew you had recorded evidence concerning Veerman, but no exact details.

As a result of that I sent out an all-points call to have you brought in and that's how we knew you had arrived at Dover. 'So you do have another copy, I take it?'

Baxter couldn't believe it, after all this there was once again no evidence on Veerman. Atterbury had seen to that.

'No, Inspector, I don't think I do have another copy any more. Atterbury told me he had had my flat searched, found the CD which contained a copy and destroyed my computer, so, no, there isn't.'

'That's bad news; I really thought we had him this time. If only you'd given *me* that recording.'

'Sorry Inspector, I wish I had as well. Mind you, we do have the Shāqi tattoo on his arm, that must surely implicate him in some small way.'

'Sorry, Baxter, but I'm certain the CPS will say it wouldn't be enough to charge him with conspiracy to murder, or anything else, save for being affiliated to a largely unknown organisation. His solicitor will ask what crimes have the Shāqi committed?'

'Well, murder for a start.' Baxter chipped.

'And you have proof of that?'

'Wait a minute, there *is* another copy, it's on Magali's mobile, and it's the original one she sent from her transmitter after recording Veerman. That idiot Atterbury took the phone from her and then gave it back in complete ignorance of the explosive content it held. He could have so easily destroyed it and we would have been left with nothing.'

'Excellent, then we've got him.' Monroe announced with glee.

'Do you know Baxter, Interpol have been monitoring Veerman for the past ten years, but failed to dig up any dirt on him. I've been investigating Atterbury for four years now. I knew there was something in his past which was questionable, but couldn't tie him into any illegal activities. It's taken an antique dealer to finally put away not one, but two of the nastiest men on our wanted list. I can tell you now, Baxter, I shall enjoy watching Veerman go down for a very long stretch.'

CHAPTER 27

EVACUATION

Veerman leaned back in his swivel chair engrossed in his thoughts, waiting for the telephone call; the one which would either alleviate his concerns or dictate an uncertain future.

The waiting was agonizing. He was only too aware how close he was to being arrested for murder, among other things. His cohort in Scotland Yard, Terrence Atterbury, the Assistant Chief Commissioner had tipped him off about the incriminating evidence Baxter had sent him. He couldn't believe how stupid he had been to let that bloody woman Magali record him admitting to conspiracy to murder. He now realised she had led him on, all that pussy footing around begging him not to kill Baxter. He wished he had ordered his killing earlier, that man had been the bane of his life, but surely not anymore.

He checked his watch, Atterbury should have finished the deed by this time and the two of them must be pushing up the daisies now, or at least what was left of them. But why was it taking so long?

He had few doubts Atterbury would carry out the killings because the man knew only too well that if he, Max Veerman went down, then so would many faces in high places. Being Assistant Commissioner wouldn't give Atterbury any protection at all if everything went pear-shaped, and so in order to protect himself and his interests in the cartel, he had volunteered to end the problem once and for all.

Veerman got up and his chair swivelled around several times. He paced his office, waiting impatiently for the call. Why was it taking so long, if he didn't hear from him soon he would have to telephone the man, but that was a risk he didn't want to take.

An intermittent buzz sounded and he rushed back to his desk

and snatched up the red secure line telephone. 'Yes,' he shouted impatiently.

'Jun Chang here.'

'Chang, what do you want at this time of night?'

'I've just been informed by my contacts in London that your eyes and ears in the Yard, Terrence Atterbury is dead.'

'What!' Veerman was stunned; a sudden sense of total exasperation took over from his previous state of irritation.

'Are you still there Veerman?' the voice at the other end asked.

'Yes. I'm still here. What happened?'

'The details are still coming in, but I gather a certain Inspector Monroe, complete with blue light cavalry, was spotted on their way to the farm. At this point the police were less than half a mile away, so the chances of Atterbury being caught in the act were very high. The controller at the scene wasn't prepared to take that sort of risk so he instructed our agents who were monitoring the situation from nearby, to make certain he was out of the equation before they arrived.'

'That saves me a job; I had a contract out to have him killed before he reached home, but I was hoping to have confirmation all the recordings were destroyed. What about the targets, Baxter and Magali?'

'I gather they were rescued just before Atterbury's bomb in the barn exploded, I don't know how they managed it, but there it is.'

'Damn it, I should have got the Shāqi to take care of Baxter and that bitch. Even they could have made a better job of it than that pen pushing idiot Atterbury.'

'I'm not quite certain where that leaves you, and more to the point, the cartel,' Chang said thoughtfully.

'There's no real problem as far as I can see.'

'What about Baxter and the incriminating recording?'

'Atterbury told me categorically that he had destroyed all copies, so once I've had Baxter eliminated, that will definitely be the end of the matter.'

'I hope for your sake you're right, Max. Anyway, I'll let you get to bed and speak tomorrow. Oh, and Max.'

'Yes.'

'Do keep me informed of any further problems, I don't like being kept in the dark.'

'There will be none, I can assure you, good night, Chang.'

The following morning Inspector Monroe stood in front of the magistrate, not in a court room but in his private chambers.

'I am led to believe you wish me to issue you with a search warrant for twenty one Jermyn Street, is that correct, Chief Inspector?' the Magistrate said, with a hard stare which softened slightly after a few minutes.

'I do, sir.' Monroe respectfully replied

'As I'm sure you're aware, I require you to present evidence that probable cause exists and demonstrate that it is likely to be relevant proof and admissible as evidence in a court of law. So on what grounds do you seek this warrant?'

'We have evidence that the premises known as Gallery Twenty One situated at twenty one Jermyn Street are a front for a major international cartel.' Monroe handed over an evidence summary.

'Who is the named person on your search application Inspector? Monroe cleared his throat. 'It's Maximillian Aalus Veerman.'

'And his connection with the said premises is what?'

'We have direct evidence that he's head of the London headquarters of the Beaux-arts d'Asie, which we believe is, in effect, a major cartel dealing in illegally exported works of art. We also have some evidence which suggests that the cartel have committed a number of murders.'

'I see' said the Magistrate thoughtfully. 'You use the words *believe and some evidence*. I have to say phrases of that nature always concern me. I don't like them and view them with great caution. But still, fill me in with details of your investigation.'

Monroe cleared his throat. 'Over the past four years I've been liaising closely with my opposite number at Interpol and we now have irrefutable evidence that Max Veerman has for many years been illegally exporting art from China and Hong Kong as well as creating a cartel which controls the sale of artworks in contravention of European law. Veerman has always been one step ahead of the legal system, not just here in the United Kingdom, but he has constantly danced around the outer reaches of international law and cleverly tested the parameters, but rarely crossed the boundaries himself. We have long suspected he is responsible for ordering acts of execution, but we've never, up until now, had any direct evidence. He has people, some in the very highest places, who do his dirty work. The illegal activities are handled by Shāqi agents, a secret organisation of very dubious and, we think, criminal nature.'

The magistrate looked over his glasses, clearly sceptical of these accusations which at best might imply complicity, at worst a case of over zealousness by the Metropolitan Constabulary. 'So what do you expect to find as a result of your search, inspector?'

'We expect to find paper and electronic evidence which will show a direct link between the cartel and Veerman's headquarters above Gallery Twenty One in Jermyn Street. But we also believe that in order to maintain a clear path for his nefarious activities; he has on his payroll: policemen, Revenue and Customs operatives, and enough lawyers to re-write the entire legal system.'

'And you have evidence for all these allegations?' the Magistrate raised his bushy eyebrows.

'We certainly do, Sir, or at least in the matter of murder. We also have this tape recording, which I feel confident you will find sufficiently incriminating to grant the warrant.

He took his I-pad out of its sleeve and turned it on.

The judge listened intently as the incriminating words of Veerman filled the room.

The Magistrate scribbled a few notes, scratched his head and then leant forward in his chair. 'I accept your submission has grounds for a warrant, but because there may be international and possibly political implications here, I have to pass this application on to the Lord Provost first. I will need to keep this recording so he can listen to it and make his own judgement, based on its content.'

'I'm sorry Your Lordship, but I can't do that, it is evidence and so I would have to ask you for a court order before surrendering it. That is as you'll know, normal practice.'

'I see,' the Magistrate muttered.

'But,' Monroe added. 'I do have a typed transcript.' He handed it to the Magistrate, who nodded.

When the Justice had finished reading it, Monroe asked 'What about the serious Organized Crime and Police Act two thousand and five?' Monroe was desperate to find a way of acting sooner, rather than later; He feared the latter might see him missing his prey.

'I don't feel that would be procedurally the correct interpretation in this case.' The Magistrate gathered up the paperwork putting it into a blue file and rose from his chair. 'Be back in front of me, here, at nine o'clock sharp tomorrow morning.'

Max Veerman had assembled a hit squad to track down and kill Baxter. He didn't have a clue of his whereabouts, but had been given the tap on Baxter's mobile from the Parisian Shāqi who had used it to track him in Paris. It was now just a matter of waiting. He felt confident the man would sooner or later use his phone and when he did, they'd be listening in.

His red telephone suddenly buzzed to life and he rushed to respond.

'Chung here again'

'Good afternoon Chung and how are you on this bright and sunny day?'

'It is not such a bright day for you, Max,' Chung said.

'Why, what's wrong?' he snapped.

'This afternoon I received a tip-off from our friendly Magistrate warning me he had been requested to supply a search warrant for Jermyn Street.'

'Well, surely he can say no, can't he?'

'He could, but he knows Monroe would ask another Magistrate. That man doesn't give up you know.

'So it seems.'

'The problem is, if he were to turn the application down, it would cast doubt on our magistrate's judgement and therefore his reliability as a justice of the peace and that could end his relationship with the cartel, and we need him on our side.'

'Is there any way we can get at Monroe?'

'No, we've tried that one, but he's long demonstrated that he's incorruptible, I know there are not many of them about, but he is a rare example of a straight cop.'

'Doesn't he have a wife or children?'

'Forget it, Max, it's too late for that, but the Magistrate has promised to reserve permission for a search warrant until tomorrow morning, so that gives you less than twenty four hours to clean up your act.'

'Wait a minute, I still don't understand what evidence they think they've got on us.'

'Not us Max, you.'

'Rubbish, they've got nothing on me.'

'Just shut up and listen. The judge says Monroe is in possession of the recording which you insisted no longer existed, you know, the one which implicates you to several murders.'

'I don't believe it, even the original copy was destroyed.'

'You're not listening to me, Max. You might have destroyed Atterbury's copy and maybe the original, but the Magistrate heard the recording from Monroe himself. But that in itself doesn't worry me, that's for you to sort out, but in Jermyn Street there will be direct links back to the cartel, and those must be severed. '

'But they can't.'

'Shut up, Max, and listen. You've strayed outside the boundaries of responsible behaviour and you're about to take all of us with you to account. I'm not prepared to let you do that; you've crossed the line for the very last time.'

'So what do you intend to do then?'

'I've called an emergency meeting of the cartel committee and we'll be convening later this afternoon in Hong Kong. We also need to inform the working group members of Omega West.'

'Omega West,' Veerman exclaimed in horror. 'Now you really are going to create a storm in a teacup. Why on earth do we have to involve them?'

'You're not only a liability to the cartel Max, but there are people in very high places all over Europe who could be compromised by this unravelling situation. Omega West will want to ensure all the politicians, judges and police who've been involved in collusion are safe and not at risk of exposure.'

'That's my death knell then isn't it?' he said sharply.

'As long as you keep your mouth shut I don't see any problem, but if I were you I would consider getting out of Europe and double quick. Anyway that apart, I'm ordering you to vacate the twenty one Jermyn Street premises tonight.'

'What happens to all the stock here?'

'Don't worry about that, I have a specialist team on their way to you right now. They will pack and crate everything from the vaults and showrooms and ship it overnight to Belgium. They will even move your personal possessions as well, if you want. Just clear up the loose ends, Max, and do it now.'

Veerman could feel his face draining of colour. Rage was building inside. How could the cartel treat him like this, he was Max Veerman, a founding member of the executive committee. He doubted if the other members would agree to his expulsion, and although those words had not been said, expulsion was going to be the end game, of that he was certain.

Veerman strained for a last ditch reason in order to avoid having to lose Jermyn Street. 'We can't leave just like that,' he said 'we've too much invested here; it's just not possible and I have to say it's totally unreasonable to expect me to do so.'

'This is not a request, Max,' the man from Hong Kong said. '*The engine has already been oiled,* so to speak. Even if I wanted to, I couldn't save you now, it's far too late for that. Gallery Twenty One will no longer exist after midnight tonight and all evidence of its existence will be eradicated. Do I make myself clear?'

Veerman softly acknowledged his understanding of the orders

and reluctantly agreed they take his collection as well and hide it in Europe. He had never told anyone in the organisation about the diamond, that was his bonus, his farewell parting gift from good old London. But he still had to find a way of smuggling it out of the country.

Chang said, 'Our friends in the Shāqi have had all contracts in the UK cancelled and as I speak they are on their way back to Paris. So there will be no more killings, Max, the Shāqi organisation will no longer be able to help you.'

'What about Baxter, I'm so close to having him eliminated.'

'Just listen to yourself, Max. Your infatuation with that man is precisely what has brought you down. Forget him and think about yourself before it's too late.'

'So what's next then, Chung? Do you want me to end it all with a Cleopatra style flourish with an asp clutched to my breast?'

'Don't be ridiculous, Max. Now listen to me. I've mobilized a professional team to go in at midnight to carry out a deep clean of your entire building.'

'So where does that leave me, where do I go? Or have you got plans to clean my existence from your inconvenienced organisation.'

'As I said, if I were you, I would get out of England as fast as you can. Whatever you do, never make contact with the cartel again. You will be monitored, covertly of course, but I'll do all I can to ensure your safety for the next few days, provided you don't come under my radar again. Goodbye, Max, and good luck.'

The meeting room above Gallery Twenty One was full, with all the members of the London-based cartel. Veerman had called an emergency meeting with all his cohorts and staff. A whisper was going around the room suggesting there was going to be a resignation. A few of his lieutenants, his commanders who directly controlled the hit men and assassins, had a fair idea that the game was probably up; they'd been half expecting it for some time now. The Falcons, who were his eyes and ears on the streets, were not there and neither were any Shāqi agents. They had already been deployed elsewhere by the secret Shāqi organisation in Paris, for whom they *really* worked.

The room had a buzz of excitable speculation, but fell silent as soon as Max Veerman entered. 'Our work here has recently been compromised by other parties' Veerman told them in a stern, yet regretful voice 'and so you must vacate this building immediately. Section commanders will each be allocated an office, store room or utility and will be responsible for removing every scrap of paper, waste bin, shredder, ledgers and accounts, books, laptops and computers, printers and especially memory sticks. I also want the removal of all dictaphones and telephones, dvd players and any other recording devices. Every table top that can be, must be removed, otherwise complete tables will go.'

'Why the tables?' The question on everybody's lips was asked.

'People write on tables, don't they?' Veerman said, 'it leaves invisible, but recoverable evidence. One other thing, security will remove all hard drives and collect memory sticks and dvds and pack them in this trunk, we'll be disposing of that material at sea.'

'What do we do with all the rest of the office equipment?' someone asked from the back of the room.

'I was just coming to that. A fleet of skips will be in the rear loading bay in an hour's time, so start moving everything down to the basement. Jeff, I want your team to dismantle the security alarm system, especially the voice wave detectors.'

'No problem,' came the reply. 'They all have a thirty second or less destruction programme which totally destroys their functionality, but I have to warn you, Sir, it will be irreversible.'

'That's exactly what I want, now see to it.'

The activity for the next few hours was hectic, but organized in a military fashion. Everyone rapidly emptied the contents of their desks, filing cabinets and shelves into wheelie bins, which were placed on each floor just outside the lift entrances. Technicians went from office to office removing all hard drives from computers, memory sticks, telephones and any other data recording items. Maintenance went from room to room removing electrical and recording equipment, as well as table tops and piling it all into the wheelie bins.

As the noise of evacuation reached a peak, many were overcome by the din and drama which was unfolding. The wheelie bins were soon piled high with the paraphernalia which had been the

Beaux-arts d'Asie organisation, and the respectable Gallery Twenty One, and when full, were sent down in the lift to the basement loading bay, where they were emptied into the skips.

Several hours later when all was completed to the satisfaction of the departmental heads, the skips were taken away to an isolated Norfolk farm; the contents dropped into a dis-used quarry and buried under many tons of soil.

The professional cleaning team arrived at midnight precisely. They were used to this sort of operation. Every one of them was well aware that they might be illegally removing evidence, but this is what they did for a living; it paid considerably more than any other legitimate cleaning job. They were regularly employed by gangs to deep clean properties after serious crimes, or even torch a building if it had been used as a hide-out and contained fingerprint or DNA evidence.

By the time the first signs of light were breaking on a new day, they had finished the job. It had taken the team of ten men just six hours to go through the entire building. Every surface had been thoroughly cleaned, from walls and floors to doors and windows and all remaining furniture and filing cabinets. Even the lifts, washrooms and outside smoking areas were de-fingerprinted.

At six am the team signed the contract off, the building was now one hundred percent sterile. No matter how much effort a scene of crime team might deploy, they wouldn't find a single fingerprint, scrap of writing or any electronic data. In fact, apart from a few pieces of furniture, the building was effectively empty.

CHAPTER 28

THE RAID ON 21 JERMYN STREET

Veerman left Jermyn Street just before midnight. With his chauffer at the wheel, he travelled across London to Curzon Street to meet the French Cultural Attaché. The Diplomat was understandably irritated at having to stay up late in order to meet with Veerman, but he was under the wing of the cartel. Over the years he had been paid very well for facilitating a vital link for the transportation of illegal Asian Art via Paris.

The Attaché put the parcel containing the diamond in the midnight diplomatic bag bound for the French capital, which by this time was already late. He was ignorant as to what Veerman had entrusted to him; he didn't want to know; he felt less involved if he wasn't privy to such information.

Veerman arrived at Paddington station in plenty of time. He gave his chauffeur last minute instructions and handed him a box containing forty five thousand pounds, money which he trusted to his long serving driver to look after until he was established abroad. At check-in he breathed a sigh of relief when his passport went through the border control scan without a problem. As he passed through the image resolution x-ray machine, he counted his lucky stars at his decision to send the diamond by a safer passage and one which would not be picked up by the sophisticated image processing software used by customs and security personnel to detect smuggled or threatening items.

Veerman caught the one thirty Eurostar and arrived in Brussels just after five in the morning. He had travelled light, as the bulk of his possessions along with the cartel holdings were already in Harwich, waiting in the hold of a container ship bound for Belgium.

He crossed the station concourse and asked for a ticket to

Cannes, which he paid for with his credit card. He then walked briskly outside, screwed up the ticket and dropped it in a waste paper bin.

'Taxi' he waved his hand and a cab moved forward. 'Paris s'il vous plaît,' he shouted through the open window to the driver, who nodded.

The following morning Monroe met the magistrate at nine am.

'Take a seat Inspector,' the magistrate said and held out his hand. He looked briefly through his papers.

'It seems this investigation of yours has attracted attention from other interested parties.'

'I don't quite understand, Sir,' Monroe replied.

'I feel certain you do, Inspector. I have mentioned it to no one.'

'When you say other interested parties, who exactly are we talking about?'

The magistrate eyed him with suspicion, but Monroe really didn't know who else was taking an interest in this case. As far as he was concerned he alone had it red-flagged.

The magistrate checked his notes. 'Yesterday afternoon I had a visit from a SOCA field director.'

'How on earth did the serious organized crime agency get involved in this one?' Monroe exclaimed.

'I am equally in the dark as far as *their* involvement is concerned,' the magistrate said, 'but on a more serious note, late last night I received a deputation from the Secretary of State for Justice and I can tell you now, that is unprecedented.'

'This affair gets stranger by the moment,' Monroe said softly. 'Obviously Max Veerman has upset someone's apple cart.'

'Well the subtleties of this investigation don't really concern me, but I think you had better execute this warrant without delay,' the magistrate said, handing the signed document across the desk.

A convoy of police cars, support team vans and forensics were waiting outside as he left the court building.

'We're on,' he said leaning into the lead car, 'let's get operation Dragon underway.'

As was the normal procedure, his admin officers had tried to contact Max Veerman or his secretary to inform him they were on route with a search warrant. However, all telephone lines appeared to be disconnected. Monroe was concerned about this revelation as it begged the question; Were they going to be too late to catch Veerman? If that was the case, then somebody must have tipped him off, giving him the opportunity to carry out the suppression of evidence. Monroe could only think of one person who had the inside information and opportunity and that was the honourable Magistrate James Pearson, who, with a reason which was highly suspect, had made them wait; an action which may have provided Veerman with enough time to flee his lair.

At ten thirty five Monroe gave the orders to begin Operation Dragon. Three police cars were sent to the Bedford Square underground car park to block the entrance to the Jermyn Street car lift, while Monroe and twenty officers assembled in front of Gallery Twenty One. It was immediately obvious they were likely to be too late as the plate glass windows which were normally a showpiece of Oriental splendour, today fronted an empty gallery.

The electric door bell was rung several times, not surprisingly without response. As it was impossible to communicate with the occupier, the police were empowered to break down the doors, even if such action was likely to cause moderate to excessive damage. Monroe, as senior officer, sanctioned the use of the police Enforcer, the manual battering ram which could deliver three tons of kinetic energy from every blow.

It took three attacks with the enforcer before a loud thud sounded and the heat-tempered glass shattered into a tight-knit network of pebble-like pieces. The glass resembled a crystalline structure as it stubbornly remained in the frame. A final thrust with the enforcer and the glass crumpled onto the floor.

Monroe and his officers spent two hours searching the building.

The vaults, whose doors had been conveniently left open, contained nothing whatsoever. The offices had likewise been stripped of all but the odd chair, filing cabinet and table legs which were discarded on the floors. The fact that even table tops had been removed left Monroe doubting they would find very little evidence here, if any at all.

Monroe left forensic teams in the building to carry out an inch-by -inch search. If there was so much as a single piece of written or electronic information he wanted it bagged and any fingerprints were to be cross-referenced with the building plan and recorded. He wasn't interested in the staff or general workers, but desperate to find prints belonging to faces, people who would have to justify what they had been doing there.

Back in his office at police headquarters he contacted FATF, the Financial Action Task Force concerned with money laundering, who had been closely investigating Veerman and had built up a substantial dossier over the past two years. He felt certain they would now find evidence of this in his bank accounts. The search warrant allowed them to acquisition these confidential records for the very first time, but only U.K, and offshore British protectorate banks.

Monroe next initiated an all-ports call on air and sea ports, with orders to apprehend Veerman should he still be in the country and try to leave. Meanwhile he waited to hear from Border Control Agency to find out if he had already exited the United Kingdom. Next he sent detectives around to the magistrate's residence to question him. Even though he doubted they would be able to pin anything on him at this stage, he wanted to put the wind up the man. He had already put a tap on his telephone and was intending to keep a watch on his movements, which he hoped would make him break cover. Monroe was convinced the Magistrate had been the whistle blower to the cartel and, if threatened, was likely to contact Veerman, or possibly someone else they might find very interesting.

Veerman was in a bad mood this morning as he flopped down on the lounger in his Paris apartment. He was unaware Magali and Baxter had surreptitiously stayed there, but then he had no reason to suspect that. He was still trying to come to terms with what had taken place over the last twenty four hours. It was only now beginning to dawn on him that he had lost his respectability and power. Thanks to Atterbury's fouled up attempt to dispose of Baxter, and the Honourable James Pearson's inability to put the brakes on Monroe, he was on the run with few options left open to him; probably, his best bet now was to re-locate to Hong Kong. This wasn't something which particularly appealed to him, but at least once he had his money from the sale of the diamond and his chattels had been sent on from storage in Brussels, he could lead a comfortable enough life in retirement, even if it was in the Orient and without any of the power he loved so much.

Later in the day he made his way by Metro to Avenue Daumesnil, the Paris prefecture administrative building, and waited until the courier arrived with the diplomatic bag.

The woman at the information desk was unhelpful from the start.

'You will have to make an appointment if you want to speak with the culture secretary,' she said in a brusque officious tone. Without even looking up she flicked through the appointment diary, rapidly dismissing the first few pages.

'I urgently need to see him today, this afternoon at the latest.'

'This afternoon!' she repeated in a sour voice. 'I can't give you an appointment for today, but I can fit you in on Thursday at....' She ran her finger down the column 'eleven am.' She looked cynically over her glasses.

'But it's highly important, I cannot possibly wait that long, can I speak with him on the telephone?'

'You will need an appointment to do that.' The self-righteous receptionist seemed to take great delight in saying those words. Veerman was furious, he had a lot of clout, even here in Paris, but unfortunately it didn't extend to the French prefecture. Because for obvious reasons he had destroyed his mobile, he asked to use her telephone and she pointed to a row of booths.

'You can ring from over there, but I doubt anyone will speak with you without an appointment,' she barked across the hall.

After several attempts, he eventually got through to the cultural Attaché in London. The man was most apologetic and promised to contact his counterpart in Paris straight away.

'Mr. Veerman.' the woman at the counter was now charming and all smiles. If you would like to go up, Monsieur Lafayette will see you now.'

Finally in possession of his diamond, Veerman jumped in a taxi and went to his St. Germaine Bank in the Luxembourg Quarter of Paris, where he deposited the stone in his safe deposit box.

By midday Inspector Monroe had a report on his desk from border control. He only had to read the top line, that was all it took to unleash a mixture of anger and dismay. The bad feeling he had been harbouring in the pit of his stomach all morning was suddenly justified; Veerman had boarded the early morning Eurostar train to Brussels, and then just after five o'clock used his credit card to purchase a ticket to Cannes.

Monroe wasn't fooled by this apparent evidence of Veerman's flight. The train journey to Brussels was one thing, but the ticket to Cannes in France, no he didn't believe that for one minute. That man was too clever to leave a trail as easy to follow as that. Monroe was convinced Veerman had laid a blind trail, and would now be in Paris.

He alerted Interpol and eager to assist, they swiftly circulated Veerman's picture to all Belgium and Paris police stations, marked *Most Wanted*.

His detectives had just returned from their attempt to interview the Magistrate. Monroe hadn't had dealings with the magistrate before, but was now convinced the honourable James Pearson was corrupt. There could be no other explanation as to how Veerman and the entire Beaux-arts d'Asie organisation, or cartel, could know about the imminent search warrant. He had told no one, not even his own officers, fearing the possibility of an in-house leak. When detectives arrived at the magistrate's smart Kensington house, they found him in his office, slumped across his desk with half his face missing and a discharged shotgun where he had dropped it.

Veerman spent an hour sitting in a restaurant speaking on his new mobile phone to various diamond buyers. He had compiled a comprehensive list of potential dealers, but was becoming more and more frustrated by the lack of any serious interest. Most claimed they were not able to finance the acquisition of such a large stone, others were too keen and therefore suspect. He finally found a Vietnamese dealer who could source backing from the diamond cartel in South Africa via Amsterdam. The man assured Veerman he could produce the money in bonds within twenty four hours and would get in touch with them straightaway.

Veerman wanted to take the stone to the jeweller's shop in the Chinese quarter today, but the jeweller said no, not until Amsterdam confirmed they were interested.

Veerman had not divulged his name or location as he would be an obvious target for any gang wanting to waylay him. He took some strength from his assumption that cartel agents would be keeping a close eye on him, even though so far he hadn't spotted them.

At three thirty Veerman climbed the steps to his Montmartre apartment building, weary and disillusioned. As he opened the front door and entered the hallway he noticed a couple of men standing chatting by the complimentary newspaper table, but took only a passing interest in them. Veerman made for the stairs and as he turned the last flight on his floor and turned the key in the lock, he was suddenly confronted by French Gendarmes. He quickly backed and fled down the stone staircase but was apprehended in the front lobby by the two men he had spotted minutes before.

When asked if he was Max Veerman he returned a hard stare and said no, he wasn't, and anyway what was this all about? He tried to put on an act of displeasure at the way in which he was being treated, but when they searched his inside jacket pocket and found his passport complete with picture, with a look of total acquiescence he admitted perhaps he was indeed, Max Veerman.

Veerman's one big mistake was to presume no one knew of the existence of his Montmartre apartment, it wasn't even registered in his own name. But of course Magali and Baxter knew it well and had been quick to put Monroe in the picture. The Inspector passed the information on to Interpol who in turn informed the Paris police who had waited several hours in the likelihood that he would sooner or later turn up there, as he did.

'Baxter, some news for you; Magali said, shutting the hotel room door behind her. He put his newspaper down and looked up.

'I've just had a call from Inspector Monroe, she said.'

'Oh really, what did he have to say?'

'He's received word that the entire cartel organisation here in London has been closed down.'

'Wow,' is all he could say.

'Yes, the Inspector says all Shāqi agents have been sent back to Paris and all contracts and activities here in the U.K. have been cancelled.'

'Well that's great news, isn't it?'

'There's even better than that.'

'Veerman?'

'Yes, they've got him. He was only using his Montmartre apartment to hide up, I thought he was cleverer than that.'

'And the fake diamond.'

'Actually, no, they didn't find that, I bet he's hidden it away.'

'So,' Baxter said, 'presumably it's now safe for us to get out of this hotel and go back to my cottage.'

'The Inspector has suggested we go home now.'

'Well, what are we waiting for?' he said, throwing the suitcase on the bed and grabbing his clothes.

CHAPTER 29

THE TRIAL

The judge entered the court and Veerman was told to stand.

For the past five months Max Veerman had been in detention in Pentonville prison awaiting trial. It had now been three weeks since his trial had commenced and he had been transported here, five days a week, to listen to the cases being brought against him.

The prosecutor for the Crown had selected thirty two cases to answer, saying he considered these to be just the tip of the iceberg. He had been ticked off by the judge for this last comment.

The most serious charges were conspiracy to murder which were nowadays considered in the same light as murder itself. Money laundering, fraudulent monopolization and operating an illegal cartel in violation of European and International law, were also cited against him.

Number six Cadogan Place, London, was a prestigious white painted five storey house, but it did not stand out in the elegant terrace of Georgian mansions, but merged comfortably in the townscape and could so easily be dismissed as being of little importance by the passer-by.

However, the property was red-flagged, meaning it and its occupants were afforded total diplomatic immunity, in other words, like foreign Embassies it was autonomous and therefore strictly out of bounds to inquisitive police and governmental eyes.

Lord McKinnon banged his hand loudly on the long conference table and the room fell silent.

This was an emergency meeting of Omega Group West, with representatives from most European countries.

Lord McKinnon, as president of this highly secretive and technically illegal organisation, had called an emergency meeting of western government protection representatives. These were a group of high ranking people who had the power to make and enforce actions deemed necessary to protect high status people in their own and neighbouring countries.

'Gentlemen, we have a potential problem which requires measures and therefore your ratification. I take it everyone has read the report in front of them?'

A resounding nod and throat murmurs from around the room confirmed they had.

McKinnon continued. 'Max Veerman, as you will have read, is in possession of critical information which he could use to lighten his sentence. He knows far too much about the faces, and not just here in the UK, but also representatives in your own countries. And I don't need to remind you that many are people in high places, whom you would not wish to be exposed.'

The German representative stood up. 'Perhaps, Mr. President, I might be permitted to clarify.'

McKinnon nodded.

'There are concerns within the international body that the forthcoming trial might put certain organisations and not just the Hong Kong cartel who, are critical to the success of European trade, but other bodies who are important to the west.'

McKinnon went on, 'The problem is we don't know how Max Veerman is going to fight his corner. He might take all the blame personally and keep quiet about the international money laundering and illegal importations. But, on the other hand, he could play another scenario, the one which concerns me greatly. Veerman could put names to faces, not just ordinary faces, but politicians, ministers, cultural attachés and big wigs in legal institutions. There is no end to the damage he could cause to the European Union; in fact such disclosures could even cause its collapse. So far there have been no whispers suggesting he has brokered a deal with the prosecution, but I am concerned he might if it resulted in a much reduced sentence. Are we all agreed that action must be taken, and swiftly?'

The room heartily concurred with McKinnon.

'What kind of action do you have in mind, are we talking about a full tactical unit?' the commander of strategic defence asked.

'No I think a local agent will do. It would be very convenient if Veerman could be removed, but that may not be possible at this juncture. The main thing is to let him know that if he did talk, then we would silence him for once and for all. I will point out that none of your governments will be informed of this action, it will be taken on their behalf by Omega Group West. Suffice to say, the minutes of this meeting will not be recorded, and officially never took place.'

It was nothing short of a miracle that he was here at all. Ninety days ago Max was brought here for the first time. His legal team, who were acting on behalf of his Barrister spoke to him briefly outside the courtroom with requests for any last minute instructions, but pointed out that he would only be required to plead his innocence or guilt.

The courtroom was packed for his first hearing, a surprising turnout as it was only committal proceedings, yet his notoriety had interested press and general public alike. When the judge asked Veerman how did he plead? he replied with a confident 'Not guilty, Your Honour.' He then did what few people would find strange in a warm courtroom. He took off his jacket and then discreetly rolled up his shirt sleeve, just a few inches, but enough so that the judge could see the batwing symbol tattooed on his forearm. Veerman had no idea if the magistrate was one of them or not, but a few high court judges were affiliated to the cartel, and or the Shāqi.

The judge merely nodded with a knowing look on his face, but even if he were one of them, he could do nothing to help Veerman now.

With tongue-in-cheek his counsel asked for bail to be set, but the request was rejected without any consideration whatsoever.

Veerman was on his way back to Pentonville, a dreary London prison, but one where he had certain clout. Among the inmates were several people he knew very well and these included an exhenchman of his who was serving a six year stretch for arson, a financial adviser who had at one time worked for Veerman, he had gone on to misappropriate two point five million pounds from his banking employer, and there were also several in for fraud and money laundering.

Word had quickly spread, his reputation was such that he enjoyed a certain position in the prison, a kind of respect that he didn't have in the same way outside. He was well aware it was his money which spoke, it bought him not only favours, but commodities like alcohol and edible treats. Within days of arriving here, he had bought a tip from another inmate for an I.O.U of fifty pounds. He followed the lead and quickly secured the services of a warder who agreed to meet with his chauffeur once a week, thereby ensuring he had sufficient money with which to barter. In that sort of situation, where money was involved, there was always going to be a prison officer who was willing to stick his neck out, should he need anything from the outside.

His legal team had told him to expect a trial in four to five months' time, so he could do no more than sit it out.

The prison escort vehicle, on its return trip from court to Pentonville, had just rounded the corner of Constance Road when without any warning the van jolted, violently sending those inside sliding to their right.

The high security vehicle driver fought to control the van but it careered into a brick wall. On impact Veerman was thrown against the police guard on his left. Had it not been for seat belts, the three of them, handcuffed together, would have been catapulted out of their seats and across the floor. One of the guards grabbed his mobile. 'Jack, what the hell was that, what's going on mate?'

'We've been hit Murray, we've been bloody rammed.'

'Hit! by what?'

'We've been rammed by a mechanical digger, I didn't see him coming, he came out of a side road when I stopped at the lights.'

'Well, get us out of here fast, while I ring for assistance.'

The driver managed to reverse, but before he could turn the security vehicle around, the machine with its toothed bucket raised, came at them again, this time folding in the rear of the van. Veerman could see a gaping crease which was now letting in daylight and a rush of cold air blew into the vehicle.

Gun shots followed, at least half a dozen from an automatic weapon. The onslaught concentrated on the rear of the vehicle rather than the driver at the front. In the back, the guard who was speaking to the security office requesting assistance suddenly shouted. He dropped his mobile phone and grabbed his arm.

'Bloody hell, I've been hit,' he said with a look of incredulity on his face. A trail of blood made its way down his arm and collected between his fingers. A dark patch on his blue uniform was getting larger by the minute. Veerman now knew that this was far from being a rescue attempt; someone was determined to silence him and for good.

He turned to the other guard. 'Are you carrying?'

'What, a gun?' the man replied,

'Yes, a gun, what else?'

'No, we're not allowed to.'

'But you always have access to one in the back, don't you.'

The guard didn't answer, but looked away.

'Look, he's going to kill us unless we do something about it and fast. Do you want to die here in this miserable van?'

'Backup will be here shortly,' the man cried.

'What, in fifteen minutes, it'll be too late by then.'

'But I can't let you have a gun,' he murmured, his voice now slurred and suddenly he slumped unconscious. It was only then Veerman realised that the second guard had also been hit by a bullet and this one had impacted with the man's chest.

Veerman looked around and spotted a small square door above the back of the driver's panel. Another impact slammed into the rear doors. On this occasion several tines bit through the steel and he could even see the distinctive yellow metalwork of the bulldozer's bucket.

He found the dead guard's keys, undid the handcuffs and stood up and unlocked the gun safe, but it remained closed. A small keypad next to it was denying him the option of doing something to stop the onslaught.

'What's the code?' he demanded of the other prison officer, but the man just looked back at him blankly. Veerman grabbed him by his neck. 'If you don't tell me the code I'll break your bloody neck, do you hear me?' The officer seemed to come to a sudden realisation that the time had come to forgo his loyalty to H.M prison service and secure his own preservation. 'Two four two four six eight,' he said, 'but it will only have one bullet.'

Veerman tapped in the code, the gun safe door swung open and he took out a hand gun. It was a GlockG-19 "Safe Action" semi-automatic Pistol, and although this was a lighter version than he was used to, he knew the gun well. He checked the chamber and saw it did contain just one bullet.

He peered out between the jagged metal. He could see the bulldozer reversing and its bucket raised and ready for what would surely be the final assault.

The van was now firmly jammed into the brick wall so it was no longer capable of being pushed by traction on its four wheels, which otherwise would have absorbed up to thirty eight percent of the impact. The next attack was going to be catastrophic, as the vehicle had lost too much of its horizontal strength and was likely to crush like a tin can.

Automatic machine fire opened up further holes and Veerman hit the deck fast as bullets ricocheted around him. He heard it first and then saw the bulldozer once again coming towards him.

He knelt and pointed the gun through the gaping hole in the steel, steadied his gaze and waited. He was nervously aware he had just a one-shot opportunity. The digger drew closer and then he pulled the trigger. His bullet shattered the windscreen of the bulldozer which imploded in showers of glass; the driver slumped against the open window, his eyes wide open as his machine continued coming towards them. Veerman dived to the front of the van seconds before it impacted once again, burying the iron bucket deep into the back and only yards from Veerman's crouching position. This stopped the bulldozer in its tracks, although its engine continued to tick over until a passer-by switched off the ignition.

If Veerman had been presented with a way of making a run for it, he would have jumped at the opportunity, but even though the van was buckled and distorted, it remained the prison it had been designed to be. Even the driver with his keys would be unable to open the doors now. This type of two-cell custodial vehicle had multiple and highly sophisticated locking systems and the escape hatches, that could be used for evacuation purposes in the event of a major accident, were firmly jammed.

Three police cars and a firearms response unit arrived less than five minutes later, too late to apprehend the bulldozer driver who was by then dead with a single bullet through his temple. The police were accompanied by an ambulance and fire engine, but it took the London fire brigade over an hour to cut Veerman and his injured guard from the high security vehicle. The dead digger driver and the officer, along with the two injured security guards were whisked off to hospital with a fanfare of blaring sirens and blue flashing lights.

As Veerman sat in the police car en route back to Pentonville, he now had time to reflect on who had carried out this attempt on his life?

The driver was not Asian, as he might have expected, but even so he was certain either the Shāqi or cartel would have been behind it; or perhaps even the two organisations had jointly ordered the attempt on his life. He was of course slightly wrong about those assumptions, being unaware that Omega West had ordered the ambush following discussions with the Hong Kong headquarters of the cartel. Veerman knew only too well that he had vital information on people who had wavered in the face of corruption and who were undeniably guilty of benefitting in some way from the proceeds of organised crime. One assistant commissioner of police had already been silenced and a magistrate had saved them the job by shooting himself. His name was next on the list for elimination.

Once news of the failed ambush reached Omega West and the cartel, they knew only too well that the security net around Veerman would be tightened, and indeed it was.

Their only option now was to corrupt the jury, a fall back they had used successfully many times before, but one that very much relied on a 'friendly' judge.

The jury who were sitting in front of Veerman today was the second one appointed. Early on in the proceedings information leaked to the judge had revealed how five of the juror's had been approached by someone acting on behalf of an anonymous organisation. Checks on their bank accounts revealed large cash payments had been made to each and every one of the five. The judge immediately declared a mis-trial and called for a new jury to be appointed. Because of the nature of the case, these new twelve men and women were confined to a London hotel for the duration of the case. The five jurors, who accepted the bribes, would face another judge in another court sometime in the future.

Horace Macmillan Q.C, had worked hard on Veerman's defence, picking up on every point the prosecution made, constantly denying the suggestion his client had been complicit to murder. He attempted to discredit the recording, claiming Magali had deliberately set a trap and had lured his client into making certain statements which were not true, but had been made up in order to impress her. The jury however, were not predisposed by the weak defence explanations Horace Macmillan presented to them.

The tape recording was the prosecutions prima facie, but Macmillan claimed it was a rebuttable piece of evidence. Ironically, this sole surviving copy of the recording had been on Magali's mobile, the one Atterbury had taken and then handed back to her. Had he known, he could have so easily destroyed it and paradoxically instead of guarding Veerman's back, he had handed the judiciary the evidence on a plate.

Another piece of damning evidence was the photograph Baxter had taken with his mobile when in Jermyn Street, whilst attempting to rescue Magali. The prosecution were in possession of clear images of the signed book with a Beaux-arts d'Asie

calendar hanging on the wall behind. They asserted it had been taken from Hadley's room the day he was murdered.

As the case neared its end, it was obvious to one and all in the Old Bailey that the distinguished Macmillan had run out of defence options. He had also lost much of the will to fight the remaining charges, but these were the most damning as they were multiple counts of conspiracy to murder.

'Maximillian Veerman.' The judge began 'you have been found guilty of twenty one counts relating to the illegal exportation of works of art. You have also been found guilty of two counts of kidnap with intent to endanger life and five counts of false accounting. On a more serious note, you have been found guilty of four counts of conspiracy to murder.'

The judge looked up from his notes. 'I have nothing before me to take into consideration.'

Veerman looked ahead with stolid indifference.

Magali and Baxter were in the gallery watching the final moments of Veerman's trial. Baxter had earlier in the proceedings been called to give evidence concerning his kidnap, although everything else had been deemed inadmissible including his dealings with Professor Hadley. When Magali gave evidence telling how she made the incriminating recording, Veerman gave her the most disdainful and murderous look imaginable.

The judge flicked through his notes again. 'We have heard evidence of how you were responsible for conspiracy to murder four people and the kidnap of two others. We have also listened to compelling evidence for the concealment and disguise of the true nature, source, location, disposition and movement with respect to ownership of property, knowing that such property is derived from illegal offences or from unlawful importation.

Our world is unfortunately characterized by greed and selfishness, we see it here in this court every day, but rarely on this scale.

We have heard evidence of your selfish ambitions, ambitions driven by a strong desire for more money and personal gain.

It is clear you have behaved in a dishonest way to achieve those goals and in total disrespect for law and order. You have been responsible for creating a toxic regime and one which has resorted to murder, corruption and fraud on a grand scale.

You have refused to help the police with their enquiries and so you'll be dealt with as the sole offender, although I do know others were involved; persons who, thanks to you, may escape the arm of the law.'

The judge looked once again towards Veerman, searching for any signs of remorse. Even though that wouldn't change the mandatory sentence, it would give the judge some comfort to see some sign of repentance or atonement. Veerman stood in the dock motionless, with a censorious expression which made it clear that he didn't recognise the court and wouldn't accept the validation of any sentence handed down to him.

'Maximillian Veerman, you will go to prison for a minimum of fifteen years, do you have anything to say?'

The weight of the verdict may have been considerable, but for Veerman this was by no means final. He said nothing, just smiled, licked his index finger and held it up. He was saying 'that was one to the judiciary; the next point would be his.'

CHAPTER 30

BREAKOUT!

With a prison sentence of fifteen years under his belt and the likelihood that he would be serving at least ten, Veerman was desperate to secure an early release. His wealth, which he had tucked away in bank accounts in Paris, London and Geneva was duly confiscated under the the the Proceeds of Crime Act 2002.

He had no way of knowing the fate of his Chinese collection in storage in Brussels; there were no guarantees since the attempted assignation on him. His one and only remaining asset was the diamond which was safely locked away in a deposit box in a Paris bank. This was his only safety barrier, his sole means to ensure his freedom and escape from assassination.

Being in prison was a considerable inconvenience for Veerman, but it wasn't difficult for someone like him to get a message to the outside world. His chauffeur had been loyal to him for more than twenty five years and he was now repaying that loyalty by way of a generous retainer, in return for acting as a mail-point messenger. In his letters to his driver, Veerman discussed life in prison in such a way that no censor would suspect the content was in any way surreptitious. On the back of one letter he wrote *'A few sketches for little Amelia, I hope she likes them. Tell her to show them to Auntie Betty.'* Amongst the words and drawings he carefully drew the batwing symbol, but not conjoined as was normally portrayed, but in parting flight. He knew full well that when his chauffeur read it, he would know Auntie Bettie was Veerman's Shāqi contact; they would recognise the symbolic meaning behind the sketches and know he needed their help to escape.

Despite the Hong Kong cartel's cancellation of all Shāqi involvement in U.K affairs, Veerman harboured few doubts that they would honour his wishes, for the right sort of money; money which he could produce with their help. The first step was to appoint a mediator, and the Shāqi had the perfect man in mind.

Within a month Max was granted permission to receive his first visitor. Major Horton was the respectable face of the retired British military, a breed which was immediately recognizable by stance, speech and impeccable dress. Horton had long been in the pay of the cartel; he was their eyes and ears at the Ministry of Defence and so was easily corruptible for a tempting sweetener, and more so if someone like Veerman had damning evidence which could put him away for a long spell.

Inspector Monroe had indefinitely left open his offer to put in a good word with the parole board if Veerman ever decided to give the police some of the names in high places, names which Monroe knew existed within government departments, the legal system and police. But without testimony from Veerman, every one of these was a tag without a name, or a name which couldn't be tagged.

Horton had been tagged years ago, but there had never been any direct evidence to prove he had been involved in any illegal or dishonest practices. His name just seemed to crop up far too often during criminal investigations, but his presence was always side-stepped by his enormous circle of associates and in particular his old chum the late Assistant Chief Commissioner Atterbury.

Horton knew only too well how dangerous Veerman could be. He had witnessed the man's ruthless behaviour many times over the years. Veerman could provide enough information to people like Inspector Monroe, evidence which would guarantee Horton served a long stretch at her Majesty's pleasure, and what's more, the Major was in no doubt that Veerman had little to lose if he did.

Following the prison visit Horton agreed to speak with the right people who could get Veerman out. This wouldn't be the cartel but a private assemblage of technicians and tactical planners, and there were a few possible contenders for the job. He did however, remind Veerman that the Shāqi organisation was already involved and would provide the heavy side of the operation, but also the escape would require considerable financial backing and only the Shāqi were able to produce that.

Veerman told Horton the reward on offer was fifty percent of the value of the diamond, a sum likely to be several million pounds.

A fortnight later, Horton returned and gave Veerman the good news. Through his ministry of defence contacts he had located three English engineers with sufficient technical ability to carry out the contract. However, the Shāqi organisation in Paris who were financing the escape were demanding not fifty but seventy percent of the value of the diamond. Veerman was in no position to argue the point, so instructed Horton to give them the okay.

Four weeks later a bright yellow van pulled up less than a mile from Grantmead Prison, an eye-catching vehicle with blue logo, a distinctive T symbol. Few passers-by would take a second glance at the telephone engineers dressed in high visibility yellow jackets, complete with hard hats, as they erected a rectangular canvas shelter over a B.T. inspection pit. But if they had been able to take a close look at the other two men sitting quietly inside the British Telecom van they would straight away see they were Chinese and not normal blue bibbed workers.

The engineers were all British and recruited personally by Horton. One was a senior lecturer at a top London institute of electrical engineering, another was a research technician from British Telecom and the third a computer expert of some note. All had reasons for doing the work, every one of them had a history of 'working outside the box,' but as usual money was the overriding factor.

The small team along with their Chinese heavies had just arrived outside Grantmead Prison. It was exactly half past ten. Timing was critical for this operation, as was precision in their setting up. They knew they couldn't make a single mistake if this task was to succeed. There would be no second chance if anyone in the prison so much as sniffed something was not quite right. The prison authorities were expert in the field of security and so one slip up, no matter how small, and the whole operation would be over in seconds.

They finished erecting the genuine B.T telephone engineer's tent, accessed the subscriber loop-carrier switching box and then set about installing a pre-set mini telephone exchange, finally linking it to the computer in the van.

At ten forty five Prison Officer Joseph Knight received a telephone call from a supervisor in the maintenance department, or so he thought, telling him they were about to carry out the replacement of search lights over at the east wing.

Maintenance was situated in the north block, which was outside the main prison compound so they would need entry into the high security access road. Knight was told to report to gate three and wait for the maintenance van to arrive. As per the required procedure he rang the supervisor back and received confirmation of the orders, but of course the call didn't go through the British telecom SLC box, but was intercepted and answered by Horton's engineers, rather than by the real maintenance department.

The electrical engineer and computer expert had re-configured the telephone numbers and could now fully control the traffic between several parts of the prison.

At about the same time the central control officer of the prison watch, received a telephone call which he believed was from the kitchens telling him there was a small fire in the store room; but again it was from Horton's engineers. At that very moment the fire alarm zone panel in his control room showed a red light flashing in the kitchen store. There was no real fire, the alarm had been activated by the man inside the B.T van who had hacked into their computerized zoning display panel.

The control officer telephoned back to the catering department to check legitimacy of the call, again as per standard procedure.

His call like all the others had been intercepted and scrambled by the mini-exchange manned by the engineer outside.

Horton's engineers were now diverting selected conversation traffic to their computer, but more importantly they could verbally respond to all telephone calls between the three departments.

This was achieved as a result of an operation a week earlier when they had intercepted the exchanges of the operators they knew would be on duty that day. The technology available to the experts had enabled them to record the exact voice patterns and put these into the computer, so that when the engineer spoke it was in the voice of the recipient.

The engineer speaking as the prison officer confirmed there had been a small fire, now extinguished, but they needed to go out the rear door to remove smouldering debris. This seemed a reasonable request, control had no real reason to question it, and besides the rear entrance only gave access to the exercise yard, no more than that. The red light stopped flashing and control isolated the back door alarm.

Veerman had been assigned to the catering department, not because of any appropriate culinary skills he might have, but just by way of random selection. His job was not glamorous or particularly demanding, it mainly involved vegetable preparation, sweeping the floors and keeping the store room tidy.

At precisely ten fifty five Officer Joseph Knight, waiting outside gate three, spotted the approaching maintenance vehicle which he had been told to expect. With no reason to question it, he duly opened the gate and let the van in. There was no way he could have known a British telecom badge was concealed underneath what appeared to be a correct prison maintenance logo and neither would he find it necessary to question the roof rack with an extending ladder on top.

The two engineers dressed in maintenance workers uniforms had been earlier briefed and told they would be required to get out of the vehicle and have their passes checked when they arrived at the gate. Armed with this vital piece of information, they didn't wait to be told but jumped out and went up to Officer Knight. Had they not known the procedure, they might well have provoked suspicion from the guard.

With their inside information of how such an exchange normally took place, they did what most builders do and took the opportunity to light up, even offering Knight a cigarette.

If Knight had any suspicions whatsoever, the workers knowledge of the routine coaxed him into a complete false sense of security.

Veerman busied himself in the store room, constantly glancing at his wristwatch. Right on schedule, at eleven o'clock precisely, the supervisors went out the front of the building for their unofficial cigarette break. Veerman looked around; the coast was clear as he opened the now alarm deactivated back door. He slipped out quietly and wandered casually across the exercise yard, whistling to himself and kicking the odd stone as he went. A group of twenty or so men, mostly lads were kicking a ball about over by gate three. This wasn't a lucky coincidence but a preconceived part of the escape plot. On cue, the ball was kicked in Veerman's direction and as soon as he tapped it back, one of the other inmates sneaked out of sight behind the catering building. Veerman sauntered up and joined the others, kicking the ball back and forth but at the same time taking note of who was in the yard. The two supervising prison officers in the centre of the exercise compound had been talking to each other. The senior officer checked his watch and blew a whistle. The inmates stopped where they were while the officers carried out a body count, something which was mandatory every fifteen minutes. There was no question of checking faces and so the prison officers had no idea there had been a body switch. Identity checks were only carried out when prisoners were escorted back to the main prison building.

A small group of prisoners wandered over towards the centre of the compound, doing very little other than strolling with hands in pockets.

Veerman kept a keen watch on the unravelling situation, his eyes never leaving the engineers, who continued to lean against their van, chatting and sharing a cigarette with the guard at the gate.

Knight was just cross checking the last of the identity passes when, at precisely eleven twenty, the two Chinese agents jumped out of the rear doors of the van and overpowered officer Knight, swiftly bundling him into the back of the van.

The van and engineers were still on the wrong side of the fence from Veerman, detached by the high wall of wire which separated the exercise yard from the high security access road. The engineers slowly drove the van through gate three and then stopped.

A fight suddenly broke out towards the other end of the exercise yard, a fairly common occurrence, but this one was staged. The prison officers ran over to intervene and this was the cue for the escape to begin.

The engineers in the van accelerated hard and then parked close to the security fence. The two Chinese clambered onto the top of the van and the ladder on the rack was swiftly slid across the roof until it extended over the edge. A tug of a rope and the extension fell vertically giving Veerman an easy climb up the ladder and on to the van.

A security camera must have spotted this activity because a siren suddenly wailed into life, a warning which galvanised them into urgent action. Veerman was now alone on the van roof tugging at the ladder in an attempt to free it from the rack. He pulled the ladder up and threw it clear of the fence. He banged loudly on the vehicle roof, hanging on to the rack as the van reversed, turned around and then shot straight through open gate three.

The first police car sirens could be heard in the distance as the engineers stopped the van just outside the prison perimeter and helped Veerman slide down the side of the vehicle and scramble inside.

It was less than two miles down the quiet country lane to Saint Martin's playing fields, but a journey that had to be completed very quickly so any consideration for comfort was abandoned for reckless speed. As they drove on to the playing fields the van bumped across the neatly cut grass, sending its occupants bouncing on their seats. In a matter of seconds they looked up after hearing the familiar droning, as a helicopter began making its descent in the centre of the football pitch. Ducking low from the whirring blades Veerman shielded himself from the backdraft which suddenly whipped up fallen leaves, swirling into the air like a cyclone, until the helicopter finally touched ground. They ran towards the chopper whose engines were now idling and clambered inside, leaving the van and the trussed up Officer Knight on the field.

The pilot revved the turbines and the idling changed to a high-pitched centrifugal whine as the aircraft lifted off.

The helicopter veered away to the north as they headed for rural Suffolk. The whole operation was over in minutes, the prison authorities never stood a chance, faced as they were with some of the best brains and technical ability money could buy.

An hour later Veerman was in the port of Harwich. He had been dropped off by the helicopter in a field some five miles away and brought here, to the dockside, by a waiting car.

Security was, like every other U.K port, very tight, although there didn't appear to be any signs of heightened security as a result of his escape.

He alighted from the vehicle and immediately felt his arm grabbed.

'Keep your head down and follow me,' a lithe young man said, leading the way, bent double as he negotiated the outer perimeter of the port.

'In here,' he said opening a wooden maintenance shed door and ushering him inside. 'I'm going to lock you in, keep quiet and have a nap, I'll be back tonight at ten o'clock.'

'How do you know someone won't want to come in here today?' Veerman tensely asked.

'We used an asset.'

'An asset?' Veerman grimaced.

'Money paid out, says no one will be coming anywhere near here today, just take my word for it and I'll see you tonight.'

He had been pacing the inside of the shed for hours and now it was getting dark. Veerman was nervously waiting for his lanky guide to return and get him onto a ship. After what felt like an eternity, he heard a key cranking inside the door lock and true to his word the tall lad returned; it was precisely ten o'clock.

'Here's your new passport, identification papers and port pass. From now on you are Frank Duggan.'

'Frank,' Veerman repeated casting an expression of dismay, 'couldn't they think of a better name than that.'

'The name Frank Duggan is real, he actually works here, but at the moment he's on holiday in an expensive Cheltenham spar hotel.'

'Lucky man,' Veerman said.

'You're paying for it.'

'I see,' Veerman nodded.

'I'll tell you one thing,' the lad said, 'I would willingly lose my passport in exchange for a holiday in the luxury of a designer hotel, wouldn't you?'

'I think anywhere would be better than here,' Veerman said.

The lad said, 'The photograph has been swopped for yours, but I warn you it won't hold up to very close scrutiny by U.K border control and besides, your face will give you away if they're looking for you and I would imagine by now they're watching every port in the country.'

'What's the bloody point of it then?'

'It will be fine if you need to use the passport in Belgium or France, maybe for a flight or something like that, and you will need the port pass to board a ship.'

'So what happens next?' Veerman asked.

'Follow me, we've got to get inside the perimeter. There's a well-established rat run used by people-smuggling groups.'

They emerged from the hut and he was immediately cast into a world of swirling mist. Following the lad he crawled forward, not a continuous pace, but in short bursts as they followed the perimeter fence. The dock was floodlit, as bright as a Christmas tree through drunken eyes, the illumination distorted by the enveloping fog. He jumped in alarm as a fog horn boomed, the lad cackled.

'Come on,' he whispered, 'no time to lose.'

They took care to keep in the shadows of the huge ship-to-shore cranes and terminal handling equipment which loomed out of the mist and the closer to ground forklift trucks and reachstackers. They came to a long row of huge containers waiting to be lifted onto ships bound for Belgium, Holland, Scandinavia and North Africa.

The lad stopped at a point he obviously knew well because it looked no different from the rest of the perimeter, yet it was clearly a place of particular significance. He lifted out a section of fence and the two of them crawled through to the other side.

They were now on the sea board side of the port, as they paused in the shadow of an administration block.

'What happens next?' Veerman asked.

'We wait for the bus' is all he said.

'We're waiting for a bus!' Veerman replied exasperated. He was beginning to think this part of the escape plan had been written by an idiot.

'See that vessel over there,' the lad said pointing to a container ship which was in the final throes of docking. 'The crew will be off-loaded in a minute and bussed back here to Border Control.'

Minutes later a bus crossed the tarmac and stopped close-by. The retiring crew jumped out, snatched their holdalls from the luggage compartment and hurriedly disappeared into the custom's hall.

'Come on, we must be quick, and keep your head down,' the lad urged, as he beckoned him on.

They skirted the admin building and once again paused. A bright light fell on the pavement as the door to the customs block opened. A group of men came out of the building, chatting amongst themselves as they stepped onto the waiting bus.

The lad pushed him into the group. 'Good luck,' he whispered as he left Veerman to board with the others.

After crossing the tarmac, the bus stopped at a gangplank which extended up to a gangway in the side of a large ship. One by one the crew members alighted, and Veerman followed them up the steps to board the Feedermax Break-bulk cargo container ship Atlantic

Voyager. At the top, he handed over his pass for inspection, but was waved on perfunctorily.

The captain was known to Major Horton and had been used many times both by the cartel and the Shāqi organisation, but this particular booking was just between Horton and the captain. Although Veerman was now in possession of a forged passport, there were no guarantees that his documentation would stand up to the sort of scrutiny which might well be implemented in the light of his escape, so he was secreted on board and made comfortable in a hidden room in the hold.

It was a further hour before the ship was fully loaded and ready to set sail for Antwerp. Before the ship departed it was boarded by police and Border Control officers who carried out a brief search of the accommodation decks and checked all passports, while Veerman remained hidden in the hold.

The 1.30 am voyage was for the most part uneventful, although a choppy sea and heavy rain made the crossing, without stabilizers, uncomfortable. The ship docked just after first light. Alarm bells rang when the manifest was queried by Belgium customs on account of its particularly light load, but nothing more dramatic came of it.

It was a further two hours before Veerman was smuggled off the ship in a reefer container holding a consignment of carpets. The ship-to-shore crane lifted the container and put it down in the cargo berth. The Belgium freight customs officer didn't bother to check the contents; he had already received a suitable remuneration for making this deliberate oversight.

A taxi was waiting to take Veerman straight to Paris and two and a half hours later he was in St Germain du Pres walking up the marble steps of his Luxemburg quarter bank.

He risked using his real passport as a form of identity, and from his deposit box he grabbed the small bundle of cash, only a few thousand euros, but enough to see him through until he cashed in on his gem. He carefully wrapped the diamond in newspaper and dropped it in his carrier bag. He took out the large brown envelope, the one that had been locked away in the safe for the past eight years. He opened it to check the contents and skimmed down the names of people who, over the years had been complicit with the cartel. He muttered to himself 'This will teach those bastards not to mess with me.' He chuckled, 'they won't know what hit them when this comes out, it's going to bring down names in high places and a few honourable faces in the judiciary as well.'

His eyes lit upon the handgun which he kept in the box in case of emergencies; he stuffed that in his top inside breast pocket.

One thing he had learnt over the years was never trust a Shāqi agent if you don't have all the cards to play with, and he certainly didn't have too many. However, the gun gave him those cards, and whilst he hoped he would never have to use it, he was now a desperate and wanted man and would play his last hand if he had to, no matter what the outcome.

Veerman booked into the Intercontinental hotel in the St. Germaine district of Paris. He discussed with the concierge his requirements for the following day, which involved a taxi to and from his appointment. He then handed the man the sealed brown envelope together with a fifty euro note, requesting suitable stamps be put on it, but, he stressed, it was not to be posted before tomorrow morning.

The envelope was addressed to the Editor of the Times and contained fifteen pages summarising everything Veerman knew about corruption in Government and judicial departments. The list of names was damning, he knew it would cause a sensation and result in public outcry and without doubt, the resignation of some important figures. He had inked over, obliterating Major Horton's name, partly because the man had done a good job springing him out of prison, but also because the man was very much privy to his future plans.

Veerman knew he couldn't remain in Europe and even less so once he released the incriminating evidence contained in the envelope. His plan was simple, he had booked a flight to Hong Kong in the name of Frank Duggan, scheduled to depart tomorrow evening; he intended to live out the rest of his days in the sumptuous

Kowloon Shangri-La Hotel, which overlooked the harbour in the Tsim Sha Tsui district.

Even after paying off the Shāqi, Veerman was confident the proceeds from the sale of the diamond would be more than enough to service his retirement in Asia.

It was not surprising Veerman hadn't noticed the two men reading newspapers at a round table just off the foyer, because they were professionals in their field. They and another team, following an anonymous tip off, had been trailing him ever since he arrived in Brussels. As soon as Veerman followed the bellboy into the lift, the two men hurried to the front desk.

They flashed the Concierge their identification cards which stated they were Interpol officers.

'That man you were just talking to was Mr. Max Veerman, was it not?'

'No, Sir, that was Mr. Frank Duggan,' the man hurriedly replied.

'Frank Duggan you say, well anyway, whatever name he checked in as, he left you an envelope. We will take it, if you please.'

'I…I'm not.'

'This is not a request, Monsieur, we can come back with a search warrant, but I'm certain you wouldn't wish to have your guests inconvenienced by dozens of uniformed officers coming in here heavy handed, if you see what I mean.'

The concierge reached into the appropriate pigeon hole and handed the envelope to the men.

'You won't mention to anyone that you've handed this over to us, will you?'

'No, Sir, I won't, in fact silly me, I've already posted it.'

'Good man, I'm glad you understand?'

The concierge nodded and the two Interpol men quietly turned and left the hotel.

CHAPTER 31

THE PROPOSAL

To celebrate the end of the Henri de Montaigne mystery and the long sentence handed down to Veerman, Baxter whisked Magali off to Paris, his favourite city, the cultural capital of the world and the undisputed romantic cradle of the west and for what he had in mind, the only place which could possibly fit the bill.

They were staying at the sumptuous Hotel du Louvre, an elegant nineteenth century building situated in the very centre of Paris.

Once the heart of the Roman city of Lutetia, this quarter known as the first arrondissement, lies on the right bank of the River Seine and includes the western part of Ile de La Cité, one of the two Parisian islands. Besides playing host to the legendary Louvre Museum, the area has scores of grand squares, magnificent gardens, stylish cafes and timeless architecture. It was no wonder this was Baxter's all-time favourite place in the world.

The five star Hotel du Louvre, built in the Napoleon III style, has four facades which overlook the five most emblematic monuments of Paris. Naturally the most expensive rooms here looked out on these iconic landmarks.

As their taxi pulled up to the kerb in front of the grand entrance, a purple-uniformed doorman with copious gold braid swiftly descended the steps and took their cases from the driver. The doors of glass and polished brass were opened by another doorman who nodded politely as they passed through.

The showcase front lobby was certainly reassuringly expensive. Brimming with proof of its exclusivity, it boasted exquisite ambient lighting which highlighted the rich yellow walls and elegant marble columns. The focal point was typically the reception where efficient, highly attractive women busied themselves at the counter. Nearby, a second desk with kiosk was home to the concierge, a retired military-looking gentleman who constantly barked orders to the numerous bell boys.

The grand lobby invited visitors up to the suites by way of an opulent staircase, although for the less active, a modern elevator was available just around the corner. But for those wishing to exert some energy, the ascent up the marble stairs was highlighted by the exquisite wrought iron balustrade which framed the impressive stairway as it encircled its way upwards. Mid-way, the staircase passed a wonderful classical niche containing a full length limestone figure of Aphrodite, the goddess of love and beauty.

Thanks to the sale of his Chinese vase, Baxter could now afford the luxury of a hotel of this quality, and besides, it would serve his purpose well if, over the weekend he was able to pluck up enough courage to propose to Magali. He had no idea what her reaction might be, how could he, for the subject had never been broached, but he was now very comfortable in her company and hoped she felt the same. He had, of course, considered the possibility she might say no, or perhaps wish to wait until some point in the future, but he found it hard to believe she would present him with a down right refusal, not after all they had been through together.

It was late afternoon, they had taken a brief nap after the long journey and while dozing in and out of sleep, Baxter decided today was going to be the day; this was it, he had psyched himself up and was going to take the plunge.

'Come on, Magali, wake up,' he said, giving her a gentle nudge. 'Let's go for a hot chocolate.'

'Hot chocolate! You really do know how to impress a girl don't you?' she said sardonically.

'Ah but this is no ordinary chocolate, but the most delicious fix of cocoa you've ever tasted, and in the opulent surroundings of my favourite café in the world.'

'Café,' she sighed raising her eyebrows.

Baxter could see she still wasn't exhibiting any signs of

enthusiasm, but he was insistent and as a result she easily gave in.

Once out of the hotel they walked hand in hand along the banks of the River Seine.

The Rue de Rivoli which parallels the famous Jardin des Tuileries is renowned for its arcades of shops which carry the most fashionable brand names in the world and is considered to be the very heart of Paris's arts and culture. The name 'Rue de Rivoli' came from Napoleon's eighteenth century victory over the Austrian army at the Battle of Rivoli and has been a fashionable shopping mecca ever since.

Josephina's, half-way along the arcade, was Baxter's all-time favourite salon de thé. Despite the name it also serves other beverages like coffee and chocolate and food such as breakfasts, lunches and desserts so it was more like a café, but with a difference and what a difference.

Even before they entered through the canopied reception, Magali, like everyone else, found it impossible not to be impressed by the enormous confection of cakes and pastries bedecking the front window. Very few people would pass by without stopping for just a few minutes to admire this spectacular culinary display. Also impossible to miss was the name Josephina's, set in brightly coloured mosaic in the pavement.

Josephina's was not the sort of place where you could just walk in and expect to find a vacant table. For most of the day a queue of expectant customers waited patiently outside, an endorsement of the quality of the venue.

Baxter and Magali joined a small queue, it was late afternoon and the tourist rush had largely been catered for so it was barely ten minutes before they reached the front where they were ushered in.

'Wow, now this is some cafe?' said Magali as they followed the waitress to a vacant table.

The interior décor, with its marble topped tables, gilded ironwork and sparkling crystal chandeliers was visually quadrupled by the reflections in dozens of mirrors. Large niches were enriched with paintings depicting pastoral themes, most from eighteenth century scenes by the celebrated French artist, Watteau.

Within minutes, with calm and efficient routine, a waitress in a starched white apron brought a large jug of Josephina's African hot chocolate, served on a silver tray with two pots of cream.

'So Magali, what do you think of my café now then?'

'It's wonderful, just marvellous, I love it,' she replied, holding her cup in both hands and slowly sipping the chocolate through the generous head of cream.

'It's Josephina's chocolate that's made this place so famous over the years,' he said as he leant across and gently wiped the cream from her top lip with his index finger.

'I've got something rather important to ask you.'

'Yes, go on,' she said,' throwing him a look of curious interest.

Baxter leaned across the table, took her right hand in his. Looking her straight in the eye he could feel she was ready. 'Magali' he began, 'you know we've been together now for…..' Suddenly the fire alarm sounded, a din which couldn't be ignored and of a volume which made speech impossible. Waiters ran around the tables hurriedly ushering everyone out of the building and instructing them to line up under the striped awning on the pavement.

'So tell me what were you about to say, Baxter, it seemed quite serious?' she said as they waited outside alongside everyone else.

Two fire engines suddenly screeched to a halt and heavy booted firemen rushed into the building. Magali looked at Baxter, waiting for his reply.

He had suddenly lost his nerve and besides, jostling here on the pavement with all these other people was not exactly his idea of a romantic place to propose. 'Oh, nothing important really, I'll tell you later,' he said dismissively.

Eventually after ten minutes or so, the firemen ambled out. They hadn't needed to undo their hoses, so climbed back into their vehicles and disappeared around the corner.

The manager appeared at the door and informed everyone that it was only the strong sun coming in through one of the glass ceiling panels that had activated the alarm. The white-aproned staff ushered everybody back in, promising to refill everyone's cups. Baxter, like everybody else, gratefully accepted the offer, but by this time he had lost the courage to proceed with his proposal and so decided to seek another opportunity.

While she was in the cloakroom Baxter removed the small ornate jewellery box from his pocket, the one he had been secretly concealing for the past two weeks. He had in fact bought it in London, but it was very much a French casket. He then came up with a good idea. He couldn't for one minute imagine why he hadn't thought of it before. He searched in his wallet for a business card and then grabbed his mobile and tapped in a number.

'My name's Baxter,' he said in fluent French. 'You might not remember the name, but you will recognise me when you see me. I would like a table for two if you have one, for this evening.' The man on the other end confirmed they did have a table for that evening.

'But also I would like one of your alfresco specials; I think you know what I mean?'

'The man confirmed he most certainly did.'

'And by the fountain de Rivoli if that's possible.' Baxter added

'No problem at all, Mr. Baxter,' came the reply.

Magali returned to the table and looked at him, puzzled, as he ended his telephone call.

'Just a little something I've organised,' he said, before she could ask. 'But first we're going for a walk, only a short one, but it will do us both good.'

'Why don't we just go back to the hotel, I'm feeling particularly romantic tonight,' she said, with a knowing twinkle in her eye, a look she knew Baxter would find hard to ignore.

He leant over the table and held her hands together. 'So am I, Magali, and that's why I have something very special for you this evening.'

They strolled hand in hand, weaving their way casually through the crowds. It was always busy in the Rue de Rivoli as the day drew to a close. Throngs of pedestrians were finishing their day window shopping, many stopping in the arcades where artists sat painting, their pictures proudly assembled on the ground before them. The onlookers would be deciding whether to buy a watercolour to take home, a souvenir of landmarks they had already visited, or were going to visit before their holiday was over. Dusk was on its way as tourists ambled out of the cafés, wending their way back to their hotels, effusively wishing one another a good night.

Baxter and Magali had reached one of the many bridges which span the river Seine. This was a particularly attractive and famous iron structure, the romantically named 'Bridge of Sighs'.

Half way across Baxter stopped, took Magali in his arms and kissed her passionately, savouring her company in this most romantic of places. Arm-in-arm they leant against the rail, looking up-river, where the dying light of day captured the twinkling lights of the capital in the gently rippling water. Further afield little illuminations flickered aboard early evening cruise boats.

Crossing the bridge they entered the Jardin des Tuileries.

The Italianate gardens parallel the Rue de Rivoli as they follow the River Seine for almost two kilometres. This magnificent horticultural celebration of France's military triumphs, had perfectly symmetrical shrubbery, complimented by dramatic statuary by the likes of Rodin and Maillol.

After a while he paused and suggested they rest.

Sitting on a raised dais which encircled the fountain de Rivoli, they sat hand-in-hand, listening to the cascading water and watching the sun set over the horizon. The night air was heavy with the sweet scent of Evening Primrose whose pretty yellow blooms open at night and attract pollen seeking, night flying insects.

Darkness was rapidly falling on what had been a glorious day. In the distance the sky slowly turned red and the fading light silhouetted the Eiffel tower in the distance. A myriad of lights confirmed the whole of Paris was coming to life in preparation for the evening lightshow, for which the French city was so famous.

A slight Autumn chill announced the oncoming evening causing Magali to shiver.

'Are you cold?' he asked, putting his arms around her.

'I don't care if I am, I never want to leave this wonderful spot. I'm going to stay here until the birds begin their dawn chorus and the sun starts to rise in the morning sky and even then I may refuse to go.'

Two men arrived sporting gleaming white aprons. 'Good evening Mr. Baxter.' the older of the two said, as they lowered a round metal table in front of them. They returned a few moments later carrying two comfortable chairs and a white starched linen cloth was expertly floated onto the table. This was followed by the placing of cutlery, glasses and finally a candelabrum. Baxter handed one of the waiters a small wrapped package. 'I think you will know what to do with this,' he said with a wink.

Magali looked at Baxter; on her face he could see surprise and confusion, but most of all happiness, something he had rarely seen in those big green eyes before.

Baxter stood up. 'If madam would care to take a seat,' he said, as he helped her sit at the table.

The moustachioed maître d' swiftly returned with a bottle of Champagne. Magali raised her eyebrows when the wine waiter tipped the bottle so she could approve the label; it was Dom Perignon Oenotheque rosé 1990. *But how did Baxter know it was her favourite tipple?* she exclaimed to herself. She had never mentioned it, far too expensive for anyone other than the likes of Max Veerman, who from time-to-time had enjoyed showing off to influential clients.

As they began their meal, several people stopped to look at them, for even though alfresco dining was not an unusual sight in Paris, here in the Tuileries, next to the Fountain de Rivoli would seem an unusual location.

Baxter pulled out his trump card by clicking his fingers. A musician walked over and with violin under his chin began playing the haunting strings of *Plaisir D'Amour.* The Pleasure of Love was composed in 1784 and took its text from a poem by Jean de Florian and appears in his romance *Célestine.* The music was originally written by the Romantic French composer Hector Berlioz. The man began quietly singing. 'Plaisir d'amour ne dure qu'un moment Chagrin d'amour dure toute la vie.'

Baxter felt sudden warm pleasure as he observed a look of total contentment on Magali's face.

As the musician finished his romantic rendition, the waiter returned with another offering, this time a silver dish with domed cover. The waiter smiled, an infectious grin, as he placed it in front of the bewildered Magali.

She gasped as she lifted the lid and took out a small glass and ormolu box. It was not so much the box which made her gasp, but set in the glass lid a coloured image of the Eiffel Tower standing proud, with the Tuileries Gardens in the fore front. The scene depicted on the casket had been painted from here, the exact spot where they were sitting right now; the scene they had been admiring throughout the meal.

Baxter pointed to the sky, it was crystal clear, alive with a thousand stars, contrasting with the ambient light from the moon which made the Eiffel tower in the distance look quite surreal.

'How romantic,' she said softly, 'I just love it.'

He could already see a tear making its way down her right cheek.

'You'd better open it,' he said. Her hesitation made him think she might just suspect what was coming next and might not want to have to embarrass him.

She gingerly opened the lid and looked in, then stopped motionless.

He said, 'Marry me Magali?'

The look of utter amazement on her face suggested she hadn't, after all, expected that. Had he got it all wrong? How was she going to react? So far she just stared at the ring.

'Damn, you, Baxter, how can I possibly say no to you after this.'

Tears began forming in the corners of her eyes and then slowly rolled down her cheeks; she wiped her eyes with the back of her hand. He leant over, taking the ring from the silk buttoned box and tenderly placed it on her index finger.

'I've wanted to ask you to marry me for so long.'

'So why have you been dithering then?' she said.

'I was frightened you might not want to. So is that a yes then?' he asked nervously.

'Of course it is, you silly man,' she said, throwing her arms around his neck and planting a long lingering kiss, her way of sealing the bond between them.

A sudden clapping brought them to their senses again. Both waiters stood at a discreet distance, applauding the proposal they had been waiting for and expecting. But even more embarrassing was the small group of onlookers who joined in the applause.

CHAPTER 32

DEATH ON THE STREETS OF PARIS

The following day Baxter wanted to pop over to the Quartier Chinois, the Chinese quarter, in the thirteenth Arrondissement on the south east side of Paris.

They'd risen early and rather than spending valuable time eating in the hotel restaurant, they grabbed a couple of hot croissants from the Boulangerie opposite and consumed them on the way.

It was nine fifteen and in the elegant surroundings of Cadogan Place, London, Lord McKinnon banged his hand loudly on the long conference table and the room fell silent.

This was the second emergency meeting of Omega Group West concerning Max Veerman and consisted of representatives from Germany, Italy, Belgium, Holland, France and Great Britain.

Lord McKinnon, as president of the highly secretive organisation, had called this emergency meeting of western government protection representatives. The summit was in the light of evidence which had been acquired from Max Veerman. Evidence which had been intended for newspaper circulation, and evidence which would implicate the European governments represented by those in attendance.

'So how did we acquire this document?' McKinnon asked.

One of the men who had commandeered it from the concierge at Veerman's hotel stood up. 'I was part of a four man Interpol operation, deployed to follow a target by the name of Veerman.'

A man on McKinnon's right explained that it was one of their anonymous faces who had tipped them off.

'Carry on,' McKinnon said.

'When the target arrived at the Intercontinental Hotel in the St. Germaine district of Paris, he handed the concierge an envelope and unknown to Veerman we requisitioned it and that's the document you have there.'

'Has everyone looked at their copy?' MacKinnon looked around the room and there was a collective nodding of confirmation.

'Do we know his itinerary, where he's going, for what purpose and more to the point, his long term plans?'

The French member rose to his feet. 'He's booked a flight for this evening to Hong Kong in the name of Frank Duggan.'

'Anything else you can tell us Commissioner?'

'He paid a visit to his St. Germaine bank yesterday and accessed his bank deposit box. We know he collected the envelope containing the document in front of you. We suspect he has another unfinished task which he intends to complete today, but more than that we won't know until he makes his next move, ah one other thing I should mention. We've not been the only ones following him. He has a Shāqi tail, which he doesn't seem to have spotted. I would imagine they've been deployed by the cartel.'

'The cartel has gone,' someone in the room pointed out.

'They may have resigned their position on this board,' said McKinnon, 'and moved lock stock and barrel back to Hong Kong, but their legacy is likely to remain for some time.'

The noise levels in the room rose dramatically as members discussed what they'd been told and the damning and destructive implications contained in the document in front of them.

McKinnon called for order. 'I also have a communication from the British organized crime agency. They apparently have an officer in the field who has been briefing us via SOCA U.K, but the officer is not assault rated. I think we all know it is down to us to initiate the appropriate measures that have to be taken if we're to stop Veerman fleeing Europe. I'm certain you all fully comprehend the potential consequences if we were to allow him to leave our radar. He's far too dangerous in his present state of mind. The information he carries in his head casts a serious threat to all the ministers and officials we serve in our respective governments. He may not have all the necessary proof, but that sort of disclosure of Government and judicial conspiracy on a European scale, will have far reaching consequences and must be avoided at all costs.'

A consensus of opinion had been reached and the room was filled with nodding heads and mumbled agreement.

The voting cards were sent round and every one came back with a large cross.

Lord McKinnon rose to his feet. 'We, as the executive protecting power of the Governments of Europe West, authorise the execution of Max Veerman, by this name or by his pseudo name Frank Duggan. It will be carried out here in France by taskforce Omega Group West and completed before eighteen hundred hours. There will be no mention of this deed to any of your respective governments and no record will be made of this action or its outcome. If for any reason the action is not successful, we will regretfully be forced to take drastic steps which may involve destroying the aircraft he will be travelling in this evening. If any one of you has a problem with that, say so now, otherwise the action will be considered to be ratified.'

There was no dissention in the room.

A short train journey and Magali and Baxter broke into daylight from out of the Tolbiac Métro stop.

In order to get to the Chinese quarter, it was necessary to navigate around the incredibly busy Place d'Italie, an immense traffic roundabout that tethers La Butte aux Cailles to the rest of the city. Here was a subway interchange, a bus terminus and the home of glass-fronted shopping malls, but the predominant feature which couldn't possibly be missed was the very large fountain encapsulated within the roundabout.

The present conglomeration of high rise concrete, largely emerged out of the refugee crisis at the end of the Vietnam War. Baxter commented how it would be pretty well impossible from the hundreds of Orientals out on the streets here, to spot a Chinese Shāqi agent.

On foot they took the turning down Avenue d'Ivry which led

them into La Butte aux Cailles, a charming district within a district, with little cobbled streets all leading up to the hill in the centre.

The area is known, among other things, for its jewellers, restaurants and antique shops, along with an inimitable collection of street stalls and vegetable markets. This district of Paris was very urban with little interesting architecture to speak of, but despite that, it provided a priceless experience. If the street style was lacking in refinement, it was more than compensated by its distinctive character. There was nowhere else in the capital where the visitor would be treated to such a cacophony of chants from shopkeepers, each with their unique Oriental accent whether in Chinese, Vietnamese or broken Asiatic French.

Le Petite caverne antiquités is a well-known haven for Oriental art, although these days not everything was by any means genuine or old. In past visits Baxter had profited well from his acquisition of Vietnamese ship-wreck porcelain and other Oriental antiques; unfortunately today he came out empty handed.

Chez Gladines is a corner cafe with a Basque menu and a notable buzz of familiarity and was most definitely always on Baxter's must visit list.

He ordered Gambas Biscayana and a beer to wash it down and she, after much deliberation chose a Danish pastry with Perrier water.

This was one of a handful of quite unique venues known as Café Philosophique where people enjoy a drink while watching other folks who are discussing philosophy in a very orderly but often passionate manner. Its basic principle is to make philosophy accessible to all, in an attempt to revive the Socratic period in Athens, where philosophers would publicly dialogue amongst themselves.

This was another of Baxter's favourite bars and cafés in Paris. The Spanish family venture was run by the Moralee's and their stunning young daughter. The Spanish couple never seemed to forget a face and always gave the impression they loved to see their customers happy. Unlike many commercial-minded establishments, it was considered quite acceptable to linger over a single coffee for an hour or more and even bring in your own croissant, and if you contributed to one of the chosen discussion topics, then you would be considered heroic.

The noise levels were rising on the raised seating area where a group of young men and women in avant-garde dress were thrashing out some philosophical debate with a couple of mature and obviously sophisticated men.

Baxter and Magali, over towards the other side of the restaurant were discussing what to do that afternoon when Magali suddenly froze. 'Sh...' She held her finger to her lips. 'Don't say a word,' she said, grabbing Baxter's arm and pointing to a figure sitting with his back to them.

'That's Max Veerman,' she whispered.

'It can't be, he's in prison.'

'But I tell you it is, I'd know that balding head and broad shoulders anywhere.'

'But he's got his back to you, so how can you be so certain?'

'Just trust me that's Max Veerman,' she maintained, sporting a new look, one of fright.

The balding man she thought was Max Veerman suddenly stood up to welcome two men who came in and walked over to his table. The men were clearly of Oriental extraction which made Baxter uneasy, wondering if perhaps she was right after all, for although there were hundreds of eastern Asians living and working in this district, particularly Vietnamese, few were dressed in expensive suits from Saville Row. The three men shook hands and then sat down at the table. The bald man clicked his fingers and when the waiter appeared he turned very slightly and ordered drinks. Baxter could see she was right, it was undeniably Max Veerman.

'I do believe you're right,' he said.

Just at that moment Veerman half turned to check who was behind him. Baxter spotted the sudden danger and grabbed the large street map, holding it high above both their heads.

'That's definitely him, I caught enough of his face to be certain,' she said

'So what do we do now?' he asked.

'Call the police,' she replied.

'But how, he'll hear me from there.'

She pointed to the cloakroom. 'In there,' she said 'now go quickly.'

'I'm not leaving you here.'

'I'll be alright; I'll keep my head down.'

'No, I'm not going to leave you here, and that's all there is to it.'

'Alright I'll come with you,' she said

'Which one?'

'Which one what?' she snapped

'Which toilet, Ladies or Gents?'

'Does it bloody matter?' she said. 'Just go in which ever takes your fancy.'

'Now this is the tricky part,' he whispered rising to his feet.

'Wait until the waiter brings their drinks,' she suggested.

'Good idea,' he said, sitting down again.

The waiter spun the round tray in the palm of his hand as he stopped at Veerman's table.

'Right let's go.' Baxter whispered, at the same time grabbing her hand, but as he reached the toilets he hadn't reckoned on the waiter intervening.

'But, Sir, that's the Ladies' toilet, the gent's is next door,' he said with a large expanding smile. This prompted Veerman and his colleagues to turn round in their seats, in time to see the two of them disappearing into the ladies toilet.

'Did he spot you?' Baxter asked

'I don't think so, but I'm not certain,' she replied, as she locked the cubicle door. Seconds later their concerns were confirmed by the sound of doors being pushed open and slamming back loudly.

'Come on let's get out of here,' he whispered, pushing her through the small cubicle window.

They ran down the back alley and into the main street. He looked back, but couldn't see any sign of pursuers, but knew only too well the degree of danger they were now in.

The street here had few pedestrians, but looked out on the busy Place d'Italie roundabout. He pushed her into a bar, called for a coffee and hot chocolate and then headed straight for the toilets. From there he rang Inspector Monroe, telling him how and where he had seen Veerman, although confided the man was probably no longer in Chez Gladines, but possibly searching for them in the nearby streets.

Monroe confirmed Veerman had escaped from prison and with an edge of excitement in his voice, promised to alert his opposite number in the Paris police department. Until they arrived, he strongly suggested they keep their heads down.

When he returned, he looked around the café and quickly spotted Magali who had taken a table which was a discreet distance from the window. She saw him seconds later and hurriedly ended a call she was making.

'Anyone interesting?' he asked.

'I was just checking for any e mails, but there were none.'

He passed on what Monroe had told him and was just finishing his coffee when, amazingly, he spotted Veerman once again.

'There's Veerman,' he said pointing across the road, 'and he's still accompanied by his heavies.'

'Well keep your head down,' she said firmly.

They watched Veerman go into an Oriental jewellery shop across the road, which was directly opposite them.

'You know what he's doing, don't you?' Magali asked.

'No not really, so tell me?'

'What does it say above that shop?'

'What the Chinese characters?'

'No silly, the English sign.'

'Best prices to pay for gold, silver, jewellery and diamond.'

'He's trying to sell the diamond!' Baxter announced with glee. He won't be very happy when he finds out it's a fake.'

'He will be furious. He'll go ballistic; believe me he really will.',' will, she said with a cheeky grin on her face.

Baxter reached inside his jacket pocket and tapped a number into his mobile phone, 'I must ring Monroe again and tell him Veerman's in that shop over there, so he can get his French colleagues around here fast.'

'So,' asked Veerman impatiently 'how much are you prepared to pay for the diamond, the famous rock of Batuta?'

The Vietnamese jeweller had good contacts with the South African diamond cartel, no one else could cut and market stones outside their monopoly, or at least not successfully. He picked the stone up, turning it over in his hand. 'Quite few carat here,' he said in broken Asiatic English.

'Seven hundred and sixty five by my reckoning,' Veerman said cockily.

The jeweller whistled. He inspected the stone through his lens. It had a few reassuring flaws, that was good. He put it under the U.V tester and it had an excellent fluorescent blue.

'It look good so far,' the jeweller said

'Well of course its bloody good, now just give me a price and I want a good one,' Veerman snapped.

'Not to be so fast Sir, we have make more test.'

Veerman sighed in frustration as he turned to look at his companions.

The Oriental jeweller reached under his bench and produced a portable Presidium Duotester. When the green light flashed, the jeweller beamed.

'It thermal conductor, so not Cubic Zirconia.'

'I could have told you that,' barked Veerman. 'I tested it myself. Now come on, I haven't got time for all this.' He put his newspaper on the counter and picked up the stone, holding it high. 'If you don't want to buy this say so, there are many others here in China Town who will want it I can tell you.'

'Not to be so fast please.'

Veerman dropped his hands, placing the stone on the newspaper. The jeweller stared at it, his face dropped with dismay.

Seeing the sudden change in the expression of the jeweller Veerman rolled his eyes upwards 'What is it now?'

'Look.' he said. 'I can read print of news.'

'So?'

'This not diamond, it carborundum. You not read print through diamond, never.'

'Impossible,' Veerman flared 'there must be other tests you can do?'

The jeweller scratched his head. 'There no point really.'

'You've made a mistake you idiot,' Veerman shouted. He then composed himself and said in a quieter tone. 'Look, I can assure you this is a real diamond, so do some more tests.'

The jeweller hesitated and then shrugged. 'Velly well there just one more test I try.' He carefully wiped his fingerprints off the one hundred and twenty five facets and then placed the rock on a Mohs scale test pad. It took him ten minutes to enter the programme into his computer, but when the analysis finally came in he pointed to the monitor screen.

'See,' he said pointing, 'absolute hardness reading on right. Your stone have seven hundred. Diamond always have one thousand six hundred. It not diamond. Sorry, take and go.' He handed the rock back to Veerman.

'Look you stupid…' He stopped in his tracks when the jeweller pressed an alarm button and an audible whine sounded in the rear room. The door crashed open and two of the largest sumo-looking Oriental giants appeared. Their size was intimidating enough, but the bulges in their jackets left little doubt they were armed as well.

Veerman snatched up his stone, wrapped it back in the newspaper then looked sideways at his two Chinese companions. Their organisation was going to want payment for springing him out of prison that's why they were by his side, the only reason why they'd been trailing him for the last couple of days. Not that he'd seen them, not even once, but he had known they were there in his shadow, silently following his every move.

The problem was that the Shāqi organisation had shelled out maybe a hundred thousand pounds, or even more, to execute the rescue operation. What with hiring a helicopter, paying for probably the best technical engineers money could buy, a false passport and documents, not to mention the passage across to France, it certainly wouldn't have been cheap.

He was thinking fast, as were his companions who suddenly looked decidedly edgy. He knew how unpredictable Shāqi agents could be, he could see on their faces they were obviously wondering what to do next, and that was when they were at their most dangerous.

Veerman dashed out of the shop, slamming the door violently behind him and then rushed down the street, parallel to where Baxter and Magali were sitting a little way from the window.

Veerman didn't spot them, and for that matter wouldn't have had time to react even if he had, because he now knew he needed to get as far away from the Chinese agents as he possibly could. He knew only too well they wouldn't have any qualms about killing him now; their organisation had lost far too much money springing him from his prison cell. Like all Shāqi agents they had been trained by the cartel and had learnt much from Veerman himself and the one lesson he always drummed into them was '*When someone has outlasted their usefulness, dispose of them before they dispose of you.*'

Suddenly the air was filled with the sounds of sirens wailing from all directions, followed by the loud screeching of brakes as dozens of police cars came to a halt in front of the central fountain. Cars stopped in the confusion, people peered out of the windows of buses as they joined the traffic meltdown. Car horns added to the mayhem as they blared out in protest as more police vehicles blocked off every exit point.

Baxter and Magali continued to watch the events unfold through the safety of the café window. Veerman had stopped, he was looking around furtively and obviously aware the reception committee was there for him. For probably the first time in his life he looked frightened, his face portrayed a hunted man, but did he have the animal instincts to survive? He straightened his lank frame and then melted into the shadows of an old carriage gateway. There was no sign of his Chinese agents, in fact they hadn't even been spotted coming out of the shop.

The Shāqi had telephoned their organisation controller and he had instructed them to stay where they were, he told them the situation was being handled by another party.

Baxter shot up from his seat.

'Where are you going?' she demanded

'I have to show the Gendarmes exactly where Veerman is. They'll never spot him hiding in that dark gateway, I'm not going to let him get away this time.'

'No, Baxter, leave it to the police,' she pleaded, but her words fell on deaf ears for he was out of the door and on his heels before she could even leave the table.

Here we go again she said to herself. By the time she reached the open door he had quickened his pace to a run and was half way across the road and then a moving bus swallowed her vision of him.

'There he is, over there, in that gateway,' Baxter shouted to the police as he pointed to a silhouette in the shadows of the entrance. Magali saw Baxter and at the same time spotted Veerman emerging from his hiding place.

'Baxter, watch out,' she shouted.

Veerman heard her, turned, saw Baxter and fired his gun twice. Baxter heard the first crack before he felt any pain and that was only a minor tingle, but it was after the second loud crack that a hot searing sting hit his chest. The impact of the second blow spun his frame sideways, he fought to keep standing, but his legs were struggling to support his body. He caught the brief sight of Magali emerging from the bar, '*sorry*' he whispered.

He went numb, he felt no pain but he knew he had been

seriously injured. His legs finally buckled and he crumpled heavily to the ground. Through an enveloping fog that was rapidly closing in, he heard the far off sounds of screams and recognised them as belonging to Magali. Darkness was creeping up on him; he knew he was slipping into death or unconsciousness, he knew not which. He fought to keep control, but was aware he was floundering, everything had become dark. He reached out to her with outstretched hands but he couldn't find her; he was travelling into a deep dark void and now no longer cared.

By the time Magali reached Baxter he was sprawled on the ground with blood pouring from a wound in his chest and another from his right arm.

'Baxter.' She screamed 'Damn, you, why did you have to do that?' but of course he couldn't reply. His body lay motionless on the granite setts, a pool of blood forming on the pavement by his side.

Suddenly a helicopter could be heard approaching and like everyone else, she looked up, but couldn't see it. Veerman was sprinting away, but now watched by a smart suited man with mobile phone against his ear, talking to someone, giving instructions to an unseen third party.

All of a sudden the chopper came into view, swinging in from between the rooftops, and then momentarily hovering. Magali spotted a figure leaning out of the cockpit window, a flash of light reflected on the barrel of a gun as the chopper dipped precariously low. She realised the suited man was communicating with the helicopter. She guessed what was about to take place and so reacted by spreading her body over Baxter's, protectively, desperate to save him from any more bullets. The sound was deafening as a two second volley from a machine gun spit out a line of bullets, kicking up tiny stones, several hitting her on the head. This sent everyone on the street diving for cover, police crouching behind their vehicles, clearly uncertain what was unfolding in front of their eyes.

When the sounds of the chopper faded into the distance, Magali released her tight grip from around Baxter, but he didn't move.

Two police officers were now trying to pull her off the body, she clung on desperately, but eventually was hauled away sobbing.

As the policeman took her away, she noticed the bullet riddled body of Veerman, sprawled in the gutter, his hand still clutching the fake diamond and the folded newspaper, stained red with his blood. There would at some stage, be questions from the French police as she was a prime witness, but before that she had an important call to make. What she was planning to tell them had to be authorised by section control. She wanted to hold out her cards and reveal the whole sordid tale, but she knew she would never be allowed to go quite that far.

Following a reply to her telephone call, she spoke with the French chief of police, who had already been briefed about her. She described in detail the entrance to the caverns under the Montmartre cemetery and suggested they waste no time if they wanted to catch the other conspirators, especially the Shāqi organisation members. She wanted them all caught now, every one of those evil killers.

She was relieved Veerman was dead, he deserved all he got and more, but not poor Baxter. Her brave English hero, who thought he had brought her in from the cold and sinister world of the cartel and Shāqi organisation. If only he knew the truth.

For the first time in her life someone had shown her what is was to be loved, and oh, how she had been made to feel so special. But she wondered if she had done enough to return those sentiments? In this hour of anguish, those were doubts that she had.

CHAPTER 33

CONFESSIONS

'How is he now?' she asked the doctor who had at last finished writing up his notes. He looked up as he hung the observation board on the end of Baxter's bed.

'He'll be fine.' The doctor grinned. 'We removed a couple of point twenty two calibre bullets, one from his chest and the other from his arm; the one in his chest was a close call though.'

A nurse came in and checked the IV tubes which were Baxter's current lifeline. She spotted Magali's worried expression and squeezed her arm, giving a reassuring smile, but saying nothing.

'So' she turned to the doctor. 'He *is* going to be alright then is he?'

'Oh yes,' he confirmed with a smile. She sighed with relief. 'He's lost a lot of blood; in fact it was touch and go at one stage in the theatre. You see we didn't know he was on blood thinners, so that made things a bit tricky.

'But when will he wake up?' she asked, desperate to find a sign of revival which would confirm the doctor really *was* right, because after all, Baxter was originally thought to be dead.

'I think you should go home now miss and come back again in the morning. The amount of anaesthetic he's had would be enough to keep a stallion out for ten or twelve hours, so don't expect any response before tomorrow morning, at the earliest.'

Magali refused to go home, but opted to sit by Baxter's bedside. She planned to hold his hand and cool his brow on the odd occasion when, during the long night, he might momentarily come-to.

Nurses came in every five minutes, or so it seemed to Magali, but in fact he was on thirty minute observation checks for his early warning score chart; but even so these visits relieved some of the boredom.

Magali had desperately tried to maintain her all-night vigil, but shortly after midnight she lost the battle to stay awake.

She didn't hear the early morning observation checks, or respond to daylight filtering into the room, but she did feel the pressure and warmth of a hand tightening in hers. She opened her eyes just in time to see Baxter stirring. He was rewarded with tender hands on his cheeks and a kiss.

'You damm fool Baxter,' she said, shaking her head, 'I thought you were dead when you were lying on that pavement. Don't ever do that to me again or I'll kill you myself.'

He tried to sit up, but couldn't lift his body, it refused to move.

'Where am I Magali?'

'In hospital,' she replied.

He looked around and could now see tubes connected to his body, the other ends tethered to suspended bags of liquid. Over to his right an array of monitoring machines were constantly blinking green and blue numbers, accompanied by fluctuating graphs.

'What in England?'

'No you're in Paris. The La Croix Saint Simon

'What about Veerman?' he asked

'Dead,' she replied nonchalantly, 'and good riddance is all I can say,' she quickly added.

'Ah the patient has woken up,' declared a familiar voice. Baxter felt flattered to see Inspector Monroe standing in the doorway with a poorly wrapped bunch of grapes.

'The wife said I should get you these,' he said, putting them on the bedside table.

'Pity she didn't tell you to bring in a decent bottle of Scotch.'

'Well I'm sure we can…'

'Don't you dare bring him in whisky' Magali scowled.

'Okay officer de Couvegne, point taken,' Monroe said.

'Wait a minute,' Baxter struggled to sit up, but the burden of pain held him down. 'What's all this officer de Couvegne lark?'

Magali shot Monroe a disapproving scowl and Baxter noticed it.

'Oops,' said Monroe putting his finger to his lips. 'I think I'll leave the two of you to have a chat while I grab a cup of coffee in the canteen,' he said tactfully as he made a hurried exit.

'So, I think you have something else to tell me Magali.'

Baxter narrowed his gaze.

'I'm not certain that this is really the best time,' she said, desperately trying to put off the inevitable confession, the one she had always known would have to be made one day.

'I can't think of a better time, can you,' he said.

'I was going to tell you the whole truth, I promise, but I wasSnot I wasn't permitted to, however, I've made a decision which means I can can I can now tell you the whole story.'

'So you really are a police officer then?'

'No, I'm not a police officer,' she said in a wavering voice but her body language said otherwise, her face betrayed shattering denial.

Baxter raised his eyebrows, waiting for an explanation.

'Well, not exactly,' she said. 'Sorry'.

'So?' he could see she was finding it difficult to explain herself and needed further coaxing.

'Actually I work for OIPC. That's Organisation Internationale de Police Criminelle.'

'What sort of French outfit is that?'

'In simple terms, Interpol.'

Baxter roared, 'Interpol! I don't believe it, you're a secret service agent.' He was struggling to work out how this revelation fitted into the jigsaw, but now all of a sudden he realised it held the whole thing together.

'No, I'm not exactly a secret service agent as you put it. Although we *were* carrying out blue ticket work for SOCA, the British Serious Organized Crime agency. The department I work for is an investigative and fact finding undercover observation unit and no more.'

'So that means I was set up right from the beginning.'

'No, you were never part of any official enquiry. The only reason you came into the frame was because of Veerman's plot to get hold of your vase. And before you ask, yes you really did save my life.'

'But wait a minute, I still don't understand. Tell me, how did you come to be working for Veerman?'

'That's simple. You see I did work for Revenue and Customs here, as I told you once before, but as an OIPC officer going through the motions. You see as Interpol officers we can be designated the authority of a police officer, customs or immigration officer, or any combination of these three sets of powers. My department was carrying out a two-pronged investigation which involved Veerman and the cartel along with suspicions of corruption in police forces both here and in France, not to mention others in high places.'

'So you were after Atterbury then, were you?' he interrupted.

'Well no, the British Serious Organized Crime Agency suspected there was corruption in the Met, but didn't know at what level and, keep this to yourself,' she looked towards the door to make certain no one else was in earshot, 'we and our British counterparts are convinced there are other senior police chiefs who are being protected in order to hush up their past indiscretions. Look I can tell you now there's at least one government minister who's been in the pay of the cartel and not to mention a judge or two. Atterbury, as Assistant Commissioner, was comparatively small fry.

'Well, all I can say is, if he was small fry, then there must have been some very big fish in the pond,' Baxter exclaimed.

Magali said 'Don't laugh, but at one stage we even had Inspector Monroe under surveillance. It wasn't until after he rescued us from that barn that I realised he was someone we could trust, and I can tell you now, there were few of those in the force.'

'Wait a minute, I don't quite understand. How long has Monroe known you were an Interpol agent?'

'Yesterday, that was the first he knew about it, and he was as surprised as you were.'

'I can imagine he was.' Baxter chuckled.

She went on 'We were able to lure Veerman into suborning me to cease my phoney Revenue and Customs investigations into his business affairs. After that it was an easy task to put him off his guard by letting him seduce me and then my agreeing to do some snooping for him.'

'And your presence at Bourge-Vilaine and the police station in Avranches, they were times you were wearing your police hat, were they?'

'Yes, and the time I fired that shot to save you from those thugs who were beating the hell out of you outside the Rat de Cave bar.'

'And that's why you were carrying a gun.'

'Actually that was not standard Interpol issue; I am not a certified assault officer and shouldn't have been carrying. As I told you once before, Max gave it to me. Whatever you do, don't mention it in front of Monroe, or I could get into serious trouble,' she said softly.

'So wait a minute, you *are* a Couvegne after all, then?

'Yes, and that *was* my real grandmother.'

'I don't understand, what was all that business with the letters and the diamond then?'

'Let me try and explain. It's complicated, but you see, the letters were nothing to do with the investigation. My only interest was in Veerman and the cartel. I was deployed to find evidence which would expose their nefarious activities in France and Britain and evidence which would lead to a criminal conviction. Veerman was only interested in the Chinese vase, which, by a completely unrelated coincidence was being sold at the same time as the letters in the Bourge-Vilaine auction rooms which as you know is less than a kilometre from my grandmother's chateau. She herself had no idea that the missing Henri de Montaigne vase was being offered for sale there, in fact she didn't even know it still existed. But after she successfully bought the Montaigne letters, she discovered the Count had hidden a diamond inside the last piece of porcelain that he shipped over. It was easy to find the shipping docket and after a search of the Chateau we found the base and the real diamond. As you know, Grandmother had a copy made of it and all because I believed Veerman would do her harm if he got his hands on your vase and consequently cracked the code.

So I tipped Veerman off about the whereabouts of the stone and went through the charade of running off with it and then presenting it to him.'

'So where did I figure in this whole affair, why did you take me along as well?'

'I had to come up with a plausible explanation as to how I knew the whereabouts of the diamond. I couldn't just make the story up. Veerman didn't know about my true identity or for that matter my real name and neither did he know about my connection with the Countess.'

'So you thought, I know, I'll use good old Baxter to get me out of trouble,' he said flippantly.

'There was a bit more to it than that. You see I thought that if Veerman believed you had helped me get the diamond, then he would leave you alone.'

'Fat chance of that.'

'Yes, I conceived that part of the scenario completely blindly. Anyway, I couldn't go through the motions without actually involving you, because as you know I was covertly escorted by the two agents who died on that mountain road.'

'So.....' Baxter was mulling over the wider implications of Magali's revelations. 'Am I right in thinking that all this time you have been reporting back to your people at Interpol?'

'Yes, my handlers were always only a phone call away and over the last couple of weeks we have been under constant track and trace.'

'Via your mobile?'

'yes.'

'But why didn't you tell me all this before, you know the truth is something you don't have to lie about, and especially not to me.'

'I'm sorry, but you're so very wrong about that. Sometimes the truth is something you *do* have to lie about,' she said bitterly.'

'Explain that one to me, please.'

'Well, for one thing, I was and still am bound by the official secrets act. Also, I was afraid it would damage everything we have together, although I knew it would surface one day because the past never stays where it should.'

'I'll say one thing for you, Magali, as a chameleon you certainly blended perfectly into each of your environments.'

'That's precisely what I was trained to do, but I didn't take any satisfaction from concealing my true identity from you.'

'So you were a reluctant chameleon then?' he said half-jokingly.

Inspector Monroe returned. 'Is it safe to come in now?' he quipped holding up his hands.

'So tell me, Inspector, did you catch the others then?'

Monroe smiled; the man he once thought was corrupt and on the pay role of Max Veerman. The Inspector did his party trick of unwrapping a sweet with one hand still in his pocket, then held it up. 'You don't, do you?' he said

'No.' Baxter shook his head.

Monroe popped the sweet into his mouth and rolled it between his teeth in his characteristic way.

'Yes, thanks to what Magali here told us, a visit was paid to the Shāqi secret underground hideout, deep below the Montmartre cemetery, and Paris' 'finest' along with forty armed officers carried out a dawn raid. Anyway, they brought out twenty one Chinese alive and four dead. Quite a gun battle at one stage so I'm told, I think we can safely say the Shāqi cell is no longer in existence in France or England for that matter.'

'I wish I'd seen that, it sounds very exciting.'

'I think you had quite enough excitement actually.' interrupted Magali.

'Did anyone mention anything about little people in the underground caves?' Baxter asked.

'Little people! No why?' said the Inspector chuckling?

'No reason,' he replied with a sigh of relief.

Baxter gave Magali a knowing look and she winked back.

'I suppose it was inevitable Veerman would be killed once he was of no use to the cartel,' Baxter said, 'but how on earth did he manage to get out of Grantmead prison in the first place?'

'Ah now that's simple. By helicopter.'

'Helicopter! That would have been expensive.'

'Precisely, you see the only way Veerman could escape from a British prison was with the help of his former Chinese associates in the Shāqi organisation. They alone had the financial means and the resources to carry out such an operation. He undoubtedly offered them a substantial reward if they were prepared and I might add able, to spring him, and you may depend that reward was going to be a large part of the money from selling his diamond.'

'Of course, that's why he was trying to sell it in Paris,' Baxter said.

'We think,' said the Inspector, 'when the jeweller told him it was a worthless fake, he ran out of the building to escape the angry Chinese who were waiting for payment.'

'And so they shot him dead,' he cut in.

'No, Baxter you're jumping the gun. On hearing Magali calling your name, he spotted you and opened fire, shooting you twice.'

'I'm so sorry, that was my fault,' said Magali, with a look of regret.

'It wasn't your fault at all,' Baxter said putting his hand in hers and giving her a reassuring smile.

'But I did call your name and nearly lost you as a result.'

'You don't get rid of me that easily,' he said. 'So it was the French police who got him them.'

'No, but boy did you miss one hell of an execution.'

Monroe then went on to tell him about the daring helicopter swoop and the way Veerman was gunned down in a hail of machine gun fire.

'So wait a minute Inspector, who did kill him then?'

Monroe threw a look across to Magali who nodded in response. Baxter realised she was giving Monroe approval to continue.

'It was a professional operation, mounted extremely quickly and ordered by someone in a very high place, a very high place indeed,' he reiterated.

'So are you saying it was special forces then?'

'It was most certainly a special task force and if I was to make an educated guess, I would say it was carried out by Omega; would you not agree Magali?'

'Yes,' she concurred, 'and to be more specific, I would say it was most likely Omega Group West, as they reputedly have a fast response unit based somewhere in the French capital.'

Monroe said 'No other organisation would have automatic military and government clearance to operate like that over the streets of Paris. '

'Omega?' Baxter queried

'They're the agency that people are talking about when someone says '*orders came from above the Government*'.

'I've never heard of them before.' Baxter commented

'Of course you haven't,' Magali said. 'Few people know of their existence and although they have agents around most of the modern world, they don't officially exist.'

'You see, Baxter,' Monroe said 'There are the usual mumblings around the corridors of power; people speculating about the likelihood of a secret agency like Omega, but the murmurs are just that and so faint no one dare question the possibility of such an organisation operating in the very shadows of modern governmental security services. I can tell you now, there isn't a single European government which would admit to their existence, but having said that, they all turn a grateful blind eye when it suits them.'

'That sounds like justice from a very high level then,' he said

'Precisely,' said Monroe, 'it's easy to forget that under the cloak of wealth and respectability, Max Veerman was a gangster, he had people murdered, and there were many shady assassins who had him in their sights. But in the end his execution was carried out solely to protect people in higher places, representatives from several European governments, nothing more, nothing less.'

'So, Inspector, I take it the cartel is finished for once and for all then?'

'No, no, no,' he replied with a heavy sigh, 'the English and French wing was only a small cog in a very large wheel. The cartel as a worldwide organisation is protean, as has been exemplified by the closure of the Anglo-French section. It can move very fast and over the past fifty years, has, on many occasions, shown that it's beyond the reach of accountability.' Monroe rubbed his chin, chewing over the question. 'I predict that in China and Hong Kong the cartel will continue to grow more and more powerful as the economic balance shifts away from the West and Asia rises to become the dominant power. China will one day achieve its long fought passion which is to *keep the dragon in the box*, as they like to put it and Asian cultural art will be once again returned to what they rightly consider its rightful home.'

'Just one last point, Inspector.'

'What's that?'

'How on earth did Atterbury get away with his dodgy dealings for so many years?'

'Have you never heard the saying 'Satan walks in very silent shoes?'

'No, that's a new one on me,' Baxter confided, 'but I like it, sums up Atterbury perfectly.'

'Well,' Monroe went on. 'Atterbury, when in his evil guise, was almost invisible; and of course, it's very difficult to investigate an officer of that rank. We had a few suspicions, but the trails always lead to dead ends, and never to Veerman or the cartel. Atterbury was totally ruthless and had no qualms about killing the two of you. Max Veerman was equally illusive and even more brutal, although he probably never committed murder himself. Men like them don't get caught because there is always somebody higher up in the chain of command who will sever all contacts once someone poses a threat. Both Atterbury and Veerman became that threat and so they were eliminated. It makes you wonder where the buck stops, it has to somewhere,' he said, shrugging his shoulders.

'So that's it,' Baxter said, 'but what about you Magali, where will you be working next? And... what secret operation will you be risking your life to unravel,' he added sardonically.

She gave Monroe a sideways look; he had a wry expression which suggested he was fairly certain about what she would say next.

'Well,' she began slowly. 'I never was a very good field operative.'

'I don't think I would agree with that,' Baxter said generously, 'anyway Interpol is no place for a woman.'

'What…' Magali screamed, 'I'll have you know the French Chief Commissioner of police is a woman?'

'No, really.'

'Mireille Ballestrazzi. She is also vice president of Interpol's executive committee.'

'I bet she doesn't get her hands dirty though.'

'Actually she made her mark battling organised crime in Bordeaux and on the violence-torn island of Corsica. Now shut up and just hear me out. I don't want to do this sort of work anymore and certainly not for an organisation that treats its operatives as dispensable, and believe me, unofficially, they do. Anyway, I've decided I'm leaving Interpol so I can keep an eye on you, Baxter.'

'That's wonderful news Magali, but I think life might be a little bit less exciting without the cartel and the likes of Mr. Max Veerman; will you be able to cope with that?'

'Don't rely on that Baxter,' Magali said with a wicked twinkle in her eye. 'From now on I intend to make every minute of your life exciting.'

Baxter smiled and rubbed his hands together. 'Now that sounds good to me, don't you agree Inspector?'

Monroe, noticing the green L.E.D. digits on the Omron automatic measurement monitor rising rapidly, dramatically cut in. 'I think we'd better change the subject, we don't want Baxter's blood pressure going through the roof, now do we?'

Magali slowly nodded her head in agreement.

'I meant to ask you earlier; What happed about the diamond?' Monroe enquired. Magali grinned broadly.

'Grandmother tells me it is, at this very moment en route for China along with the base and will be in pride of place in a Beijing

Museum by the end of the year.'

'That's great,' said Baxter. 'Which one?'

'I think it's called the Cultural Relic Exchange Museum.'

'Ah, yes, now that *is* a fitting place for it, as the museum is situated in the Zhi-Hua Temple in the Dongcheng District, and that's close to where it was concealed a century ago.'

'So, the rock of Batuta is finally in safe hands then,' Monroe said pragmatically, with a contented grin.

'Yes, and you can be certain of one thing Inspector.'

'What's that then Baxter?'

'From now on the Chinese will be keeping *that* particular dragon firmly in the box, I can guarantee it.'

'Well at least something good came out of the shadow of evil that Veerman cast over everyone, and everything he touched,' Monroe said drily.

'Well, I wouldn't say that was the only good thing to come out of this whole escapade,' said Baxter, looking at Magali. 'It looks as though your wish of the other week is going to come true after all.'

'So what wish was that,' She shot a sideways look at him.

'You know, the one you made in the barn, just before we were about to be roasted alive by Atterbury's homemade bomb.'

'Enlighten me.' She gave him a sheepish smile, which meant she knew full well what those last rite wishes had been.

'You said you wished we could have grown old together, well I think you and I will, don't you?'

'Yes, I do, Baxter, and I can't wait to begin.'

'*Begin*! Don't you think we've already begun, we've long passed the end of the beginning, this Magali, is the beginning of the rest of our lives together.'

'Promise me, Baxter.' she threw a suspicious glance at him.

'I promise we'll grow old together.'

'At last,' she said 'and I have a witness here, don't I Inspector?' she gave him a knowing look. A broad smile formed on Monroe's face which for the first time softened the solid line of his eyebrows. He didn't answer as he rotated his toffee around in his mouth.

'So don't ever forget your promise Baxter or I might have to kill you,' she said stiltedly.

'By the way Baxter, what *is* your first name? You can't keep secrets like that if we are going to spend the rest of our lives together?'

'Baxter, just call me Baxter, besides, if we are talking about secrets, you've never told me where you actually live,' he said cocking his head sideways.

'You wouldn't want to know, besides its classified information, I'd definitely have to kill you if I told you, so don't ask me again,' she said laughing. He noticed Monroe was guffawing quite loudly from the opposite side of the bed.

'Well, that's a pity then, because I don't know where to tell the garage to deliver that Austin Healey; the smart red one that has your name on it.'

'You've bought me a car! You darling man, just tell them to drop it off at your cottage. That will do nicely, but we will need something bigger once the children begin to arrive,' she said beguilingly.

'Children!' he shrieked.

'Just shut up and kiss me.' She said.

'Yes, officer de Couvegne.'

'Baxter, just call me Baxter,' she said mockingly.

He had never understood women, and he doubted he ever would, but Magali had rewritten the code female for him and he liked it, he liked it very much indeed.

THE END

CPSIA information can be obtained at www.ICGtesting.com
Printed in the USA
LVOW01s0845240114

370727LV00006B/22/P